THE WORLD TO COME

THE
WORLD
TO
COME

A NOVEL

DARA HORN

W. W. NORTON & COMPANY

New York | London

For information about permission to reproduce selections from this book,
write to Permissions, W. W. Norton & Company, Inc.,
500 Fifth Avenue, New York, NY 10110

Manufacturing by Quebecor World, Fairfield
Book design by JAM Design
Production manager: Amanda Morrison

Library of Congress Cataloging-in-Publication Data

Horn, Dara, 1977–
The world to come : a novel / Dara Horn.—1st ed.
        p. cm.
ISBN 0-393-05107-2
1. Art thefts—Fiction. 2. Chagall, Marc, 1887– —Appreciation—Fiction. 3. Fugitives from
justice—Fiction. 4. Brothers and sisters—Fiction. 5. Loss (Psychology)—Fiction. 6. Parents—
Death—Fiction. 7. Jewish families—Fiction. 8. Twins—Fiction. I. Title.

PS3608.076W67 2006
813' .6—dc22

                                                    2005014586

W. W. Norton & Company, Inc., 500 Fifth Avenue, New York, N.Y. 10110
www.wwnorton.com

W. W. Norton & Company Ltd., Castle House, 75/76 Wells Street, London W1T 3QT

1 2 3 4 5 6 7 8 9 0

For my siblings,
Jordana, Zachary, and Ariel—
my fellow artists and my lifelong friends,
in this world, in prior worlds,
and in every world to come

THE WORLD TO COME

1

THERE USED to be many families like the Ziskinds, families where each person always knew that his life was more than his alone. Families like that still exist, but because there are so few of them, they have become insular, isolated, their sentiment that the family is the center of the universe broadened to imply that nothing outside the family is worth anything. If you are from one of these families, you believe this, and you always will.

Lately it had begun to seem to Benjamin Ziskind that the entire world was dead, that he was a citizen of a necropolis. While his parents were living, Ben had thought about them only when it made sense to think about them, when he was talking to them, or talking about them, or planning something involving them. But now they were always here, reminding him of their presence at every moment. He saw them in the streets, always from behind, or turning a corner, his father sitting in the bright yellow taxi next to his, shifting in his seat as the cab screeched away in the opposite direction, his mother—dead six months now, though it felt like one long night—hurrying along the sidewalk on a Sunday morning, turning into a store just when Ben had come close enough to see her face. It was a relief that Ben could close his office door.

Ben was a full-time question writer for the quiz show *American*

Genius, where he had worked for the past seven years. Long ago, he had loved it. He had loved the thrill of working for TV, loved telling people he worked for a network, loved thinking up new questions, loved wondering which contestant he would stump next. Secretly, he had dreamed of someday becoming the show's host. The fact that he was five-foot-six, weighed 123 pounds, spoke in a near-monotone, and was legally blind without his glasses never struck him as an impediment to this goal, even though the only reason most people watched *American Genius* was for Morgan Finnegan, the show's hunky, Texan, redheaded, hilarious, charming, and (Ben had noticed over the years) intellectually underqualified emcee. But before he turned thirty a few months ago, Ben had maintained full faith in logic. If he, Benjamin Ziskind, was the smartest person on the staff, then his intelligence would eventually be rewarded. His specialty was in the thousand-dollar-plus category, questions that no one but the true champions could answer. In the past few months, though, his questions had been repeatedly rejected, and now they were interlaced in his mind with questions he asked of himself:

What acclaimed Russian writer, author of Odessa Tales *and* Red Cavalry, *was executed in 1940 under false charges of treason?*

During which of the following incidents in the past year did Nina lie when she claimed that she loved me?

Which 1965 battle in the Vietnam War, code-named Operation Starlite, was successful enough to inspire the Pentagon to send thousands more Marines to the war?

For how many of the eleven months of our brief and pathetic marriage was she actually sleeping with someone else?

To the nearest power of ten, what is the number of American soldiers who have lost limbs in combat since the end of World War Two?

Among American males who have twin sisters, what percentage are as jealous of them as I am of Sara?

Once Sara sells our parents' house, what will be left of them?

What is the probability that my dead parents are disappointed in me?

Ben did not try to answer these questions. In the past few months, he had condensed his life into the few things that still belonged to him: his pitiful job, his twin sister, the apartment his former wife had stripped of nearly all its furniture, and a stack of children's picture books his mother had written. And, as of last night's theft, a $1 million painting by Marc Chagall.

————

IT WAS SARA'S fault, really. She was the one who persuaded him to go to the singles' cocktail hour at the museum. In the weeks since his divorce, Sara had begged him to try to meet someone new, to make at least some vague effort toward being happy—perfect, productive Sara, hopeful enough to have just gotten married in their mother's hospital room two weeks before their mother died, and tough enough to already begin picking up the shards. It had been easier to say yes to Sara than to explain to her why he had no hope or interest in going.

But when he passed through the museum's metal detectors and entered the crowded gallery, he saw that the other people at the exhibit of "Marc Chagall's Russian Years" were little more than walking ghosts: his mother, his father, preserved in other people's skin. Glimpsing the side of a woman's head—a younger woman, of course, but another remarkable thing about the dead is that they are all ages, preserved at every age you ever knew them, and at no age at all—he had to fight the impulse to glance at the profile again, unwilling to feel the sick relief that came with confirming an unfamiliar face. It was easier to look at the art.

Ben edged away from the crowds at the center of the gallery, toward the paintings on the walls. He stopped alongside a giant canvas titled— he stooped to read the caption—*The Promenade*. A man stood in the middle of the painting, legs apart as if striding with confidence, one hand at his side holding a small bird, the other in the air, holding the hand of a woman—a woman who flew in the air like a flag on the flagpole of his wrist, her magenta dress fluttering in the wind. Another large canvas, called *Over the Town*, cast both man and woman into the sky, wearing different clothes this time, a green shirt for the man, a blue dress for the woman, with petticoats flying at her ankles. The two of them soared over the town below, in a sky pure white, as if the flying people, ruling the air, hadn't yet decided what to fill it with. For a moment Ben wished he could fly. And then, as he turned around to cross the gallery, someone called his name.

"And what about you, Benjamin Ziskind?"

Ben looked up, startled. Had someone from the show tracked him down? But as he scanned the unfamiliar faces of the three women who had closed in around him beneath the flying woman, he realized that everyone was wearing a name tag, and someone had just read his aloud. He was trapped.

The three women laughed, and Ben forced a smile, wincing as he remembered why he was ostensibly here. He glanced at the name tag of the woman who had spoken: "Erica Frank, Museum Staff." A shill, he thought. Too bad; she was the most attractive of the three. She was slightly shorter than him, with curved hips, long hair the color of damp rope, and (Ben was captivated and then ashamed to notice) a glimpse of shadowed skin that shimmered between the buttons of her bright blue blouse. Her green eyes were watching him. In the glass covering the painting behind her head, he turned away from his own reflection: short, dark, unworthy. He remembered how he had first met Nina two years ago—at a party like this one, but in Sara's apartment. He was happier then, less fearful. He had told a joke, a bad one, some horrible pun, and she had laughed. Ben wasn't used to people laughing with him instead of at him. He would have married her on the spot. On the night two weeks after his mother died, when his wife failed to come home from work, he had assumed she had been kidnapped.

"We were just talking about languages in museum work, translations, that kind of thing," Erica Frank was saying. "Do you speak any foreign languages?"

Ben resented being forced into this inane conversation, but he remembered Sara pleading with him and knew he owed it to her to try. He in fact spoke several languages, but he tried to pick the one that would end the conversation the fastest. "Yiddish," he said. He immediately wished he had lied.

He regretted it more when Erica Frank, Museum Staff, appeared suddenly intrigued. "Wow, I didn't know anybody knew Yiddish anymore," she said, staring. *Yes,* Ben wished he could announce, *I am a freak, a relic, a generational error, a leftover shard from a broken world. Now please let me go home.* But he was caught. "Why did you—I mean, where did you learn it? From your grandparents?" she asked.

Ben looked at the three women and felt as if he were facing a panel of judges. "From my father," he said. Erica was looking at him, absently brushing a strand of golden hair away from her cheek. For a moment he felt hopeful, but then he remembered where the conversation had lurched. He was beginning to wish he could leap over their heads and vanish into the sky.

"Do you still speak it with him?" Erica asked, a wide smile on her face.

"He's been dead for almost twenty years, so no."

Ben hadn't meant to snap at her, but he was strangely happy that he had. The smiling faces on the panel seemed to fall to the ground, like dropped masks. The air yawned between him and the three others, stretching into a wide, blank space of empty canvas.

"I'm so sorry," Erica stuttered.

Everyone looked at the floor for the obligatory seven seconds before someone changed the subject, a ritual deeply familiar to people whose parents die young. Ben waited for the obligatory seven seconds to pass. It had been years since he had felt embarrassed during those seconds. By now they felt to him like time spent waiting for an elevator: boring, wasteful, a chance to run errands in one's head. Sara had mentioned that she was going to stop by his place after he got home, he remembered. She claimed to have news, and she promised him that it wasn't about selling their parents' house. But it was impossible that it wasn't about selling the house, Ben thought. What else was there to talk about?

"What's really interesting about Yiddish," Erica was saying, the first courageous soul to break the silence, "is how much humor there is in it."

Her smile, which had seemed so promising just moments before, was beginning to sicken him. "No more than any other language," he muttered. But what it really does have, he thought—what you don't know it has, because it isn't in any Woody Allen movies—is a world of the dead built into it, a true fear of heaven, an automatic need to invoke the presence of God whenever saying anything good or bad about anyone or anything, an absolute trust that the other world, if one could call it that, is not separate from this one, that eternity is always breathing over your shoulder, waiting to see if you will notice. But Ben didn't say anything more. Instead he glanced at Erica and then looked at his feet, noticing for the first time that in the haze of changing his clothes after work and going to the Chagall exhibit, he had somehow ended up wearing two slightly different shoes.

"You'll have to excuse me," he announced, and pushed his way out of the circle into the very crowded room.

———

HE MOVED TOWARD the sides of the gallery, staring up at the paintings that interrupted the walls like gigantic plate-glass windows, offering views beyond the room. Some of them, he saw, hung limp on the gallery walls, tired and derivative, a parade of boxy men like early Cubist works, or distorted interiors with absurdly bright wallpaper borrowed from Matisse. Ben became more interested when things started to fly: first clouds, then words, then angels, then goats, and finally men and women, soaring through the air. The more things flew, the better the paintings became. Occasionally, as he moved along the gallery walls, he thought of Erica Frank. He stared at the flying goats and resisted the impulse to search for her again over his shoulder. A few times, he allowed himself to turn around and scan the crowd for her face. When he didn't see her, he was surprised to find himself disappointed. He stared at the paintings until they seemed to dissolve into blank white space.

A man near the door at the end of the gallery cupped his hands to his mouth, trying his best to roar above the crowd. "The band will be starting up downstairs in five minutes," he bellowed.

A band? Sara must not have known about the band, Ben thought. He wasn't about to listen to music; the year of mourning wasn't over yet. For a moment he panicked. Then, as the hordes of jabbering singles began to flow down toward the door on the opposite end of the gallery, he realized, grateful, that he now had an excuse to go home. The room emptied quickly, and soon he was the only person in it, standing at the far end of the gallery next to a series of tiny paintings. He was about to turn around when a woman's head leaned back into the room from a nearby doorway, a blur of light brown hair. Erica Frank.

"Going downstairs?" she asked.

He was surprised to see that she was smiling. Had she forgotten their awkward conversation before? No, it didn't look that way. Her smile was different from before: dark, canny, her upper lip slightly curled as if they had shared a private joke. Suddenly he felt as though he were seeing an actress backstage, shifting from playing a part to being herself. She was forgiving him, it seemed. Or was she just laughing at him? He searched for something to say to make her stay a moment longer, to test her, to see. "I'll be down in a minute," he answered, and for a split second he wished it were true.

But it wouldn't have mattered. "I can't stay for the music," she said, and Ben briefly wondered why. But only briefly, because she was already moving away. "Have fun," she said with a wave.

Ben watched as she vanished from the room, cutting back into the gallery and through a white door marked "Staff Only." The door hovered open for a moment, framing the back of her hair, which glimmered gold in the shadow within the outlines of the doorway. Then the door closed behind her, a blank white wall. Ben felt the entire wasted evening draining through his gut. Well, Sara, he thought, surveying the empty gallery, I tried. He turned to leave. And then he stopped.

It was a painting of a street. The street was covered with snow, and lined by a short iron fence and little crooked buildings whose rooftops bent and reflected in all directions. Above the street, a man with a beard, pack, hat, and cane hovered in the sky, moving over the houses as if walking—unaware, in murky horizontal profile, that he was actually in flight. The painting was tiny, smaller than a piece of notebook paper. The label next to the painting offered its date as 1914 and its owner as a museum in Russia, titling it *Study for "Over Vitebsk."* This intrigued Ben, who despite his mastery of trivia on all topics, including modern art, had never before known this particular painting's name. All he knew was that it used to hang over the piano in the living room of his parents' house.

Now in the silent white gallery, in front of *Study for "Over Vitebsk,"* Ben stood still. He looked at the floating man with the cane, the dark late autumn or early winter of the painting's twilit evening, and thought of fall evenings long ago, years when his father would take him and his sister trick-or-treating. He and Sara used to take turns carrying a folded artist's stool along with their candy bags for when their father got tired and needed to rest, which was usually at every house. As the long night of house-to-house waned, Ben would try to walk more slowly, self-consciously copying his father's eternal limp, dragging his right leg deliberately through the heaps of leaves on the side of the road as if only for the joy of crunching leaves beneath his foot, but really, as the evening grew darker and the circle of trees drew the horizon closed like a drawstring bag around them, tightening the early evening sky with wrinkles of naked branches, he was thumping out his father's perpetual four-legged pace: left leg, two crutches, bad foot, left leg, two crutches, bad foot, left leg, two crutches, bad foot. His father, he thought as he looked at the painting, had probably wished he could fly.

Ben stared more closely at the painting. It had been over fifteen years since he had last seen it. There was no way it was the same one. Artists often paint the same picture over and over again, he told himself, thinking of Sara in her paint-splattered apartment. Even the idea that it might be theirs was just a momentary deception, like the people on the street or at the cocktail hour, dead ringers for his parents only because he wanted them to be.

Ben breathed out slowly and took one last look before turning again to leave, this time for good. But then he noticed, in the painting's lower right-hand corner, a tiny glossy area that gleamed white under the gallery lights—the same place where Sara, at the age of seven, had once tried to coat the painting with clear nail polish until their parents caught her. And then Ben's entire body started shaking with rage.

He read the label again, still stunned. *On loan*, it read, from a Russian museum. He stretched his arms toward the painting without even noticing that he was doing so, reaching for it, ready to grip the bottom of the frame like the rung of a ladder. In his mind he saw his feet walking up the wall until he could step into it, sliding through the frame and out and up and away. Instead he caught a glimpse of his own hands out of the corner of his eye and stopped himself, lowering his arms and turning his head to see if anyone was still around.

No one was there, not even a lingering guard.

Strange things happen to paintings that no one looks at. They start to sing. In the absence of people, the empty room reverberated with the colors humming on its walls. Ben stood alone and listened as each wide flash of color vibrated at a different pitch: wistful wavering high notes for the airborne woman, deep resonating low tones for the *Lovers in Blue*. The dark little picture rattled the air with the banging of piano keys like the ones that once lay below it in his parents' living room, a minor chord struck by accident in the middle of a song.

He stepped closer.

With all his strength, he grabbed the painting's thin frame and yanked the whole thing off the wall. It was so light that he nearly flew backward. And then he left.

2

—

ORIS KULBAK had been in the Jewish Boys' Colony in Malakhovka just outside of Moscow for only three months, and he remembered very little from before then. It was 1920 and he was eleven years old, and from the entire first ten years of his life he could recall almost nothing but a single incident. One day long ago, in the town where he used to live—he could see, in the clarity of a single framed memory, that it was a beautiful day, one of those spring days when the air becomes like clear water rippled by a breeze and the ground loosens its grip and you feel as though you are not walking but swimming in air, flying, weightless, over the town—he had seen a group of boys beating a horse. The horse was old, a mare, and her right front leg was broken. Boris had just noticed her lying there when a group of boys, big boys, older than he was, strolled by, swinging big wooden sticks they must have been using for a game. When they noticed the horse, they approached her slowly, making gentle cooing noises. But then one of them suddenly raised his stick and struck the horse on her side. She neighed, a long, agonizing sound. Then the other boys each took a turn smacking the horse. One of them struck her in the eye, and a stream of blood oozed out. This excited the boys to the point where they began beating her in earnest, laughing and jeering as they clobbered her over and over until Boris, who until then had been riveted to his spot by morbid fascination, could no longer watch. Later, in Malakhovka, he remembered that the whole scene had confused him, upset him. But he could no longer remember why he had been upset or confused.

Many of the orphans had brothers who lived with them in the Boys' Colony, running around in pairs or trios or packs. These boys tended to be mean, fond of taunting outsiders, unwilling to play with anyone else. Boris envied them. He envied the boys who had sisters, too, girls who would visit from the girls' home down the road, though the girls' home was much smaller, and the girls who lived there much younger; girls older than twelve or so being in a category with parents, people who no longer existed.

When the other boys asked Boris, he told them that he had never had brothers or sisters, that he had always been an only child. But that wasn't quite true. He remembered, in a thought that he could hold no tighter than one can grasp a stream of water, that there had once been a baby brother, years ago, a baby who hadn't even learned to walk before he began coughing, and coughed and coughed and coughed all the way through summer and autumn and into the winter, when one cold night Boris heard the coughing stop; the dark house was silent for a moment in the dim kerosene light, a silence one could feel like the presence of a person in a room, and then the cough was replaced, suddenly, with his mother's wail. And he was going to have another little brother, too, or a little sister. He had hoped for a boy, but he still wasn't sure, when he saw it torn from his mother's knifed-open belly and thrown through the smashed bedroom window, whether it was a boy or a girl. He had watched this with his hands tied to the bedpost and his mouth stuffed with a scrap of his mother's underwear, his father already strangled in the next room. In the seconds before the man who had tied him up clubbed him across the forehead and left him for dead, he had seen it—the not-yet brother or sister, slick with water and blood, but with a fully formed head and limbs, its legs uncurling as it was pulled through the air. Before it took flight, he had seen its face, its tiny thumb wedged between its lips.

After that everything turned into a long dream. Months of crawling around the city, stealing food, stealing money, stealing anything, sleeping in stables, sleeping in alleyways, eating trash. He joined a

gang of boys he had known from his school, back when there was a
school; they had bullied him then, and now it was worse. He would
go on missions for them, stealing rolls and eggs, and they would beat
him until he gave up the portions he had saved for himself. One night
when winter came he ran away from them. He kept himself up deep
into the night, until he knew they were dead asleep, and then raced
to the city's edge. He thought of going to the forest, but there were animals there, and bandits, and he was too afraid. Instead he went to the
Jewish cemetery. He had once been afraid of the dead, but now they
seemed benign to him, familiar. In the cemetery he stumbled in the
premorning dimness between the stones until he found an empty
grave. Boris lay down inside it, covered his arms and legs with dirt
until he managed to stop shivering, and closed his eyes against the
falling snow. At dawn he was discovered, half frozen, by someone
from the burial society. The burial society paid his passage to
Malakhovka.

The Jewish Boys' Colony in Malakhovka was like an enchanted
island, a private Soviet republic where no one was over the age of sixteen. Fifty boys lived in a cluster of wooden huts where they ruled
themselves, cooking their own meals, growing their own vegetables,
chopping their own wood. They even had a little Soviet, a council of
older boys who ruled the colony through a central command.
Mornings were spent in the colony's school, in classes taught by
adults—math, science, socialism, literature, art—after which they
would file out for the afternoon's labor. Evenings were spent in one's
communal house, around the fire, debating chore divisions in the
colony council and singing hymns of praise to the Red Army. All this
amazed Boris, stunned him. He didn't know how to talk to the other
boys, and so he was silent, but no one seemed to make fun of him for
it; there were a number of silent boys there, and no one seemed to
mind. He moved from one moment to the next on this magical island
dazzled by daylight, by the food that no one stole from him, by the
warm blanket that wasn't his coat, by his shaven head that was no
longer full of fleas, and most of all by the boys around him, busy
shaven-headed boys who buzzed away at their daily tasks as if nothing
else had ever been. And in those busy days, he found, it was impossible to imagine that anything ever had. Except at night.

Each night, the boys in Boris's hut stood in rows beside their army-style bunks, sang the "Internationale," and climbed into bed with military precision. Once the lights went out, silence would hover for a few moments like a cloud bearing down on the earth, waiting for release. And each night, slowly and steadily, the silence cracked and the rains came down. It usually began with a boy on the far end of the room, a small boy, much smaller than Boris, who over the course of several months had managed to reduce his bawling to a careful sniffle that began the evening's performance. Then the smallest boys would start really crying, one by one, the sobs getting louder and louder like waves of rain slapping against the windows until the noise was so loud that the older ones would shout at them, insult them, even get out of bed and hit them, and then they would quickly shut up. But that was nothing compared to the real thunder and lightning of the evening. That happened with the older boys, after the little boys had finally stopped crying and everyone, including the older boys, had at last fallen asleep. Then the tempest would begin. First, one of the bigger boys would rise, still sleeping, and start shouting that the house was on fire. He usually kept shouting for several minutes, jumping up and grabbing his brothers from the neighboring bunks and dragging them toward the windows. On some nights he made it halfway out the window before he woke up, still shouting. Later another boy, who worshipped no god but Lenin by day, would stroll around the room in his sleep until he found the eastern wall, where he would stand in the humbled posture of his fathers, his back crooked and his shoulders hunched, chanting the entire Hebrew evening liturgy aloud until someone nearby found the energy to get out of bed in the cold night and slap him awake. A third boy would regularly get up in his sleep and attack people, shouting his older sisters' names and vowing revenge, pummeling the boys in the beds near his and anyone else too stupid to get out of his way. His victims would wake with bruises. But he was far from the worst. The worst, in Boris's opinion, was a boy about Boris's age, two beds down. This boy would fall asleep in perfect silence, an enviable peace hovering over his thin, motionless body, almost the sleep of the dead. He remained quiet each night until all of the other thundering had stopped, long past midnight. After the final incident of the night had come and gone, several minutes would pass in a deep, weary silence. And then, every single night, the boy would let out a high-pitched, blood-freezing shriek, after which he would scream, "Mommy! Mommy!" over and over without stopping until one of the boys next to him shook him awake. Then the dormitory would settle down again into the gentle sounds of small boys breathing in their beds, and Boris Kulbak would fight to stay awake for as long as he could until he was forced to surrender, as if cringing before a beating, to his own mangled dreams.

And then he met Comrade Chagall.

———

SINCE BORIS HAD arrived at Malakhovka, there had been no art class; the teacher had fallen ill, and had departed for Moscow. But that early spring day, for the first time, art classes were scheduled to resume.

Boris had never been in the art room before, which doubled as a classroom space for boys older than him. When he entered that morning for his first art class, the artwork by the students from three months earlier still hung on the dirty walls. Their paintings were full of grinning workers, muscular boys and girls hauling bales of hay, Red Army soldiers waving proud fists in the air, a red dawn always rising in the background. Boris looked at the pictures and thought they were ugly. But he sensed that this might be a wrong thought, a bad thought, the kind of thought that—he had learned in his socialism class—led to things like horses and boys being beaten, though Boris could not understand the connection, and he tried to look at the pictures with an appropriate amount of awe as he filed into the room with the rest of his class. Boris sat near the back of the room, behind several long rows of shaven heads. Suddenly the boys in front of him jumped to attention, standing beside their seats. Between their heads, Boris saw that a man had come into the room.

"Please, sit down. You make me nervous that way," the man's voice said.

The boys sat down in unison, their backs straight. Now Boris could see the man clearly. He was a tall man, younger than most of Boris's other teachers. He wore clothes that none of his other teachers wore— gray pants with thin white stripes on them, and bright red suspenders over a dirty white shirt. His head was covered with dark curls, which made Boris jealous. He looked at the class, his eyes wide, then glanced at his own hands. He coughed once, and the noise was still bouncing off of the concrete floor when he began to speak.

"Good morning, boys. You've probably guessed already that I'm your new art teacher for the term. I'm Comrade Chagall." He coughed again, into his fist.

The boys answered in a chorus, and Boris joined them: "Good morning, Comrade Chagall."

The teacher pressed his thick lips together and leaned back against the wall. A hiccup of air escaped his lips, and he quickly turned to the side, pretending to fix the cuff of his sleeve as he cupped his mouth with his palm. He glanced back at the class and stuck out his lower lip like a child, blowing air up so that a lock of hair on his forehead rose and quickly fell. Then he began to pace around the edge of the room, looking at the paintings on the walls. The boys watched him, motionless.

"These," he said suddenly, sweeping his arm across a broad wall of red dawns. "Who painted these?"

The class was silent, unsure of what was coming next. Finally the boy directly in front of Boris raised a finger. "Students, Comrade Chagall."

"What students?" the man asked. "You students, or other students?"

The boys glanced at one another, their eyes narrow. Was it a compliment? Boris leaned back slightly in his seat, relieved that he had never had an art class before. "Some are from us, some are from the other boys," a big boy next to Boris volunteered.

The man nodded slowly, still looking at the walls. "I asked," he said, turning to face the class, "because I know that you can do better than this."

Boris watched as the pale neck of the boy in front of him turned red. The boys in his row squirmed in their seats, their eyes on the floor.

"How many of you have had art class before?" the man asked.

The boys looked at each other and bit their lips. A few raised their hands, carefully, as if afraid to disturb the air, staring into their own laps.

"What did your last teacher tell you about how to paint?"

A pause hung heavily in the air, until a boy Boris hated spoke—a cruel boy whose head sprouted the shaved beginnings of orange hair. Boris had seen him throwing rocks at stray dogs. "He just told us to paint what we see," he said.

"To paint what you see," the teacher repeated, as if he were the student. "To paint what you see, or to paint what you look at?"

The orange-headed boy looked at the teacher and opened his mouth, but said nothing.

"Just because you look at something doesn't mean you can really see it," the man said, looking first at the boy and then at the class. "Look at my hand, for example," he said, waving his left hand in the air. "If I were to cut myself, the blood that would come out of my hand would be red. Blood is red, right?"

Boris cringed. There wasn't a boy in the room who didn't intimately know the color of blood. He glanced around quickly, noticing how the other boys hid their wincing—drawing their eyebrows together, rubbing their shaved heads, pressing their palms against their cheeks. The red-fuzzed boy looked down at his desk, his lower lip lodged between his teeth. No one spoke or even whispered. The entire room sat in silence, waiting.

"But look at my hand right now," the man was saying. With awkward, jerky motions, he rolled up his stained sleeve and revealed a pale left arm. "See the veins?" He traced a dirty finger along the back of his hand, holding it out to the class. "This blood isn't red. It's blue!"

The man turned to the jars of paint resting on the table in front of him and chose a brush, dipping it first in blue, then in green. Boris leaned to one side to see around the head of the boy in front of him. While the boys stared, the man put the brush to the back of his hand and began running it along his skin, tracing branching rivers up from his fingers along his forearm, all the way onto the edge of his shirt cuff above his elbow. Boris watched as the man leaned forward with both hands on the table in front of him, his two arms like twins, one clothed and one naked. Boris's eyes traced the paths of blue blood running up from the man's knuckles like water through the roots of a tree, up through his forearm and elbow and shoulder and toward the man's heart. "I don't want you just to look, or even to imagine," the man said. "I want you to see."

The man gathered a pile of large papers up in his arms and began quickly distributing them along the sides of the room, and then started passing out brushes and jars of paint. The boys, unable to understand the concept of someone doing something for them, got up out of their seats and began distributing the supplies themselves. "Today I want you to paint something you have seen yourself," the man said.

Boris glanced around the room again and saw the other boys—the ones passing out supplies and the ones still sitting down—avoiding each others' eyes. He couldn't think of anything he had ever seen that he would want to paint.

But the man kept talking, and Boris saw a smile creeping up over his face as the boys in the front row began to wet their brushes. "Whether you saw it yesterday or years ago, I don't care. It doesn't matter what it is, either. Or how you paint it. It could be a person. A tree. A rectangle. I don't care. So long as you paint what you really see."

Boris's row finally got its supplies. There wasn't much, and they would have to share the colors. The boy on Boris's right began painting a thick blue stripe along the bottom of his paper. Then Boris thought of something he had seen that seemed to fit what the man had said, something inside, like the blue blood in the man's veins. And he began to paint a picture of a womb.

Most people have never seen the inside of a womb—or, rather, everyone has seen it, but almost no one remembers it. Boris had been reminded of what it looked like on that night the previous spring, but that was just red blood, like the man said. Instead he painted what he had seen, inside, before. He made an outline of a body, bulging at its center, remembering something his mother had told him. For the past three months at Malakhovka, he had remembered nothing, but now he discovered that his thoughts were like the man's veins, suddenly and clearly rising to the surface.

The baby had been kicking a lot that day, she said. He saw her very clearly now: she was sitting beside him on his bed, her heavy body pulling the blanket tight. It was a spring night, and cool. Her bulging blouse glowed gold in the light of the lamp. She took his hand in hers (did he see the blue blood flowing in her fingertips as she took his hand, or was he only imagining it?) and placed it on her stomach. "Feel it," she said.

Boris tried very hard, but felt nothing, and was so embarrassed to have felt nothing that he pretended that he had felt it. There was a quiet shame in lies like these, not-quite lies that were only not-quite lies because they would never be noticed. A silent shame. Afraid of the silence, Boris strained to say something, anything. "What's the baby doing in there?" he asked, suddenly realizing that he did not know. "Why is he taking so long to come out?" And so his mother told him what happens to people who are waiting to be born.

Before being born, his mother explained, babies go to school. Not a school like Boris's, but a different kind of school, where all the teachers are angels. The angels teach each baby the entire Torah, along with all of the secrets of the universe. Then, just before each baby is born, an angel puts its finger right below the baby's nose—here she paused to put her finger across his lips (could he see the blood under her skin, or did he only imagine it?)—and whispers to the child: *Shh—don't tell.* And then the baby forgets.

"Why does he have to forget?" Boris had asked, moving his lips beneath her finger. He didn't want to know, not really. But his mother's back had stiffened, and he could feel that she might get up at any moment, put out the light, walk away, disappear.

She pulled her hand away from his face, resting it on her own stomach. "So that for the rest of his life," she said, "he will always have to pay attention to the world, and to everything that happens in it, to try to remember all the things he's forgotten."

Boris thought about this for a moment, but his mother was already leaning forward, about to kiss him good night. Please, he thought, don't leave. "Have you ever remembered anything?" Boris asked desperately. "I mean, any of the things you forgot?"

"Only a few," she whispered, brushing her lips on his ear. But before he could ask her what they were, she put out the light and vanished.

The womb Boris painted was dark inside, cavelike, with painted stalactites dripping down from its sides, and illuminated only by a single ray of narrow painted light. But inside it was a treasure house, like the one he had once heard about that explorers had found in Egypt, an underground hideaway filled with everything necessary for the next world. Bookcases climbed up the back wall of the womb. Its bottom was cushioned with piles of old scrolls. In the middle of it all was a small table—it was difficult, Boris found, to make the table straight, with the brush trembling in his hand—where a little baby sat on a chair. A thick pink baby (Boris, by accident, had made him a little thicker than he should have been), bald, as if he were already an old man. (Boris wondered: Do some people grow young before they are born, the way some people grow old before they die?) The baby was sitting in front of a large book, but he was looking straight ahead, a gaze that was unintentionally unnerving. Next to the baby floated an angel. Not like the ones he had seen carved onto the doors of churches, with two wings, but like the ones his father had once described, with six wings: with two it covered its face, and with two it covered its legs, and with the final two it flew. In the womb on Boris's crowded page, the angel hovered just to the left of the baby, a feathered cloud of white and blue paint. As he finished the angel's final wings, Boris was annoyed to see that a drop of blue paint had fallen, by accident, just beneath the baby's nose.

"It's marvelous," a voice behind him said.

Boris looked up. He hadn't noticed everyone else leaving the room. Now the room was empty except for him and the teacher who stood behind him, blue paint wrinkling the skin of the hairy forearm that he leaned against Boris's desk. Boris shivered. He hadn't been alone with an adult since that morning in the cemetery, when someone had found him in the grave.

The man leaned in closer over the table, examining the painting. To avoid looking at the man, Boris examined it, too, and realized that none of it had come out the way he wanted. The baby was far too fat; the beam of light looked more like a sheaf of straw; the angel looked more like a cloud than a bird. And then there was that blue mark below the baby's nose, exactly where it shouldn't be. The cheap paint had already begun to dry. Boris waited for the man to speak. The man kept looking, though, and suddenly he started whistling. Afraid to move, Boris listened to the thin blue melody rising from the man's heavy lips. It sounded less like a whistle than a wail, crying condensed into a narrow beam of breath. Then Boris recognized it. It was the tune for the prayer El Maley Rachamim, "God Full of Mercy," the one sung in cemeteries. In the past year Boris had often stolen money from the pockets of mourners at crowded funerals, while they listened, bawling, to cantors howling out that song.

The whistling stopped. "Marvelous," the man repeated. "What's your name?"

"Comrade Kulbak," Boris answered.

The man coughed, and in the cough Boris thought he could detect a hidden laugh. He felt his face becoming pinker than the fat baby's. Noticing a blotch of paint on his own hand, he wondered if his face, too, was marked beneath the nose. He rubbed his upper lip. "Comrade Kulbak," the teacher repeated. "I would love to have this painting, if I could. To put on the wall for the class."

Boris swallowed, and pressed his dirty hands down along the painting's edges. "What'll you give me for it?" he growled. This was what he always did, ever since his first beating, whenever someone wanted to take something from him. Months earlier, someone had asked for his shoes, and he had gotten four rolls and two pieces of candy for them. He still had no shoes, but it had been worth it.

This time the teacher laughed openly. "Comrade Kulbak, you're a little capitalist!"

Boris kept his eyes on his painting, his grip fierce. He didn't understand what the word meant, exactly, though it had been explained to him many times. All he knew was that it was something terrible.

But the man didn't seem to care. "You're very smart, Comrade Kulbak," the man said. "If it's a trade you want, fine. That's fair. Come with me, and we'll see if I have anything to trade."

The man offered Boris his hand, the one with the blue-painted veins. Boris looked at the hand, then at the man's face, and then back at his hand again, unsure of what to do with it. After a long time, the man laughed again and took hold of Boris's hand. Boris felt his chapped palm rubbing against the man's hard slab of a hand, like chalk writing on stone. The touch made him shiver. With his other hand Boris clung to the edge of his painting, careful not to drag it against his side. Silently, the man led him out of the room, across the muddy lawn, and toward the main road. As they walked across the mud, Boris looked at his own bare feet and saw the blue blood beneath his skin. He looked at the mud and saw the things it was made of: fallen leaves, bits of bark, melted snow, pieces of bone. In a few moments they were standing outside a large stone house that Boris had seen many times before, one that the younger boys said was haunted. But Boris wasn't afraid of the dead.

———————

"I'M SORRY ABOUT the smell," the man said as he pried open the wooden door. "We don't use the ground floor. We keep the windows open all the time, to try to air it out. It's still too dirty to live in."

Boris followed the man inside, his eyes growing wider to let in the feeble light. The man's comment shocked him. Three months ago, he would have considered this a palace. There were two dark rooms, with a narrow wooden staircase between them. Empty medicine bottles were scattered over the floors, interspersed with heaps of animal dung. A cold breeze blew through the open windows, and the smell—a familiar smell from the streets where he once slept, sickness condensed into a breath—coated the air around him like a layer of paint. It smelled orange, and green. The man pinched his own nostrils closed as he led Boris up the stairs. "My wife and daughter aren't here now," he said, his voice ringing through his nose. "They went to visit my wife's family in Vitebsk." At the top of the stairs, he opened a door, and Boris followed, allowing the door to slam into the smell behind him. And suddenly Boris was standing in a place that reminded him of a womb.

It was a long, narrow room, with light pouring in like a river of gold through a single window on one side. Under the window an easel was set up with a canvas propped on it, its white radiance untouched. Bookcases climbed up the back wall of the room, the middle and high shelves sagging with books of all colors and sizes, while the bottom shelves were taken up with rolls of canvas. There were two tables scattered with dozens of tubes of paint—real tubes, metal tubes, not like the watery jars they had used in class—and with drinking glasses filled with green and brown and orange water. Large paintings hung on the side walls one after another—a woman flying on a man's hand like a flag, a man and woman flying together through the air, a bride and groom held together by an angel, the bride with a little person embedded in her cheek. Along the edges of the room, stacked canvases leaned against the walls, the uppermost of which were vertical portraits

of people who looked to Boris like they had been broken into pieces—
a man playing a violin, a fat woman clapping her hands, and last, an
unfinished pale man in profile, writing on a scroll. In one corner was
an iron bed like Boris's, stretched to a width longer than its length by
a stack of old wooden boards that were rotting like railway ties. There
was a sink and a stove, and a few wooden chairs. Pink and yellow dolls'
clothes were strewn across the middle of the floor, which was stained
with blotches of blue paint. Boris looked at the clothes and imagined—
no, he didn't imagine, he saw—the absent dolls (had there been many
dolls, or just one well-dressed one?) lining up to leave the womb. The
angel from the painting of the wedding came down from the wall and
stood by the door as each of the dolls went by, pressing its finger into
their little lips, to make them forget.

Someone knocked at the door.

Boris looked up at the teacher, who was rolling his eyes. "He never
leaves me alone," the teacher muttered under his breath. Then he
shouted toward the door, "You know it's open, so don't pretend."

The door flew open with such force that it almost slammed into the
wall. Behind it was a man about the teacher's age, also with a head of
dark hair. But this man was far shorter and even more shabbily dressed,
in a dark suit worn to a shine. He had a long nose growing out of dark,
furry eyebrows, a thick mustache like a third eyebrow that covered the
dent below his nose, and a bristling smile. He noticed Boris, grinned
at him, and then looked back at the teacher, waving a torn envelope in
his hand.

"You have a telegram from Shloyme Mikhoels," he said, holding the
envelope high in the air. "He needs you to come back to Moscow and
finish the theater sets as soon as possible. He really means it this time,
my friend. 'As Soon as Possible.' That doesn't mean next month. That
means as soon as possible."

"Thanks for reading my mail." The teacher reached over and
snatched the envelope, a gesture the short man took as an invitation to
enter, which he did.

"Always a pleasure, Comrade Chagall," he sang as he strode into
the room. Boris watched as he navigated around the dolls' clothes
until he reached an empty wooden chair. He plunked himself into

the chair like a man in his own home, tipping backward against the bookcase. Suddenly he looked at Boris again and sat up straight, the chair's two front legs landing with a thunk. "I don't believe we've met," he said.

The teacher smiled a forced smile and turned to Boris, speaking in an overly loud voice and beating his chest with his fist. "Forgive me for failing to introduce our most honored, welcome guest. This," the teacher said, with a theatrical bow in the short man's direction, "is my upstairs neighbor, the illustrious Yiddish writer Pinkhas Kahanovitch, better known as Der Nister." *Der Nister*, Boris thought. *The Hidden One*. Boris looked at the Hidden One, who seemed even shorter than before now that he was perched in the wooden chair, and imagined for a moment—or saw?—that this strange little man was actually hidden among the books and paintings behind him, his human form merely the dullest of the portraits. "He teaches literature in the colony, to the older boys," the teacher explained. Der Nister smiled, his teeth poorly painted in layers of gray.

"And this," the teacher said, nudging Boris forward, "is Comrade Kulbak, an incredibly talented artist." Boris felt that the room had suddenly become uncomfortably cold. He looked down at his feet, scratching his left foot with the toes of his right. "Show him your painting, Comrade Kulbak," the teacher said, slapping him on the back.

Boris brought forward his picture and reversed it so that Der Nister could see it. To him, it now looked far worse than before, not even the palest shadow of the paintings on the walls. He wondered if, in some deep hidden way, he might actually be blind.

"Stunning," Der Nister said. Boris couldn't tell whether he really meant it. Der Nister turned to the teacher and asked, "Why are children so much smarter than adults?"

"The boys in Malakhovka are not really children," the teacher said, his voice low. "They are adults trapped in children's bodies."

"True," the Hidden One said. He looked at the painting carefully, and then, even more carefully, at Boris, until Boris suspected that he could see beneath his skin, down to his blood, his brains, his breath inside his lungs. "My daughter is just a few years younger than you," he said.

Boris said nothing, holding his breath.

"What is your real name, Comrade Kulbak?"

Boris looked at him, confused. "Boris," he tried.

"No," the man said. "I mean your real name, your Jewish name."

Boris thought a moment, frightened. Had he forgotten his own name? He stood in silence, almost for too long. "Benjamin," he finally said. No one had called him that in over a year.

"Benjamin," Der Nister said. "What's your full name? Benjamin son of who?"

Boris thought again, even more frightened. What if he couldn't remember? His mother had once told him that only with his full name would he be admitted to the world to come. What was it? "Benjamin son of Jacob," he blurted, relieved.

Der Nister smiled. "Benjamin and Jacob. *Nafsho keshura benafsho.* You know what that means?"

Boris shuddered and shook his head. He was used to speaking Yiddish with his teachers, even though the boys usually spoke Russian among themselves. But Hebrew he had long forgotten.

"It's from Genesis, about Jacob and his son Benjamin," Der Nister explained. "*Nafsho keshura benafsho*—'His soul was bound to his.' That's how it is with a father and son. What happens to him, happens to you."

Boris froze. His body became rigid and numb, like that morning lying in the grave, as the smile dissolved from Der Nister's face. He saw, without feeling it, the teacher's blue-streaked hand on his shoulder.

"Never mind him," the teacher said to Boris with an uneasy laugh. "He enjoys being cryptic."

Slowly Boris began to thaw. He looked at the teacher standing above him, and at the Hidden One sitting almost below him, at the teacher's forced grin and at Der Nister's eyes that peered at him with pity. Their two faces—the sneering grin of one, the earnest sad smile of the other—confused and frightened him. It was as if he were looking at the faces of the other boys in the orphanage, or of the boys in his town before he was brought to Malakhovka. The teacher's face suddenly reminded him of the mean boys, the ones who laughed at mean jokes and beat up the others, while the Hidden One's face seemed to him like the faces of the boys who cried too easily and were invariably bullied and beaten, with no one to save them. It doesn't change, he thought. He bowed his head, saw the blood inside his own bare feet, and trembled.

"Comrade Kahanovitch and I collaborate sometimes," the teacher said loudly, breaking the silence. "We write children's books together— he writes the stories, and I make the pictures."

"That's nice," Boris said, in order to say something. He braced his feet against the floor.

"Why don't you show him one of our children's books, Kahanovitch?" the teacher asked Der Nister, his voice a preternatural shade of bright green. "I have them all right on the shelf behind your head."

"But you said these boys aren't really children," Der Nister said, his mouth pulled down in concern as he contemplated Boris. Suddenly his eyes brightened. "Why don't I read him one of my real stories instead? Here's something I just wrote this week." He got to his feet, pulling a few folded pages out of his inside pocket as the teacher groaned.

"Oh, God, spare us. Not a performance," the teacher begged.

"I wrote it for a longer story, but this is part of it. Tell me what you think," Der Nister said, unfolding the sheets.

"There's just no way to shut him up," the teacher muttered to no one, and then sighed loudly, a deliberate, sharp puff of breath. The Hidden One carefully ignored this as he began, in a voice that seemed accustomed to lullabies and bedtime stories for a little girl about Boris's age, to recite his tale.

This is the story of the All-Bridge, the bridge which leads from the deepest depths of the abyss to the highest heights of heaven. Did you know there was such a bridge?

"I don't think you meant to write 'bridge,' " the teacher interrupted. "It sounds more like a ladder to me. Don't you think so, Comrade Kulbak?"

Boris shrugged, pretending not to care. But he was intrigued. Was there really a bridge like that? He looked at Der Nister. A moment earlier, the writer had seemed commanding, powerful. But now he looked strangely embarrassed, folding and unfolding the pages between his fingers, wordlessly opening and closing his thin lips.

The teacher sighed again, this time with a smile, and sat down on the floor. Boris lowered himself to the floor beside him as the story continued.

Well, there's a reason you've never heard of this bridge.

The bridge was created at the very end of the week of creation, on Friday evening, at twilight—the very last thing God created before he completed the world and rested on the seventh day. But he didn't spend much time on it. It was made hastily, and then immediately abandoned as God went off to celebrate the sabbath. So the bridge was alone on the very first night of the world. Its form stood silent in the darkness, its feet sunken into the abyss, and its head aloft in the bright heavenly shrine, where a sacred stillness rested.

And in that heavenly shrine, there was a door that led into another door, and the second door was closed, and behind it, that night, God planned to celebrate the sabbath after his week of world-weariness, leaving the bridge alone.

The bridge was very pleased with its head, which rested at the door of the heavenly shrine. But its feet were sunk into the abyss, where they rested amid cold, dark slime, and strange reptiles were swarming all over them. So the bridge began to complain. He complained so much that God hurried away from him right after creating him, retiring behind the heavenly door. And after hearing the complaints, Satan made his very first nighttime visit to the world.

"So here you are," Satan said to the bridge, "with nothing to do. It's nighttime, it's the sabbath, and God has shut himself up in his heavenly shrine. Why don't you come with me, down into the abyss?"

"That's just where I don't want to go," the bridge said. "I'm already covered up to my feet in muck and slime. Why would I want the slime to reach up to my head?"

"Because it's going to happen anyway," Satan told him.

"What do you mean?" the bridge asked.

"What," Satan sneered, "haven't you heard what your job is?"

"My job?" the bridge asked.

"Yes, your job. What, don't you know what it is? It's incredibly unfair! Why should everything in the whole world be created for its own sake, except for you? Why should you alone be created just for the purpose of others, so that everyone else gets to walk all over you?"

And then Satan explained the bridge's task: that from the very first generation of the world and for all the generations to follow, people would be traveling on him from the depths up to the heights. And all of the people ascending him would bring with them their damp and disgusting bodies, and drag their dirt and slime all over him, until he was so covered with muck that his entire body might as well have sunk into the abyss, enslaved to other people's filth. The bridge listened and became nauseated.

"So, aren't you insulted?" Satan asked.

The bridge shuddered, disgusted. "But what if I am? What can I do?"

Satan stepped closer and whispered in his ear. "Break yourself! Right now! God won't notice—he's shut up in his shrine. And then you and I will establish our own kingdom in the depths, and you'll be a regular bridge, just spanning the length of the depths, without connecting at all to the heavenly shrine. Who needs God and his heavenly shrine when we could rule ourselves?"

The bridge listened, but didn't answer.

"I'll let you decide on your own," Satan said, and went away.

The bridge wavered, hesitating. A cold shudder ran through his entire length, and his feet trembled in the abyss.

The sabbath day passed, and when it ended, God appeared on the threshold of the heavenly shrine.

"A good week!" God said to the bridge, using the post-sabbath greeting for the very first time.

And the bridge felt filthy, and suddenly he pulled himself up and broke off the part of himself that was stuck in the abyss. Though he felt no more slime on his feet, the light of his head became dim, like the eyes of a beaten man.

"A good week!" the bridge said, echoing God's blessing. And his eyes were downcast and ashamed.

Der Nister stopped reading, but Boris wasn't sure that the story was actually over. How could that be the end of the story? Was there really no way out of the slime? Boris remembered something he had heard in school, not in Malakhovka, but a long time ago. The world was made of vessels (the teacher had said "vessels"; Boris, unsure what it meant, had always pictured clear glass jars), one within another, with God at the center. But God had to shrink himself to make more room for the world, and when he did, the vessels shattered into pieces. Standing among the paint stains and scattered dolls' clothes, Boris felt like the foot of the ladder, a broken, abandoned piece of a dark and shattered world.

"I'm telling you, Kahanovitch, stuff like that is a one-way ticket out of the USSR."

The Hidden One pursed his lips as he folded the story into his pocket. "It's symbolic, you pest. Don't you understand symbolism?"

Boris looked at Der Nister and then at the teacher, wondering what "symbolism" meant. But the teacher only grunted, an inelegant sound, and scratched at the paint on his forearm. Bits of blue flaked to the floor like shards of pottery. The veins below the paint were dark, obscured by curly dark hair. "The symbolism isn't even the problem, artistically," the teacher said, his voice gruff. "The problem with your stories is that you start writing them with one little moment like that, but then you keep adding more and more pieces to it until it really stops making sense."

"That is exactly where you are wrong, Comrade Chagall. It is only after I put together the rest of the pieces that the story starts to make sense."

"Mmph," the teacher said, still scratching his arm. The floor around his arm was now covered with shards of blue paint, as if his skin had shattered. Boris glanced to the right of Der Nister's chair, at the portrait of the shattered musician and the pale unfinished man, who now seemed to Boris to be writing on a broken scroll, a scroll torn in two by a set of scored pencil lines below the paint.

Suddenly the teacher leapt to his feet. "I almost forgot!" he said. "Comrade Kulbak was about to choose one of my paintings. I'm trading one of mine for his."

"A little capitalist art dealership," Der Nister said, his eyebrows raised. "Does the colony council know about this?"

"This is between me and Comrade Kulbak," the teacher snapped. "It would have happened a long time ago, if you hadn't barged in with your heavenly shrine routine." He turned to Boris. "Take a look around."

Slightly startled, Boris began to wander around the room, dodging the dolls' clothes, with the teacher's voice following behind him. He eyed the painted wedding couple with visible envy. "I'm sorry, but I can't give you any of the larger ones," the teacher said behind him, throwing his hand across the bride's face. "I need them for an exhibition. And the ones on top of those piles I can't offer you, either," he added, waving his hand at the portraits of the broken men with the violin and the scroll. "They're for the State Jewish Theater. They're being used for the play next month."

"Only if you actually answer that telegram," Der Nister interjected, pointing to the envelope the teacher had set down on the table.

The teacher ignored him, turning toward Boris. "It's going to be very exciting," he said. "They're performing stories by Sholem Aleichem. Do you know his stories?"

Boris thought hard, seeing his mother sitting with a book by his bed, struggling with something that would not become a memory. "There was a story about—about a goat?" he asked softly. "About a man whose goat keeps getting stolen, but the man doesn't notice?"

The teacher looked at him, his eyes blank. But the Hidden One's voice soon filled the air. "Oh, yes, 'The Haunted Tailor,'" he said, almost singing. "One of my favorites. Do you remember how it ends?"

Boris shook his head.

"Allow me to remind you," Der Nister said.

"Please, spare us, just this once," the teacher begged.

Unruffled, the Hidden One stood up and declaimed:

" 'Don't force it, kids! The ending is not a good one. The story started very happily, and turned out, like most happy stories, very sadly. And since you know the author of the story and know that he's not the depressive type, and hates miserable stories and much prefers happy ones, and since you know that he hates stories with a "moral" and that preaching isn't his thing—therefore the author will take leave of you laughing instead, and wishes for your sake that people all over the world would laugh more than they cry. Laughing is healthy. Doctors prescribe laughter.' "

The words shrank as Der Nister recited them, becoming softer and softer until the final sentence came out almost under his breath. From someone else it would have seemed pompous, but Boris could see that Der Nister wasn't doing it on purpose. It was simply as if he had forgotten that any of them were there. He was speaking to himself. Boris watched in awe as Der Nister lowered himself, carefully, back into his seat.

"Maybe they should do that one at the theater," Der Nister said to the teacher, his voice still low. "It's not so bourgeois like the others. Less likely to cause problems."

"But it doesn't have a real ending," the teacher protested. "People like real endings. Redemption, that sort of thing."

"How is that not a 'real ending'?" Der Nister snorted. "There are no real endings in life, either. Since when do things end?"

"I suppose it would be a good example of socialist realism," the teacher said, and Boris heard something snide in his voice, a dark edge.

"I'm telling you, this is as realistic as it gets. 'Laughing is healthy. Doctors prescribe laughter.' That's the best way for anything to end." Der Nister turned to Boris, his own story refolded in his hand. "What do you think, Comrade Kulbak?"

"I—I don't know," Boris stuttered, though it seemed to him that in fact things did end, and that when they did, it wasn't funny at all. He looked at the Hidden One, at the space below his nose where his thick mustache completely covered the dent in his upper lip.

"Comrade Kulbak doesn't care about those stories," the teacher said loudly, resting his hand on Boris's shoulder. "He's here to pick one of my pictures." He turned to look at Boris. "As I said, I can't give you the larger ones. But I will let you have a study, since you're giving me a study," he said, leading Boris toward several piles of canvases beneath the portrait with the scroll. "Look through these studies and tell me which one you want."

Boris looked, and was surprised to find a series of miniatures of the larger paintings on the walls, as if the larger ones had been broken into pieces replicated on separate little canvases: the musician drawn individually, without his violin; the bride split apart from the groom. There were some that he lingered over, like the two women bathing a baby, and others that he flipped through quickly, like the cartoons of wounded soldiers. But most of them were too bright, the colors too imaginary to be real. And then his eye stopped on a tiny dark painting, darker than all the others, a deep brooding street that looked very much like the street where he used to live, with a man who looked very much like Boris's own father hovering in the air over the town. This, he thought, was what he had once seen.

"This one," he whispered.

"That one?" the teacher asked, and in the question, Boris thought he heard a tinge of disappointment. But then the teacher pulled it up from the ground, recognizing an old friend. He smiled. "I think of this one as *Going Over the Houses*," he said, his voice soft, as if he were sharing a secret. "When I was a boy, beggars used to come to the house all the time, and people would call it 'going over the houses.' When they said that, this was what I saw."

"He loves to play with words," the Hidden One said. "If you look, you'll see that most of his painting are little jokes with words."

The teacher held Boris's own painting up in the fading sunlight. "I would call yours *El Maley Rechamim*," he said. That was the name of the Hebrew cemetery prayer he had been whistling earlier, Boris remembered. *God Full of Mercy*. Except the teacher had pronounced it wrong.

"He loves to play with words," the Hidden One repeated. "He should be the writer, not me. *Rechamim* instead of *Rachamim*—you understand?"

Boris shook his head.

"*Rachamim* means 'mercy,' but if you pronounce it *rechamim*, it means 'wombs.' *God Full of Wombs*."

Full of wombs?

"So that's it, then. Take it," the teacher said, clamping his blue hand on Boris's shoulder for the last time. "A fair trade. You'll see your picture on the wall in class tomorrow morning."

Before Boris could take the painting, Der Nister leapt from his seat. "Wait," he cried. "I'm not about to be the only unrepresented artist here. Take this, too." He reached into his jacket pocket and pulled out the crumpled paper with his story, grabbing the painting from the teacher's hands. "I have it all in my head, so you can keep this," he said. Turning the painting around and balancing it on a shelf behind him, he folded the paper into a long thin strip and then slipped it underneath the wood of the canvas frame.

"Don't stretch the canvas like that!" the teacher shrieked, then blushed, lowering his voice. "It loosens the tacks. In twenty years the whole thing will fall apart."

Der Nister held it tight and laughed. "Don't worry, I'm sure our apprentice artist will take even better care of a pregnant painting." He grinned as he faced Boris, turning the painting back around and grandly presenting it to him. "I trust you will be an excellent curator of *two* works of art."

Boris took the canvas in his hands. "Thank you," he said, and began edging his way toward the door.

"Won't you stay for supper?" Der Nister asked.

But Boris looked at his smile and the teacher's grin and saw the boys' faces again. He suddenly needed to leave, to escape this strange clarity, which was becoming fiercer than a bad dream. "I have to—I have to go back," he stuttered, acutely aware of his lie. "The council will be angry if I don't get my chores done."

Der Nister frowned. "Spoken like a true Marxist. From each according to his ability. Workers of the world, unite and break the little artist's back!"

"Shut up, Kahanovitch," the teacher hissed. He turned back to Boris, who was now clutching the painting in both hands. "I'll see you tomorrow," he said, opening the door for him with a laugh.

"Thank you," Boris murmured again, and stepped out of the room.

"The pleasure was ours. You have a wonderful imagination," Der Nister called behind him as the door swung shut.

But Boris was already running down the stairs as fast as he possibly could, descending into the abyss of the house's ground floor and the mud below, hoping the last of the stairs wouldn't break beneath his feet. For what he had seen up above was now seared forever into his mind: the man who laughed at him, who he knew would last, and the man who praised his imagination, who he already saw disappearing.

3

—

THE PAINTING was even more beautiful than he remembered it, Ben thought as he propped it up on the headboard of his bed later that evening, lying on his stomach in front of it. With his head at this level he almost felt as if he were walking down the painting's street. He looked at the painting and found himself feeling very light, as if, lying prone on the bed, he were actually floating through the air. He wondered if this was what people felt like when they were finally freed of their bodies. There was a strange ache in his cheeks. He sat up and caught a glimpse of his face in the mirror next to the door, one of the few things his wife had failed to take with her when she left. To his surprise, he was smiling.

He wandered around the apartment that his former wife had denuded of everything but the bed, a desk, and one small bookshelf. On the desk was a stack of papers he had taken home from work, articles he had been assigned to edit for the *American Genius Online Encyclopedia*, a pathetic piece of pseudo-scholarship whose only purpose was to provide fifth-graders with material they could plagiarize for school reports. At the top of the pile was a recent encyclopedia submission on the subject of "Schrödinger's Cat," a paradox in quantum theory that had impressed him as supremely logical when he had first read about it as a teenager. In a hypothetical experiment, a cat is placed in a box, Ben fondly recalled, with a potentially self-opening

pellet of cyanide that creates a fifty-percent chance of feline death. As
the encyclopedia article rather inelegantly explained it,

> Subatomic particles are often described as existing simultaneously in
> two contradictory states. But this is a paradox, like the idea that the cat
> in the box is "fifty-percent dead" up until one opens the door of the box
> to find out the cat's state. On the macro level of the non-subatomic
> world, it is impossible for something to be both dead and alive at the
> same time, or to be "half dead."

Ben glanced at the unedited article and smiled. It suddenly seemed to
him profoundly possible for something to be both dead and alive at the
same time. Half dead, surely. He turned to the floor, which was covered with old stacks of paper, whole categories' worth of questions that
hadn't made it onto *American Genius*:

Which Aztec deity is considered the Lord of the Land of the Dead?

*What name have scholars given to the compilation of spells discovered
on scrolls that had been placed between the thighs of Egyptian
mummies?*

What is the Greek term for the transmigration of souls?

In the Book of Genesis, what guards the path to the Tree of Life?

He was in the habit of leaving questions lying around the apartment,
scribbling them down whenever they occurred to him and then forgetting about them until he would return to the bathroom and pick up
a tissue that asked him for the dates of Stalin's first Five-Year Plan, or
open a kitchen drawer and find a shopping list requesting the date of
George Washington's birthday according to the Julian calendar. His
wife used to laugh at him for that. Sometimes she would append the
notes with questions of her own:

Does your Five-Year Plan include cleaning the bathroom?

What do you want for your birthday?

Do we really have to visit the hospital every single weekend?

Have you ever noticed that your sister is always covered with paint?

And once, toward the end, beneath a question about Egyptian kings:

Why should I care?

Only later did it occur to Ben that she wasn't just referring to the
pharaohs.

One day in recent weeks while he was slogging away at *American Genius*, she had returned to the apartment in his absence and relieved him of all of their furniture. Sara told him he should sue. He settled for changing the locks, but not before she returned again and took all of his books, for what reason he didn't know—and there had been hundreds upon hundreds, cherished memorized volumes from the days when he had been a child prodigy, before he had learned the horrid truth that there is no such thing as an adult prodigy—except that she was thoughtful enough or resentful enough to leave behind the series of picture books by Ben's mother. In the past few months he had barely been able to look at them. Now, though, with the painting lying on his bed as he waited for Sara to arrive, he took his favorite off the shelf and opened it.

It was a masterpiece: a beautiful melding of ink and watercolor, solid inked drawings of real things and then imaginative watercolor tracings of things in the story that had disappeared. The illustrations had won a prize. She had always been an illustrator, even before she began publishing her own books. But this time, as he opened to the very first page, it was the text that drew him in. He sat on his bed, more fully awake than he had been in weeks, and began to read the book called *The Man Who Slept Through the End of the World*.

He was always sleepy. At every opportunity he slept. Everywhere: at all the big events, concerts, parties. Everywhere. He just sat and slept.

One night while he was sleeping, it seemed to him that it was thundering outside. But he didn't wake up. When his bed shook, he thought in his sleep that it was raining outside, and his sleep only became more delicious. He snuggled up under his blanket and kept sleeping. But when he woke up, he had quite a shock.

His wife was gone. His bed was gone. His blanket was gone. He would have looked out the window, but there was no window to look out of. He would have run down the three flights of stairs and yelled for help, but there were no stairs on which to run and no air in which to yell. He would have just gone outside, but there was no outside!

For a while he stood there, confused. Then he decided he would just lie down and sleep on the ground. But then he saw that there wasn't even any ground to sleep on.

"What a mess," he thought. "I've slept through the end of the world. How do you like that!"

Then he was annoyed. No world, he thought. What would he do without a world? Where would he work? And how would he make a living? Especially now that everything was so expensive and eggs were a dollar and twenty cents a dozen and who knew if they were even fresh? And where was his wife? Was it possible that she had also disappeared, along with the world and the money in his pants pocket? She wasn't the type to disappear, he thought. And what would he do if he wanted to sleep? What could he lie on, if there was no world?

"Well, there's no world! Too bad," our hero decided. "What can you do? I might as well go to the movies and kill some time." But to his great surprise, he saw that along with the world, the movie theater had also disappeared.

"Look what I've gotten myself into!" our hero thought. "If I hadn't been so fast asleep, I would have disappeared right along with everything else. Now where am I going to get a cup of coffee? And what about my wife? Who knows who she's disappeared with? Maybe she's disappeared with the guy from the top floor. . . . And what time is it, anyway?"

At these words our hero would have taken a look at his watch, but it had disappeared.

"I always drink a cup of coffee in the morning," he thought. "Where am I going to get a cup of coffee? And here I went and slept through the end of the world!

"Help! Help!" he shouted into the emptiness. "What was I thinking? Why didn't I keep an eye on the world and my wife? Why did I let them disappear? Help!"

And our hero began banging his head against the void. But since the void was a very soft void, he didn't hurt himself, and he lived to tell this story.

When Ben last read it, years ago, the story seemed the same as always: amusing, absurd. But this time, as he looked around his empty apartment, he was suddenly astonished by how possible it was to let your wife and your life slip through your fingers simply because you didn't hold on tight enough, how normal it was to assume the best of people, how common it was to foolishly count on others to guard you while you slept—how very, very easy it was to sleep through the end of the world. He was still thinking about it, banging his own head against the void, when Sara arrived at his door.

———

THAT NIGHT SARA was radiant. Her radiance came from confidence, from a failure to care about what anyone else thought of her, and Ben envied her for that. She was a doctoral student in art history and an artist herself, ten minutes younger than Ben, and she wasn't what anyone, other than people who knew her well, would call attractive. Tonight, for example, it was clear that she hadn't been teaching, only working alone: her right hand was encrusted with blue paint, and her hair was pulled back with a white garbage tie. But Sara had the kind of beauty that would sneak up on you, catching your eye only when you saw her burst out laughing, her blue eyes crinkling into dark slits in her face, or when you saw her with her head dipped into a book, her perfect fingers resting on the pale nape of her neck, or tracing the edge of her forehead where you could see the tiny dark brown hairs emerging from her skin, held in absurdly straight lines by her tight ponytail until they were allowed to race into wild curls. And then you couldn't believe that you hadn't always thought she was beautiful.

They were long past the point where they bothered saying hello to each other. Even phone calls between them generally started with a brutal question, going straight for the jugular. This time, she looked around the room, kicking lightly at the piles of questions on the floor. She plucked one off the rug, read it, and smiled.

"*The Book of the Dead*," she said.

It was the answer to the mummy question. "You're an American Genius," he told her.

She snorted, then glanced at Ben's lap and smirked. "How's the book?"

He slammed it shut on his knee, trying to think of an obnoxious retort. But he found that he couldn't even growl at her the way he wanted to. He couldn't help it; he was still smiling.

Sara looked him in the face. "What's so funny? Did you meet someone at the museum?"

Ben glanced at the mirror built into the wall behind his sister, and saw what Sara had not yet noticed: the painting resting on the bed behind him. And then all of his usual resentment of Sara—of her talent, of the competence that made their mother give her power of attorney, of her brilliant marriage to the brilliant husband whom Ben himself had long ago deposited in her lap—evaporated. Tonight, at least, he was the one with the bigger news.

Ben turned to the treasure lying behind him, picking it up and turning back toward Sara as he stood, holding it against his chest. "Do you recognize this?" he asked.

It took her a moment to respond, and when she did, it was as if someone else were speaking in her voice—as if, Ben thought, she were only a shell of herself, and the real Sara was floating freely around the room. "From the house," she murmured. Ben grinned as he watched her gazing at the painting, mesmerized. It was a long time before she looked at him again. "You bought a copy of it?"

"It's not a copy. It's the one from our living room," he said. "Look, you can even see in the corner where you smeared nail polish on it."

Sara leaned toward him and peered at the painting's corner. "Oh, God, you're right," she breathed, and stayed there, staring at it. "Where did you find this?"

"On the wall in the museum."

"What?"

"It was part of the exhibit."

Sara snapped her head up and stepped back until she had her back against the wall. She stood there, silent.

"There weren't any alarms or anything. I was kind of surprised."

Ben watched her face tremble as she struggled to speak. An eternity seemed to pass before she managed to form a word. "Ben, this is a crime," she said slowly. "A crime. This is not like shoplifting in a drugstore or something. You're going to go to jail for this."

"Only if I'm caught."

"Only if you're caught?" she shrieked.

He ignored her, turning the painting back toward himself and sink-ing to the floor. Sara squatted beside him, still fuming. He pretended to be entranced with the painting, avoiding looking at her until she glanced away. Sara leaned her head back against the door and stuck out her lower lip, blowing air up toward the loose hairs on her forehead to make them fly. Sitting on the floor with her, Ben suddenly had the strange feeling that they were eight years old again, when sitting on the floor was completely expected, admiring a painting which, he had to admit, could have been an eight-year-old's work. A vague memory entered his mind of sitting with her on the floor like this once, using paints to cover the wall of her room with fake paw prints, until their parents discovered them. The warm wave of longing that ran through his body embarrassed him.

But Sara was still shocked. "You can't just—you can't just—"

"Why not?" Ben asked. "You mean it's wrong for me to steal it, but when it gets stolen from us, then that's perfectly—"

"You know we can't prove that," Sara interrupted. "And even if we could—"

Suddenly Ben slammed the side of the painting down against the floor. The man in the painting lay prone, rattled but intact. "Sara, I'm sick of it!" he shouted. The pitch of his voice surprised even him. It was the way he should have shouted at his wife, but he had never had the courage. "I am sick, sick, sick of having things taken from me. Don't you get it? Our family is finished, Sara. This is the one thing we have left." He took a breath, and the man in the painting shuddered. "You know you only came here to talk to me about selling the house. There's nothing left anymore."

The man in the painting trembled beyond Ben's squinting eyelids. But Sara's body was solid and steady, barely moving as she tilted her head back against the wall. "I didn't come here to talk about the house," she said.

Ben swallowed, feeling blood thumping in his neck. "What do you mean?"

"I came to tell you that I'm having a baby, my dear dumb brother." She smiled, and then, when Ben didn't say anything, began to laugh.

Ben stared at her, watching her laugh and wondering if it was some

kind of joke. But as he raised his eyebrows at her, he saw her nodding
her head, her lips trembling.

"Leonid is working late tonight, but I couldn't wait to tell you. I'm
due right after Passover."

It was a long time before Ben was able to speak. His shock slowly dissipated into a thin, wavering jealousy, blurring the air in the room.
The whole world was leaving him behind. When his voice finally
came loose from his throat, he tried to congratulate her. Instead he
blurted, "But Sara, are you—are you sure?"

"Of course I'm sure."

He stuttered, choked, struggling to find something to say, anything
that would hide how he really felt. "No, I know, but it's just—I mean,
you just got married, Sara. Are you sure you wanted—"

Sara looked up at the ceiling, and Ben suddenly noticed a drop of
pale blue paint in the dent below her nose. "We planned it that way,"
she said softly. "I was hoping that Mom would—" She looked at her
hands. "Well."

Ben looked at his sister's hands, and then glanced again at the painting. God, he thought, a baby. And their parents, who would never see
it. But a baby. For all of them.

Still sitting on the floor, the two of them embraced—or, really, the
three of them embraced. In her arms Ben stammered his congratulations and then fell silent, sensing the presence of the new person, the
not-yet person within her. The three of them held each other, dreaming unborn dreams.

Sara stood up, as if breaking a spell. She picked up the painting and
placed it carefully on the bed. "They're going to come after you for
this," she said. "You need to take it out of your apartment. Stash it
somewhere else."

"Where?"

"Anywhere, just not here. I don't want you in jail when the baby
comes." The baby. "Don't worry, we're going to figure out a way to get
you out of this."

Ben grimaced. "It's our painting. You can tell me whatever you
want, but I'm not going to turn anything in—not the painting and not
myself. Just try and make me." But already all he could think about was
the baby.

"Just try and stay out of jail," Sara said.

Long after she left, Ben lay on his bed and suddenly found that he couldn't sleep. Instead he imagined himself flying, gazing at the ground far below and seeing, from his aerial view, two paths out of the necropolis that might not be dead ends.

4

—

BENJAMIN ZISKIND did not become intelligent until he was eleven years old. Well, naturally that wasn't quite true (studies have shown, Ben knew, that people's characters are more or less fixed from the age of six), but at the age of eleven, two things happened to Benjamin Ziskind. First, his father died, and second, he was locked into a cage for the next six years of his life.

The cage was actually called the Milwaukee Model Orthotic Brace, but from the moment Ben saw it—or, more accurately, from the moment the doctor and his mother helped him into it, a process that took almost half an hour, immediately after which the doctor broke the news that Ben would have to wear it for twenty-two hours a day, every day, for the next six years—he might as well have been handed a life sentence in solitary confinement. Ben had been a smart boy, in the casual way that eleven-year-old boys are called smart for always winning board games, but he had never been able to sit still, always running in mad circles around the house and, since their father died, testing the flammability of various aerosol bathroom cleaners in the backyard. During their father's illness—twelve weeks, start to finish—no one had noticed how Ben had begun walking around with his right shoulder slightly lower than his left. After his father's death, everyone and everything slumped, and once again no one noticed. It was only several weeks later, when Sara started drawing

people walking crooked on her sketch paper and performing elaborate imitations of her brother's Neanderthal clopping around the
house, that their mother realized that something was wrong. Some
people are uncomfortable in their own skin, but Ben was uncomfortable far deeper than his skin. He was uncomfortable in his own
bones.

His very first day in the cage began with forty-five minutes of humil-
iation as his mother tried to help him put it on, until she had to take a
phone call from the life insurance agent. Ben struggled alone until
Sara wandered into the bathroom where he was standing between the
sink and the toilet, naked except for his underwear and the half-
adjusted brace.

"Mom told me to help you," Sara muttered dutifully, standing in the
bathroom doorway. She was already dressed for school, avoiding Ben's
eyes.

"I don't need help," Ben snorted, and turned away from her. Sara
was ten minutes younger than him, but this was the first year when he
could no longer feel the power of those ten minutes. Since their father
died, she had become taller than him and, to his astonishment,
seemed to suddenly have the beginnings of breasts, while he was still
short, beardless, scrawny, and now, standing in front of his twin sister
in his underwear, trapped inside his scrap-metal cage. He bit his lip
and tried again to connect the brace collar that he had already given
up on, reaching for the thumb bolt at the back of his neck and ignor-
ing Sara's face in the mirror. The chin support dug into his jaw, and
soon he began to feel as if someone were choking him. He stole a
glance in the mirror and saw himself imprisoned. The steel bars of the
cage—one in the front, two in the back—ran up and down his torso,
from his neck to his stomach, with a plastic plate gagging him beneath
his chin. His waist was encased in steel-lined plastic, and additional
bars of plastic and steel ran underneath one arm. He didn't have the
courage to look at his own face.

"Let me help you," Sara said behind him. Her tangled hair brushed
against his cheek as she reached for the bolt at the back of his neck.

"I DON'T NEED HELP!" he screamed. He tried again to tighten
it himself, contorting his arms behind his head, but it was hopeless.

She watched him struggle for a moment, wincing. Then her hand moved in silence across his neck and snapped the bolt into place.

Ben could no longer turn, bend, or even slightly move his head. He looked straight ahead in the mirror because he had no other choice. He was helpless now. Just above the metal scaffolding, his face was bright red, streaked with tears.

"You're like a knight wearing armor, Ben. Now nobody can hurt you," Sara said, her voice almost a whisper. Ben saw her face beside his in the mirror and squeezed his eyes shut. His skin itched and seethed beneath the plastic sheath.

"Ben, everything is going to get better," he heard her say in the void. "Really. It has to get better, because it can't get worse."

Ben opened his eyes with a jolt, staring at himself in the mirror. That's not true, he suddenly thought. It can definitely get worse. As he nodded at Sara and pretended to smile, he understood that it was the first intelligent thought he had ever had.

————

WHEN HIS MOTHER finally locked him up properly the next day and left him alone, Ben took advantage of the moment of solitude to steal the newspaper articles she had saved about Soviet Jewish dissident Natan Sharansky, who had recently been released from the gulag, and he began reading over and over about Sharansky's days and nights in the punishment cell, blocked off from the world by freezing cement. It was around then that he started taking books out of the library about jails and gulags and prison camps and even the Hanoi Hilton, though his mother returned that one the next day, claiming that she had found it in his room and it was overdue, which was a blatant lie, of course, so Ben had to read that one secretly in the library while pretending to be researching a school report about coral. Those books led him to others, and soon he had given up on burning bathroom cleaners and lived entirely in his room filled with books. It was during his first year in the cage that Sara sent a letter to the local TV station proposing a new game show about "grown-ups challenging a nerd with a heart of gold." Ben's heart may have been golden, but it felt more to him like stone, encased in a steel and plastic cage. But that didn't matter once they aired the pilot episode of *Beat the Wizkind*, in which the twelve-year-old prodigy, in a face-off with a tenured professor of political philosophy from Princeton, trounced his opponent by over three hundred points.

At school, his fame as a Wizkind only made things worse. Few people had spoken to him before, but now he was positively taunted, tortured in ways only twelve- and thirteen-year-olds know how to torture each other. On several occasions he came to school to find his locker coated with a mosaic of used chewing gum, more of which was thrown at him as he sat in the lunchroom, praying for Tuesdays, when the two seventh-grade classes ate lunch together and he could at least take refuge with Sara, who also didn't have any friends. That stopped the flying gum wads, but not the passed notes about him that always seemed to get "accidentally" passed to him, or the burping campaign that erupted in one particular class every time Ben tried to speak (a correlation that his teacher failed to notice), or the chants of "Wizkind takes a whiz" that met him every day at the bus stop. The only reason no one tried to beat him up was because they had learned—in a school assembly about scoliosis that was held while Ben was being fitted for his cage—that the Wizkind was a cripple.

Nights were worse. Ben couldn't sleep in the cage, and no one else was really sleeping, either. His mother had taken to wandering around the house all night, pulling open their father's file drawers and emptying their contents onto the floor. Sara sometimes would sob all night long, crying for hours before giving in and going to their mother's room, climbing into their parents' bed, and falling asleep on their father's pillow. More recently, as Ben discovered when he sneaked into her bedroom late one night to retrieve a book, Sara had taken to sleeping with her eyes open, waiting for disaster to strike again. As for Ben, he would simply lie in bed in his brace as if stretched on a torture rack, fighting as hard as he could not to be crushed by the weight that he felt resting on the steel-reinforced cage above his breastbone: the horrible feeling of knowing that this wasn't a cruel joke or dream or even a misfortune of any rarity, but rather that this was simply the cost of loving, that this misery was how things were meant to be and that it could never be otherwise—and that this was only the beginning, that it would happen again and again, with his mother, with his twin sister, with everyone—that no one is anything more than the cloud that vanishes, and the best anyone could hope for was not to be the last.

And so it was two years later, while the Wizkind blossomed on local TV and the Ziskind festered in his cage, that Leonid Ilych Shcharansky first came into Ben's life.

———————

FOUR MONTHS BEFORE his bar mitzvah, Ben was assigned to Leonid Ilych Shcharansky of Chernobyl, Ukraine, USSR—an unfortunate Jewish boy living in terror behind the Iron Curtain and forbidden from celebrating a bar mitzvah—as his own personal Soviet bar mitzvah "twin." On the day of his own bar mitzvah, Ben would be called to the Torah not only for himself, but a second time in Leonid Ilych Shcharansky's name, so that Leonid would have the opportunity to celebrate a bar mitzvah even if he couldn't be there himself. It was the same kind of pairing that had been given to Jewish children all over America for the previous ten years. Generally the bar mitzvah boy or bat mitzvah girl was provided with an address and told to write a letter, without expecting a reply. The previous year, for Sara's bat mitzvah (which, as a girl, she celebrated at the age of twelve instead of thirteen, just another step in the process of leaving her twin behind), Sara had mailed off a friendly greeting card to her assigned victim of religious intolerance and then threw away the address. An hour later, she couldn't even remember the Russian girl's name.

But when Ben received the address of Leonid Ilych Shcharansky, he thought of his horrible school, where nothing had changed in the two years since he had lived in the cage, and then looked again at the address, which was printed on a piece of paper with a logo from a Soviet Jewry activist group, a Star of David intertwined with a hammer and sickle, along with the words "If Not Now, When?" And he was determined that he would write to Leonid Shcharansky until Leonid Shcharansky wrote back.

Dear Leonid,
    Greetings from the Land of the Free and the Home of the Brave. I am Benjamin Ziskind, your bar mitzvah "twin." I am looking forward to

our bar mitzvah, and I am sorry you cannot be here with us. The Torah portion I will be reading for us is about the freeing of the Israelites from Egypt and the crossing of the Red Sea. I hope that you will also make it out of the Red Sea and cross to the Promised Land.

Your friend,
Benjamin Ziskind

Ben was very proud of his subtle reference to the "Red Sea." He had considered creating a more elaborate code to foil the Soviet censors but decided against it, since he couldn't be sure how perspicacious Leonid might be at reading these things, or even how good his English was. So he signed it, sealed it, sent it off, and waited.

Leonid didn't respond.

When he didn't hear from Leonid, Ben wondered if the letter had gotten Leonid and his family in trouble. His mother assured him that that sort of thing didn't happen anymore, but still, Ben feared for Leonid's safety. After entertaining various scenarios in his mind in which Soviet mailmen confiscated the letter, presented it to the KGB, and had thirteen-year-old Leonid arrested and exiled to the far out-skirts of Novosibirsk (the city with the ninth lowest mean daily temperature in the world, selected from cities of over a million inhabitants), Ben dismissed the idea and began to wonder if perhaps Leonid simply didn't understand English, even though Ben had tried very hard to use only short, easy words in his letter. At the risk of having Leonid's entire family dragged off to the gulag, he decided to try again.

Dear Leonid,

Greetings again from your bar mitzvah "twin," Benjamin Ziskind. I wrote to you a while ago, but I don't know if you got my last letter. I know that it might be hard for you to write to me, so I don't mind if you cannot write back.

I wanted to tell you a little about myself. I am in seventh grade. I guess you are in seventh grade also, if they have seventh grade in the USSR. I have read a lot of books about the USSR but none of the books ever explained if they have grades in school there the same way we do.

You probably think I am reading these books about the USSR in school. Actually school is very easy for me, and mostly I learn things outside of school. I am on a TV show called "Beat the Wizkind" where I have to go against grown-ups and answer quiz questions.

Last night at the taping I won, as usual. One of the questions near the beginning was, "Which of the following was the cause of the nuclear meltdown in Chernobyl?" I have read a lot about Chernobyl since I got your address, so I kind of should thank you for knowing the right answer. I figure you probably don't have the opportunity in the USSR to have your own personal game show on TV, so instead of just being your bar mitzvah twin, I can also be your game show twin. So congratulations for living in Chernobyl and getting the question right.

I was wondering if you have any mutations from living there.

> Your friend,
> Benjamin Ziskind

Leonid still did not respond.

After watching him checking the mailbox every day, Ben's mother suggested that he stop writing to Leonid. "There's no point in writing letters to someone who doesn't write back," she told him one afternoon, inking the drawings she had penciled onto the page. In between other projects, he knew, she had been working on her own children's book, something that she had taken up and thrown away many times. It had pictures of a town filled with slimy-looking mud, and a little boy in the town square at night, holding a fading lantern. The boy was mired up to his waist in mud, waving the lantern for help.

"But Sara sticks letters to Dad in the mailbox every day," Ben said. "Every day for two years, and counting."

His mother sighed. "That's different," she muttered, and continued inking the picture. On the drawing's dark horizon, Ben noticed, a man on horseback was approaching.

Ben could see that she was too tired to argue. But he didn't care. "The only difference is that Sara's letters are a real waste of stamps," Ben said. He knew he was walking along the edge of a cliff, but he felt bold. "I mean, at least with my letters, it's possible that this Leonid guy might write back someday, right? But as for Sara's letters, I can absolutely guarantee that—"

"Ben, stop it." Now his mother was watching him, her facing turning red.

"—nobody is going to read those letters, nobody, it's not like she's going to get an answer from the other world or something—"

"Ben, stop!"

But Ben didn't stop. Instead, he turned his head as best he could and aimed his voice down the hall, where Sara was in her room. "Hey, Sara," he shouted, "haven't you heard? Dad's dead! Dead people don't read their mail!"

His mother's face, burning, suddenly ignited in rage as she flung her right hand into the air.

Ben cringed. The two of them froze, she with her eyes burning, he shrunken into his cage. Then he saw her eyes shift to his shoulder, where a strip of steel pushed beneath his shirt. The pity in her expression was more horrible than if she had hit him. Ben watched her as she slowly lowered her hand, and his own gut curled with the shame of being too crippled to be slapped.

"Go to your room," she said, her voice a cage confining a roar. "Just go to your room."

Ben tried to think of something to spit back at her, but it was over. Everything was over. She turned back to her drawing as he shuddered in his cage like an animal, humiliated, impotent. He walked away as slowly as possible, muttering under his breath, "Dead people don't read their mail."

———

BUT LIVING PEOPLE don't read their mail, either, as Ben was fast discovering. Months passed, and the bar mitzvah approached without any word from Leonid. Not that it particularly mattered, though. After all, for the purposes of the bar mitzvah, Leonid was just a symbol, an Oppressed Boy, a blurred figure floating above a white background. But in Ben's mind Leonid grew more and more vivid, like an embryo or fetus that becomes more recognizable each day, fingers and lips and spine and eyes and hair coming slowly and smoothly into focus. In his brief moments each day outside of the cage, he borrowed Leonid's body: small, lithe, gentle, yet quietly enduring, with the world's straightest spine.

And after discovering a mailbox near the school, he continued sending letters.

Dear Leonid,

I told you a little about myself in my last letter, but I thought I should tell you more about my family because you might think it is interesting.

My mom says that our family has a long history of fighting for freedom. My mom came from the USSR when she was a little girl, which is still almost impossible, and my mom says it was even harder then. Her dad was put in prison in the USSR, not for killing anybody or anything but for no reason, which my mom says happened a lot in the USSR. My mom and my grandmother got out and they didn't find out what happened to her dad right away but later they found out he was dead.

My dad also has a history of fighting for freedom, because he served his Country in Viet Nam. If you want to know more about that I really can't tell you, because that's something else people don't talk about much. I told you already how we never learn anything at school. We have to learn American History every year, but only up to 1945, because I guess nobody thinks that anything important ever happened after 1945. There are sometimes chapters in the back of the textbook from after 1945, but the school year always ends before we get to them. I found some books in the library about it, but when I try to bring them home my mom gets in a bad mood and yells at me for no reason.

Once when I was eleven I found metal name tags in a drawer with my dad's name on them. My mom told me they were for in case he got killed there and his face got blown apart and nobody could tell who he was. Luckily for you that didn't happen, because then I wouldn't have been born, and you wouldn't be having a bar mitzvah.

Your friend,
Benjamin Ziskind

Dear Leonid,

I forgot to say in my last letter that my dad died a few years ago.

I also forgot to say the most important thing, which is that our bar mitzvah was last week. As expected I read everything perfectly with no mistakes at all, the way you're supposed to do it, and I read your part perfectly also, so you can tell everybody that you had a perfect bar mitzvah with no mistakes. Which is pretty good considering that I did all the work for it and you didn't do anything. Afterwards there was a dumb lunch at our house, and that was pretty boring because everybody just said the same things again and again, congratulations, and you're a real man now, and what a great job you did, and how proud your dad would have been, and how sorry they were that he couldn't be with you today, over and over again. So you didn't miss much.

I am sorry you weren't at the bar mitzvah but I have to say I missed my dad more than I missed you.

Your friend,
Benjamin Z.

Dear Leonid,

School is a terrible place, I have decided. There is nothing good about it except for math class. Everything else is a total waste of time. As I mentioned before I have done a lot of reading about prisons, and I notice that they always describe them as painted in very dull colors, and my school is also painted in these kinds of colors, with greenish lockers and brownish walls and grayish floors. Actually they recently fixed up one wing of the school, and now that part of the school is just the opposite — all the colors are really bright, with bright red and yellow lockers and blue doors and shiny white floors that are already all scuffed up. It's funny because I thought the other colors were terrible but these are much worse, because they make it seem like it's normal to be happy there when it isn't.

I am actually not sure if it is normal to be happy anywhere. I think that I used to feel happy most of the time, when I was little, but now I notice that being happy is more like an exception than what usually happens. Sometimes I feel like the time when I was happy was sort of like the time before I was born — like I wasn't even born yet then, but I didn't know it yet. I know I was happy living there, in some place I don't remember anymore, but now I've been born already and there's no way to go back.

I was just wondering if you ever felt that way or not. But you don't have to answer.

Your friend,
Ben Z.

Two years passed, and Benjamin Ziskind's unanswered letters continued. But then one day the Soviet Union collapsed, the exodus from the Red Sea commenced, and what seemed like half the Jewish population of Chernobyl was relocated by an American Jewish refugee agency to Benjamin Ziskind's New Jersey town, including Leonid Shcharansky. And Ben's mother, recognizing the name when she spotted it on the list of immigrants looking for host families to help ease them into their new lives (the list included both Leonid's mother, who had been an English teacher in the USSR, and Leonid himself, who would be entering the ninth grade in Ben's school), decided to call up Leonid and invite his family to dinner.

When the doorbell rang, the Ziskind twins and their mother assembled in a row beside the door, and Ben was relieved to be wearing a new kind of brace that at least (merciful God) didn't have a chin support and fit almost completely beneath his shirt. When the door opened, a large woman with dark hair and a brown dress stood on the threshold. Someone else stood outside on the porch, but Ben's view was obstructed by Sara, who lately seemed to always have paint smudges on her cheeks and arms. She was still taller than him.

Their mother stretched out her hand. "Hello, Mrs. Shcharanskaya."

"Please, call me Raisa," the woman answered. She had a deep voice, and slurred her words.

"You can call me Raisa, too," their mother said with a smile. "That was my name, when I was a little girl."

Raisa Shcharanskaya opened her eyes wide, drawing up her heavy painted eyelids, and said something very loud, in Russian.

Their mother laughed. "I used to know Russian, but I don't anymore. I'm sorry," she said. But Ben knew that was a lie, because he had noticed that their mother spoke Russian often—in wild shouts, late at night, in her dreams.

Raisa made a noise that sounded something like a grunt. "It's better to forget it," she said. "Rats and thieves, all of them."

Their mother smiled uncomfortably before turning to face Ben and Sara. "Let me introduce everyone," she began, but Ben didn't hear anything else she said, because at that moment, Leonid emerged.

There are two kinds of fifteen-year-old boys in the world. The first are the kind that look like they are twelve, and the second are the kind that look like they are twenty-four. Benjamin Ziskind was the former. Leonid Ilych Shcharansky was the latter.

Leonid was beyond big. Leonid was colossal. It was even possible, Ben reasoned as he tried to strain his neck against the shoulder straps of the cage to take in Leonid's tremendous form, that Leonid was suffering from some sort of glandular condition that explained his massive size. Acromegaly, Ben thought to himself, his game-show buzzer finger twitching. Or cretinism. Marfan syndrome, perhaps. (Marfan syndrome, of course, was the disease Abraham Lincoln had suffered from. Its symptoms included abnormal height, an indented chest cavity, elongated digits, heart murmur, and premature death in one's thirties or forties, though not usually at the hands of a Rebel assassin.) Or maybe even a mutation of some kind, from Chernobyl.

Leonid was at least six and a half feet tall, perhaps even closer to seven. He had to duck his head to fit in the doorway, which his giant frame filled completely, since in addition to being tall, Leonid—as Ben quickly registered while the straps of the cage dug into the skin on the back of his neck—also had a tremendous physique. His massive arms were forced into a flannel shirt whose sleeves barely reached past his thick, hairy elbows, his chest was encased in a tight black T-shirt that seemed about to burst, and his monumental legs, one now inside the house and the other outside, straddled the threshold like (Ben thought, finger on the imaginary buzzer) the Colossus of Rhodes. On top of it all was a giant face crowned with flaming red hair like a burning halo, and drooping blue eyes that looked, more than anything else, bored.

The face surveyed the Ziskinds, a slight smirk crossing its handsome lips as the droopy eyes paused on Sara, lingering with a strange curve of the lower lip that just might have been the shadow of a smile. When his glance came to rest on Ben, Ben stuck out his hand, uncertain as to how high he might have to reach to offer a handshake, and struggled to form a word. But just as Ben was about to squeeze out a hello, Leonid turned around and looked down at his own left foot, still outside the house. Ben peered over the threshold and watched as Leonid spat and crushed the butt of a cigarette on the Ziskinds' front porch.

"I DO NOT know what they feed him in the school, but all we eat in Chernobyl is cabbage all the time and he does not stop growing," Raisa said as they sat down at the table. "Look what will happen to him when they give him American food. Who knew I would have a giant in my house?" Ben looked at Leonid, who grunted from the heights. "Of course, you know how boys are," Raisa laughed, eyeing Ben across the table. "Little beasts. You are lucky not to have more men at home."

Ben saw his mother wince, a subtle gesture, a slight blinking of the left eye, a slight biting of the lower lip, that Raisa Shcharanskaya failed to notice. Leonid had settled into what used to be their father's chair.

"And is Leonid's father here in America, too?" their mother asked delicately.

Raisa snorted. "Lenya's father is—I don't know how you call it. A *mamzer*," she said. "Two years ago he ran away with a Georgian whore."

Sara, who was in the middle of a sip of juice, suddenly inhaled the liquid, choked, and spewed it out through her nose onto the table. Then she began gagging until their mother and Raisa, both clearly thrilled by the distraction, simultaneously jumped up to beat her back and offer her water. Ben wondered if Sara had choked on purpose. Soon, to Raisa's visible relief, everyone was laughing, except for Leonid, who at long last grinned.

For the rest of the meal Ben watched Leonid closely. It was clear that Leonid understood English, because he responded to everything that was said with an appropriate snort or grunt. Meanwhile, he shoveled food into his mouth with reckless abandon. His hands were so large that they might more rightly have been called paws. There was no way, Ben thought, that this could be the same Leonid he had been imagining all these years. His Leonid was small, gentle, patient, daring. Not this behemoth. It couldn't possibly be. Ben was so fascinated by Leonid that he barely heard most of the conversation—that is, until Raisa Shcharanskaya suddenly mentioned his name.

"I read the beautiful letters Benjamin wrote to Lenya," Raisa said. "Not all of them, only the recent ones."

"Recent ones?" Ben's mother leaned forward. "But he was just writing to him for the bar mitzvah. That was two years ago."

Raisa laughed, the flabs of fat in her chin moving in slow waves. "Oh, no. Our last letter came only three days before we left. Maybe there are even more coming that we have missed."

Sara leaned over to look at Ben, who was trying as hard as he could to shrink himself into the cage concealed beneath his shirt.

"I brought them all to my school to show my students," Raisa continued, pausing to show off her dull little teeth in a wide smile. "It was such good experience for our class—to see how a true American boy writes English. And to learn about life in America, from the view of this true American boy, in this personal way—it was a very great opportunity for my students." Ben felt himself turning redder than borscht. The room around him became blurry, sliding out of focus.

"Didn't Leonid read the letters?" he heard his mother ask through the haze.

Raisa Shcharanskaya let out a theatrical laugh, five descending notes. "Oh, you know boys," she said. "They would rather watch girls on television. Isn't that right, Lenya? Lenya would rather look at girls."

Raisa bared her teeth again and turned to face Leonid, who gave what looked like a slight sneer. Ben's mother, changing the subject, asked Raisa something about her language students as she got up to clear the dishes, and everyone followed with their own plates into the kitchen. This did not prevent Ben from wanting to crawl under the table and die.

"I felt terrible to leave my students, but I know this was the right— the right decision," Raisa said as they circulated between the kitchen and the dining room table, carrying coffee and fruit. "Now the whole country is corrupt."

Leonid had stopped midstream in the flow of food, his enormous body hovering by the desk in the kitchen where a pile of papers had accumulated under a loose photograph. Raisa stopped beside him, and Ben watched as Leonid whispered to his mother, picking up the photograph and pointing at it. Raisa quietly scolded him, slapping his hand until he put the photograph back down on the desk.

"It's a painting by Chagall," Ben's mother said, leaning over Raisa's shoulder.

Raisa crouched, ashamed. "I thought—yes, Chagall," she muttered. "But I did not know he makes small pictures like this." Ben stood on his toes and saw the picture over Raisa's shoulder, a snapshot of the painting from the living room, with his mother's hand along the side. Leonid slunk away into the dining room, sulking alone in his seat.

"It's small because it's a study—a practice for a bigger painting," Ben's mother said, pointing at the picture. "And that's my hand. See, that's my wedding ring on that finger."

Raisa looked at their mother's ring finger in the picture, then at the same finger alongside the photograph, and then looked up, alarmed. "You have a painting by Chagall?"

Ben's mother shook her head. "No, not anymore. It's a long story," his mother said. She seemed to suddenly regret mentioning it. She took the photograph and the pile of papers and quickly stuffed them into the desk drawer.

Raisa let out a snort. "Rats and thieves, all of them," she repeated as they returned to their seats around the table. "Now is only worse than before. Even my students there, now they are turning into thieves. Bad for Lenya, too. So many bad children. We try to make children good, but who can know? You cannot know how children will turn out. Parents, teachers can only do so much."

"So are you teaching here, too?" their mother asked, passing a bowl of grapes.

Raisa sighed. "No, I am not. I am . . . I am . . ." She paused for a moment and bowed her head, closing her eyes and pinching them together with her thumb and forefinger, over her nose. She continued rubbing her eyes this way, long enough for the three Ziskinds to notice it, before raising her head. "I am working at beauty parlors," she said, her lips tightly pursed between words. "Near the school. There is someone there from Russia who found this job for me."

For a moment no one spoke, until Sara broke the silence. "You could still teach here," she said, speaking for the first time that evening. Ben marveled at how much she sounded like their mother, and suddenly felt more ashamed of his own high cracked voice. "You might have to go back to school or something, but I bet you still could—"

"No, I am afraid, I think it is over for me," Raisa said, looking down at her plate. Her breasts heaved under her dress before she looked up again. "Lenya, though, it is not over for him yet. He is smart, but more important, he is good. At least Lenya is a good boy."

Everyone looked across the table at Leonid, who was busy lighting a cigarette.

As Leonid and his mother left the house that night, it occurred to Ben that he still had not heard Leonid's voice.

———

THAT WEEK, THE teachers at the high school announced that all the students in advanced-level math and science courses were now required to purchase TI-82 model scientific calculators. Most of the students in such classes had driver's licenses, or at least friends who could drive them to the electronics discount store on the highway to buy one, but child prodigy Ben had to have his mother take him calculator shopping—only to discover that in the discount store, along with every other store they tried, the calculator was out of stock. The next day, Ben arrived at school early to find a crowd of students gathered in the hallway, and saw Leonid's red hair towering above them. Ben remembered that Leonid had just been placed in precalculus— along with Ben, he was the only other ninth-grader in the class—and he wondered if Leonid had also had trouble buying the new calculator. He didn't have to wonder long.

"TI-82s for sale," Leonid called to the crowd. "Discount price." At Leonid's feet, Ben saw as he pushed his way through the crowd, were cartons of TI-82 calculators. Calculators were flying out of the box as students grabbed for them, and Leonid's pockets were bursting with cash.

"Hey," Ben said, unsure whether to try to make his voice friendly or not. He failed to control his anger; his voice trembled as he spoke. "You can't sell those like that."

Leonid looked down, noticed Ben, and laughed, crushing a smoldering cigarette butt on the floor. Someone elbowed Ben to the side. Ben watched for a moment, embroiled by a tangle of fascination and fury. He glanced down at the half-smoked cigarette next to Leonid's enormous black sneakers, its paper already uncurling.

"Smoking inside the school is illegal," Ben said as he shoved his way back toward Leonid. "People could die of lung cancer." People like Ben's father, for example.

Leonid, busily taking orders, managed to pull another cigarette out of his pocket, light it up, and blow the smoke in Ben's face. "Sorry," Leonid slurred at a hand emerging from the crowd, "I do not give change. Buy two, give one to friend." From a boy nearby, he took three twenties.

"The math teachers are going to hear about this," Ben said, scanning the crowd for a face of authority. But the crowd was already thinning out; first period was approaching.

"Yuri!" Leonid suddenly yelled, twisting his giant head to the right. Nearby, a boy with a belly like a forty-year-old's, a shadow of a mustache, and fingers covered with thick rings was pinning another boy to a wall of lockers. The big boy looked up and dropped the second boy, who fell to the floor in a heap.

"You see this guy?" Leonid asked Ben as the boy with the big belly approached.

Ben started to repeat his own threat, but Leonid clearly wasn't listening. Instead, Leonid muttered something in Russian to Yuri, who grabbed Ben by the chin and lifted him off the floor—not entirely, but enough to force him to stand on his tiptoes. Ben felt his torso stretching painfully, loosening within the steel and plastic cage.

"This is Yuri," Leonid said as Yuri released Ben's chin. Ben rocked back on his heels, his spine aching. "You tell people what we do, Yuri, me, we beat you up."

Yuri turned and said something to Leonid in Russian, pointing at Ben. They both laughed, Leonid so hard that he almost choked, but he still managed to step on a wayward hand that tried to grab a calculator out of the box. Sales were tapering off. Yuri lumbered down the hall and disappeared into the boys' bathroom, and Leonid looked down at Ben and laughed.

Ben swallowed, trying to make his voice sound lower, tougher. "What do you think this is, a bad TV show?"

Leonid grinned as he bent down to close the calculator crate. The bell for the first class had already rung. "I think this is a bad TV show," he said in his thick, deep voice, slurring his words. "You are the star."

LEONID SHCHARANSKY HAD only been in school for a few weeks before he succeeded in forming the very first gang Benjamin Ziskind's high school had ever seen. Its members were exclusively Russian immigrants. Leonid was the linchpin of the group, with the afore-mentioned Yuri as his sidekick (with an emphasis on the kick, since one of Yuri's favorite things to do was wander the hallways of the school, seeing how many freshly painted lockers he could kick in with his steel-tipped shoes). Besides them, there were six other boys—puny boys compared to the colossal Leonid and the bulging Yuri, all dark-haired and with long, thin noses, like a flock of ravens. There were also four girls, girls with enormous breasts who walked around with painted mouths and spiked bangs in a style American girls had stopped wear-ing years earlier, yet they managed to pull it all off with a sort of sleazy panache. Among themselves they spoke exclusively Russian, though sometimes, to Ben's shock, he would pass them by and overhear, in the middle of Russian sentences, a Yiddish word. They had no official name, but the rest of the school had begun to refer to them, behind their backs, as the "Meltdown Gang."

As a gang, they specialized in theft and resale, their stock consisting primarily of items like calculators and marijuana but also, increas-ingly, car radios and other auto parts from the school parking lot. The boys' bathroom had become a veritable chop shop. But they also were not above threats. Each day as he sat behind Ben in math class, Leonid would kick Ben's chair and then toss a small note onto his desk. The note, in a curly capitalized handwriting and with daily variations in spelling that Ben found extremely irritating, always consisted of exactly the same words:

WATCH OUT WIZKIND — SOON I BEAT YOU UP.

For the first time in his life, Benjamin Ziskind was afraid. He didn't talk to any teachers about it, or even to his mother. Yet each morning in class when he received Leonid's daily warning note, he felt something more than mere dread. It was as if Leonid were finally responding to all the letters Ben had sent him over the past few years, and the sick swaying of Ben's own stomach—the nausea he felt whenever he tried not to remember how he had poured out his own guts and mailed them off to Chernobyl—made him feel as though he himself were at fault, as if he had desecrated something.

He lost interest in his schoolwork. Instead of coming home and sitting down to his physics problems, Ben now found himself wandering into the living room, where a picture of his father sat on a bookshelf. He stared at the picture for as long as he could before his mother or sister discovered him. One time, with a freshly crumpled note from Leonid in his pocket, he went into his mother's bedroom and took out his father's dog tags from where she had hidden them in a box in the closet. The pressed metal reminded him obscurely of the school lockers dented by Yuri's shoes—bulging, bestial Yuri, who, he later discovered, had been the bar mitzvah twin of someone else in Ben's math class. As he ran his fingers along the reverse side of his father's name, he remembered his own bar mitzvah and then thought of that moment when he had first met Leonid, the way Leonid had spat and used his toe to grind his cigarette butt into the front porch.

And then the day came when Leonid decided, at long last, to beat him up.

———

IT WAS A winter day, and Ben liked winter days, then. He had hated them for a long time, since it had been cold the day his father died, but now he found cold days to be a relief, days when he could wear thick sweaters that covered up the cage completely. It was cold on those days, cold enough to snow, but so far there had been no snow that year. Instead, the grass had died and the ground was coated with dead leaves that eventually dissolved into a carpet of mud, thick brown mud that seemed to cover the entire town. The days shrank one by one, curling around the edges like dead leaves. Ben had stayed late at school to take a test for a math contest, and found himself faced with a long walk home alone.

But as he made his way around the side of the school, Ben had something new on his mind. His mother had just finished her own children's book, with the ridiculous title of *Young Tongue Brat*, which she had shown Ben and Sara the night before. Written entirely in rhyme, it was the story of a boy—"Young Tongue Brat," as he was apparently known in recognition of his quick answers to any grown-up's question—who was renowned for his brilliance and courage. The poem began with a description of the town where the Young Tongue Brat lived, which despite its horses and thatched-roof houses seemed to Ben deeply similar to his own town, because the main problem with this town was that it was covered with mud.

In the story, it was the beginning of winter, but no snow had yet fallen. As a result the streets were covered with a thick autumn mud, so deep that people could be sucked into it and never be heard from again. The townspeople's only hope was for snow to cover up the mud, but none came. On one afternoon of deep and early darkness, Young Tongue Brat and his friends were walking home from school, carrying their lanterns to guide them (here the pen-and-ink illustrations glowed, the tiny lanterns suffusing just enough light to illuminate the boys' little faces with their terrified expressions, along with their feet held gingerly above the mud as they took their terrified steps). But on the next page, Young Tongue Brat tumbled into the mud, trapped, his lantern snuffed. His friends—some friends, Ben thought—ran off into the night, too horrified to help, but the Brat simply stayed in the mud, unafraid. As luck would have it, soon a nobleman on horseback discovered him and pulled him out. The nobleman asked Young Tongue Brat why he hadn't cried, and the Brat simply said that he hadn't been frightened at all. The nobleman was so impressed that he made the Young Tongue Brat an offer, which the Brat accepted as only he could. The nobleman began:

> "I have a horse that cost me plenty
> Who might as well be flame and fire!
> He flies by faster than an arrow,
> Twelve miles a minute, if I desire.

And I have a ring of magic, too,
Just the ring for a boy like you:
Spin it seven times around
And then the snow will coat the ground!

And you yourself can be my guest
And choose which one you like the best.
Choose the ring, or choose the horse,
But just don't think too hard, of course!"

All this alarmed our Young Tongue Brat.
The horse, or the ring? This one, or that?
He didn't think too hard, of course:
"I'll take the ring AND take the horse!"

Amazing things can happen, it seems, if you ignore the rules. The nobleman, impressed once more by the Brat's courage, gladly handed over both horse and ring, and the Young Tongue Brat wasted no time in taking off into the wide world on his flying horse, scattering snow in his wake with his magic ring. A few of the final stanzas from the book were running through Ben's head as he walked home that day, sliding in the mud along the side of the school:

Young Tongue Brat flew like an arrow!
Riding on the horse, he raced
Farther, farther from his hometown
Off to somewhere out in space.

But when, each year, from distant ways
The winter comes with rainy days
And there is still no snow to see
And snow just seems not meant to be . . .

Whoa! The horse stands above the ground
As Young Tongue Brat's ring spins around:
Seven times it spins, and then
The snow falls to the ground again.

The trouble, Ben thought, was that the whole thing seemed so familiar to him. The words weren't familiar—he couldn't say that he had heard those silly rhymes before—but the story, there was something about the story. Where was it from? Ben was navigating the muddy path along the school's brick wall, racking his brain for remnants of the Young Tongue Brat, when a deep voice bellowed into his ear:

"Today is the day, Wizkind."

Ben didn't even have time to turn around before someone grabbed him by the neck and threw him against the wall, backside first. He landed on his feet and found himself facing the male members of the Meltdown Gang, raven-boys on both sides and Leonid at the helm. Yuri grabbed Ben's arm and pulled off his backpack, casting it in the mud.

"You think I do not mean it? I do," Leonid said. "I beat you up myself."

Ben glanced around at the raven-boys' beaked noses and Leonid's giant face, towering above him. He had had this dream before, many times. But this did not seem to be a dream. He bit his lip, tasting sweet blood as his chapped lip cracked under his teeth, his vision reeling. And then suddenly, like in those blissful moments during tapings of *Beat the Wizkind* between hearing the question and realizing that he knew the answer, a hushed thrill rushed through Ben's body, carefully contained beneath his skin. He was no more frightened than the Young Tongue Brat.

"Go ahead," he told Leonid. "I dare you." For a second he felt anxious, the familiar panic of the game show contestant who instantly realizes his response might have been wrong. But Ben hid his panic, staring Leonid in the eye.

The Meltdown Gang exchanged puzzled glances until Leonid finally laughed. "Okay, I fight you," he bellowed. "But Wizkind, I show I am fair. You cannot tell people you were beat by giants. I will kneel in mud for you, and I will still beat you up."

"Be my guest," Ben said, his voice shaking. He leaned back against the wall.

Again the Meltdown Gang paused, the flock of ravens exchanging fevered whispers. But then Yuri picked up Ben's backpack and pulled out his trigonometry textbook, dropping it in the mud at Leonid's enormous feet.

Leonid fell to his knees with an audible thud, the textbook sinking into the mud under his weight. As Leonid straightened his back to face him, Ben was reminded oddly of the way his father used to look during High Holiday services at their synagogue, the one time of year when he—also a tall man, but much thinner—would drop to his good knee, pause briefly before he lost his balance, catch himself on his palms, and then press his own forehead to the floor until Ben helped him up. But he quickly forgot that as he faced Leonid, whose head seemed even larger now that it was at Ben's eye level. He noticed that Leonid's eyelashes were the same color as his hair, drowsy red.

Leonid's smile vanished. He lightly punched his own chest, a gesture that made Ben think of a gorilla, and then drew back his arm. Ben cringed and covered his face with his hands, spreading his fingers just slightly so that he could still see Leonid screwing up his ruddy face, drawing a deep breath, and balling his gigantic fingers into a fist.

It happened so fast that Ben didn't even feel the punch. All he saw, an instant later, were the large eyes rolling backward as Goliath blacked out and fell to the ground, having shattered five different bones in his hand and wrist from the impact of slamming his fist directly into the cage.

———

BEN WAS SURPRISED the following day to find that Leonid's apartment, which Leonid shared with his mother and also with an unrelated elderly Russian woman and the elderly woman's seven-year-old granddaughter, was hardly bigger than Ben's parents' bedroom. His mother had forced him to go there to apologize, no matter how many times he had tried to explain that it wasn't his fault. When Sara insisted on going with him, he found himself feeling a mixture of embarrassment and relief.

The elderly woman who answered the door at Number Sixteen— whom Ben first assumed must be Leonid's grandmother, though he later learned otherwise—opened it only a few inches, stretching the chain lock. She didn't speak.

"Hi, I'm Ben Ziskind," Ben said, trying to make his voice sound lower. "I came here to—"

The woman slammed the door shut. Ben turned around to look at Sara, but then they both heard shouting behind the door. Ben recognized Leonid's thick voice, firing in rapid Russian. The old woman unlatched the door, pulled it open, then stepped aside. Ben tried to thank her, but she quickly disappeared, retreating into a room that, in the brief glance Ben caught before she closed the door, looked more like a large closet, its tiny space filled almost completely by a double bed.

Inside the apartment there were just two small rooms, as Ben could see from the open door next to the one the old woman had entered, which revealed a closet crushed full of broken boxes. The kitchen was entirely contained in a small counter next to the door. The door to the tiny bathroom had also been left open, exposing a jungle of women's underwear stretched along crisscrossing laundry lines. A person would have to duck to use the toilet, Ben thought. The main room, where Ben and Sara found themselves standing, was filled with packing crates and stacks of photo albums and, between two tall columns of boxes, a cheap foam cushion of the kind that opens out into a mattress. A blanket lay in a pile on the ground beside it, covered with a sheet of clear plastic. On top of the plastic was a full ashtray. In a small stack beside it were a notebook and a worn Russian-English dictionary, along with the same edition that Ben had from their English class of *The Pathfinder*. Ben realized with a jolt of shame that this must be where Leonid slept, and maybe his mother, too. The mattress probably wasn't even long enough for Leonid. The air in the room was full and thick with strange smells, sandpaper smells of burnt ash and old books and something sickly sweet that Ben could not identify until he noticed a browning apple core on the floor in the corner. Ben removed his coat and placed it on a nearby crate. His sweat dripped underneath the brace, a slow water torture.

Leonid was sitting propped up on the mattress cushion, leaning against the wall with his long legs stretched out on the floor in front of him. His club of an arm, encased in yellow fiberglass, rested in a canvas sling. His droopy blue eyes focused on a small TV set a few feet away, where a game show was playing softly. He didn't look up.

"I'm here to apologize, Leonid," Ben said. He had rehearsed his lines with Sara on the way over, practicing not being enraged. "I'm really sorry about your hand. If there's anything I can do for you, like carry your books or help you take notes in class or something, I, uh . . ."

Leonid remained silent, his dull eyes focused on the screen. Ben's glance wandered to the TV set, where a game of *Jeopardy!* was on. The volume was so low that Ben could hardly hear it. His eye caught a question as it was blinking off the screen, asking for the scientist who introduced the periodic table.

"Mendeleyev," Ben and Leonid said together.

Ben jolted. Taking a careful step forward between the packing crates, he angled his body closer to the TV. The next question asked for the capital of Uzbekistan.

"Tashkent," Leonid and Ben said in unison, Ben a few notes above Leonid.

Ben felt his blood pumping through his body, the way it often did when the competition became tight, his skin sweating profusely under the cage. Leonid had leaned forward, doubled over his cast. Ben was barely prepared when the next question appeared: "The composer of the *New World Symphony*."

"Dvořák," Ben and Leonid said, Leonid slightly earlier. Ben was drenched in sweat, his lips slightly shaking. He tried to focus, feeling himself beginning to slip. Another question flashed across the tiny screen: "The author of the classic novel *Fathers and Sons*."

Ben stared at the words, reading them twice, racking his brain, his heart pounding.

"Turgenev," Leonid said.

This time Ben stared at Leonid, who still hadn't taken his eyes off the TV. Only the cage prevented Ben from shrinking into his shirt.

"Wow, even Ben didn't know that one," Sara suddenly said.

Leonid jumped, startled at the sound of another voice. At long last he turned his head. He glanced at Ben, but he seemed amazed at Sara. He looked at her so carefully that Ben couldn't help but look at her, too. Her coat was draped over her arm, and she was wearing a new sweater that she had gotten as a present for their birthday, a blue V-neck that showed off her shape. Leonid grinned.

"I beat the Wizkind," he said.

"I thought the Wizkind just beat you," Sara answered with a smile. Ben glared at her, but Sara didn't seem to notice. To Ben's surprise, Leonid burst out laughing.

"Do you watch this show a lot?" Sara asked.

"Oh, yes," Leonid said. "Questions are difficult about American things, but I—I improve."

"You and Ben should play against each other sometime." Sara smiled, then glanced around the room. "At our house, maybe. It looks like you don't have much space here."

Ben grimaced. What the hell was she thinking? The last thing he needed was Leonid coming to his house, armed with a fiberglass club.

But Leonid seemed not to notice the invitation. "Here is better than Chernobyl," Leonid said slowly. "There we have five people in two rooms. Here only four."

Ben wondered for a moment about Leonid's father, who had run off with the Georgian whore. It occurred to him that he and Leonid had something important in common, living lives-minus-one. And surrounded by girls. But Sara cut off his thoughts. "I bet you could move some things around to make it feel more spacious here. Like those boxes," she said, pointing to the packing crates in front of the window. "What's in them?"

"Them?" Leonid shrugged. "Books. Clothes. Things."

"It would take up a lot less space if you got rid of the boxes and just put some shelves or drawers under the window. That way the room would feel a lot bigger because you'd get more light. And this wallpaper makes it feel even smaller," she added, pressing her hand against the dark green patterned wall. "If you painted the room white, it would probably look twice as big."

Ben looked around the shabby room and wondered what Sara was talking about. It didn't look to him like it had any potential. Besides, the room reeked of cigarette ash. It was a smell that reminded him obscurely of being a very little boy, his mother yelling at his father to smoke outside, to stay away from the twins.

"We cannot buy those things," Leonid mumbled, looking at the floor.

Ben instantly realized Sara's mistake. How could she be so stupid? He felt himself turning red on her behalf. He tried, again, to say something, anything. But Sara seemed animated by an unaccountable grace. "That's all right, we have some extra shelves at home," she said. "And I know we have some leftover paint in the garage. Ben and I could come over and we could all do it together. Right, Ben?"

"Right," Ben said with a crack in his voice.

A few moments later, Ben and Sara were walking home, without speaking. It was a still winter afternoon, the kind of afternoon where the air is cold and gray and solid and immobile, like hardened cement. Even the muddy path from the building to the street seemed hard, dead leaves resting on it like fallen birds. But then a slight, cold breeze blew, lifting up the dead leaves and circling them in a little round dance in front of them. Sara gazed down at the ground as she walked, and Ben noticed as he walked beside her that the corner of her mouth had turned up, just slightly, as she walked down the muddy path.

———

"WIZKIND, CAN YOU take notes for me?" Leonid asked Ben the following week in math class.

Ben always made an effort to arrive early to math class, but Leonid walked in late so regularly that the teacher barely noticed it anymore. Today, though, Leonid was in his seat before Ben even arrived, waiting with an open notebook. Ever since the injury, Ben had noticed, the Meltdown Gang had been avoiding Leonid, shunning him in the hallways. At some point, a coup had apparently taken place. Yuri was their leader now. Oh, Ben thought, how the mighty have fallen.

"Sure," Ben answered, feeling a familiar fear surging and then retreating under the cage. Leonid's smile seemed different this time, more honest. Still, Leonid had been sitting in math class for the past few days without bothering to take notes. It seemed a little odd that he had suddenly abandoned his pride.

With his hulking left arm, Leonid passed Ben an open notebook. Across the top of the page, a short sentence was scrawled in large block

letters, far more clumsy and childlike than any of Leonid's old threatening notes. Leonid must have written it with his left hand.
Anticipating some new threat, Ben was shocked when he saw what it
actually said:

HEY WIZKIND—YOUR SISTER IS HOT.

Ben almost laughed out loud—first, because it was so absurd, and
second, because he thought it was a joke. Sara was hardly what anyone
would call pretty. She might have been, if she had bothered wearing
something that wasn't covered with paint more than once a year, or
even just brushing her hair, but she didn't.

Ben hesitated before turning around, staring at the bulging letters
and wondering what it might mean. His first guess was that this was the
entry point for some sort of elaborate and embarrassing scheme—and
one even more unpleasant than any of the earlier humiliations,
because now Sara would somehow be involved. It could clearly be
nothing but the worst, though Ben was too frightened to imagine what
the worst might be.

But when Ben finally worked up the courage to turn around, he saw
that Leonid wore a strange expression—his eyebrows raised slightly, his
lower lip caught between his teeth. Hopeful.

Leonid's reddish eyelashes fluttered. He nodded at Ben, then
reached with his left hand toward the notebook. "Wait," he muttered,
then pulled the notebook back onto his own desk.

For a few long moments he struggled with a pencil in his left hand,
sheltering the page with his cast. Ben reached into his own bag and
began taking out and arranging his textbook and calculator, fighting
not to turn around. Then Leonid's notebook landed on Ben's desk
again, with a second clumsy sentence underneath the first. No longer
afraid, but burning with curiosity, Ben seized it and struggled to read
the new, wavering words:

PLEASE TELL ME, IF SHE HAVE BOYFRIEND.

Ben realized then that power lay in his hands.

You cannot know, he later would remember Raisa Shcharanskaya saying, how children will turn out. Ben could not know then, for instance, that his sister would come to him now, years later, to tell him that she and Leonid were going to have a baby, that he would surprise himself by dreaming of the child who would be given his mother's or father's name—that in this yes or no lay the entire future, the entire world. On that morning in math class, all that lay in it was trust. He paused for a moment, and then wrote:

NO. CALL HER.

As he turned around to pass the notebook back to Leonid, Ben glanced out the classroom window and noticed that the first snow of the year was beginning to fall to the ground.

———

BUT TONIGHT THERE was no snow on the ground, just the thick silence of the house where Ben had grown up, when he arrived there after Sara's visit to stash the painting he had stolen (or, as he thought of it, *rescued*) from the museum.

The silence in the house had smothered Ben for the past six months, following him through the halls every time he took the train out to New Jersey to clean up another room, and following him back to the city every time he left. It lay in heavy layers on every object, like thick dust. On the days after the funeral when he had woken up in the morning in his old bed, he felt it resting on his upper lip, collecting in the dent below his nose during the confusion between sleep and waking, when the morning sounds that filled his morning dreams—a car starting in the garage, a shower running in the bathroom, his mother calling him from down the hall—vanished into heavy air. Every time he entered a room he found himself waiting, listening, expecting someone to call his name. When no one called he felt as if he had been drugged.

He put the painting back on the wall where it had always been, and took down the picture that had replaced it, a framed photograph of Sara and Leonid—Leonid, who had finished college in three years and his applied math Ph.D. in four, who had held fellowships at universities around the world, who turned down a professorship at Cambridge in order to finally marry Sara, and who now worked for an investment bank, making a fortune doing some kind of mathematical modeling for asset pricing. It was like a joke. Ben could hardly be jealous of him, though. Sara's mother-in-law was right: in the end, he was a good boy. You cannot know how children will turn out. Not to mention the new child, the not-yet child.

But as he held the picture of Leonid and looked up at the floating man in the painting, Ben suddenly thought of the last time he had seen Leonid and the floating man together—on that night when Leonid had first come to America and held the photo of the painting in his hands—and then remembered the piles of papers that had been underneath the snapshot. And then he went down the hall to his parents' studio, where all of the family files were kept in a set of cabinets on the wall, and knew what he needed to do.

5

—

WHAT DOES a child resemble while it waits in its mother's womb? As a boy, Der Nister had been taught the answer: a folded writing tablet. Its hands rest on its temples, its elbows rest on its legs, its heels rest on its backside, and a lit candle shines above its head. And from behind eyelids folded closed like blank paper, it can see from one end of the world to the other. There are no days in a person's life that are better or happier than those days in the womb. When those days must end, an angel approaches the child in the womb and says, *The time has come.* But the child refuses—wouldn't you? (Didn't you?) *Please*, the child begs, *please don't make me go.* And then the angel smacks it under the nose so that it falls from the womb and forgets— which is why babies are always born screaming. But before that, they are happy, and they wait.

Everything Der Nister had done that day was just a show, for the child. After he had eavesdropped through the door and heard one of Chagall's students in the artist's studio, Der Nister had bounded in and tried his absolute best to be funny, witty, boisterous. He believed he owed it to the boys to amuse them at every opportunity, that the orphanage school was their very first chance at happiness since before their birth. Not that he and Chagall hadn't seen the same things. In Der Nister's hometown of Berdichev, there had been a massacre the previous year, children and old men butchered. In Vitebsk in the same season, Chagall's wife's family home had been sacked, the valuables pillaged and the rest smashed to pieces while his mother-in-law was held at gunpoint. By then it was standard. But somehow Der Nister—unlike Chagall, who only pretended to be charmingly naive—still trusted the world. And Der Nister, the Hidden One, had chosen his name in part for reasons of character. By nature he was timid, a quiet believer that the happiness from the world before birth was still waiting for him.

The incident with Peretz was more typical of Der Nister. Years earlier, an editor had sent some of his stories to the famous Yiddish writer I. L. Peretz. To say that Der Nister worshiped I. L. Peretz would be inaccurate. One cannot worship the air one breathes. When the editor informed him that his stories had earned him an invitation to visit Peretz—Peretz! Peretz, the greatest Yiddish writer alive, Peretz, the latter-day prophet whose stories had turned literature into a new religion, Peretz, whose words were a bridge between the living and the dead, Peretz, who deigned to meet only with young writers of the most astronomical talent—when he heard that he had been deemed worthy of visiting Peretz, Der Nister started trembling, and kept trembling all the way from his own apartment in Kiev to the crowded third-class cars on several long overnight train rides to Warsaw and then to Number 1 Ceglana Street, where at the appointed hour (after pacing the street in front of the building for the entire afternoon) he finally summoned the courage to knock on Peretz's door.

When the door opened, Der Nister only shook harder. Standing before him was not a servant or editor or fellow admirer, but the master himself. Der Nister recognized him immediately from the bookplates: a big man in his sixties, with bushy hair and an enormous mustache. Years later, Der Nister would notice how much Peretz—not to compare them—resembled Stalin.

"The Hidden One, hiding in the hallway!" the prophet's voice boomed from the doorframe. Der Nister was astonished: it was the first time anyone had actually called him by his pen name. He hadn't eaten since the train arrived the night before, and now he nearly fainted. But Peretz already had him by the arm, steering him through the foyer and into his modest three-room apartment. (No Yiddish writer in the history of the world, not even Peretz, had ever supported himself through his writing. It was a fact that Der Nister, then a starving bachelor whose only food came from inconsistent tutoring jobs, knew very well.) The master looked him over. "Perhaps I am too gray for you," he said, motioning to his hair, "and you are too green for me. How old are you?"

"Twenty-four," Der Nister answered, shrinking into his shirt. They were the only words he would speak all night.

"Let's change that," Peretz said.

He was joking, but Der Nister heard the subtext of the joke: youth is like a good card, which one can either play or hide under one's vest. Der Nister tried to hide his as Peretz sat him down in his study. "Now, about your stories," Peretz began, but then interrupted himself, standing up and leaning toward a box on a desk crowded with papers, books, notebooks, albums, and loose cigarettes. Der Nister looked on in disbelief. Could this be Peretz's writing desk? The desk where the world was created?

"Would you like a cigar?"

Der Nister nodded, dumbstruck, unable to stop the manic spinning of his head. As the crisp brown paper of the cigar glided from the prophet's fingers to his own mortal palm, he clutched it so tightly that it nearly crumbled in his hands. A souvenir of paradise! Yet here the prophet was already offering him a light. How could he smoke the cigar and still keep it forever? He had no choice but to lean forward and use the prophet's flame, but he only pretended to smoke it. In a few minutes, he decided, he would snuff it out and save it. Working through these details in his panicked mind, Der Nister began listening only after Peretz had already begun his critique.

"What's remarkable about your work is the bridge you build between good and evil," Peretz was saying when Der Nister finally listened. "Most people don't believe in evil. For them, every act of cruelty is just a misunderstanding, and if we only understood the motives behind it, we could eliminate those motives and make it disappear. I believed that, too, when I was young." Smoke leaked between the writer's lips. "I was a lawyer, you know."

Der Nister knew, of course. The lost souls in Peretz's stories often found themselves being judged in front of a divine tribunal, and usually the prosecutor had the last word. "In a way I'm sorry that you don't still believe it," Peretz said. He leaned back in his chair, tapping his cigarette on a plate on the table next to him. "You know about the irrationality of evil, and the humanity of it. It's in everything you write, and it's necessary."

Der Nister allowed himself to smile, but the smile proved premature. "But you are too indulgent," Peretz declared, waving his hand to brush away a smoke ring along with Der Nister's ego. "You are seduced by beauty, and you think that if you can write a pretty sentence about something, then it doesn't matter where the story goes or how it ends. Your greatest weakness is that you write as if you are painting a picture instead of telling a story. A painting doesn't have to mean anything, but a story does."

Der Nister had splurged on a new vest for the occasion, but he suddenly felt as though he had been stripped naked. His thin, hesitant fingers fumbled with his cigar, then carefully slid it into his new vest pocket at the moment when Peretz moved in his seat. He wanted to vanish into his chair.

"Remember the story you learned as a child: When the hour arrives for us to proceed to the next world, there will be two bridges to it, one made of iron and one made of paper," Peretz intoned. His words were heavy, but his voice floated on rings of smoke, a breath of fire and ash that hovered over the room full of Hebrew and Yiddish books, as if waiting to descend and consume them. Der Nister swallowed, breathing in the master's air. "The wicked will run to the iron bridge, but it will collapse under their weight. The righteous will cross the paper bridge, and it will support them all. Paper is the only eternal bridge. Your purpose as a writer is to achieve one task, and one task only: to build a paper bridge to the world to come."

Der Nister was so awed by Peretz's presence that he had to struggle to understand what the master said. He felt as if he were seeing the sound and hearing the light in the room. Meanwhile, in a split second of lucidity, he had glanced at the table to his left to marvel at a scrap of paper with what could only be Peretz's handwriting on it. It read, "Buy eggs." Der Nister planned to pocket it at the earliest opportunity. But suddenly Peretz's gaze, until then burning into Der Nister's eyes, dropped to the young writer's chest.

Peretz cleared his throat. "Let me go see if I can find the source for that story," he announced. He rose quickly from his chair and left the room.

It wasn't until Peretz had left the room, and Der Nister had slid forward in his seat to grab the scrap of paper on the table beside him, that the young author smelled something burning. He looked down to see the enormous hole that the still-lit cigar had burned through the pocket of his brand-new vest. For the rest of his life, he never owned a better vest. And he never smoked again.

———

A painting doesn't have to mean anything, but a story does. Just barely, but it does. Der Nister often thought about that in the years that followed, as his own writing grew more and more tangled and obscure. And he wondered: Why should paintings be exempt from meaning? Didn't everything need some sort of meaning, some purpose? Or did meaning emerge from what stories had and paintings lacked—a beginning and an end? But the Hidden One was timid, and afraid of asking questions. Ten years passed until, in the year when he was living in the orphanage, he summoned the courage to ask his artist neighbor about it. It was the day after one of the boys had visited the studio, and something about the strange quiet child among the paintings had haunted him. He stopped by in the afternoon on his way up to his top-floor apartment, slipping silently toward the open door on the second floor.

Chagall was busy with the theater paintings, making studies for the murals that would soon plaster the walls of the State Jewish Theater in Moscow. They hadn't paid him yet, which infuriated him. Chagall was constantly concerned that his four-year-old daughter was going to starve, even though he had had more success than almost anyone else in their circle. The artist had been taking more commissions lately, while Der Nister struggled to feed his family on the pittance from the orphanage school. Chagall had stooped to all levels, even taking on a project for the Yiddish hack poet Itsik Fefer—illustrations for a long poem praising the new Soviet-Jewish republic in Birobidzhan on the Korean border. As poetry it was trash, even if you believed the propaganda, which Chagall apparently didn't. Nor did he much care, as far as Der Nister could tell. Already he was making arrangements to move himself and his family to Berlin. But the artist offered Der Nister a friendly indulgence, a consistent flattery that the writer was willing to believe was real. "I love your work," Chagall had once told him, not long after they completed their first children's book together. "You've inspired me. You know, I've secretly put your name into every painting in this room." It was a joke, Der Nister was sure, but he glanced around the room at the paintings, just in case. He noticed nothing, and the artist laughed at him. "Someday when people buy them," the artist announced theatrically, "I'll say I couldn't have done it without my brilliant upstairs neighbor, the Hidden One." Now Der Nister watched him in his studio, envious of the way the artist seemed to shrug off life with a laugh.

"This painting," Der Nister ventured, trying to sound casual as he gestured toward a picture of a man and woman—Chagall and his wife?—kissing against a blue background. The blue seeped into the lovers' skin until foreground and background were one, the man's gloved hand tentative on the woman's neck and cheek. "This picture you made. I was wondering—what does it mean?"

Chagall turned around, following Der Nister's pointing finger with his eyes. He gazed at the picture, and seemed about to say something profound. Then he shrugged.

"Blue," he said, and went back to painting.

Der Nister stared at Chagall's back. "What do you mean, 'blue'?" he demanded when he regained his breath. "I can see that it's blue. But doesn't it mean something more, even if you don't want to tell me what? Something about love? Or comfort? Or—or—" He stumbled on the word, strangely embarrassed. "Or sex?"

Chagall groaned, jamming the tiny brush he was using into a cup of orange water. He spun around. "It means blue," he said again. He folded his paint-stained arms across his chest.

"Blue?"

"Just blue," Chagall repeated. He wore a narrow circle of reddish paint on the skin beneath his nose, like a wound. "Why does it need to mean something? What does your daughter mean, Kahanovitch?"

The Hidden One bit his lip. He thought of Hodele, almost eight years old and already brilliant, solving puzzles, writing full sentences in three languages, ready to take over the world. For an instant his imagination simulated the brush of her hair against his wrist. Did gifts from God have the right to be meaningless? "But she does mean some-thing," he heard himself say. "She means—she means the future. Someday she'll light a candle for me on the anniversary of my death, and her grandchildren will be given my name."

"And what if they're not?"

The Hidden One repressed the atavistic urge to spit three times, the way old Jews did whenever someone said something about the future. Chagall did it for him, sarcastically spitting air with all the fervor of an old woman.

"What if they're not? Then what will she mean?" Chagall asked. He picked a shard of paint off his thumb and cast it on the floor. "Or how about Boris Kulbak? Does he mean something?"

Der Nister stared at him, surprised to hear the child's name. He thought of the boy's little painting—that round circle filled with a blob of a creature which, with the help of Chagall's hints, he realized was meant to be a fetus in a womb. The fetus's bald head had strangely resembled the boy's shaven one, his unborn face equally frozen in fear. At least Hodele liked to smile.

"I looked at his records this morning in the office," Chagall said, rubbing a bare foot against an orange spot on the floor. "Eleven years old, from Zhitomir." Hodele had been born in Zhitomir, Der Nister remembered, in their dark apartment in the middle of a night full of fog and rain: screams of agony and blood, followed by pure light. "They dug him out of a grave in Zhitomir last winter," Chagall added. "Apparently he had buried himself alive."

The Hidden One gulped at the air. It seemed to him that the boy did mean something, and something specific: a revival of the dead. He imagined the boy grown up, married to Hodele, the two of them paint-ing pictures and making puzzles for their children.

"It doesn't mean anything," Chagall declared. Der Nister saw with relief that the artist was gesturing toward the painting. "It's just color. And light." Chagall turned back around, taking the little brush out of the water. "A little happiness. Do yourself a favor and don't beat it to death." He began to paint, his back facing Der Nister. "So when are you going to give me the next children's book to illustrate?"

"I—I need to work on it a little more," the Hidden One stammered. But his mind was elsewhere, dreaming of the boy and of Hodele.

"Good. Go disappear and leave me alone. And don't come back until you have a joke to tell me."

The Hidden One vanished from the room. As he walked back up the narrow staircase to his own home, he wondered if it was even possible to have happiness in a story, when one was required to imagine both a beginning and an end. He walked faster up the steps, hoping that Hodele was waiting for him.

6

W HEN ERICA FRANK took the job at the Museum of Hebraic
Art, she discovered two things that made working at a Jewish
museum different from the other museums where she had worked
before. First, nearly the entire museum security budget went to protecting people instead of protecting art. Orientation for new employ-
ees included a security brochure listing various attacks on Jewish
institutions, selected from among hundreds of others as helpful exam-
ples: Buenos Aires (Jewish community center bombing, 1994; 85 dead,
300 wounded), Istanbul (double synagogue bombing, 2003; 25 dead),
Casablanca (quintuple bombing with targets including a Jewish community center, 2003; 41 dead), Djerba, Tunisia (synagogue bombing,
2002; 14 dead), Kallingrad, Russia (Jewish kindergarten bombing,
2003; 1 child injured), Montreal (Jewish school bombing, 2004; no
injuries reported), Terre Haute, Indiana (arson attack on a Holocaust
museum, 2003; museum burned to the ground). By the time Erica
started working there, entering the museum was like going through an
airport checkpoint, complete with X-ray machines, metal detectors,
security guards, and pat-downs. Faxes came in regularly from the FBI,
warning of recent threats from fuel truck bombs and suggesting that
the museum set up hideous cement barriers outside on the sidewalk
like every other Jewish institution in the city, despite its status as a land-
mark building. The barriers hadn't been ordered yet, but they would

be. In the meantime, someone had lifted a million-dollar painting by Marc Chagall off the wall during a cocktail hour, and there wasn't a single camera or alarm to stop the thief on his way out.

The second thing that made this job different from the others, Erica had slowly realized, was that everybody knew everybody. There was hardly a person on the staff who didn't know everything there was to know about her dating history, her brother's children, her father's depression—and every day, someone new had to tell her how sorry he or she was to hear about her mother's death. After a while it began to feel like a punishment.

Erica had just seen her mother the night before. In a dream, as usual. This time her mother was in a crowd at night, maybe for the fireworks or something, fighting her way through masses of people as she tried to make it to wherever she was going, but everyone else was moving in the opposite direction. Erica spotted her and grabbed her hand. "Mom, what are you doing here?" she heard herself ask. "You're supposed to be dead."

"Just keep moving," her mother answered, turning around and allowing them both to be carried by the crowd. "Just keep moving. No one's going to know."

Lately Erica was having trouble waking up in the mornings. Waking up meant coming out of dreams, smiling with her eyes closed until she would catch a glimpse of the wall in front of her and find herself yanked through the very same moment she had experienced every day for the past several months, the sudden, clobbering realization that her mother, for yet another day, was still dead. She was surprised to find that, despite all her attempts to prepare for this—knowing it was coming three months before it happened, steeling herself each day, expecting the worst every time the phone rang—every morning since it happened had gotten harder, not easier.

During most of the previous year, at the last museum, she had been dating her boss. His name was Saul, a tall man with narrow, wiry muscles, divorced. He had interviewed her for the position and had hired her on the spot, without even making her wait for a phone call. She knew it was because of her looks, but she took the job anyway. For a time she enjoyed how he used her, his new, beautiful girlfriend, to get back at his ex-wife. Later she began to like him, though she had trouble determining if she enjoyed being with him or if she just enjoyed being with someone whose every thought didn't revolve around postoperative radiation therapy. He was Jewish, had a small earring at the top of his left ear, and was an excellent cook.

She moved in with him quickly, without telling her mother, claiming that she had changed her phone number because of telemarketers and insisting that Saul let her use her voice on their answering machine. She never even mentioned him to her mother, though in the final weeks she suspected that her mother knew something was up. It was as if she were practicing, testing out what it might be like not to be able to tell her mother things. They had only started dating about three months before her mother died, and all she had told him was that her mother was ill. She didn't tell him about her mother's death until several days after it happened; she didn't want him at the funeral. He was crushed when she told him that he had missed it, and when she returned to the city after the seven days of mourning he began to treat her like a queen. She started to hate sleeping with him, and hated herself more when she enjoyed it.

Saul's parents were also divorced, like Saul himself. He hadn't spoken to his father in fifteen years, and he hated his mother. But after Erica's mother died, he began calling his own mother from home once a week, forcing Erica to speak with her for a few minutes each time. She knew he meant well, but that didn't matter. Burning, flaming jealousy consumed her, enraged her. She felt herself casting the evil eye.

A few months ago, Erica went to Saul's brother's wedding—actually a stepbrother, from his mother's husband's first marriage, and it was the stepbrother's second wedding, too, or possibly his third; Erica couldn't remember. In the ladies' room, as she was about to leave the stall, she heard the nasal voices of Saul's mother and another woman by the makeup mirror.

"Her mother just passed away, and now we're really all she has," she heard Saul's mother say as the other woman clucked her tongue. Erica thought she was talking about the bride, about whom Erica knew absolutely nothing, except that the bride had walked down the aisle alone.

But then the other woman said, "Saul's just a knight in shining armor for her. Is it serious?" Serious, Erica thought. Like a disease.

Saul's mother smiled a self-satisfied smile that Erica could hear in her voice as she replied, "Saul's a fool if he doesn't want it to be. People like that girl are just looking for love. And you know Saul—he needs someone who will eat out of his hand like that."

Two sets of high heels clicked along the marble tiles, and then Erica was sitting inside their conversation as they took their places in the stalls on either side of her, their words arching over her bent neck. "My father's second wife was like that," the other woman called through the wall of the stalls. "Her first husband had died on her, and she just latched on to my father like she couldn't breathe if he wasn't around. I thought she'd suck the life out of him, but it was just the opposite."

Erica heard the toilet on her right flush as Saul's mother answered, "This girl is like that. She's good for Saul."

"Such a pretty girl, too," the other woman said. Fawning, almost. "Drop-dead gorgeous."

"Mmm," Saul's mother muttered, and Erica could picture the tight wrinkle between her eyebrows before she spoke again. "And if it works out, it means the grandchildren will be mine. Usually they go right to the girl's mother. We're at an age where we have to think about these things, aren't we?" Erica trembled, taking care not to lean forward so that the automatic toilet wouldn't flush. "And it means he wouldn't have a mother-in-law!"

Erica waited on the toilet for a long time after that, long after both of them had left. She sat with her elbows on her knees, her eyes fixed on the shining green marble floor. The bathroom was made of the finest materials, but underneath it all was nothing but shit.

One morning she woke up before dawn, involuntarily, jolted by Saul's snores out of a dream where she was standing in the kitchen with her mother, waiting for her mother to tell her which plates to use to set the table, meat or dairy. She had trouble falling back to sleep. Saul moved in his sleep, once even throwing his arm around her. She pushed it off. At last she fell asleep again. This time, she was at a wedding—it looked like the place where her brother had gotten married, years ago, but now somehow Erica was the bride—and her mother was helping her into her dress. She woke up before seeing the groom. The third dream didn't even involve her mother. She was lying in bed with Saul beside her—it was hard to tell, until the end, whether or not it really was a dream—when she heard someone open the apartment door. She woke Saul and whispered to him that someone was in the house. Saul didn't believe her until the man entered their bedroom, a tall man in a dark coat, holding a long knife. Saul sat up in their bed and offered the man Erica's body in exchange for leaving them both alive. The man was about to take up the offer when Erica woke again.

It was still dark outside when she woke up. Saul rolled over beside her, letting out a low rumble from his throat. Erica swallowed a sob. She had never cried in front of Saul, because she knew that if she did, Saul would have to put his arm around her, talk to her, change the subject, distract her, tell her stupid jokes to cheer her up, caress her shoulders and then gradually move to stroking her breasts—anything, in the guise of comforting her, to avoid listening to her cry. She decided that nothing could possibly help her except to leave. Not for good, of course. Just for now, for a few hours. She didn't know where she would go, but it didn't matter. Anywhere.

Erica slipped out of bed and into the bathroom, careful not to let herself look in the mirror. In the shower she let loose a few low sobs as the water ran over her face. She stepped out of the shower, wringing out her hair with her hands before wrapping herself in a towel and then bending down briefly to dry her feet. When she did, she noticed another pair of feet, large and dark, behind hers.

"You have a beautiful body, Erica. You know that, right?"

Erica stood up and turned around, seeing Saul first reflected beside her in the bathroom mirror. He was squinting at her without his contact lenses, grinning a strange grin that she had sometimes seen him wearing in his dreams, drunk on sleep. His stubble made him look older than he was. He was naked except for a pair of boxer shorts, the front slowly rising away from his skin. The breeze from the open door made her shiver. She picked up the ends of her towel and began to wrap herself in it again, her skin feeling tight.

"I want you, Erica."

Saul stepped toward her, running the palms of his hands along her cheeks and neck and then down to her shoulders, nudging her arms away from her chest. He had taken hold of the corner of her towel and was slowly pulling it away from her, sliding it from underneath her arms until it fell to the floor. She stood motionless, watching him. For a moment she thought to reach down for the towel, but Saul had already moved in front of her, planting his feet on the towel and bracing his arms against the sink, her body wedged between them.

"I love you, Erica."

Saul began kissing her, the fingers of his right hand tracing a line from her cheek, slowly, down to her breast. Erica tried to speak, but her tongue was caught in his mouth. He took hold of her wrist and pressed her palm against his stomach. She felt his breath moving beneath it, rising from below his chest and seeping into her own mouth as he pushed her hand down beneath the waistband of his shorts. Erica leaned back against the sink. His left hand clutched her breast, slowly circling her nipple with its forefinger and then pressing against her, trapping her hand between them and sliding his right hand downward until his finger crept between her thighs, just barely grazing her skin. She moaned, out of habit. They had made love only hours earlier. She suddenly felt incredibly tired, eager to crumple to the floor. "I want your children, Erica," Saul whispered.

This was something new. She opened her eyes, her skin suddenly cold against the edge of the sink. Saul looked back at her, and a jolt of terror struck her as it occurred to her that he might be waiting for a reply. *And if it works out, it means the grandchildren will be mine,* she heard Saul's mother repeating in her head. She was silent. Saul smiled and closed his eyes, pressing his body against her and leaning in toward her ear. Brushing his lips against her earlobe, he whispered, "Marry me, Erica."

"No."

She looked up to see if he had heard her. He had. He stared at her, his gentle fingers stopping short. Then, without warning, he pinned her to the edge of the sink and thrust into her, crushing her with his full weight. A moment later, as Saul arched his back and gasped for air, Erica took the opportunity to slip out from under him, pushing him back with all her strength. She slipped and plummeted to the floor, knocking her head against the toilet as she fell. Saul followed her to the floor, a mad demon, lying down on top of her like a heavy blanket, or a shroud.

Afterward it was as if nothing had happened. She let him pull her up off the floor and back into bed, where he promptly rolled away from her and fell asleep. Erica lay silently beside him until she heard his first few snores. Then she crept out of the bed, her movements careful and silent. He was a lighter sleeper than she had thought. She was afraid even to open a drawer. Instead she slipped on a pair of sweat-pants and one of Saul's T-shirts that had been lying on the floor, grabbed her purse, and left. Outside, the sun was just coming up, and the only people on the street were more homeless than she was. She wandered for almost twelve hours, pacing the streets, until she found the courage to knock on her brother's door.

After three days of doing almost nothing but sleeping on her brother's couch and reading children's picture books to her brother's little daughters over and over again, she finally found the courage to go back to work. There she discovered a letter on her desk, signed by Saul and two other museum administrators, informing her that her efforts at the museum had been weighed in the balance and found wanting. And so, one month later, she found herself at her new job, sitting in her depressing basement office at the Museum of Hebraic Art.

ERICA'S BOSS AT her new museum was a man named Max—a happily married grandfather in his sixties, to Erica's relief. But her relief didn't last long. Max was enraged by the theft, and he blamed Erica for it. At an emergency meeting the day after the heist, he made a point of asking who on the curatorial staff had been responsible for the cocktail hour logistics, even though he clearly knew the answer, humiliating Erica into raising her hand like a child. Later that morning he barged into her office, foaming at the mouth.

"Let me put this right on the table," Max growled, not bothering to sit down. He carefully kicked aside her extra chair, making way for himself to hover over Erica's desk. "You're new here. You organized that cocktail hour. This happened on your watch."

Erica took a breath. She had been dragged through dirt before. "The problem wasn't the event," she said slowly. "I followed the protocol exactly. The problem was that we have no alarm system. You can't hold a major exhibit like this without securing the objects and alarming them. Every other museum knows that. It's absurd. We have a huge security budget, but all those metal detectors aren't going to—"

"Erica, you know that we have security concerns here that other museums don't have."

Erica closed her mouth. There was no point in arguing, she saw. She looked down at her desk. Saul had left her with a fear of bosses, and she couldn't afford to lose another job.

"Here's what I want from you," Max said. He was leaning down toward her now with his hands on her desk, breathing in her face. "You have the lists of everyone who bought tickets. Hell, you made the god-damn name tags. I want you to call every single person who came to that event and interview every last one of them about everything they saw that night. In person."

Erica stared at him. This was insane. "Aren't the police doing that?"

"Yes, but there's a limit to what the police can do. They don't know what to ask. We're supposed to be helping them out. And frankly, I think certain people would be more, let's say, *open* with someone like you." He gave her a disgusting wink.

Erica shuddered, but Max didn't give her a chance to refuse. "Start making your calls now," he said, and left.

So Erica began. And after three days, she had gotten nowhere. Most people didn't even bother to return her calls. Those who did had paraded into her office one by one, each with the same lines, as if they were reading from a script: *Wow, stolen? Wow, that's too bad. Lemme think. No, didn't see anything. Wasn't looking for that kind of thing, if you know what I mean. Wow, sorry. Wow, good luck.* There had been articles in several newspapers with photographs of the painting, soliciting tips, but none had emerged. The police investigation was already focused on the possibility of an inside job, but Erica looked around at her colleagues—old men whose offices were plastered with family pictures, suburban women always running off to pick up some child, administrative assistants who spent half the day playing computer solitaire—and found it hard to believe. Meanwhile, the museum was wallowing in industry ridicule, had an irate Russian gallery and a far more irate insurance company on its back, and would be lucky if it could ever hold a major exhibition again. Even Saul had left messages for her at work about the theft, expressing his own museum's condolences, apparently for no other reason than to gloat. And then at last she came to the end of the

alphabetical list, and waited in her basement office for Benjamin
Ziskind.

————

HE WAS FIVE minutes late. No, ten. He was her last appointment of
the day, and she had already turned off her computer, eager to leave.
But now he wasn't showing up. Irritated, she decided to give him five
more minutes, and began to doodle on the legal pad where she had
written his name at the top. Ziskind, she thought. Why did the name
sound familiar? She didn't remember him from the cocktail hour; no
matter how hard she tried, she couldn't recall a face from that evening
to fit that name. No, she had heard the name somewhere else. Then
she knew where she had heard it: it was the name on the cover of the
picture books she had read to her nieces, during her involuntary stay
at her brother's home and on several visits since then. Her nieces
seemed to have an endless supply of books by that one author, and they
refused to let Erica read them anything else. Thankfully, the books
had been pretty good. Her phone rang: a different Ziskind was on his
way down.

There was a knock at her office door. "It's open," she called, almost
forgetting who she was waiting for. Then the door opened, and Erica
held her breath.

Standing before her was the one person from the cocktail hour that
she actually remembered, though she had forgotten his name—the jittery man who had snapped at her. He was a slight man, thin, with dark
hair and thick round glasses, not much taller than she. Yet there was
something unnerving about him, captivating, both then and now. He
hesitated at the threshold, holding the door open with his fingertips
without stepping closer. It was as if he couldn't enter without her
magic word.

"Nice to see you again, Mr. Ziskind," she said, trying to sound busi-
nesslike. "Please, come in. We're just doing a routine follow-up here
after the theft. I know you mentioned on the phone that you'd already
talked to the police. That's great. I just need to take down some details
about you and what you saw."

"Okay," he replied softly. There was a stillness in his voice that surprised her. He entered her office and sat down on the chair opposite

her desk, the one that Max had kicked aside during his tirade. He took off his glasses for a moment, rubbing one eye before opening both and looking right at her. His eyes were large and brown, almost black. With his glasses, she had barely noticed them. She fumbled with her pen, and it fell to the floor. Embarrassed, she reached for another one from the corner of her desk. He leaned forward and pushed it toward her, sending it swiveling across the surface between them. When she caught it, he smiled.

Flustered, she stared down at the paper and asked him for his address. She found herself taking more time than she needed to write it down, spelling out the letters of the street name. It looked beautiful like that, she thought. *West Seventy-eighth Street*. But she was being ridiculous.

"Occupation?" she asked. She looked up again, eyeing him across her desk. Here in the depths of the museum, under harsh fluorescent light, his pale skin glowed thin, revealing dim blue veins along the sides of his neck. Yet he looked older than he had seemed in the gallery that night, and more confident. There was a firm clarity in the way he glared at Erica that reminded her of her father, on her father's better days.

"Television," he said.

This seemed hard to believe. He was attractive, she admitted to herself, but hardly glamorous. She noticed he straightened his back as he said it, almost with pride.

"Doing what?" she asked.

"I write questions for *American Genius*."

Erica stared at him, waiting for him to smirk, or to otherwise let on that it was a joke. "That's a full-time job?" she asked.

But the man didn't smile. "I write several hundred questions a day," he told her, deadpan. "For every question on the show, there are hundreds that are rejected."

She was about to laugh when he awkwardly raised his hips in his seat, wresting a thin wallet from his pocket. He pulled out a ragged business card and slapped it down in front of her: *Benjamin Ziskind, Staff Writer*. The network's logo gleamed on card stock. He was serious, it seemed.

"Interesting job," she said. "I've seen that show a couple of times.

Isn't that the one with the really annoying host? That fake cowboy guy? I hate him."

To her surprise, Benjamin Ziskind laughed. It was a ridiculously loud laugh, and she had to stop herself from laughing at his laugh. "That's the one," he said, when his wild laughter had settled down.

She tried to hold back her grin. With people like Max and Saul, she had begun to think that she was crazy—inadequate in some way that others saw immediately but that she herself insanely couldn't see. But Benjamin Ziskind seemed to be even crazier than she, even more oblivious to the world, and that fact soothed her. "Let's get down to business," she said, allowing herself to smile. "What do you remember about the cocktail hour?"

He had stopped laughing, sipping slow breaths. Now he leaned back, stricken. "Look, I already talked to the police," he said. His hand gripped the chair's armrest like the gnarled roots of a tree. "I told them everything you would want to know. I didn't see anything suspicious. I didn't even recognize the painting you're talking about when I saw it in the paper."

Erica tapped the pen on her desk and sighed. It was the same thing everyone else had told her, only more concise. Max was an idiot, she thought. But then she remembered something. "You were in the gallery right before the music started, weren't you?" she asked. "Did you see anyone lingering there before you went down to hear the band?"

She watched as he moved in his seat, fidgeting with a finger as if twisting an invisible ring. Amazing how harmless certain men looked to her after Saul, she thought. And how gentle. She remembered thinking he was short at the cocktail hour, but in his seat he looked taller, his posture so perfect that he seemed almost regal. In another context, she might have reached for his hand.

"I really don't remember," he said. "I was on my way out."

"You didn't stay for the music downstairs?" she asked.

"I had to go home to meet my sister," he said. "The police already called her, if you don't believe me. I'm sure she'd be delighted to hear from you, too, if there are other interrogation cells available."

Erica winced. She was surprised that the sarcasm bothered her, but it did.

"I'm sorry," he said softly. He hunched forward, his hands in his lap, looking down at his knuckles. "I've had a difficult week."

"We all have, I suppose," Erica said, hiding her astonishment. It had been a long time, perhaps years, since she had heard a man apologize. She smiled.

"Do you have anything else to ask me, or can I go?" he asked.

She looked down at her legal pad, wondering what more she could say to prolong the conversation. Then she saw his name again, the doodle lingering between the letters of his address, and glanced at him again. "I was just wondering: Are you related to Rosalie Ziskind?" she asked.

As soon as she said it, she heard how irrelevant it was, absurd. But the man sat up in his seat. At first Erica thought he recognized the name, but then his face resumed its grim, tight-lipped pallor. He looked disappointed, as if he had been hoping for another chance to proclaim his innocence and had lost it. He watched her, waiting for more.

Erica made herself smile, surprised to find herself embarrassed. Why had she said anything? But now she was forced to explain. "This is going to sound silly, but—well, my nieces have this huge collection of picture books by someone named Rosalie Ziskind," she said. "They have the whole series, and I really like those books. Anyway, I'm sure there are thousands of Ziskinds in the world, but I was just wondering if you were related." She grimaced, unable to sustain the smile.

The man's lower lip hung open for a moment. He moved his head slowly, as if the room were moving and he were trying to steady his vision. Erica opened her mouth, ready to tell him to forget it, when he finally spoke. "She's my mother," he said.

"Your mother?" Erica repeated. She looked at him, stunned. When she started talking again, she almost couldn't stop. "Well, please tell her for me that I absolutely love her books. My favorite was *The Dead Town*. That was amazing. Usually ghost stories for kids are just gory or stupid, but that one . . . I mean, a town where people don't even notice that they're dead? Or where the dead come back to life because they aren't *worthy* of being dead? I read it to my nieces as a bedtime story, but then I couldn't sleep for days. I just couldn't get past that line near the end, where the man from the dead town says, 'No one in our town has ever really died, because no one in our town has ever really lived!' I mean, God, that's not a kids' book. That's—I don't know what that is."

Erica realized that she was babbling, letting down her guard, and for no good reason except that she had talked to almost no one in weeks except for a few coworkers and her brother—and she didn't want the man to leave. She held her breath, then considered the person in front of her. He was sitting like a statue, and for an instant she caught herself admiring him, her eyes tracing the tension in his arms and shoulders as if he were one of the sculptures in the galleries upstairs. But when she finally let herself smile at him, he didn't smile back. He watched her from behind his glasses with a puzzled look, and then backed his chair away from her desk. Suddenly she was sorry she had said anything; clearly she had said something wrong. "Your mother is incredible. Really," she said, swallowing a seeping taste of shame. "I'm looking forward to reading whatever she writes next."

He coughed, then suddenly stood up. "I have to go now," he announced, glancing at his bare, hairy wrist as if he were wearing a watch. "May I please leave?"

Erica had barely nodded her head by the time he reached the door. "Sorry to take up your time," she called after him. But the door had already swung shut.

Erica stared at the closed door, wondering if she should invent a reason to follow him out. But the opportunity had passed. She looked again at the legal pad with his name on it, her few sparse notes taken along the sides of the doodle, and she found herself thinking again of the picture books she had read to her nieces so many times, with their rivers of watercolor and deep shadows of ink. Her own mother had been an architect, and Erica had always loved to watch her work: careful, steady hands laying out lines with purpose, each perfect angle braced with potential, with a world waiting to be built. What was it like growing up in the Ziskind house, she wondered, with a mother making those books? Was it like growing up in hers? But here she was, daydreaming, wasting time with other people's memories. *Your problem, Erica,* she heard her brother lecturing in her head, *is that you take other people too damn seriously. You believe everything anyone ever tells you, and then you end up taking all their shit.* Her brother's only problem, it seemed to her, was that he was always right.

Erica tore off the sheet from the legal pad and reached for a file folder on her desk, the one where she was storing all her notes from these pointless Max-induced meetings. She would have to copy it over later, minus the doodle. On top of the folder was a stack of documents about the stolen painting, papers that she had barely had time to skim. She tugged at the folder from underneath the pile, but it wouldn't budge. She leaned over to move the stack instead. On top was a piece of paper listing the painting's provenance. She was about to push the pile over to get to the folder when she saw the words at the top of the page:

"Study for 'Over Vitebsk,' " by Marc Chagall, 1914.
Earliest known owner: Private collection, Rosalie K. Ziskind.

7

W HEN TWINS are in the womb and one of them is born—Sara remembered hearing once—the twin who remains behind watches his sole companion vanish and suffers an agony almost too devastating to bear. Only a moment later, he will understand that his twin has not died, but quite the opposite, that his vanished friend is closer to him than he can know. This, according to a story Sara once heard, is also the way of real death and the world to come. Just because we think people have disappeared doesn't mean they have. They are closer than we think.

Sara was the younger Ziskind twin by a matter of minutes. But even before she heard this story, Sara had been aware of a silence within her bones, a residual sorrow that flowed quietly in her blood—the legacy of the ten minutes before her life began, when her twin brother left her behind. Those ten minutes also gave her something that few others had: a knowledge, a hard fact that she carried within her like a dark and polished stone, that people who were supposed to have disappeared really hadn't. She had seen Ben disappear and knew better. Vanished people were a breath away. One only needed to breathe.

It began on the eighth day after her father's death, her first day leaving the house after the seven days of mourning, during which she and Ben had been taught the ways of the week. Ripped clothes, sitting on little low chairs that the funeral home had given them, covered mirrors, no shoes, sleeping on the floor, the endless stream of people bringing tasteless cookies to the house, the services held with the guests every evening, and worst of all, the mourner's prayer that they all had to recite every day for the rest of the year, the one that—as their mother had explained to them—said nothing about death at all but instead spoke only of the greatness of God, saying how God was blessed and praised and glorified and exalted and extolled and honored and lifted and lauded, blessed be the holy name. She and Ben missed a whole week of school. In the endless services held in the house, the strange clothes, and the boring board games she played with Ben in his bedroom to avoid the awkward silences in the living room, Sara realized that none of the events of the week had anything to do with her father at all. Even the funeral had simply been a box, and then, after everyone, even she and Ben, had added their requisite shovels' worth, a box covered with dirt. Whenever Sara was in the room with the guests, she had noticed, the adults in the house avoided mentioning him. It was as if they wanted her to forget him.

But on the eighth day after he died, when Sara returned to the fifth grade, her class took the same field trip that Ben's class had taken two weeks earlier—a forty-minute school bus ride to New York's Metropolitan Museum of Art, where she saw things whose relevance to her life her teacher could not possibly have imagined. Mummies.

Of course, Sara knew about mummies already; all eleven-year-olds do. But while her classmates flocked to the glass cases filled with human-shaped painted caskets, thrilled out of their skulls over the five-thousand-year-old bodies preserved inside, Sara avoided them. A box, she knew from the previous week, was just a box. What intoxicated Sara was something else. Most of the mummy galleries, she noticed, were not actually filled with the mummies themselves, but rather with other things—bowls, plates, cups, necklaces, combs, rings, vases, fabrics, models, pictures, scrolls. And all of it was for dead people.

Dead people had boats to ride in, food to eat, clothes to wear, games to play. Dead people had maps and directions to the underworld, and pictures and models of servants who would travel with them and help them to find the way. Dead people had friends to keep them company and jobs to keep them busy, painted in careful profiles on sandy stone walls. Dead people even had books to read: on one wall of the museum was a long unrolled scroll, called *The Book of the Dead.*

It wasn't until Sara had left the museum and had gotten on the bus—emerging from the dark galleries to find that the day had vanished, unnoticed, into a frighteningly early winter evening, the sky already the color of dark blue ink—that a thought struck her, as she sat surrounded by children raving about the extraction of a mummy's brains through its nose. The previous week, her father had been buried in a box, with nothing. Nothing. Even the box had been unmarked and bare, made of pale unpolished wood. They wouldn't even put a stone up on his grave until eleven months later, her mother had said, and when they did, all it would say was his name. Her mother had even told Sara, after she asked repeatedly, that he wasn't even wearing any real clothes inside the box, only a white shroud. How, she thought in a panic as she stared out the bus window at her own reflection, would her father ever survive in the underworld, without a map to take him there, without a job to do there, without a single picture to take with him on his journey?

And so Sara decided to build her father a tomb.

The location of the tomb, she determined, would be in the studio: a small room at the back of the house, filled with filing cabinets and drafting tables, where her father had often worked at home. Her mother, too, had worked there. But on the eighth day after Sara's father died, her mother had gone straight to an art store and purchased a new drafting table for herself, a smaller one, which she had set up in another room. The door to the studio hadn't been opened since his death. For that reason it was all the more appropriate for Sara's purposes, since it was unlikely that her mother or brother would wander in. Even Ben, she had decided, shouldn't be told about it. Secrecy was essential. As she had learned at the museum, one always had to be concerned about people robbing the tomb. As for when to work, Sara decided that early afternoons were best, when she and Ben were supposedly busy doing their homework, and Ben actually was. But Sara had recently discovered that homework, once the only thing that mattered, was simply no longer necessary. When she stopped handing things in, her teacher didn't even ask her about it. All she did was stop

Sara daily on her way out the door, after the other children had left, to tell her that "I know how you feel," to which Sara would nod, and to ask if "everything was all right at home," to which Sara would also nod, and to add that she hoped Sara would tell her if there was "anything I can do to help," to which Sara would nod again and then leave the room, because Sara had figured out that all she ever needed to do at school anymore was nod, particularly when she was asked to agree with something that wasn't true. So now Sara had both space and time to make the tomb.

The first thing her father needed was transportation to the under-world. Maps would help. These she had to dig out of the glove com-partment of the car—which, she discovered, was a small pocket of the world where time had stopped, where the maps were still folded the way no one but her father knew how to fold them, with the road trips they had taken together carefully marked with highlighters and out-lined in detail in her father's capitalized handwriting just off the paper coasts, as if they might any day now pile back into the car and take another trip with him. For the trip itself, Sara helped herself to a few of Ben's toy cars, which she dug out of his closet one afternoon when he was at a doctor's appointment. Her father could now choose between a Lamborghini and a Ferrari to take him to the underworld. Other supplies were also essential. Piece by piece, so that no one would notice, she began sneaking into her mother's bedroom and con-fiscating her father's clothes. Not all of them, of course. Just underwear and socks, a few pairs of pants, a heavy armload of shirts, a tie (in case it was fancy there), and a sweater (in case it was cold). Food, too, didn't need to be overly elaborate—merely "symbolic," as the museum had suggested. She stole a box of raisins and a bag of almonds from the kitchen and stashed them in the tomb.

But the major feature of the tomb would be the murals, and these required serious preparation. Sara began observing her mother and brother, watching them surreptitiously in the evenings. She sketched them, first in her mind and then later on paper, and eventually right in front of them, telling her mother that it was part of her homework, an art project. (Ben knew better, but he was too busy squirming in his new brace to care.) She was surprised at certain things—how difficult it was, for example, to draw someone's arm from the front, when it was angled forward, or the problem presented by noses, which in Ben's face seemed to grow straight out of his eyebrows, but only from certain points of view—and she began to appreciate the murals in the real tombs, where the people were perpetually in profile. But once she started drawing she knew that profiles weren't good enough, that her father deserved better. Her mother, believing Sara's claim that this was a school assignment, showed her how to draw things in "perspective" by drawing lines on the page before starting, and Sara discovered to her satisfaction that some of the problems with noses and arms were slowly resolved. Her father she had to create from memory. But Sara discovered that the range of the mind's eye—or at least her mind's eye—was enormous, opening up to an endless landscape of things that she couldn't even remember having seen in real life. After a few nights of lying in bed with her eyes open and trying to remember what he looked like, she discovered, to her joy, that she could picture her father—not "imagine" him, but actually see him—at all ages, knew what he looked like from every angle even in the years before she knew him, could see the tilt of his head or the position of his arm even at times when he had been out of the house, or with someone else, or alone. She drafted these first in a sketchbook, then with paint on paper, and finally—after moving some furniture out of the way, and raiding her mother's supplies—in paint that she applied directly to the walls of the room.

Her first painting was of her father in his usual position, sitting at a drafting table, drawing on a large piece of paper covered with rows of numbers. She wanted to make sure he would have a job in the under-world. But the other paintings were more fun. In paintings that filled the studio walls as high as she could reach, she re-created every room in their house, with her father taking his proper place in each. In the living room, he sat on the piano bench next to her, one hand on the keyboard and the other on her shoulder as she tried to follow his lead. In the kitchen, her father and Ben played checkers together, laughing, their painted mouths open. And in her parents' bedroom, she painted him into bed next to her mother, their eyes closed and his arms wrapped around her mother's body like a warm cocoon, as she had once seen them in their sleep.

The paintings wound their way around the room, and Sara was

pleased with her work. But she still thought her father ought to have a *Book of the Dead*. She began to look around the house for an appropriate one, but few of the books on the shelves seemed suitable, and those that did—a Bible, a yearbook, a photo album—might well be missed. It would be best to make one from scratch.

There was a story that Sara remembered her father reading to her, not once but many times, called "The Dead Town," and she decided that it might be a good thing for her father to read in the underworld. She had liked it so much that she knew the main parts of it by heart. She took a few pieces of paper, cut them into strips, taped them together into a scroll, and began to copy out the story as best her eleven-year-old brain remembered it, sometimes embellishing it with new details, like an ancient scribe. It was only a shadow of the original story, but it was the best she could do.

Once upon a time I was traveling around the country, and I saw a man walking by the side of the road, dragging his feet step by step in the sand. He looked like he could hardly walk. I thought I should be nice to him and give him a ride, so I did. We started talking, and soon I asked him, "Where are you from?"

He answered, "From the dead town!"

"Where's that?" I asked him. "I never heard of it."

The man laughed at me and said, "Just because you never heard of it doesn't mean it doesn't exist. Not every place in the world is on the map. Believe me, it exists. It's a regular place, with houses, stores, schools, and everything. Just like any other town."

"So why do you call it the dead town?" I asked.

"Because it IS a dead town!" he said. "It's a town that from the very beginning was hanging by a hair, and then the hair broke and it just hung in the air, with nothing holding it up. And while it was hanging there in the air, it became a dead town. If you want, I can tell you why."

"Tell me," I said.

The man started to tell his story.

"In the beginning, the town hung by a hair, because it was built in a place where it was against the law to build a town. That's why it's not on the maps. People started moving in, and so they built houses, and a school, and a cemetery, until the government found out about it. Then everything in the town had to be sold. But when they tried to sell the cemetery, the dead people got very upset, and started coming up out of their graves."

That was what the man told me. Then he asked me, "Do you believe that?"

I wasn't sure. It was hard to believe that dead people could come back to life. So I told him, "I believe that people's souls live forever. But their bodies? No way! Once you die, your body is in the grave, and that's it."

"But what happens to your soul?" the man asked. "You say the soul lives forever. Okay. If the person was good, the soul is rewarded in the world to come, and if the person was bad, then the soul is punished. But why are there rewards and punishments at all? I'll tell you why. Because as long as a person lives, he has choices. He can do good things, if he wants, or bad things, if he wants. But what happens to a person who never does anything good or bad, who never makes any kind of choice? A person who isn't really a person, whose life isn't really a life? What happens to that person's soul?"

"I don't know. What happens?" I asked.

"Nothing!" he said. "It just keeps living in its own imaginary world, like it did before. No one in our town has ever really died, because no one in our town has ever really lived! No one ever made any choices, no one ever did anything good or bad. No one ever did anything at all! A lot of towns are like ours, actually. When people in our town die and come back, they don't remember anything, and no one remembers them, because there is nothing to remember. They just crawl out of their graves, go home, put on their pajamas, and go back to sleep!"

"But don't the living people think that's a little weird?" I asked.

He laughed at me and said, "The living people? They don't notice! They're busy with their own stupid fights and problems. Why should they notice? The people are the same, alive or dead! After a while, the dead people took over the whole town. It was easy, since they don't need any food or air. And they never have any worries, because what makes a person worry? Knowing things, making choices! They don't know anything, and they never choose anything, so they never have any questions, never any doubts, never anything to make them sad."

I looked at the man next to me, and I asked him, "And what about you?"

"I'm half dead," he answered. Then he jumped back onto the road and disappeared into the woods.

———

Sara copied over the words in ink, and the book of the dead was complete. But the one in the museum had had little illustrations in it, she realized, and now she had written on the whole scroll without leaving room for anything else. So she taped on another strip of paper to the end and made little drawings of the three remaining things that she knew her father would need, but that she was too afraid to search for in her mother's bedroom: his two crutches, and his leg.

———

SARA HAD LEARNED about her father's leg years earlier, when she was six years old, on a night when she couldn't sleep. She had tried her best to close her eyes, following every single suggestion she had ever heard for falling asleep: counting sheep, counting goats, just plain counting, pretending she was on a raft floating in the ocean, pretending she was flying, but somehow none of it worked. Soon she gave up and wandered down the hall to her parents' room, where she saw that the light was on beneath the closed door. Without speaking, she leaned against the door and gently edged it open.

It was a hot summer night, and her parents were lying on the bed. Her mother was wearing the shirt she had been wearing during the day, but no pants, just white underwear, her bare legs stretched over the sheets. Her father, hairy and wearing nothing but a pair of white briefs, was lying on his side, facing her mother, his fingers rising in ripples underneath her mother's shirt, his eyes closed, and his lips moving along the edge of her mother's ear, like he was tasting it. Her mother's eyes were also closed, and she was laughing—a strange laugh, a smile filled with short airy breaths. What was so funny? Sara watched

as her mother wrapped an arm around her father's waist. Her mother
sat up a little with her eyes still closed, still laughing that funny airy
laugh, and began running her fingers along the waistband of her
father's underwear, sliding two of her fingers underneath it. Then she
opened her eyes, and her laugh stopped. "Sara," she said, her voice
dark.

Sara stood in the doorway, her white nightgown trailing on the floor.
She opened her mouth to speak, but then her father turned his head
and looked at her. He started to smile, and then suddenly laughed out
loud. What was so funny? Her mother wiggled her fingers out of her
father's underwear, the waistband snapping against her father's hip as
she let out a tight burst of breath. Sara stood in silence, her mouth still
open. Her hand was sticky, pressed against the door. She felt like she
had been eating candy, the gummy fruity kind that made you feel
sticky afterward, outside and in.

"It's okay, Sara, come on in," her father suddenly said, his tone
unusually bright. He dislodged himself from his perch against her
mother's body, kissing her mother's eyebrow as he moved. Her mother
frowned.

"I—I can't sleep," she said as her father rolled himself over on his
back. And then she held her breath.

She had seen the prosthesis before, since discovering it the previous
year—he had rolled up his pant leg to show it to her one day when, sitting on his lap, she had slipped onto his hard plastic shin. She had
never been terribly curious about it. She had thought it was something
all fathers had, like rough cheeks and wrists ringed with fur. But
recently she had noticed other men, fathers even, who seemed to have
two regular legs, like her mother. There were people on television, of
course, but you couldn't really count them because they were all imaginary anyway. What confused her in particular was the man who lived
across the street. Mr. Eriksen often stood outside in the summertime
with his kneecaps shining in the sunlight, wearing shorts as he watered
his plants. His legs were both exactly the same color, she noticed. One
time she had crossed the street to get a closer look, and she had seen
that not only were his legs the same color, but both had fur on them.
That day he was watering his plants barefoot, and she could see, as he
stood on the deck on the side of his house, that both of his feet even

had toes. (Her father's hard leg, as she thought of it, was smooth, with no fur, more pink than his other leg, and it didn't seem to have any toes; it went straight into a sock and shoe.) She had tried to sneak up a little closer, walking out onto his lawn and pretending that she was looking for a lost toy. Then her mother had called her back to the house, urgently, and she had wondered if there was something dangerous about men with two legs. But what she had never seen before was what she was seeing right now, in her parents' bed, as her father rolled over onto his back: her father's right leg in its natural state—a narrow thigh, a twisted red and purple knot in the place of the knee, and then nothing.

Sara knew that it was a matter of time before Ben woke up, heard them talking, and broke the magic circle. But for that reason the moment had to be seized. She listened for a second, trying to hear if Ben might be in the hall behind her. But she heard nothing but blank sounds, crickets rustling the air outside and the buzz of her brother turning in his sleep. She took a few careful steps into the room. Then, watching her parents watch her, she asked, "Daddy, can I see your leg?"

Her parents froze. Sara watched as her mother's face emptied of color, her lips and eyes drying up like the yellowed grass in the yard, parched and pale. A lock of her hair, loosened from its ponytail, fell down over her left eye. Her father lay motionless beside her, staring, balanced on his elbows behind him. Their two faces hung in the air like portraits framed on a wall. Her mother turned to look at her father, but he didn't look back. Instead he looked at Sara, his eyebrows raised as if in fear.

Her father blinked twice and glanced down at his stump of a leg. The leg shuddered involuntarily, as she had sometimes seen it do before, beneath its sheath of pants. Sara saw it move and trembled along with it. Then her father pressed his hand down on his thigh, holding it down, kneading it with his thumb. The shuddering stopped. He looked back at her, forcing a smile.

"Sure, Sara. Come on up," he said, patting the mattress alongside his leg. Her mother sat up beside him, her face empty and blank.

Sara pulled herself up on the foot of her parents' bed, amazed by the wide expanse of mattress and sheets that stretched between her and them, the vast elevated continent where her parents slept. She moved cautiously across the mattress, pulling herself along the length of her father's good leg—it was strange even to see her father's good leg with its toes, weird long and hairy toes, with the second toe longer than the first, because her father almost never removed his socks and shoes— until she came close enough to see the other leg, with its strange, ugly bulge of darkened flesh.

It was mottled in color, red in some places and an almost bluish purple in others, with deep indentations in the skin, some of them nearly black, like cracks filled with dirt. The indentations traveled in a row, forming a ring around the limb near its end. The hair on his leg only began growing a few inches up from where the leg stopped, and even there his thigh was misshapen, concave on the sides where it should have been round. Like a bone. The thigh quivered again, and her father pressed down on it with his hand. She heard him swallow a groan.

Sara sat quietly for a few moments, looking. There had been a big storm the previous week, and a large branch from the tree in the yard next door had fallen down across their driveway. She had noticed the following day how horrible the rest of the tree had looked, severed and deformed, the place where the branch had fallen off now swollen into a damp, dark lump on the tree's flesh. Maybe, she thought, her father had been out in a storm, or struck by lightning.

"Why is your leg like that?" she asked.

Her parents looked at each other. Her mother began to open her mouth, searching for words. But before she could speak, her father said, "I was in the jungle once, and a tiger bit my leg off."

Sara stared at him, searching his face for a hint of a joke; she couldn't find any. She was stunned. "Really?" she whispered.

Her father nodded, solemn. "Really! I was fighting with a tiger in the jungle, and he bit it right off."

"Did it hurt?"

"Daniel, stop it," her mother snapped, rolling over until she had turned away from him. As her mother moved, Sara noticed a dark line of curly fur along the inside edge of her mother's underwear, peeking out while her mother shifted on the crumpled sheets. The sight of it disturbed her. Why were some people covered with fur?

Sara looked again at her father's stump of a leg. Now she could see what she thought might be the teeth marks in the pinched, purple skin, on what would have been his knee. "Can I touch it?" she asked.

Her father hesitated, glancing at her mother. But her mother remained curled on her side, just barely turning her face to keep an eye on Sara. "Sure, if you want," he said. He raised the stump slightly, and Sara heard her mother draw in her breath.

Sara trembled for a moment, and then reached out her hand. She touched it, first with her fingertips and then caressing it in her palm, running her hand along the distortions in the skin. She was surprised to find that it was warm, the skin thick and taut like her father's palm. She traced her fingers along the dents in the flesh, and then caught a glimpse of her father's other leg lying next to it, long and full, as if it belonged to a different person, lying beside him. Suddenly Sara felt a deep and heavy weight within her, a leaden pendulum swaying slowly as it settled in her chest. "I bet it hurt a lot," Sara said softly.

"Yes, it hurt a lot," her father answered, with a weariness she had never heard before, and clutched her hand. She knew then that it was true, all of it.

Her father released her hand and then shifted heavily on the bed, pulling himself up and balancing on one elbow to grab a box of cigarettes from his night table. He tapped one out, wedged it between his teeth, and turned back toward Sara, one hand still groping for the lighter. Sara's mother turned over, sitting up beside him.

"Why did you go the jungle?" Sara asked.

Her mother looked at her father, and then suddenly yanked the cigarette out from between his spluttering lips and threw it on the floor. When she spoke, she looked at Sara, though it was clear that she was talking to her father. She curved her words to the side, throwing them at him. "That's a really good question, Sara. I wonder if your dad can answer that question." Now her mother turned to face him. "Dad, can you answer that question?" she asked. "Because I don't think I know the answer."

Her father forced a grin, looking at Sara, away from her mother. "To fight the tigers, of course," he said.

"But the tigers won?" Sara asked.

A strange look crossed her father's face, as if he had just bumped his foot against something. His eyes pinched into thin slits. It was a face he made frequently, Sara realized. Her mother sat up and took her by the shoulder. "Sara, you need to go to bed," she said.

Sara curled up closer to her father, unwilling to break the magic circle. She shook her head. "What if tigers come to my room?" she asked, although she knew they wouldn't.

"Tigers are not going to come to your room," her father told her, his face relaxed again. "They only live in the jungle, remember?"

Her mother groaned as Sara clutched her father's arm. "What if I have dreams about tigers?" she asked. She was afraid even to mention what she really feared, in case saying it might make it come true: What if she had dreams about legs, legs without people attached to them, legs wearing shoes, legs kicking at her bedroom door, legs running after her?

Her father opened his eyes, letting out a sharp breath. "You're not going to have dreams about tigers," he told her, holding her briefly before letting her go. "Go to sleep, kid."

"Good night, Sara," her mother said, leaning back, her eyes already closed.

Sara edged carefully off the bed and then walked slowly to the doorway. "Good night," she repeated, closing the door behind her. When the door was fully closed, she walked down the hall as loudly as she could, slapping her bare feet against the floor. Once she had reached the door of her own room, she turned around and walked with quick, delicate steps back to her parents' door and sat down silently behind it, leaning her head against the wooden frame.

"Daniel, you have to stop lying to the kids all the time," she heard her mother say from inside the room.

She listened as her father coughed, a throaty wheeze that lasted too long. The mattress creaked. Sara pictured her father's ruined leg brushing up against her mother's thigh, and shivered. "What should I have said?" she heard her father answer, clearing his throat. He made a strange noise that Sara couldn't quite identify, spitting maybe, and then his voice grew louder, almost shouting. "Tell me, Rosalie, what would you have me say? Something about the road? About the cave? About the trap? What would you prefer? Should I mention the shit they smeared on the spikes?"

"Quiet, she's still here," her mother whispered.

Sara held her breath, balancing her head on her knees. Perhaps if she thought hard enough she could become invisible, a pair of floating invisible ears. She waited, listening to her father listen.

"How do you know?" her father whispered back.

"They always stay," her mother said, her voice warmer now. "Why don't you put her to bed, King of Nightmares?" she asked. "We'll be lucky if we hear about anything besides tigers for the rest of the year."

Sara thought of running back to her room, but decided not to. Instead, she listened as her father moved, hearing him hoist himself out of bed and onto his metal crutches. When he reached the door, his legs newly covered with a pair of pale blue pajama pants and his chest still bare and furry above them, she stood and raised a hand. He offered her one of his fingers, the rest wrapped around the crutch, and she took hold of it. And the two of them walked on together.

Sara moved at her father's side, matching his slow, three-legged pace, and wondered how she could ask what she wanted to ask. She looked at the right leg of his pajama pants alongside her, an empty flap hanging beside his right crutch, fluttering gently in the light that crept out from under her parents' door, and she felt as though she could see through the cloth to the knotted knee beneath it. Her father's good foot, its bare toes like long hairy fingers, pushed hard against the floor between the thump of his crutches.

"Should I be afraid of tigers?" she asked as they neared her room. Or of roads? she thought. Or of caves? Or of—what was it, a spike?

"No," he said as they entered her room, "you should definitely not be afraid of tigers."

He leaned his good leg against her bed, propping himself up with one crutch as he freed his other arm. Then he took her hand in his strong, warm palm as she climbed into bed. He sat down beside her, leaving the crutches leaning against the bed. "Good night, Sara," he said softly. He leaned over and kissed her hair, and then slowly sat up, reaching for his crutches. Please, she thought, don't leave.

"Sing the song about Mom," Sara said.

Her father paused and brushed his fingers against her cheek, glancing toward the doorway in the dark room. Her twin brother was visible through the door across the hall, twisting in his sleep. "That would wake up Ben," he whispered, his voice near the inside of her ear. The touch of his fingers against her cheek was so exquisite, like being wrapped in a silk blanket, like swimming in warmed water, like floating on a cloud.

"Sing the song," she repeated.

"You're too big for stuff like that, kid."

His hand against her cheek reminded her of a game they often played, in which she would fill her cheeks with air and he would try to "pop" them, tapping one side of her face and then another, back and forth and back and forth, until she could no longer hold in her laugh. Suddenly, in the beauty of his hand on her cheek, Sara felt a seeping sense of dread, a still small voice telling her that this astounding sweetness might vanish at any moment, like breath released from the inside of her cheek, if she didn't hold on to it as tight as she could.

"I won't go to sleep until you sing the song."

Her father sighed, a sigh that was not frustration or exhaustion but mere breath, thin and calm, like a cloud that vanishes, or a fading breeze. He leaned even closer to her, so close that his lips were almost resting on her ear. His breath stirred her skin. His out-of-tune voice, without any of his usual pauses for coughing or clearing his throat, floated into her head as if it were her own thoughts. The words, which Sara had heard hundreds of times, on hundreds of sleepless nights, were in Yiddish:

> *Shteyt zikh dort in gesele*
> *Shtil, fartrakht, a hayzele*
> *Drinen, afn boydem-shtibl*
> *Voynt mayn tayer Reyzele!*
> *Yedn ovnt farn hayzl,*
> *Drey ikh zikh arum,*
> *Kh'gib a fayf un ruf oys, Reyzl:*
> *—Kum! Kum! Kum!*

> Standing in the little lane,
> A little house, bemused and plain.
> At the attic window, she'll appear:
> My Reyzele lives there, darling dear!

Each evening by this little house,
I pace and wander 'round,
I whistle and call to Reyzele:
"Reyzele, please come down!"

There is a moment that has happened over and over again, in every place children have ever slept, on every dark night for the past ten thousand years, that almost everyone who was once a child will forever remember. It happens when you are being tucked into bed, on a dark and frightening night when the sounds of the nighttime outside are drowned out only by the far more frightening sounds in your head. You have already gone to bed, have tried to go to bed, but because of whatever sounds you hear in your head you have failed to go to bed, and someone much older than you, someone so old that you cannot even imagine yourself ever becoming that old, has come to sit beside you and make sure you fall asleep. But the moment that everyone who was once a child will remember is not the story the unfathomably old person tells you, or the lullaby he sings for you, but rather the moment right after the story or song has ended. You are lying there with your eyes closed, not sleeping just yet but noticing that the sounds inside your head seem to have vanished, and you know, through closed eyes, that the person beside you thinks that you are asleep and is simply watching you. In that fraction of an instant between when that person stops singing and when that person decides to rise from the bed and disappear—a tiny rehearsal, though you do not yet know it, of what will eventually happen for good—time holds still, and you can feel, through your closed eyes, how that person, watching your still, small face in the darkness, has suddenly realized that you are the reason his life matters. And Sara would give her right leg and her left just to live through that moment one more time.

———

SARA'S MOTHER HAD not yet discovered the tomb when she announced to Sara one day after school that she was going to New York on an errand and wouldn't be back until the evening. The announcement—which luckily came just minutes before Sara finished eating

her after-school snack and proceeded as usual into the tomb—took
Sara by surprise. Her mother hadn't been to New York since Sara's
father died. When Sara asked what the trip was for, her mother simply
sighed, "Business. Very boring, I promise." Probably a meeting about
one of the books she was illustrating, Sara figured. But Ben had stayed
late at school for a science competition, and as her mother stepped out
the door, Sara suddenly felt the entire empty house weighing down on
her shoulders. It was one thing enclosing herself within the tomb
when she knew her twin brother was suffering in his own new cage a
few rooms away. But being alone in the house for hours was something
else. When she heard her mother's car starting up outside, she raced
out, waving her arms in the driveway. Sara didn't need to explain. Both
of them had spent enough time alone already. Her mother stopped the
car and let Sara in. They had already been on the highway for twenty
minutes when Sara finally found the courage to ask, more specifically,
why they were going to New York.

"To meet the person who bought the painting we're selling," her
mother said, her eyes distant as she stared out at the road.

"What painting?" Sara asked. The "we" near the end of her mother's
answer surprised her. For a moment she panicked, thinking that someone had discovered the murals in the tomb.

"The painting from the living room, the little one with the man
floating in the sky," her mother said.

Sara thought of the painting, which was almost impossible to picture outside of where it hung in the living room. She used to look at
it fairly often, since it was above the piano, but since her father died
she had stopped playing. She couldn't believe that it was gone. She
glanced in the back seat, thinking that perhaps it had just been taken
down now. But she wasn't entirely surprised that it wasn't there. She
had been missing cues for a while at home, spending too much time
in the tomb. "Someone is buying it?" she asked.

"Yes, a man from Russia is buying it."

Sara looked at the road, confused. "So why are we going to New York?"

"Right now there's a person there who has it, a man who buys and
sells paintings. An art dealer," her mother explained. "He's been trying
to sell it for me, and he found this person to buy it. Actually I already
signed the papers, so it's already sold."

Sara looked at her mother. "So then why do we have to go?" she asked. Now she was annoyed, wishing she had stayed behind in the tomb.

Her mother sighed. "I just wanted to meet the buyer, because the buyer is only going to be in New York for today. He works for a Russian museum," her mother said, her voice getting softer. "I wouldn't have wanted to at all, except that that there was something I forgot when I gave the painting to the dealer. There were some—some papers stuck in the back of the frame. I was hoping the buyer would agree to give them back to me. Not the painting, just the papers. I just forgot to take them out before I . . ." She paused, blinked. "I told you it was boring," she said quickly.

Sara looked out the window, watching the weedy lawns of the houses by the highway before glancing back at her mother. "Why are we selling it?" she asked. It was strange, this use of the word "we." She liked the way it sounded. Very grown-up.

Her mother grimaced, clutching the wheel. "Because the artist just died last year, and now it's worth a lot of money, that's why," she said. "This way we can keep the house and you and Ben can still go to college."

This was more than Sara wanted to know. Pretending to be bored, she examined herself in the passenger-side mirror and noticed how curly her hair had become in recent months, the subtle changes in the shape of her jaw and cheeks. Already she looked different than she had when her father died. After a few years, she thought, he wouldn't even recognize her. She glanced back at her mother, whose mouth was hanging slightly open, and remembered the painting. "Don't you like that picture?" she asked.

Her mother paused a moment. "Yes, I do," she said, her voice stiff.

"So why can't we just keep it?"

Sara's mother stuck out her bottom lip, blowing a strand of hair away from her face. "People don't always get to keep what they like," she said, staring out at the road in front of her. "Sometimes you can only have something you like for a short time, and after that you just have to be happy to have had it when you did, and enjoy the memory of it. Like—like a library book," she finished.

Or like a person, Sara thought. She bit her lip and looked out the window. They were on the ugliest part of the highway now, the part that passed through miles and miles of nothing but brown swamps and abandoned buildings. The sky had changed color, from blanched gray to the sort of sad blue that shines forth on cloudy days just before the day dies, a burnished brassy color that laughs at the ugly day behind it and at the long nighttime to come. Seeing the sky getting dark so soon after school ended made Sara feel sick, and thinking of how the days would continue shriveling up into nights, each day shorter than the last, made her feel even sicker. And it didn't matter that eventually the days would get longer, either, Sara thought, because all that meant was that eventually they would also get shorter, and shrivel and die again.

It was a long time before she wanted to speak. When she did, she practiced her question to herself first, in her head, making sure it would come out the way she wanted it to. Few things did, now.

"Do you believe in reincarnation?" Sara asked. She had first heard the idea when someone in her class had talked about it. It was a few days after the field trip to the museum, where they had also seen an exhibit about knights and armor. The boy had explained to his friend that he was really Sir Galahad, a famous knight, who had been born again in a different body. He was a smart boy, liked by teachers and despised by students, and Sara was inclined to believe him.

"No," her mother said.

"Why not?"

"Well, it doesn't work, if you think about it," her mother said.

Sara thought about it, but she couldn't understand what her mother meant. Still, an unexpected excitement coursed through her body at her mother's answer. She hadn't had a real grown-up conversation with her mother since her father got sick. Here, now, sitting in the passenger seat at the front of the car, the place of honor, she almost didn't care that she didn't understand. Her mother had taken her seriously. "Why doesn't it work?" she asked. She tried to make her voice sound curious, but she could barely contain her joy, a joy that surged ever so slightly above the sorrow of the weeks that had swollen into months, just to be alone with her mother, to sit beside her and drink in her words.

"Well, let's say the whole world started with Adam and Eve," her mother began, drumming her fingers once on the steering wheel.

"Okay," Sara said, hesitant. The boy who said he was really Sir Galahad had also told his friend that the Bible was made up.

Her mother moved the car quickly into another lane. "Or if you don't like that, then at least the world started with fewer people than we have now. Right?"

"Right," Sara agreed, wondering what might be coming next.

"Well, if that's true, then how can people's souls come back to life, if we only started with two souls? Or even if we only started with a few dozen, or a few hundred, or even a few thousand? There wouldn't be enough to go around."

Sara thought for a moment. This was becoming complicated, far more complicated than the boy at school had made it sound. The conversation was turning into a math problem. "But for the people who get the old souls," Sara objected, plotting it out in her head, "for them, it would still be the same—"

Her mother gripped the steering wheel. "But the same what?" her mother asked. "What makes the soul who it is, if not the choices the person makes while he's alive? Isn't part of who I am that I'm your mother? If I wasn't your mom, and Ben's mom, if I was someone else's mom, or nobody's mom, do you think I'd be the same person?"

"I—I don't know," Sara said, although it occurred to her that her mother hadn't always been her mother, and before she was her mother she was the same person. Or was she? Sara suddenly realized that she had no way to know, that even the photographs of her mother from before she was her mother were mostly black and white, and besides they only started when her mother was about five or so, the earlier ones having been lost, and anyway even color pictures didn't include things like the way a person's voice sounds, and even if they had had home movies then, it still wouldn't be good enough, because they still would be missing the way a person would answer a particular question, or the smell of the person, or the taste, or the touch.

"Let's say that every time the soul gets born into another life, it has another chance to make better choices," Sara's mother was saying. "But then how can a person's life mean anything at all? How can the first chance matter, if you always get a second chance? How can anything you do in your life matter, if it's always just a rehearsal, just another try, if it's never the real thing?"

Somewhere along the road, Sara had gotten confused. It had sounded simple to her the way the boy had explained it, but for some reason it seemed to upset her mother and she couldn't understand why. She was sorry she had mentioned it.

"Sara, do you remember why people were kicked out of paradise?" her mother suddenly asked.

Her mother was beginning to frighten her. The boy from school clearly could no longer be trusted; better to go with what she knew. "Because of eating from that tree?" Sara asked.

"That's what most people think," her mother said. "But I once found something in that story that no one seems to notice. It doesn't actually say that they were kicked out of paradise for eating from the tree of knowledge. Not at all! Instead, after they eat from that tree, God says, 'Oh, no, they just ate from the tree of knowledge—now what if they also eat from the tree of *life*, and live forever?' So he kicks the people out of paradise, and then he puts a bright, revolving sword in front of the path to the tree of life. Just to keep people from living forever!"

A revolving sword?

"No one can live forever, see? Not even in someone else's body. No one can get past that sword. There are no second chances, Sara," her mother said, staring straight ahead. "I want you to remember that. Everything counts. Don't ever let anyone tell you that you're just rehearsing for your life."

They were entering the tunnel now, the car edging slowly between the rows of bathroomlike tiles and orange filmy lights. Usually the tunnel was Sara's favorite part of the drive—watching for the distance markers and the big mosaic "New Jersey/New York" dividing line, guessing when they would finally reach the curve in the road where the light from the other end would come streaming in, and best of all, her father explaining to them how the tunnel had been built, describing the pumps and pylons and air compressors that had been used to help displace thousands of pounds of dirt to construct the path beneath the riverbed. She had never really paid attention to the details, but it amazed her just to listen to him, to imagine how all of the secrets of what seemed like every road in the world were packed into her father's head. But now she sat in the dark of the orange lights, thinking about that revolving sword. If God thought no one could find a way past the sword and on through to the tree of life, he clearly hadn't met her father.

Her mother rubbed her own right eye, tracing her finger along the edge of her eyelid, where she was wearing makeup for the first time in many weeks. "No, I don't believe in reincarnation," she said. "You want to know what I believe?"

"Okay," Sara said, although she suspected that her mother was no longer talking to her, but rather to herself, or to someone else entirely, someone who wasn't in the car at all.

"I believe that when people die, they go to the same place as all the people who haven't yet been born. That's why it's called the world to come, because that's where they make the new souls for the future. And the reward when good people die"—her mother paused, swallowed, paused again—"the reward when good people die is that they get to help make the people in their families who haven't been born yet. They pick out what kinds of traits they want the new people to have—they give them all the raw material of their souls, like their talents and their brains and their potential. Of course it's up to the new ones, once they're born, what they'll use and what they won't, but that's what everyone who dies is doing, I think. They get to decide what kind of people the new ones might be able to become." She brushed a loose bit of hair away from her face. "That's why your children will be lucky, Sara, because Dad is going to help make them who they're going to be—just like my father helped make you."

They emerged from the tunnel and into the city. Sara and her mother sat in silence for a long time after that, as her mother navigated through the streets and then searched for a place to park. Since the last time Sara had been to the city with her mother—months and months ago, before her father got sick, when they had all gone to see the circus—the city had lost its gleam. Outside the tunnel, men holding little mops tried to clean the car's windows and wouldn't go away, no matter how many times Sara's mother leaned on the horn. As they drove through the streets, Sara looked out the car's sponged windows at the buildings tattooed with scribbled nonsense words, storefronts clouded with the black breath of spray paint. Later, when they got out of the car, all Sara noticed were the dark splotches on the sidewalk, and the piles of garbage bags on the curbsides, and the trash blowing in the cold wind, and the bundled dirty old people with beards filled with bits of food, lying curled up like babies over metal grates. She followed her mother into a tall building, where her mother had to sign her name in a book at the front door, and then into an elevator where it was so warm that both she and her mother took off their coats. And then they entered a series of rooms that reminded Sara of a tomb.

———

THE ROOMS WERE small and dark, and crammed with all sorts of things, weird furniture and fancy tables and chairs, but mostly they were filled, like the tomb, with sculptures and paintings. Sara looked around in awe. Every inch of every wall was covered with pictures, some of nothing, just colors and shapes, but many of them of people. Most of the people in the pictures were weird and distorted, with baggy watery bodies or bodies that were divided into circles and squares, but some of them had the kind of accuracy she had been trying so hard to achieve in the tomb. The same was true of the sculptures that crammed the floor. Some of them were just shapes, twisted bits of stone or metal or wood like one of the construction sets she used to play with, but she could see that some of them were twisted versions of people, people with nothing but blobs for heads, or plastic cylinders for legs. Others, the ones she like the best, looked like real people— ugly people, yes, but real people, ready for the underworld. Sara had barely had time to look around before a short man with a thick mustache and a big smile came into the room.

"Rosalie!" his voice boomed. "We were worried you wouldn't make it. And you brought a guest!"

"This is my daughter Sara," her mother announced, and then, to Sara, "This is Mr. Komornik. He's the man I told you about."

"It's good to meet you, Sara," the short man said, and stuck out his hand for her to shake. "Your mom talks about you and your brother all the time. I hear you two are real troopers," he said.

Sara wasn't sure what he meant, but she shook his hand and nodded. The skin on the man's palm was warm and taut, like her father's. "Are you from Russia?" she asked. He didn't sound like he was, but then neither did her mother.

The man looked confused for a moment, then laughed. "Russia?

No, I'm not from Russia. But if you want to meet someone from Russia, look no further," he said, and began to walk toward a doorway on the opposite side of the room, taking hold of her other hand. She almost had to skip to keep up with him. It felt strange, holding hands with a man who could walk faster than her. Her mother followed close behind.

The second room looked to Sara even more like a tomb. Every corner was piled high with sculptures and paintings, the walls lined with pictures so old-looking that she was sure they were from dead people, pictures of things that had happened to dead people while they were living, like the paintings on a tomb's walls. There were faces everywhere. Sara looked around the room, her eyes so occupied with all the different heads—heads carved in stone, heads in bronze, heads in oils, heads in watercolors, heads in ink—that she jumped when one of the heads moved, attached to a large body seated in a chair.

"Sergei, this is Rosalie Ziskind, whom I've told you about. Rosalie, this is Sergei Popov."

The old man stood up, rising from his chair as if facing great resistance. When he drew himself to his full height, Sara saw that he was not merely old but mountainous, one of those older people who seem to accumulate mass over their years. His head was like a cragged, whitened peak above his enormous brown-suited body, avalanches of flesh sliding down over his immense white-shirted waist. His tie was short over his massive stomach.

"Mrs. Ziskind," the old man said, his voice deep and his accent heavy as he extended his hand to Sara's mother. "It is a pleasure to finally meet you."

The short man dropped Sara's hand and stepped to the side, angling himself between the old man and Sara's mother. Sara watched as her mother took the old man's hand. Then the old man stooped down, his body moving in waves as he lowered himself to squat in front of her. His large, wrinkled face was red under his thick white hair. Sara noticed, once he was at her eye level, that his eyebrows moved independently of each other, like hairy caterpillars crawling above his eyes. "And what's your name?" he asked, singing the words in a high voice, like a little girl.

Sara didn't answer or even smile. She never answered when people talked to her like a baby. Besides, the man exuded a faint odor, like how the bathroom sometimes smelled after Ben had come out of the shower now that he was wearing the brace, the dense rotten flavor of sweat and plastic still lingering on the bathroom counter. She could hear the man breathe.

Sara glared at him, waiting for her mother's prompting. Usually, when she refused to talk to someone, it was a matter of seconds before her mother reprimanded her for being rude. But when she glanced up at her mother, she saw that her mother wasn't even looking at her. Instead, she stood staring at the old man, a deep line drawn between her eyebrows, her lips tight.

"Popov," her mother said. "I thought I recognized that name."

Sara saw the short man walk across the room, turning his head back briefly when he heard her mother's voice. But soon he was standing by a table in the corner, his back to them, flicking switches on a coffee machine and casting jittery glances around the room. Earlier he had made Sara think of her father, but now she saw that he was more like Ben: jumpy, distracted, trying his hardest to look the other way. He fumbled with a tower of styrofoam cups.

The old man straightened up, squinting as he looked at Sara's mother. "Have we met before?" he asked.

Sara's mother shook her head. But her head moved back and forth a few too many times, changing from an answer to a motion, a swaying movement that gradually slowed to a stop. Her mouth opened slightly, her tongue edging out between her teeth. Still staring at the man, she murmured, "Sara."

Sara jumped but didn't answer, unsure of whether her mother had really said her name. Then, without looking at her, her mother spoke even more softly, in Yiddish. "*Sorele, zog zey az mir darfn geyn—itst,*" she said, her eyes still focused on the man. *Tell them we have to go—now.* He had taken off his jacket, and now Sara noticed how the man's shirt was stained dark in the underarms, damp from sweat. It had been freezing on the street, but now Sara suddenly felt uncomfortably warm, as if the room were running out of air.

"Why?" asked Sara. And why was her mother speaking Yiddish? Sara glanced across the room at the short man. His hands were filled with coffee cups.

"*Zog zey,*" her mother answered, "*zog zey az ikh khalesh.*"

"Really?" Sara asked. Her mother felt faint? If she was, then why couldn't she tell them in English, herself? But then she looked at her mother and saw that she was standing paralyzed, her eyes hard, wide, preoccupied—as if someone else had occupied her body, showing her something more than what her own eyes would see. And someone else had also borrowed her voice.

Her mother spoke again, shaking her head, an urgent rush of slurred words. "*Neyn, kholile, ober zog zey—zog zey—*" No, God forbid, but tell them—tell them—

A phone rang in the next room. Sara looked at her mother again, watching the blood draining out of her face, and then turned around to face Mr. Komornik, who had put down the cups and was already edging his way toward the doorway with the ringing telephone. She straightened her back and looked him in the eye. "My mom is sick," she said.

Mr. Komornik seemed startled, but he barely paused. "Just a minute, okay?" he said, stepping quickly toward the door. "I have to take this."

"My mom is sick," Sara repeated, louder this time, and glared at him. The phone rang again. "We have to leave. My mom is sick."

"I'll be back in a second, trooper," Mr. Komornik called as he reached to close the door behind him. "Tell your mom there's a bathroom down the hall on the left."

The door slammed shut. Sara looked around the room and saw all of the faces in it looking at her, most of them frowning, staring her down. She turned to the old man and tapped the back of his hand, cringing at the feel of his damp, hot skin.

"My mom is sick," Sara told him. "We have to leave now." She glanced up at her mother, whose face had turned pale. Maybe it was true, Sara thought. Why wasn't her mother saying anything? Should she take her mother to the bathroom? Find her some water? Make her sit down? It was mothers who were supposed to help children when they were sick, not the other way around.

The man, until then facing her mother, turned at her touch and looked at her, squinting in her direction. His eyebrows crept up on his forehead, and Sara thought for a moment that he might help. But then his eyebrows settled over his eyes, which slowly focused on her, as if he had just noticed something strange. "Your mother is not sick," he said, his voice rough.

Sara's stomach lurched. She glanced up at her mother, but her mother stood as if frozen, her face an empty canvas. Then the man crouched down again to Sara's height, studying her face.

Sara squirmed. She hated being looked at. The man's face was red and thick, its wide nose etched with pores. A rivulet of sweat dripped down one of his cheeks. Suddenly he smiled, a thin, slow smile, the skin shriveling beneath his eyes.

"I don't recognize your mother," the man said to Sara in his baby singsong voice, "but I recognize you."

The air in the room had become unbearably warm. Sara felt the spaces between her legs and under her arms and knees becoming damp. Ben had once told her that the human body was eighty percent water; she wondered if she might be leaking.

The man turned his heavy, ancient face with what seemed like tremendous effort, looking up at Sara's mother. "The girl I remember was smaller than this one," he said to her, pronouncing each word delicately. "But the face is the same. A lovely face," he murmured, his voice thick and moist. He raised his hand to Sara's eye level, and then he pressed his warm, damp fingertips against her cheek.

Sara tried to step back, but her legs would not move. She glanced at the door to the next room, listening for signs that the short man might return, but she could hear nothing except the large old man's breathing. His smell filled her face. He had begun moving a finger along her cheek, tracing his fingernail in circles along her skin. Sara's skin tightened as she stood in place, unable to speak. The man raised his other hand and cupped her chin in his palms like a broken head from one of the room's statues, pinching her cheeks with his thumbs.

"Please don't touch her," Sara's mother said, almost in a whisper.

Sara looked up and saw her mother standing motionless, her eyes unblinking and her body still, as if her breath had been sucked out of her lungs. Sara had only seen her mother like that once before, when they stood at her father's grave. Sara tried to speak, but her lips shook and her tongue would not move. The man was gripping her face now, his thumbs digging deeper into her skin. Her eyes began to leak, and she blinked hard, trying to keep herself in. "Now, this is the face I remember," the man said.

"You know who you look like?" he asked, the singsong gone from his voice. "Boris Kulbak's little girl. Raisya Kulbak."

The man looked up at Sara's mother, a long, slow smile spreading across his face. And then Sara's mother passed out.

————

BY THE TIME the ambulance arrived, Sara's mother had already opened her eyes, and it was a challenge to convince everyone that she was really well enough to drive herself and her daughter home. Besides saying that she felt fine, however, Sara's mother refused to say anything. Even in the car on the way home, she was silent, a silence so polished and strong that Sara was afraid even to open her mouth.

The next day, when Sara came home after school, she found that her mother wasn't in the house. She called out, "Mom?" as she came in the door, but no one answered. Panicked, Sara raced through the house, running from the kitchen to the living room to the bedrooms and out to the garage and the backyard and then back into the house, even flinging open the bathroom doors, screaming, "Mommy! Mommy!" until she finally decided to open the door of the tomb. And there she found her mother sitting on the floor like a child, surrounded by toy cars and men's clothes and Sara's murals of her father's life, crying, reading the book of the dead.

8

THE HAND that dents each child's face below the nose just before he is born, Der Nister had once learned, is a familiar one. The day before the child's birth, the very same hand scoops up the child and takes him on a tour all over the world, from morning until evening, showing him everything he will ever see—the place where he will be born, the places where he will live, the places where he will travel, and, at the end of the long day as the dusk slips between the fingers of the hand, the places where he will die and be buried. The child sees all this in a single day. The owner of the hand reminds the child that against his will he was created, and against his will he will be born, and against his will he will live, and against his will he will die, and against his will he will someday have to give a full and complete accounting of everything he has done with all that was given to him against his will. And the child is frightened—not of dying, but of living. He is so frightened that he refuses to be born, spitting on the hand until it smacks him across the face, removes his memory, and casts him out. Which is why so many people wander around the world, forgetting to account for where they have been and where they are going—and which is why Chagall left the Soviet Union for good, while Der Nister and all of the other Yiddish writers whose works Chagall had illustrated left only for a few years and then returned.

Chagall had been ready to leave for a long time. Shortly before his arrival at the orphanage in Malakhovka in 1920, he received a letter in the mail from a friend, a poet in Berlin: "Are you still alive? The rumor here is that you were killed in the war. Your paintings are selling for big prices here." Der Nister knew about this letter, because Chagall showed it to anyone who came into his room.

"I'm famous over there," Chagall liked to snort. "Famous! Big prices! But here's what I'd like to know: Where are my paintings? Who has them? And when do they intend to pay me? Do they expect my daughter to starve to death?"

Der Nister used to listen to this and then look down at his hands, pretending to occupy himself with picking at his fingernails in order to keep himself from scowling. By 1922, Chagall's daughter was a beautiful round little five-year-old whose baby fat Der Nister couldn't explain, while his own Hodele was a nine-year-old scarecrow, wasting thinner and thinner by the year. Chagall had already lived in France, before the war, and had starred in a one-man gallery show in Berlin. He had had books written about him, exhibits, critiques, sales. People knew his name. Once you swallowed the strange colors and flying people, there was nothing difficult about his work—nothing to comprehend, only to feel. There was no meaning, nothing that anyone needed to translate or know or understand. It was all just color and light. Meanwhile, the Hidden One had published four books of kaleidoscope stories with tiny worlds packed one inside another, mazes of symbols and layers of meanings like the puzzles his daughter loved, but Yiddish readers had already begun to disappear. And his daughter was starving.

"Big prices, I'm telling you," Chagall groaned. "In Moscow, they haven't even paid me for the murals yet. In Berlin, they're holding auctions. I've got to get back to Berlin."

And then one day, he did.

————

DER NISTER, PLAYING shadow, followed Chagall. In Berlin he founded a journal with a few other Yiddish expatriate writers, but readers were scarce and money scarcer, and he left the journal after its first issue. In Germany people burned money instead of spending it. It was cheaper than coal. Boardinghouse rooms were insulated with worthless money pasted on the walls. Chagall soon continued on to Paris. Years later, word of Chagall's daughter's eighth birthday party reached Der Nister in Germany: a lavish celebration in the artist's huge apartment on Avenue d'Orléans, where every guest was a famous writer or artist or critic or gallery owner. In a German magazine, Der Nister came across an elegant photographic portrait of the renowned painter Chagall, posing with his wife and daughter. In the photograph, very beautifully lit and composed, the eight-year-old girl was naked. Everyone talked about how shameless it was: cheap, exploitative, debased. But all Der Nister could see was the girl's pudgy belly and her chubby cheeks.

In Berlin, in the tiny, filthy room he shared with his tired wife whom he no longer loved, his scrap of a daughter, and his scrawny newborn son, the Hidden One would lie in bed at night, fighting off what might have been nightmares had he been able to sleep. But hunger kept him awake. He was reminded of his older brother Aaron back in Berdichev, who had become a follower of the dead mystic and storyteller Nachman of Bratslav. Aaron used to fast for days on end, hoping for divine visions. But Der Nister's hunger, involuntary, brought him demonic visions instead. He began to stay up all night, and as he listened to the drunken half-naked prostitutes outside his window and the whistling breath of his children and wife, he was tortured by waking dreams. And so he wrote them down.

Wide awake, he dreamed of a world-carrier, a man who dragged the entire world around with him, bearing it on his back—until he decided to hand it off to someone else so that he could go out drinking. While the world-carrier was drunk, everyone in the world carried out a suicide pact, killing themselves off one by one. Der Nister looked out the window at the lights of the city and could see the dead-drunk bodies in the street. They were clearly visible beneath the gas streetlights outside Der Nister's window where he stood behind the curtain, shivering between cloth and glass and cupping his hands to the windowpane until, above the noisy nightclubs across the street, he could just make out a star. Der Nister wake-dreamed of the constellations he had once seen in the firmament above Berdichev. The Great Star-Bear, Ursa Major, invited him to dance with her in the sky, and Der Nister climbed up a ladder and danced with the bear until the bear suddenly cast him down, down, down, into a pit where he landed in the lair of ten bears, starving bears who repeatedly demanded food. Der Nister fed them and fed them until there was nothing left to eat but Der Nister himself. The bears ate him alive, limb by limb, until the very last bear reached for his heart.

He heard Hodele scream in her sleep. He came out from behind the window curtain and went to her corner of the room, where she slept on a cheap folded mattress on the floor. He crouched on the floor beside her. What had she dreamed? "Hodele," he whispered, but she was still sleeping. It was cold in the room, and she lay on her side, curled into a bony ball under her blanket. Her mouth was stretched into a horrid grin as her teeth chattered, and in the dark room beside her cold body, Der Nister thought of Boris Kulbak, the boy who had been found in the grave. He sat down on the floor and put his arms around her, warming her, and then found himself wake-dreaming again. The drunks in the street were throwing stones at her, and he was shielding her from them. She clung to him in her sleep, clutching at his arms. On the other side of the room he heard his baby son wheeze in the shadows, and then heard the wife he no longer loved shifting in their bed, sliding half asleep toward the cardboard bassinet to nurse the baby boy. In the light from the crack of the curtains he could see his wife's bared breast, orange in the stripe of gaslight like the breasts of the prostitutes outside. He turned back toward his daughter's body and held her. She was lighter than a dry straw doll. He began to dream, wide awake, that he was nursing her, that she was suckling at his chest, but he had no milk to give her. Soon she rolled away from him, moaning, her teeth gnashing at cold air—and he no longer knew which part was the dream.

IN DAYLIGHT, WHEN he wasn't dreaming, Der Nister sometimes spotted Chagall's works in magazines. Other times, he saw them in galleries where friends brought him against his will. The paintings struck Der Nister as colorful and playful, nothing more. But no one wanted more. Chagall's paintings had become a sensation. Apparently he had invented expressionism, though Der Nister knew his old housemate had nothing he intended to express. *It just means blue,* Der Nister heard Chagall's voice repeating in his head. *What should it mean? What does your daughter mean?* But in public, Der Nister noticed, Chagall would say almost anything:

"If I weren't a Jew, I would never have become an artist." (Der Nister read that one in a Yiddish newspaper.)

"I am not a Jewish artist. A Jewish cloud is a Russian cloud is a French cloud." (That one was in a German pamphlet.)

"I am sure Rembrandt loves me." (That was in French, from his memoirs, which Der Nister read in excerpts in German translation in a magazine—rambling, incoherent memoirs, written when the artist was thirty-six.)

"The title 'a Russian painter' means more to me than any international fame. In my pictures there is not one centimeter free from nostalgia for my native land." (That was in Russian.)

"My heart is in the East, and here I am on the edge of the West! How easy it would be for me to leave all the good things here and return home, to behold the dust of the desolate sanctuary." (Did he say that, or was it part of Der Nister's waking dreams?)

"Who am I?" (From his memoirs, and from Der Nister's dreams.)

Who am I? It was an easy question, if you were sitting in an apartment in Paris that would soon turn into a house in Provence and then a visa to New York sponsored by the Museum of Modern Art, with a wife you loved and a laughing daughter and an army of defending critics wherever you chose to appear. But in Der Nister's tiny room, crowded with a wife he didn't love and children he couldn't feed and stories no one would read, the question had no answer.

"Who am I?"

Der Nister moved his family to Hamburg, but his sleepless nights only grew longer. Shards of stories moved like shadows through his family's room, like demons that danced on tightropes of light and swung down on trapezes of odors and dust, threatening to devour his children. It was better in Russia now, people were saying. The government was sponsoring Yiddish schools, Yiddish publishers, Yiddish magazines— enormous opportunities for someone like him. It was the new promised land, the papers claimed, and Der Nister almost believed it. In Hamburg they still lived on a street full of prostitutes and drunks. But now Der Nister's waking dreams were of trials, his room transforming into a dark medieval courtroom with all of his former pupils denouncing him, claiming that he was selfish, an egocentric beast, that he had sacrificed his daughter's life for his own. At the end they burned him at the stake. If Chagall had painted it, it would have been bright yellow, lurid green, pulsing red. But in Der Nister's vision, it was only black.

———

ONE NIGHT IN Hamburg—or a not-yet night, a tired late afternoon in the winter of 1926 when the sun grew weary and decided to give up early, passing the world along to the moon and going off to get drunk—Der Nister sat alone at home, writing a technical article for a magazine and fighting off dreams. His wife and the little boy (almost four years old now) had gone to the doctor, and Der Nister waited for Hodele. A friend had shown him a new card trick, and he was eager to show her, to see if she could figure out how it worked.

She always could. She was extremely clever—brilliant in four languages, a natural at math, her head always bent into a book. But she was thirteen now, and at home it had become awkward. In their one shared room, his wife insisted that Hodele couldn't change her clothes in his presence. In the mornings, he would dress quickly while Hodele slept and then leave, idling in the hallway until he heard her give three taps on the inside of the door, the signal that he could go back inside. When he opened the door, Hodele would be strapped into her ragged blouse and skirt, the new curve of her tiny breasts clearly visible through the tight clothes she had outgrown, and his wife would already be angry. "Look at her, stooped over like a hunchback," Der Nister's wife would spit. "She looks like you." But when her mother wasn't home, Hodele was brave enough to laugh about it. They had developed a little system now. Their room was on the ground floor, and its single tiny window faced the alley. But there was one small part of the wall of the room, windowless and wooden, which faced the street where Hodele walked on her way home from school. When she approached, Hodele had taken to tapping it three times with whatever book she was reading, to let her father know she would soon be at the door. An inside joke.

That early night, he was listening for Hodele when some boys began yelling outside. Nothing unusual; the drunks typically didn't appear until later, but boys from the high school often congregated on the street while waiting for the prostitutes to arrive. At least it was better than Berlin, Der Nister thought. Then he heard the three telltale taps on the wall—and a loud thump.

Through the wall, he heard a boy laugh out loud. It must just be a joke, Der Nister thought. Or more likely a coincidence. But then he listened, moving closer to the corner, where a girl's whimper reached him through the wall. "Please, no, please, please," he heard her beg, and then there was a scream. It was the same scream Hodele released in her sleep. Der Nister was too confused to move. But then the scream stopped, and Der Nister could feel, on his own body, the hand on his daughter's mouth.

He raced to the door, struggling with the three different locks; his hands shook, and it took far too long to let himself out. Once he was free, he hurried to the building's entrance. But their apartment was at the end of the hall, and the entrance was on a different street, around the corner. As he ran, he felt demons blocking his way, tripping him, dragging him down, and making him stumble three times on his mad run to the building's door. When at last he reached the front of the building, no one was there but an old man lying on the sidewalk, grumbling in his sleep. He paused, baffled. Had he dreamed it? He raced in mad circles, running down the streets nearby, ripping around every block, venturing as far as he could before circling back to his own building and then into the alley that ran alongside it, shouting her name before glancing at his own window. Someone had closed the curtain.

He ran back around the building, tripping on the sleeping man as he desperately barreled down the sidewalk and through the main entrance. The door to his room was locked. He pounded on the door, afraid to tap it, but no one answered. Shaking, he fished his keys out of his pocket and opened the locks slowly, as if solving a puzzle piece by piece.

When he edged the door open, he saw a small dark shape curled into a ball, shivering on the mattress in the corner. He moved toward her slowly, measuring the room with his steps. When he finally crouched over her, the way he had on his sleepless nights, she rolled over to face him. He saw her clutching together the sides of her ragged coat, trying to cover the stumps of thread where the buttons had been torn from her blouse, pinching the cloth closed over her scraped red skin. A small circle of blood lay in the dent below her nose. She tried to speak, mouthing words, but he couldn't understand her. What did his daughter mean?

"I want to go home," she said.

———

REPORTS OF THE Soviet promised land proved to be greatly exaggerated. Chagall had been right: once Der Nister moved his family back to Russia, he had no chance at all of publishing his stories. Only "socialist realism" was permitted. Such was the price of dancing with the bear. His previously published work was panned, denounced in all the journals as decadent and absurd. Even the children's books he had written with Chagall were gathered up and destroyed.

For ten long years he wrote almost nothing, struggled to find odd jobs, nearly starved. And then he began writing something realistic, a novel that the censors would approve. While Chagall ensconced himself in France, befriending Picasso and Matisse and painting pictures of bright green Jews, crucified Jesuses, flowers, and fruit, the Hidden One started writing the only story in the world.

It was called *The Family Crisis*.

9

—

THROUGH HIS own private family crisis, Ben and Sara's father Daniel Ziskind had once learned that time is created through deeds of true kindness. Days and hours and years are not time, but merely vessels for it, and too often they are empty. The world stands still, timeless and empty, until an act of generosity changes it in an instant and sends it soaring through arcs of rich seasons, moment after spinning moment of racing beauty. And then, with a single unkind deed, a single withheld hand, time ceases to exist.

Daniel Ziskind was only twenty-one years old in 1965, but he could already count several instances in which he had witnessed the creation of time, or its destruction. The first came when he was twelve years old and sick of the world. He and his parents had just moved out of Newark, New Jersey, to a town farther away from the city, living for the first time in a real house, with real trees—a whole forest's worth—in its backyard. It was a small house his mother's father had owned before his death, and Daniel paced the rooms nervously, wondering whether his grandfather might have died right where he was standing. But even with the move, Daniel noticed, time didn't pass. No matter how old he became, he still remained a child—short, smooth-faced, soprano-voiced, and perpetually afraid. No matter how long his mother stayed in the hospital, she still remained ill. And no matter how many years went by, his father still was and had always been a member of the

Communist Party who insisted on sending Daniel to Yiddish afternoon schools run by his comrades at the Workmen's Circle in Newark while he hung framed pictures of Stalin on his walls. After the move, though, there was no more Yiddish school—just Daniel's father's daily harangues about the plight of the workers, and his angry letters to the editor, and his endless tirades (Daniel was forbidden to repeat them in public, since his uncle had lost his job) against the neighbors, and his bosses, and the schools, and the corporations, and the doctors, and the banks, and the television studios, and the hospitals, and the government, and the country, and his good-for-nothing twelve-year-old son, instead of against the illness that had debilitated his wife. And then, one afternoon when Daniel decided to wander into the woods behind the house, time was created.

Daniel had never seen so many trees. His whole life had been spent on grimy sidewalks, or in the pathetic city park where anemic maples huddled in sad clumps. Even when they had visited his grandfather, he had rarely strayed far from the house. But that afternoon he entered the gate of the forest, looking up at the ancient trees towering like the columns of a temple above his head. The muddy floor sank beneath his feet as if he were a tree taking root. He moved in soft, cautious steps along the roots and rocks as his head reeled at the branches in the sky. How long could he walk through the woods? How far did the trees go? Would his father return from the hospital before Daniel found his way back? If he did, he would be furious, Daniel thought. His thin twelve-year-old chest constricted out of habit. But then he looked up again at the tree trunks towering overhead, and breathed out. Fine, let him, he thought. It's not like anything will change. Daniel walked until he came to a clearing, surprised to see how quickly the vast new continent dwindled. Beyond the last few trees, he could just make out a house. It was an old, rotting, broken-down house with a divided back porch— for two families, probably, or even three or four, like the way the houses were in the poorer neighborhoods back in Newark, grass growing between the cracks in the porch steps, abandoned by the world. And then he saw the little girl.

She was sitting with her back to him, under a crabapple tree whose branches scraped at the broken windows, her hair hanging in a thick black braid like a shining rope down her back. She was singing to a doll that she held in the air. When he saw her, he froze, frightened. The thick braid swung against her back like a pull for a theater curtain, closing before him, and she seemed about to turn around. He turned quickly, finding his footing to run away. But then, for a fraction of an instant that divided what was from what would be, he listened, and recognized the song.

It was a Yiddish song called "Reyzele," about a boy who circles a girl's house, waiting for a sign from her. Daniel stood at the edge of the forest and slowly turned around. He had never heard a girl so small sing in Yiddish.

He knelt behind a tree and watched her as she sang. He could see her face now, from the side, but she didn't notice him. He held his breath. Now he was staring at how the sun was scattering little drops of light through the leaves of the tree, dripping light down on her thin pale neck and the dark hair slipping out of her braid onto her skin. The dirty broken house behind her seemed to disappear. He watched her as she moved, just barely moving, swaying in place almost like praying, and he couldn't stop looking at her. There was something about her face, about her whole body, about the way she breathed, that made her different from any little girl he had ever seen. He noticed it in the tone of her voice, in the way she cast her eyes down in her lap, in the slight trembling of her little lower lip. And then he knew what it was. She's sad, he thought. It was the kind of sorrow he had never seen in any child's face, except in the mirror. He leaned forward, peering through the back gate of the world. A fallen branch snapped beneath his knee.

She stopped singing. He ducked, but it was too late: she had seen him. She dropped the doll and stared. He waited for her to run into the house, but to his surprise, she smiled—and time was created.

In the created moment Daniel stood up, and stepped out of the woods onto the weedy grass of the girl's backyard. She was still smiling at him, watching him carefully. Her lower lip gleamed in the daylight, and the glimmer of light on her little lip confused him so much that he forgot to say hello. Instead he stood on the grass in front of her, looked down at her lip, and asked, "How do you know that song?"

She looked at him, still smiling, but said nothing. She had dark eyes, he noticed, and pale little fingers that trembled like her lower lip. The doll in the grass stared into the sky.

"There's hardly anybody who knows that song," he stuttered. Hearing his own high voice shamed him, but the girl was listening. "And definitely hardly any kids. You have to tell me—where'd you learn it?"

Now she frowned, pulling her delicate eyebrows together and glancing at the ground. She pointed to herself. "No English," she said. She swung her head forward until her hair landed over her shoulder, and tugged at her braid.

The theater curtain had been drawn closed. He stared at her shining braid and felt the way he often felt now around girls at school, as if a thick screen hung between him and them, impassable. She was getting up from the grass now, picking up her doll. Please, he begged her silently, don't go! But then he thought of something.

"*Vi heystu?*" he stammered. He had never spoken Yiddish to someone younger than him before.

She stopped moving, kneeling on the grass. Her dark eyes glowed, and the curtain opened. "Reyzele," she said.

He laughed. "That's really your name?" he asked. Only after it was out of his mouth did he realize he had asked in English.

But this time the girl seemed to understand, or at least to have something to add. "In school," she stuttered in English, "they say Rosalie."

Rosalie. Reyzele. He rolled the words under his tongue. "*Ikh heys Daniyl,*" he told her. She was standing now, her head up to his chin. Her face blossomed before him, radiant eyes, luminous lips, soft skin like petals. Her nostrils curled like the pink surfaces of a seashell. But look how short she was! "*Vi alt bistu?*" he asked.

She held up nine fingers. God, he thought. Was he allowed to become friends with a nine-year-old girl?

He pointed to himself, trying hard to keep his hand from shaking. He didn't have enough fingers anymore. "*Tsvelf,*" he said. She nodded, smiled. Her lips glowed. "*Fun vanen shtamstu?*" he asked. She must be one of those Jewish refugee kids from Germany, he thought, like the ones his friends used to make fun of in Newark a few years back. But all of those kids had learned English by now. And they were older.

"*Moskve,*" she said.

She was from—Moscow? But how could that be? He thought of his father and started to sweat. "Are you here with—with your mom and dad?" he asked, sliding into English again.

"Mother," she said, and pointed to the house.

"What about your dad?" he asked, and immediately regretted it. Maybe she won't understand, he hoped.

She frowned, and looked down at her doll. "I do not know how to say," she stammered in English. He was about to tell her she didn't have to, when she suddenly said: "*Geharget.*"

He stared at her, jolted by shock. He turned the word over in his mind, searching for the slightest possibility that it could mean something other than what he thought it meant, but there was none. When he spoke, his mouth was dry. He whispered: "Killed?"

Suddenly a woman's voice bellowed from inside the house: "RAISYA!"

The *r* rolled and trilled into the backyard, flattening the grass. The girl glanced at the house and bent down to pick up her doll. She straightened, doll in hand, and looked at him, her lower lip trembling. "A *dank, Daniyl,*" she said softly. Before Daniel could speak, she rose on her tiptoes in the grass and pressed her trembling lips against his cheek.

Daniel stood, stunned. His body shook with beauty. "I'll come back tomorrow," he said quickly, fighting to control his shaking tongue. His voice was lower this time, deeper. "I'll teach you English. I will. I promise I'll come back. *Vart af mir.*" Wait for me.

The girl smiled, and ran into the house. Daniel watched her until she had passed through the door, and then backed away from the yard. He retreated without turning, slowly, as if exiting the holy of holies. When he reached the trees, he lingered in the afternoon shadows, staring at the dirty little house with its broken shutters, searching for some sign of the beauty within. But the house and yard were silent, encircled by a magic ring.

In the created moments the woods had grown dark, and Daniel had trouble finding his way back. But by the time he stepped onto his own back porch, he knew that he didn't want to do anything for the rest of his life except stand in that backyard beyond the woods, and if that meant that he would have to spend the next seven years of his life waiting for her to grow up, then he would. When his father heard him enter, he screamed at Daniel for being late, for being "lost," and then slapped him across the face. But to Daniel even the slap didn't matter in the least. There were moments beyond it to look forward to, because time had just been created.

THE SECOND INSTANCE of time's creation and destruction came seven years later—seven years during which time rumbled high in the heavens, shaking the wilderness in Daniel's backyard. Rosalie was sixteen, and had kissed him many more times. At one point he had taken her to meet his parents. She had entered their living room, with its stacks of Party newspapers and portrait of Stalin on the walls, turned pale, and made an excuse to leave. It was a long time before she came back. By then Daniel was nineteen, in college already, and there was no avoiding it. One lonely night at dinner (his mother was home but sleeping, drugged, upstairs), he decided to mention what had happened to Rosalie's father. His father flew into an unprecedented rage.

"Either that girl is a liar or her father was a criminal," he shouted, throwing his fork to the floor. She had stopped being Rosalie; she had become That Girl. "Either way, I don't want to see you with that girl ever again."

"Fine," Daniel shouted back. He was bigger now, and his voice was lower, and louder. "You don't have to see her. That doesn't mean I won't."

"Yes, it does," his father growled, confining a roar.

"It's a free country. I can see whoever I want."

His father stood up. "Only you would think it's a free country," he hissed. "You're nineteen years old, Daniel. By now you ought to know that nothing is free." He walked over to the desk in the corner of the kitchen, with its stack of unpaid bills. He flipped furiously through the stack, shedding notices on the floor until he picked out an envelope, already addressed and stamped. He waved it in the air like a flag. "Do you know what this is?"

Daniel was silent, although he could see the address on the front. This can't be happening, he thought. Mom will wake up, she'll talk him out of it. It was a fantasy he had often had since he was a boy, a dream. But his mother didn't wake up. She rarely did anymore. And when she did, she didn't speak.

"This is the check for your tuition next semester," his father announced. He tore it in half, then in quarters, then in tiny shreds that scattered in the air. "There won't be any more of them. See how you like it when it's free."

"You're joking," Daniel whispered.

"You can decide for yourself which one is the joke—that girl, or your future."

At first Daniel gave in. "Please don't ruin your own life because of me," Rosalie begged him later that night, when he sneaked out to their meeting place in the woods after his father was asleep. There was snow on the ground, and she trembled between kisses in her thin coat. "We've already waited this long. College is just a few years—it will be over sooner than you think. I'll wait for you." But when Daniel went back to his engineering classes, miserably maintaining his promise not to see her anymore, he found that time had evaporated. The months and years simply refused to pass, or even to exist. Then he realized that he wouldn't need his father to pay for college if he joined the army. When Rosalie turned eighteen, he asked her to marry him, and time was created again: thirteen whole months of it before their wedding, which he would spend waiting for her on his tour of duty in Vietnam.

———

THREE WEEKS AFTER Daniel's arrival in Da Nang, he received a large envelope in the mail containing five of his own letters, unopened, and a short typewritten note from his father claiming that he would rather rot in prison like Daniel's dead criminal soon-to-be-father-in-law than read a single letter Daniel sent from Vietnam, or write to him again. At the base in Da Nang, where the city streets were filled with thousands of men and women riding bicycles with live pigs strapped over the back wheels, Daniel was perpetually exhausted from the heat. He waited, bored, for his assignment, hoping he would be sent into active combat, if only to further insult his father. He was crushed when he heard where he had been assigned: a mobile army construction unit charged with building a road over a dirt track, euphemistically called Highway One, that ran from Da Nang up into

the mountains, through a treacherous mountain pass—the Pass of the
Ocean Clouds—and on to a place called Hue. The city of Hue ("pronounced 'Hway' "), Daniel read in one of the pamphlets published by
MACV, was "an important cultural and strategic center, one province
removed from the demilitarized zone. An imperial capital of Vietnam,
it is known for its elaborate tombs, final resting places of the rulers of
the ancient Vietnamese empire." Big shit, Daniel thought. There was
only one empire he was here to send down to the grave, and it wasn't
ancient Vietnamese.

Still, when he arrived at sunrise at the site in the foothills where construction had already begun, he saw the other men with their maps
and tools and felt hopeful. But a few days later, as he ate lunch with
five of them while sitting on the thick mud near the edge of a cliff, he
was asked his very first personal question by a fellow soldier:

"Hey, Ziskind, why don't you tell us something about your girlfriend's ass?"

The questioner was Timothy Jackson King, a direct though consid-
erably less illustrious descendant of Stonewall Jackson, the
Confederate general who once led his troops to several brilliant yet
ultimately meaningless victories in Tim's home state of Virginia. Tim
himself was Daniel's age and rank—twenty-one, lance corporal—but
much taller, and built like the sacks of cement that it was his job to
haul off the supply trucks as they built the new road. At the moment
he had just finished his can of baked beans and was puffing on a cigarette under an enormous tree, highly amused. "You've been here three
days and you still haven't mentioned your girlfriend's ass," he added,
and smirked. The four other men smirked, too, looked at Daniel, and
waited.

Daniel shrugged, trying to be casual. He swallowed a forkful of
beans and glanced down at his dog tags, which were hanging outside
of his shirt after too many hours of scratching his sweating skin. "I
don't want to talk about my girlfriend's ass," he said.

Tim grinned, then blew a ring of smoke. "Because you don't have a
girlfriend, or because she doesn't have an ass?"

Everyone laughed. Daniel tried to smile, and looked down at his can
of beans. "I have a girlfriend," he said quickly. He still wasn't used to
calling her his fiancée. "I just don't want to talk about her ass."

Wayne—eighteen, a private, and bigger than Tim—piped in. "Maybe you'd rather talk about your mom's ass," he said.

Daniel fought hard not to wince. His mother wasn't well enough to write him letters, and if his father didn't write to him, how would he know how she was? Would his father break his vow and write to him if his mother died? Or would he just come home, thirteen months later, and find her gone?

Rob, a twenty-year-old PFC whose dangling dog tag announced his religious preference as "Evang. Christ.," added, "Or maybe you're lying, and you're really a fag."

Tim laughed out loud, a sound that alternated cackles and grunts, and then pretended to regain his composure. "Now, come on, gentlemen, let's not assume," he said, his face mock-stern. He nodded to the group with a gleam in his eye. "Because remember, when you assume . . ."

The four others joined in: "You make an ass out of you and me." They burst out laughing.

Daniel smiled, feeling forgiven. In their easy laughter he heard an echo of something he had almost forgotten: friendship, and trust. Surely there was a way to say something, to be a part of it. He stirred his can of beans, then held one up with his fork. "And when you eat a legume," he said, "you make a leg out of you and me."

The men stopped laughing. All five looked at him, their faces blank.

"Legumes," Daniel fumbled, feeling a bead of sweat sliding down his temple. "Like beans. Beans are legumes."

They stared at him for a moment longer, silent. Then Tim stood up, looking at the others as if Daniel weren't there. "Let's get back to work. We've got shitloads to do."

It had started raining again. The commanding officer had yet to call them back to the road, but the others still stood up, pressing their soles into the soft ground around Daniel's legs. The beans left a sour taste in his mouth. As he rose from his spot in the mud, he watched as Rob turned his back to him, stepping toward Tim as he dropped his own cigarette in the mud. "Definitely a fag," Daniel heard him mutter.

Tim dropped his cigarette, too, and leaned toward Rob. "Definitely a Jew."

After that, Daniel tucked his tags into his sweat-soaked shirt, and time stopped passing.

THERE IS NOTHING lonelier than an unused road, Daniel decided. Particularly a half-built, poorly designed, piece-of-shit road that ran up the side of a mountain at a twenty-percent grade with hairpin switch-backs every hundred feet. As the road began to rise out of the foothills, the mirror-bright rice terraces gave way to pure jungle—tall trees, thick underbrush, clumps of bamboo, curtains of vines, biting red ants, and most of all, sluices of mud that ran in rivers down the dirt track where the road was supposed to lead. Within two weeks, they had fin-ished the more level segments and had reached an elevation where they were actually building the road into the side of a cliff, with a sheer rock face on one side and a hundred-foot drop on the other. The ter-rain was too rough for real machinery; most of the work had to be done by hand. It rained for several hours a day. Daniel slept in a leaking tent in the thick mud with the others, listening to constant speculation about Rosalie's existence and that of her genitals. He rarely spoke. In his letters to Rosalie he feigned cheerfulness. *Greetings from the ends of the earth! It's hot here, but not as hot as you! Don't worry about me, Rosie—I'm going to come home with a serious tan!* On the mountain road he started smoking, enjoying breathing in the filth of the world. It felt more honest than real air.

"Look at this thing," Tim said one afternoon as they laid down guidewires in the mud.

He wasn't speaking to Daniel, of course. But Daniel was pulling the other end of the guidewire on the edge of the cliff, and he was the clos-est. They had just come around a bend in the track to a steep moun-tain face pockmarked with caves. In front of one of the caves was what looked like a little wooden birdhouse, painted bright red—a small, red-roofed painted box perched on a wooden pillar hung with beads, with a clay bowl inside it. Daniel had seen others like it before on the road, and had wondered what they were. Some sort of path markers, he fig-ured. This one stood where the left lane was going to be. "There's too many of these things," Tim said. "They ought to send a whole unit just to get rid of them." He pressed one boot against the wooden pillar and took hold of the red house, pushing and pulling it back and forth until it dislodged from the ground.

"Where are you going to put that?" Daniel asked.

Tim looked up, the birdhouse hanging from one arm. He seemed genuinely surprised to hear Daniel's voice. "I'm going to put it in a museum and cherish it forever," he said. Rob, pulling up the guidewire behind him, concealed a laugh under a grunt.

"Seriously, what is it?" Daniel asked. "You can't just move it around. It probably belongs to someone."

Tim glanced at the birdhouse, tilting it against the mountain. The bowl inside the little house slid and thunked against its side. "Who gives a shit what it is? It's in the way." By now the others had stopped pouring gravel and were watching Tim, who had stepped over to the edge of the cliff next to where Daniel was squatting by the road, until only Daniel separated him from the precipice. Tim looked out at the jungle valley a hundred feet below, grinning. Then, clutching the birdhouse by its pillar, he swung it into the air. Daniel jumped up as the arc of the birdhouse, still gripped tight in Tim's hands, sailed above Tim's head like a red-roofed Ferris wheel, gliding toward the abyss.

"STOP IT!" Daniel shouted, and grabbed Tim's arm.

The birdhouse stopped in midair in Tim's fist, suspended over their heads like a torch above the precipice. Now everyone was watching. Tim froze, still holding the birdhouse aloft, first startled, then enraged. His eyes focused on Daniel, then narrowed in the shadow of the painted box.

"Do NOT touch me, you fucking faggot," he growled. "You have three seconds to let go before I push you off this cliff."

Daniel gulped. He couldn't back up; he was standing inches from the edge. Instead he let go of Tim's arm, then tried to move sideways until his foot slipped on a patch of rotten leaves. He landed on his knees at Tim's feet, his hands pressed into the mud. Tim's boots grew out of the ground like tree trunks, inches from Daniel's face. He raised one boot, then set his heel down on Daniel's knuckles and pressed them hard into the mud. Daniel swallowed a howl.

"If you want to go home in one piece, don't ever touch me again," Tim said, and released Daniel's hand.

Daniel pushed himself off the ground, stepping away as Tim lowered the birdhouse down from over his own head. To Daniel's surprise, Tim then took the birdhouse in both hands and pushed its pillar into the slip of ground beside the road, leaning on it and pounding on its roof until it was standing upright in the mud like before, though on the opposite side of the road. When he was finished, he looked up to find everyone staring at him, including Daniel.

"What do you people think this is, the Easter Parade?" he shouted. "Bank the goddamn curve." As the men reluctantly turned back to the road, Tim muttered, almost to himself, "Fucking Jewish faggot."

The day stood still in a haze, hovering over the abyss. Daniel slowed his pace in the heat. He started dumping gravel farther behind where Tim was working, gradually drifting backward until he was bringing up the rear on the road, half a mile behind Tim. He worked in a miasma of sweat and thought. It was all for Rosalie, he reminded himself. Just as he began to drift into memory, he felt someone's hand on his shoulder. He nearly fell off the cliff.

It was Cuong Thien Minh, the ARVN interpreter assigned to their unit—a thin man, young, with thick black hair and a ready smile. He was very quiet, and Daniel wasn't sure whether he didn't talk much because he felt limited by his English or because, like Daniel, he simply didn't want to talk. Unlike some of the interpreters Daniel had met in Da Nang, many of whom seemed more interested in bumming cigarettes than actually getting things done, this man Cuong was diligent, following the crew step by step along the mountain path, advising them on the best places to set up camp, and negotiating around the occasional mountain village that appeared alongside the road on the plateaus. Now he was standing next to Daniel, unfurling a wide topographical map in front of Daniel's face.

"Can you help?" he asked Daniel, his stilted English slightly tinged with French. "I do not comprehend what this means." He touched a thin finger to a part of the map a few miles past their current point, a clearly labeled leveled portion on a wide ledge of the cliff.

Daniel smiled to himself. It was the first time since his arrival that someone had asked him for help. "That's a future loading dock," he said. "This part of the road is going to be the major supply conduit, see, so it's going to have more drop-off points, to make it easier to transfer supplies. Refueling, that kind of thing."

Cuong's face lit up. Daniel modestly kicked at the mud, grinning. He felt useful. "For truck or tank?" Cuong asked.

"Trucks," Daniel said. "There'll be a camp set up there, too. It's important because they're going to be enlarging the base up at Phu Bai."

Cuong nodded sagely, as if everything now made sense. "To bring supplies," he said. "For Americans to come from Da Nang."

Daniel watched him. What he said seemed obvious, not worth saying, and Daniel wondered if he had said it just to practice his English. But then he realized that what Cuong said wasn't quite true. "Actually, I don't even think they expect us to use this road much in the future," Daniel said. "It's really being built for you, for the South Vietnamese. It's supposed to be a better route to the coast, harder to attack. When we're done it'll be that much tougher for the VC to break the line."

Cuong wrinkled his forehead, looking at the map. It wasn't clear to Daniel whether what he had said had gotten through. Cuong pointed again at the same spot on the map. "This place," he said delicately. "It is not good for the camp."

Daniel squinted at the paper, wondering what he meant. The elevation lines were hard to see, but it seemed flat enough to Daniel. "It's fine," he said. "The grade is less than one percent."

Cuong shook his head. "Flat, but many mudslides from mountains. Bad for the camp. Better close to the village, near Deo Hai Van."

"Near what?" Daniel asked.

Cuong leaned back from the map, pointing with one finger. "Hai Van Pass," he clarified. His finger underscored words on the map: *Pass of the Ocean Clouds*. "Better to make the camp in this place," Cuong repeated. "Easier to kill VC."

Daniel flinched. It wasn't something anyone was supposed to say, not like that, at least. But something about the way Cuong added that last phrase made Daniel like Cuong. There was a brute honesty to him, a sense of purpose. Daniel felt that he had found a friend. "Thanks," Daniel said. "I'll tell the CO."

Cuong twirled the map into a tight scroll and smiled. In the warmth of Cuong's face, Daniel found an old shred of forgotten courage. "Now I have a question for you," he said. "What are those?" He pointed to another birdhouse near the road, apparently set far enough back from it to have dodged Tim's wrath. Tim was right, though—there were a lot of them. In this one, Daniel noticed, someone had taken a stick of incense and lit it in the bowl inside. Thin plumes of incense flew out of it into the air, ascending the mountain like a smoke signal along the road.

Cuong looked at the birdhouse, furrowing his thin eyebrows. If he had seen the incident earlier, he didn't show it. "I do not know how to say," he said. "It is a souvenir of dead persons."

Daniel swallowed. "Like—like a shrine or something?" he asked. He thought of the birdhouse clutched in Tim's hands, hovering over the abyss, and hoped Cuong hadn't seen it.

But Cuong smiled. "Yes. A shrine. We worship our ancestors."

This sounded vaguely familiar to Daniel, echoing out of the dim corners of his memory. Third-grade history class in Newark, a project about China. His mother, not yet ill, helping him build a model of some Chinese tomb out of sugar cubes, laughing at him as he swallowed the cubes meant for the sarcophagi until she started eating them, too. Then they were doubled over on the table, laughing until tears came, high on sugar and laughter. His father came home and saw them and started laughing, too, bellowing jokes about the dentist and swallowing the sugar cubes with them, the three of them laughing until laughing became painful, eating their way through a sweet, sweet death.

Cuong interrupted his thoughts. "These shrines are for persons who die on the road," he said.

"Oh." Daniel nodded. "Like in accidents?" It was the logical explanation, but as he gazed up along the dirt path that they were trying to turn into a real road, he couldn't imagine any accidents happening on it. You couldn't even ride a bike through the mud. Perhaps people had died falling off the cliff?

Cuong chewed his lower lip, scanning the terrain. He shook his head. "There are no accidents," he said. It wasn't clear to Daniel, at first, whether Cuong was describing the victims' deaths or making a fatalistic statement about the universe. But then Cuong added, "Usually tigers."

Daniel stared at him. "Tigers?"

Cuong nodded. "Yes. Persons are eaten."

This combination of subject and verb had to be some sort of grammatical error. Daniel searched Cuong's face, waiting for him to notice the mistake. " 'Eaten,' " Daniel repeated.

But Cuong offered no correction. He shrugged. "Persons are eaten," he said again. "It happens often on this road."

Daniel glanced around at the caves, the trees, the vines hanging off the side of the mountain. Man-eating tigers?

Cuong saw his face and laughed. "Americans with M16s should not be afraid of tigers," he said. Cuong tucked the scrolled map under his arm and took out a box of cigarettes, pulling out two. "With tigers, it is simple. When they want to kill you, kill them first. Just like VC."

Daniel smiled. Cuong offered him a cigarette, and he accepted. They lit them and watched as the day's steaming mist lifted. The sky turned pink over the abyss.

"You like Vietnam?" Cuong asked.

Daniel looked out at the valley, into the thin sliver of air between two distant mountains where he could see a blue tongue of ocean reaching into the shore. "It's wonderful," Daniel answered. And as he watched the sun set over the valley, standing next to the first person who had smiled at him since he saw Rosalie for the last time, he believed that it might not be a lie.

LATE THAT NIGHT, Daniel had the same dream he had been having over and over since he began building the road. Like the other dreams, it took place in the grave. Not in a real grave, but in what Rosalie called "the little grave," their secret hiding place—the one he had dug in the forest for the two of them, where she first kissed him on the lips.

She was thirteen, and mature for her age. He was sixteen, and in agony. He had already waited four years for her, four years of visiting her backyard through the woods every day, of playing childish games with her, of building snow forts and waging water fights and drawing pictures and reading books together under the tree outside the house just beyond the woods. The books were usually in Yiddish. She had learned English quickly, well enough to be mistaken for an American, but she found the books from school duller than dirt. "The 'Scarlet Letter' should have been B for boring," she would mutter during their afternoons in the backyard. "Today I earned the 'Red Badge of Boredom.' " She liked stories about worlds supposedly just beyond the one they lived in but really right here on earth, stories that made you realize how different the world was from what everyone thought it was, if only you would look. Together they read all of I. L. Peretz, most of Sholem Aleichem, weird tales by Der Nister from a volume she had found in a box of her father's old things. Daniel read with her, laughed with her, threw snowballs at her, held her hand like a child. But soon he wasn't a child anymore. By the time he was sixteen, her mother was warning her about the stringy teenager haunting the backyard. One autumn day in the yard, when they were sitting and laughing together, she brushed her hand against his thigh. It was unspeakable ecstasy, but he backed off, ashamed. For days he didn't return. When he did, and she did it again—that smooth, soft palm brushing against his leg, then resting on it (there was no mistaking it now), its perfect fingers tracing slow circles on his thigh—he had leaned in toward her face, pressing his hand hard against the weedy ground to keep it from reaching for the curve of her new breast. This time it was she who backed off. But for her it wasn't shame; it was fear. "Not here," she whispered. "Somewhere where no one will see us." But then her mother called her inside and it was too late. Daniel retreated into the woods, releasing his agony on his knees in the mud and then searching, desperate, for a hiding place on the forest floor. But there was nowhere—the woods, once dark and sheltering, now seemed flooded with light. At last he found a spot where three thick trees stood huddled close, with a bit of a hollow between them. He began digging out the space in between, using rocks and branches and his hands like paws, breaking roots until he had dug a deep, narrow pit. The next day he led her into the forest. She saw the pit and laughed. "Who are you planning to bury in it?" she asked. But when he brought her down inside it and spread his jacket between her and the dirt, she surprised him—him, the one for whom she had created all those years for herself to grow up—by kissing him first. It was like molten sky pouring down into his mouth. On their last night together before he left for Vietnam, he had taken her down into the little grave, as always, and huddled close against the dark night. Toward dawn it started raining. In the soft spring rain he licked the raindrops off her skin, one by one, until he was licking away her tears.

In the dream, it was always the same. He was in the grave with her,

licking the cool raindrops like that last night. But then she began sinking into the pit, the earth dissolving underneath her and dirt pouring
over her until she had vanished underground. Then he was alone,
half buried and swallowing dirt. He would wake up with his bones
blasted, scratching his ant bites until he bled. The night after the incident on the cliff, though, a variation was introduced into the dream.
This time, shortly after Rosalie was buried alive, a tiger roared its way
into the grave, sinking its teeth into his damp flesh just before he
woke up.

———————

AT DAWN THE next day the air was already thick with heat. The commanding officer gathered them outside of their tents for a pep talk,
yelling at them about how essential it was to speed up the project, the
vital importance of their task, the necessity of keeping up morale.
Daniel listened seriously. When they went out to the road, he found
himself paired with Tim, using pickaxes to break up some of the
mountain rock on a difficult point on the road. Electric drills or jack-
hammers would have risked a rockslide, and they had to do it by hand.
It was grueling. Daniel concentrated on hacking at the rock and ignor-
ing the welts on his hands, trying his best to pretend that Tim wasn't
sweating right beside him. But after only half an hour of pounding,
Tim put down his pickax and leaned against the mountain, taking out
a cigarette. The rest of the unit was around the next bend on the wind-
ing road. Tim puffed for a few minutes, watching Daniel work. Daniel
was drenched with sweat, but somehow the effort exhilarated him. He
stood tall on his strong legs and let Tim watch him swing the pickax in
the air, smashing it on the rock.

"So how do you like this assignment, Lance Corporal Ziskind?" Tim
suddenly asked. "Glad you avoided combat?"

Daniel was startled. It was the first time Tim had asked him something since his question about Rosalie's ass. For a brief instant he
thought it might be an overture, an opening to friendship. But then he
heard the acid streak in how Tim had recited his rank, and the shame-
ful implication of the second question, and kept working. Life was easier when he pretended Tim didn't exist.

But Tim existed. He took a long drag on his cigarette and then stepped dangerously close to Daniel, blowing smoke in his face. Daniel inhaled the smoke, wishing he could have a cigarette himself. But taking an unauthorized break with Tim was the last thing he wanted to do. Instead he breathed in Tim's air. "Well, don't let any of your Jewish faggot friends back home in medical school think you aren't doing your part," Tim said, sarcasm moistening the smoke between his lips. "You heard the CO this morning: 'The future of freedom is in our hands.' Remember, it's really, really important that we build this piece-of-shit road in the middle of nowhere, because if we don't, the Commies will take over the world." Tim took another long drag, then stepped back toward the mountain face. Daniel was determined not to look up. "Like who gives a shit about Commies?" Tim concluded, his voice taking on an oddly reflective tone. Daniel wondered again if Tim really wanted to have a conversation. "Either they nuke us or they don't, but in the meantime I don't see why we should give a shit what they do."

The rock wasn't breaking, but Daniel's will was. He raised the pickax into the air again, no longer caring whether the rock broke or not. He wielded it with sheer animal fury, and decided to risk a word. "They killed my fiancée's father in Russia," he suddenly said, and slammed the pickax into the rock.

The burned stub of Tim's cigarette fell onto a heap of rock dust as his mouth drooped open. He heard Tim swallowing smoke. "You have a fiancée?"

The question was more stunned than civil. Daniel took several more swings at the rock, enjoying making Tim wait, before allowing himself to answer. "Yes, I do," he sneered, then paused. "She even has an ass."

Daniel continued pounding away at the rock, relishing Tim's silence. It took Tim several minutes to speak again.

"What, her dad was a spy or something?" Tim asked.

This time Tim seemed genuinely curious, but Daniel wouldn't take the bait. Just because he had mentioned Rosalie didn't mean he was about to become Tim's friend. "Nope," he said, tasting sweat. "Just in the wrong place at the wrong time."

Tim waited for him to say more, but Daniel refused. Instead he pressed his lips together, measuring the size of the crack in the rock with his eye before raising the pickax again.

Tim blew a mouthful of smoke-flavored air near Daniel's ear, then gave up on waiting. "So you're here to kill Commies," he said.

The acid streak in Tim's voice had returned. Daniel said nothing, and continued hammering. He swung the pickax up in the air, willing it to land on the crack he had finally made in the rock. It missed. He breathed hard and wedged the pickax between his knees, shaking out his hands. His palms burned. He picked up the pickax again and kept pounding.

"Well, good for you," Tim said. "A motivated killer. Fucking impressive. Blow 'em all away." He kicked at the mud. "Me, I couldn't give a shit. My wife's having a baby next week."

Tim had a wife? Daniel's pickax wobbled in his hand. He resisted the temptation to look up. Out of the corner of his eye he could see Tim leaning back against the side of the mountain, glancing at the sky. For Tim, Daniel realized, time existed; "next week" was not merely a set of empty days, the way it was for Daniel, but a sequence in the creation of the world. Before Daniel could wonder more—a *baby?* Tim, a father? were there other children? how old was his wife? what was her name?—Tim, still looking at the sky, opened his mouth and said, "By the time I get home, the kid's gonna be a year old. He won't even know who I am."

Daniel put down the pickax and looked up at Tim, who was still staring at the sky between the thick jungle trees. He saw the unfamiliar softness between Tim's eyebrows and decided to speak, to try. "But at least you're doing something for—for your baby's future," he said. "For the future of the world."

Tim looked at Daniel for a moment in silence. Then he laughed, a cold, caustic laugh. "Fuck that," he said. "That kid's gotta make his own damn world. This one isn't good enough."

Daniel stood still, speechless. But Tim just glanced down the road over Daniel's shoulder, and then suddenly reached into his pocket. He pulled out a cigarette and held it below Daniel's chin. "Want one?" he asked.

Daniel breathed in, desperate. The smoke was sweet on Tim's breath, the offer lingering perilously close to friendship. He threw his pride over the cliff. "Thanks," he sputtered. He grabbed it out of Tim's hand, stuck it in his mouth, and lit it. Tim shrugged, taking up his own pickax and suddenly hammering away in a fury. Daniel was just breathing in his first sweet breath of filth when he heard the commanding officer's voice boom behind his back. He spat the cigarette onto the ground and fumbled for his pickax, which he had left lying on the rocks. Sparks flew from Tim's pickax beside him.

"Progress, Corporals?"

Tim stood at attention, pickax in hand. "Lance Corporal Ziskind here has been slacking off, sir," he said, and pointed to the cigarette smoldering in the mud at Daniel's feet. "May I suggest you assign him to a task more suited to his poor work ethic, sir?"

Daniel tried not to cringe in the reeking air. He watched as the CO bent down to examine the fresh cigarette burning on the ground, then rose to spit words in his face. "We don't have time for your crap, Wizkind," he barked, blithe in his mistake with Daniel's name. "This is a goddamn war here. You can't just take a break whenever the hell you feel like it."

"Yes, sir," Daniel muttered. He could feel Tim grinning above his head a moment later as he did the requisite push-ups, his blistered palms bitten by rock dust until they bled.

"Any more shit like this and you'll be breaking rocks for the next twelve months."

As the officer abandoned them, it began raining again: thick heavy raindrops that poured down into wide rivers and washed the shards of debris down into the abyss.

———

DANIEL STOPPED TRYING after that. The days had become grueling, pointless; the nights full of redundant dreams were worse. He began to live for the few moments each night just before he fell asleep in the mud. Then he would replay memories of Rosalie in his mind over and over until they grew grainy and pale, like paintings exposed to too much light.

"I think that's my favorite thing we've read together," he remembered telling her one day. In his mind he was eighteen, and they were sitting again in her backyard. They had just finished reading a story called "The Dead Town," and the book lay open on the grass beside him. He was leaning back against the porch steps with his legs stretched out on the ground, while she was lying with her head in his lap, watching the sky.

"Why?" she asked.

He looked down at her black hair draped over his legs. "I don't know," he said. "I guess because—because it's about missed opportunities."

"My favorite was 'Beheaded,' " she said.

"You've got to be kidding," Daniel snorted. "That one made no sense at all." "Beheaded" was a long, convoluted story, ending with a bridge between heaven and hell that was seduced by the devil. Before that, though, there was a part about an innocent man who was sentenced to decapitation. At the plaza where the beheading was to take place, there was a long ladder leading from the plaza up to the heavens, constructed out of previously decapitated heads. The executioners explained to the sentenced man that beheading him was, of course, a virtuous deed for the common good, helping them and everyone else reach heaven.

"I thought it made a lot of sense," Rosalie said. "But I'm glad you didn't."

He was about to ask her to explain when she suddenly sat up, her hair swishing across his knees. God, so beautiful, he thought. And sexy. He stared at the delicate shelf of her collarbone, at the hollow dent below her nose, the way her soft skin absorbed the light and glowed, incandescent. But she was only fifteen. She twisted around him and grabbed the book out of the grass.

"You have another copy of this, right?" she asked, flipping through the thin lightweight pages that had closed in the breeze.

The book was hers, and he had seen another edition of it on his father's shelf. "Yeah, I think I—"

"Good," she said, and tore the story they had just read out of the book.

He grabbed the torn book out of her hand. "What'd you do that for?"

"If it's your favorite, we should keep it in my library," she said. Then she stood up and took his hand, dragging him into the house.

If she were anyone else, he would have assumed she was crazy. But you could never tell exactly what Rosalie was thinking; she was far too smart for that. She pulled him into the dingy living room until they were standing in the corner, where she pointed at a tiny painting hanging on the wall without a frame. "See, this is the Dead Town," she said.

He had never noticed the painting before. Like everything in Rosalie's house, it was dirty, dark, and small. A man hovered over a gloomy street, his leaden body blocking out the sun. Two little markers—tombstones?—stood in the foreground. The man floated above them in a white sky, risen indifferently from the dead.

"Did you paint this?" he asked.

But she wasn't listening. "Let's keep 'The Dead Town' with the dead town," she said. She took the painting down off the wall and turned it around, leaning it against the bookcase as she folded the torn-out story lengthwise, smoothing the folds with her fingernails until the pages were flat and thin. Then she took the pages and slid them between the wood and the canvas. On the opposite side of the backing, Daniel noticed a piece of yellowed paper peeking out from behind the wooden canvas frame. It seemed she had done this before.

"What's that, another story?" he asked her.

She didn't answer. Instead she turned the painting around and placed it back on the wall. But then she leaned toward him, standing on her toes until her lips rested on his ear. "When you marry me," she whispered, "I'll tell you everything."

As he succumbed to sleep on the edge of the cliff with Tim snoring by his side, he realized how much she still hadn't told him.

———

A FEW DAYS later, Daniel's unit heard disturbing news. A nineteen-year-old private was killed by a booby trap at the base at Phu Bai, not far beyond the pass—a sophisticated trap involving a bicycle rigged with explosives. Everyone was on alert. Even the construction unit was being sent out on patrol; the enemy was thought to be hiding somewhere near the pass, and they were the closest. After weeks of building the road, they were out for blood.

"Ziskind, it's your dream come true," Tim hissed at Daniel as they cleaned their weapons late that night. His baby hadn't been born yet, Daniel figured. Or maybe it had, and even Tim hadn't heard. "Make sure you write to your little girlfriend and your Jewish faggot friends about all the Commies you're going to kill. Your mommy and daddy will be very proud of you."

Daniel said nothing. He thought of his father and held his breath. What time was it at home now? It was a few hours after midnight in the jungle, so it must be the afternoon. Was his father at the hospital with his mother? Was his mother even still alive? And Rosalie in her illustration class—was she thinking of him? Would she be glad if he killed someone?

"Course, as we've discussed, I personally don't give a shit," Tim added, satisfied to have a one-way conversation. "Someone would have to be pointing a gun at my head for me to fucking bother. So you better cover for both of us, bastard. Got that?"

Was it a threat? Daniel wondered if Tim really meant it. If he did, so be it, Daniel decided as he picked up his pack. "I'm putting you in the line of fire, bastard," Tim repeated. He slung his gun over his shoulder and stepped forward. "Now move your ass."

But when Tim moved to push him out of the tent, Daniel had already stepped out ahead of him into the darkness, in line with the soldiers before him. They walked in silence along the banked curves of their newly built road up toward the Pass of the Ocean Clouds, and then turned off the road and into the jungle, breathing the sweet wet night air that reminded Daniel of his last night in the little grave.

———

THEY STALKED THE darkness in the jungle all night long, wearing seventy-pound packs with all their supplies, walking for hours without traveling very far at all, moving in circles. Daniel was surprised to find himself more frightened of tigers than of the enemy, scanning the buzzing forest for glowing animal eyes. When the rain lifted and the sun began to rise, light spilled in between the trees like rivers of gold, and it was decided that they were too vulnerable in their long line of men. They were told to separate into pairs to secure the immediate area, and then they would continue on through the Pass of the Ocean Clouds. The line was divided. Daniel split off with Tim, and stiffened his limbs as he realized that Tim was keeping his promise, moving a fraction of a step behind him as the two of them walked on together.

Daylight glistened on the jungle floor. In the long new shafts of

light, Daniel saw spiderwebs stretched between the trees, large enough
to trap a person—vast nets that vibrated with each of his footsteps,
transparent but for the tiny raindrops clinging to their woven tapestries
of threads. Daniel tore them down reluctantly, afraid of leaving a trail.
But staying unnoticed was almost impossible. No matter how quiet he
and Tim tried to be, every step they took resounded like cannon fire,
a blasting crackle of leaves and branches exploding underfoot.
Without speaking or thinking, Daniel and Tim began to take their
steps at the same time, with Tim moving closer until he was moving
right beside Daniel, matching their heartbeats. Now the only sounds
they heard came from the buzzing of insects, and from their perfectly
synchronized steps. That made it easy, half an hour later, to hear when
something else—something too big to be any animal but a tiger or a
man—began to move behind the trees.

The two men froze. They stared into the trees in the dim gray light
until they both saw someone standing about thirty feet away, half
obscured by trees and plants. Daniel's breath caught in his throat. All
he could see was the top of the man's head, covered by a helmet he
didn't recognize, and part of his leg. But then the man shifted in his
place so that they could see his hands, and Daniel saw that he was fumbling with something that looked about the size and shape of a stick
grenade.

Tim elbowed Daniel, a little too hard, and silently raised his rifle.
Daniel crouched over his weapon, trying not to breathe. It seemed that
Tim had been bluffing earlier about putting Daniel on the spot. But as
Daniel watched the man's hands through the leaves, it became clear
that the man was simply waiting for the right moment to pull the pin.
Had he seen them? Or was he aiming for someone else? Daniel began
to raise his rifle, but then Tim elbowed him again, urging him on, and
the gun slipped in his sweaty hands. He began to raise it again, slowly,
but Tim already had the man in his sights. Daniel watched, defeated,
as Tim pulled the trigger.

Nothing happened. The gun was an M16, the new rifle that had
only been released a few months earlier. Instead of firing, it just made
a loud clicking noise. Jammed. Tim began rattling the trigger, whis-
pering, "Shit!"

Daniel moved the man into his own crosshairs, remembering his vow. The target was so close that Daniel didn't even need to use the sights. He watched the enemy through the leaves and slipped his finger toward the trigger. But then, with another loud click from Tim's weapon, the man with the grenade suddenly looked up. His eye caught Daniel's, and Daniel saw that it was Cuong.

Tim elbowed Daniel again and whispered, "Fire, bastard! Fire!"

Daniel stood motionless, staring, trying to imagine what Cuong could possibly be doing holding a grenade. But his imagination failed him. Regaining movement, Daniel began to shake his head at Tim, to signal to him that they shouldn't shoot, that it was a mistake. But then a strange expression spread across Cuong's face, an almost-smile, and that almost-smile confused Daniel so much that he forgot who he was or where he was or why he was, because when Cuong looked at Daniel, it was as if he had suddenly removed a shell that had been covering his face for all those empty timeless days, as if the person Daniel had seen before had evaporated into that hot, thick air and what was left behind was some kind of animal, like a tiger suddenly baring its teeth into a smiling rumbling throaty roar, and Daniel watched, paralyzed, as Cuong pulled the pin and flung his arm back.

Tim screamed, "Move, bastard! Move!"

As the grenade arced through the air, Tim threw himself at Daniel, knocked him to the ground, and jumped on top of him. But in fact he only partly jumped on top of him, because when he started jumping he was Tim, but by the time he landed he was only partly Tim, from the chest down, and the part of Tim from the chest up was lying on the ground beside Daniel, screaming in a high, high voice, like a little boy's, until the screaming stopped.

An instant later the jungle exploded with bursts of machine gun fire, but soon it fell silent again. Daniel lay for a long time on his stomach in the mud, listening to the insects and the occasional explosion in the distance, with the bottom of Tim on top of him and his gun in front of him and the top of Tim next to him, which had stopped screaming but which still had its eyes open, as if it were watching Daniel. Daniel tried not to think, and he succeeded. He looked at the trees, looked at his hands, looked at the mud. Then he rolled over, wriggling his arms out of the blasted-open pack on his back that was drenched with Tim's blood, so that the bottom half of Tim fell off of him and onto the ground next to the top half. Then Daniel stood up, leaving his pack on the ground as he put half of Tim over one shoulder and the other half over the other shoulder. After endless timeless days, time suddenly began passing on Daniel's back, long moments emerging with each step he took, created like light from the void. Bright sunlight gleamed through the silent canopy overhead as Daniel carried Tim's body through the Pass of the Ocean Clouds, toward the mountain road leading to the city where men worshipped their ancestors and buried their ancient kings.

––––––––––

WHEN DANIEL ARRIVED at the road, he discovered that all the guardrails and lines they had installed the day before had been torn out, and the segment that they had paved the day before had been blown to bits. The tents and supplies were gone. The equipment had been destroyed, with all the rollers and drills blown up and the blackened frame of a jeep lying burning in the road like the bones of an ancient animal. No one was there, at least no one alive. In the distance, Daniel saw thick black smoke and knew that some Americans from another unit must have survived, because they were burning down the village.

He couldn't keep carrying Tim. His arms had started to tremble, and then to shake so hard that the body was nearly slipping to the ground. He laid Tim down, one piece at a time, underneath one of the shrines by the roadside. He bent down on his knees over the body, took one of Tim's dog tags, and closed Tim's eyes. Then he looked over his shoulders, up and down the road, for someone to tell. Afraid to leave the body, he tried to shout for help. But his voice came out of him not as a shout, but as a long, high, wrenching scream. He flung himself across Tim's body and screamed again, his scream rumbling and shaking the valley below him. A moment later, as he paused for breath, he heard someone nearby shouting back, in Vietnamese.

The wild thought crossed his mind of crawling over the cliff, of somehow concealing himself along the side of the precipice. But as he peered over the edge he saw a blond-haired body lying still in the ravine, bleeding from the head. It was Rob. And next to him, Wayne, shot in the back. Everyone was dead, he slowly understood. He had wandered into a necropolis—and then, as he looked at the shrine above Tim's closed eyes, he realized that it had happened because of him. Suddenly he replayed his conversation with Cuong in his head: Cuong's suggestions on where to build the camp, his own choice to pass the suggestions along, the ease with which he had granted his trust, how carelessly he had assumed that anything any of them planned to do—himself, his own unit, Cuong, anyone—was of course for the common good, as if they had all been building the same road into the sky. He looked again at the bodies in the ravine and almost screamed again, but then he heard a shot fired somewhere nearby. He jumped to his feet and began running down the road as fast as he could.

But where could he run? Toward the village in flames? Going in that direction meant going back into the jungle, or farther up the dirt track of Highway One. Either way there was no chance of avoiding Cuong's unit. As for going down the road, there was nothing between the burning village at the pass and Da Nang—nothing but dozens of empty miles, and dozens of shrines for the dead. But it was the only choice. Daniel started running down the road he had built, running and running, choking on air and sweat as he fled from the dead town. He would run all the way to Da Nang if he had to, back to the land of the living. The jungle flew by at his sides, green and brown and gray and hideous, and Daniel began to feel like a bird, released from the earth as he soared downhill. But as he raced down the switchbacks, he heard Vietnamese voices shouting again, closer in behind him.

Suddenly as he ran, gasping for air in the heat, he noticed a jagged hole in the mountain face near the road. A cave. Daniel ground to a halt on the muddy slope, leaning over on his strong thighs and panting like an animal. He heard the shouting again, and entered inside the rock.

Later it would amaze him how vividly he would remember every detail from the next few moments, as if all of his senses had been sharpened into knives of hearing, seeing, smelling, taste, and touch, carving every detail of those moments onto his skin and into his brain. The cave wasn't like any place he had ever been. The only other time he had been inside a cave was on a road trip with his parents when he was a little boy, and there the cave was all lit up inside, with railings

and walkways. This cave was like the inside of a womb. The floor of
the cave was thick, soft mud, and just a few feet past the mouth, the
darkness was total. Inside, it was silent, a sealed silence unlike any he
had ever heard. The only sound was the occasional echo of a drop of
water from the ceiling of the cave landing in a puddle on the floor—a
strange noise, like the plucking of a string. The air was so cool and still
that Daniel felt as if he had slipped underwater. He raised his arms in
front of him, still panting, and began to move toward the back of the
cave, where he hoped there might be another way out after a curve or
two in the rock.

He took a few steps forward and slammed his head against the ceiling. He must have taken off his helmet at some point, though he could
no longer remember when or where. He reeled a bit, almost tripping
in the mud, and he could hear his boots crunching on leaves that must
have floated inside the last time it rained, or so he thought. His hand
slipped from his momentary grip on the ceiling and landed on his forehead, and he felt something warm and wet on his face in the dark. He
was dripping. He assumed it was sweat or water or mud, but then he
realized that his whole body was painted with Tim's blood. He could
taste it in his mouth. He spat three times, ducked his head, tried to see
the ground, couldn't see anything, pushed his hands back against the
ceiling of the cave, and took one step forward. And then the ground
disappeared beneath his feet, and he plummeted down into hell.

It was a "tiger trap," of the kind the unit had often been warned
about: a pit about six feet deep, completely covered by leaves and
underbrush that hid a trapdoor of bamboo. At the bottom of the pit
were about eight four-foot-long bamboo spikes, each implanted in the
ground and sharpened to a knifepoint, and smeared with excrement.
Daniel couldn't imagine why they would have put one in a cave—the
cave must have been a training center for them, he would reason
much later, conveniently located to where the ambush had taken
place, and surely there were more traps like it set up in the jungle. But
Daniel didn't think of any of that as he fell into the pit, where three of
those spikes went straight through his right leg.

He didn't feel anything at first. It was as if he were suspended in
space, hanging by a hair, and he couldn't understand how he had
stopped falling without landing, as if the earth didn't want him and had

decided to spew him out. He reached down to feel what had happened, and it was only when the palm of his hand felt a spike erupting through his calf that he opened his mouth to scream. But then he heard a shot fired outside the cave, somewhere very close, and someone yelling in Vietnamese, and he understood that Cuong and his fellow soldiers must be nearby, that they might come and take him prisoner or execute him on the spot, and that his last remaining hope was to swallow his screams.

Daniel clamped his jaw tight, nearly biting off his tongue. His body shook so violently that he felt as if the spikes were alive, squirming and tearing through more of his flesh. He knew he had to do something before he passed out, but he had already lost so much blood that he thought it might be too late. For a moment he thought that he would just let himself die, end it, end himself. But then he thought of Rosalie, and of Tim and the others, and he braced his shaking body against the sides of the pit and hauled himself out—ripping his leg off the spikes, which tore through it deeper until the bottom half of his mauled boot ripped off, and part of his foot went with it. He was lying on his stomach and vomiting, half his body draped over the edge of the pit, and his leg, or what was left of his leg, just barely pulled out and propped up on the side. He pressed his mouth into the mud and started eating dirt to keep himself from screaming. He vomited, swallowed more mud, vomited again, and then managed to pull himself up, pour out the water in his canteen onto the dirt and blood from the wounds, and tear off part of his shirt and tie it tight around what was left of his calf before collapsing again, shaking hard, to fill his mouth with mud. He could just barely see the mouth of the cave out of the corner of his eye. And then he noticed the spider.

It was just a little spider, hanging by a thread at the entrance to the cave, dangling in the sunlight like a pendulum on a clock, swinging from side to side, slowly, as if time had slowed to a stop. Daniel stared at it as he tried to control his screams for another eternity, until he was suddenly, vaguely aware of the sound of voices at the mouth of the cave. With his mouth stuffed with mud, Daniel saw two men standing just beyond the cave's opening, ducking down and peering inside, both armed with what looked like his unit's M16s. And he recognized one of the voices and knew it was Cuong.

Daniel was certain that they had seen him, but they didn't move any closer. Then he realized that they weren't able to see inside the cave from where they stood. He wanted to pray, but his thigh began convulsing again and it was all he could do not to scream. Cuong began shouting at the other man, pointing at the mouth of the cave. The other man answered with a nod of his head, and then—and Daniel could not be sure, at first, if it really happened or if it was delirium—they walked away. For a long time after that Daniel still did not move or scream. He was certain that they had just left to bring more people with them to capture him, or to photograph his execution. It wasn't until the light began to change in the cave door that he understood that they weren't coming back. They had seen the spiderweb and thought that no one could have gone inside.

It started raining again. Daniel watched, in moments between bouts of passing out—was it seconds? hours? years?—as a waterfall of dirt began running across the mouth of the cave, followed by a thick sludge of mud, heavy wet clods of it, and then loose rocks from above, until the thin brown curtain of mud became an avalanche of heavy stones, piling one on another and fusing with a river of filth, the stones and mud piling higher and higher. The pale window of faint light was starting to close, and Daniel realized what was happening but there was nothing he could do—his body was still shaking so hard that he couldn't crawl toward the door. He stopped thinking, stopped feeling, stopped caring. Instead he watched as the entrance to the cave sealed off the last bit of daylight air, until time no longer existed. He was buried alive.

———

IT IS EASIER than it seems to sleep through the end of the world. Daniel struggled hard to stay awake, trying to scream, but after suppressing so many of his screams he found that they would no longer come out. The pain came in waves, hot irons searing his body as if he were being thrown into a blacksmith's fire, his body convulsing until his head rattled against the mud and he swallowed his own vomit, alternating with dull, quaking dread and fear of the next wave. The only difference between closing his eyes and opening them was that when his eyes were closed, he saw the top half of Tim, still screaming.

He fought hard to stay awake. He seemed to remember that it was once hot outside, but now he shivered constantly. Between his bouts of vomiting and wrenching convulsions, the hands of the cold cave air rocked him gently, stroking his cheeks. In college once, Daniel remembered in a half dream when his body stopped shaking for a moment, he had long ago read a story by some Greek philosopher about a cave. In the story, people were trapped in a cave, chained to a rock. One of them managed to leave the cave, going outside and seeing the sun and the trees and the whole rest of the world, and then he went back inside the cave to tell the people there about everything they were missing. But the ones inside couldn't understand what he meant. Instead, they became enraged and killed him. The point of the story, as Daniel remembered it, was supposed to be that everyone is living in the fake world inside the cave, and the man who left the cave is "enlightened," the only one who realizes how wonderful the real world is. What a joke, Daniel thought. He knew, now, that the fake world was the one outside. The real world was the cave, a dark place of little light. And the chill of the cave air was like a cold compress on a wound.

It was becoming more and more difficult to resist the tug of sleep, the deep seductive undertow that pulled at his eyelids each time he paused between gasps of breath and bludgeoning pain. Beneath his closed eyelids, the top half of Tim loomed over him in the cave, screaming, but articulately this time. Now he was screaming for his wife and baby. Tim's baby! Daniel remembered, anguished. Had it been born today? Daniel started sobbing, pleading, begging Tim to stop his screams. But then he heard a thundering roar, louder than the blast of the grenade, as something large appeared behind Tim at the mouth of the cave. A tiger. Daniel struggled to wake up, to scream, but he couldn't. And of course he couldn't run. He watched helplessly as the tiger began to devour the still-screaming Tim, sinking its teeth into Tim's neck like a deep sick kiss until Tim fell silent. Then the tiger looked at Daniel, licking his black lips. And Daniel, choking, unable to run away or even to scream anymore, turned around and began digging furiously in the mud, throwing clump after clump of mud behind him until he had blinded the tiger and dug himself a tunnel, burrowing like an animal into a passageway underground. In the depths of dream and delirium, in the darkest recesses of his crippled mind,

Daniel crawled through his imaginary tunnel until he reached a door, pushed it open, and entered a little room.

––––––––––

IT WAS A room of babies. Two babies, Daniel saw—tiny, scrawny babies, naked, without navels, a boy and a girl. Daniel wondered if one of them was Tim's. But these babies looked at him warmly, expectantly, laughing baby laughs, smiling toothless smiles. If either of them thought he had killed their father, they didn't let on.

The room was an underground chamber, small, unfurnished, and dimly lit. But its walls were lined high with books. Whose books were they? Daniel wondered. Could the babies read them? The floor was made of smooth, rounded tiles, and was nearly covered with books and loose scrolls that were scattered across the room. The two babies sat on the tile floor, squirming and smiling in the treasury of books. The books were dusty, ancient. But the babies were fresh and new, their pink skin glowing and their tiny hands and feet waving in the room's dim light. One of them, the girl, looked up at Daniel and beckoned him to come in.

Daniel began pulling himself on his stomach across the floor, dragging his torn leg behind him. But then the floor started moving beneath him, the ground trembling and the tiles separating from each other. When he first felt the floor move he started shaking from fear, certain it was another trap. But then he looked down and saw that the rounded tiles on the floor were not tiles at all, but turtles, hundreds of turtles, their backs like an army of soldiers' helmets in a solemn military march. The books and scrolls on the floor weren't scattered at random, but were being carried, each by a different turtle. As Daniel dragged himself into the room, the two babies watched him, crawling over to look at his leg, then back around to look at his face, staring. Daniel looked back at their tiny faces and noticed something familiar about them, but he couldn't tell what. It frustrated him. Their blank faces stared at him with deep comprehension, as if they knew who he was. Now they sat before him, leaning with their little hands against the turtles' backs, waiting. What did they want from him?

The girl baby who had beckoned to him before now crawled in front of him. She glanced at the turtles around her, then selected a book

from one of their backs. While Daniel watched, the boy baby helped
her lift it and open it. Daniel stared at them as they flipped through the
pages many times, burbling to each other as they turned the book's
heavy leaves. At first Daniel thought they were just enjoying the movement of the pages, treating the book as a toy. But soon it became clear
that they were looking for something specific. As they paged through
the book together, Daniel hoisted himself up on his elbows and tried to
see what it was. But he couldn't. At last the babies, working in tandem
as if they had done this many times, turned the heavy book around to
face him. He squinted at the block letters and saw that the book was in
Yiddish. As he jolted backward, nearly slipping off his elbows onto the
turtle-tiled floor, he caught himself and looked again. It wasn't just a
Yiddish book, but one that he had read before, many years ago, with
Rosalie. He gasped. The book was opened to a story by one of the old
master storytellers, the "Tale of the Seven Beggars." An inked baby's
handprint marked the corner of the page.

Daniel stared at the page in wonder, then looked up at the babies,
glancing at both of their quiet pairs of eyes. How did they choose this
book? He looked again at the page, at the careful baby handprint in the
corner, and silently began to read. He was about to turn the page when
the boy baby grabbed his finger, wrapping his tiny clutched fist around
Daniel's thumb in a relentless baby grip. Soon the other baby had
grabbed another of his fingers until he was trapped, blood choked from
his hand by ten tiny baby fingers. He looked at their desperate faces,
their toothless mouths puckered into almost-wails as the girl baby cried
aloud. He glanced around the room again, at all the hundreds of turtles with their hundreds of books, and wondered if it was a dungeon.
To be surrounded by books without knowing how to read!

"Do you want me to read to you?" he asked.

Smiles spread across the babies' faces. Slowly the two tiny fists
released Daniel's fingers. The two babies moved around the book and
raised it up together, propping it just below Daniel's face, and Daniel
took it. Then they stared at him, their loose thumbs lodged between
their toothless gums as they hovered over the book with him, drooling
on the ancient page. Again Daniel noticed something familiar about
them, an odd presence in the room. But the babies were silent, and
waited.

Daniel looked at the text. The dark patches of ink slowly resolved themselves into letters before his eyes, like paint taking form on canvas. " 'I will now recount for you,' " he read aloud, " 'how people once were happy.' "

It was a story with many stories inside it, he remembered now, stories within stories within stories. He and Rosalie had struggled with it, gathering the pieces together into a story that made sense. But the book the babies held before him was blotted and stained, with pages torn and missing, and the light was dim. Daniel read what he could make out and tried to remember what he couldn't, reciting the story from the bottom of the abyss.

Two children were once abandoned in a forest, a boy and a girl. A blind beggar found them there, but he could not lead them out of the forest. Instead he gave them bread. The children took it, and the beggar offered them a blessing: that they should be like him.

The next day, the lost children were hungry again. A deaf beggar offered them bread. He, too, left them with the blessing that they should be like him. By the seventh day, seven beggars had found and fed them: first the blind one and the deaf one, then a stutterer, then one with a crooked neck, then a hunchback, then one with missing hands, and finally one with a missing leg. Each of them offered the same blessing: that the children should be like them.

Years passed, and the children grew up. They found a path to a town and joined a roving group of beggars, "going over the houses," begging for alms. When the children were finally old enough, the beggars decided that they should marry each other, and the children agreed. So the beggars prepared the wedding hall in the forest.

" 'They dug out a large grave,' " Daniel read aloud, " 'and covered it up with wood and earth, and they all went down inside it and made a wedding there for the two children.' "

Suddenly he stopped reading, afraid. He glanced up from the book and saw the girl baby staring at him. He looked at her face, at her large eyes and the light glowing on her trembling lower lip, and then at the baby boy's thin smile, and suddenly he knew who they were. "I can't read anymore," he stammered, and started to cry.

The babies watched him for a moment, and he was ashamed in

front of them. Then the boy made a baby fist, and thumped it against the book until Daniel bit his lips, drew in his breath, and continued reading.

During the seven days of the wedding feast, the children wanted to see the seven beggars who had helped them when they were abandoned in the forest. On each day, they asked for one of the beggars, and on each day, one of the beggars appeared. Each one denied his handicap and told them many stories, giving the children the wedding gift of becoming just like him.

On the first day, the blind beggar arrived at the wedding feast.

"Do you think I'm blind?" the blind beggar asked. "I'm not blind at all. It's just that all of eternity is nothing more than an eyeblink to me." He then told them that he was once in a shipwreck, and he and the other survivors decided to tell each other stories—the oldest experiences they could think of, their very earliest memories of life. The others told many stories, but the blind beggar told the oldest one of all: he remembered nothingness, the place before stories. And he gave the children his gift: a long life.

On the second day, the deaf beggar arrived.

"Do you think I'm deaf?" the deaf beggar asked. "I'm not deaf at all. It's just that it isn't worth hearing a whole world full of people complaining about what they lack." He told the story of a wealthy country where people believed they were living "the good life." The country had a garden of riches, of so many sights and smells and sounds that the people in the country literally lost their senses, spoiled by everything they had already seen and heard and smelled and tasted and touched, until the deaf beggar taught them how to use their senses again. And he gave the children his gift: a good life.

On the third day, the stuttering beggar arrived.

"Do you think I'm a stutterer?" the stuttering beggar asked. "I'm not a stutterer at all. It's just that all the words of the world that aren't praise will never be worth saying." He told a story of a mountain with a spring emerging from a rock, and the heart of the world—because everything, the stutterer said, has a heart, including the world—which stood thousands of miles away. The heart and the spring yearned for each other constantly, but the spring could only live through the time the heart gave it, the days the heart created by singing songs and riddles to the spring. And the beggar gave the children his gift: songs and riddles, to use to create time.

And so the crippled beggars continued appearing at the wedding, one after another each day. Nothing was what it seemed. Each of their defects turned out to be strange gifts, talents for finding the true world behind the imaginary one and for picking up the pieces of a broken world. Daniel found himself reading faster, both eager and afraid to find out what the seventh beggar with the missing leg would bring them. He approached the last page, where the handless beggar gave the newlyweds his gift, and his mangled leg shook as he held his breath.

And there the story stopped.

Daniel stared at the book, flipping pages, puzzled, but there was nothing more to read. A large white space filled the page below the story's last line. "What about the seventh beggar—the one with the missing leg?" he asked. He didn't remember the missing ending from when he had read it with Rosalie. Had the author died before finishing the story?

Daniel looked up. The babies were smiling at him, their eyes flitting between his face and the story's last page. The boy started laughing, little baby laughs that bubbled in the room's warm air. Suddenly Daniel remembered Tim, and Rob and Wayne and the carnage outside, and his role in causing it—how he had trusted, believed, imagined, instead of seeing what was right before his eyes. Oh, to be a baby, unborn, immortal! He looked at the babies and wanted nothing more than to stay in this little room forever, reading to the babies and holding their hands. His torn leg twisted behind him, a wrenching pain that yanked at his gut, but he swallowed his moans. He didn't want to upset them.

"What happens to the beggar with the missing leg?" Daniel asked again.

But the babies were laughing so much now that he wondered if it was some sort of joke, if they had hidden the last page of the story somewhere among the little scrolls on the floor. For a moment he thought he was right. The boy, squirming with laughter, had crawled away, reaching with his baby hand for a little scroll on the back of one of the turtles on the floor. There it is, Daniel thought. The last page.

The baby crawled back toward Daniel, clutching the scroll in his tight baby fist. The girl baby watched, drooling with glee, as the boy baby offered Daniel the scroll.

Daniel rolled it open, ready to find out what would happen to the beggar with the missing leg. But the parchment was blank except for three spare words, in English this time:

GO FIND OUT.

Go find out?

Daniel was still staring at the paper, bewildered, when he heard a noise behind him. He twisted around to see the door creaking open, pushed by turtles with their helmetlike shells. As he turned again to face the babies, he saw that they had started to move away from him, waving their little baby hands in farewell. The floor rumbled beneath him, the turtles shifting under his missing leg. And then the army of turtles started to carry him away. The babies had turned away from him completely now, the backs of their fuzzy baby heads bobbing up and down, laughing with each other as if he weren't there.

"Please, don't make me go!" Daniel begged them, but they refused to turn around. The turtles carried him through the door and then back into the tunnel, up toward the cave. When Daniel saw where they were taking him, he became so frightened that he started to scream.

This time a scream came out, the loudest scream Daniel had ever screamed. He screamed and screamed and screamed, and didn't stop screaming until he saw a light appear, and saw the turtles who had been carrying him changing, slowly, into the helmets of soldiers, soldiers who were now hoisting him up and bringing him out into daylight, fumbling at his neck, reading his tags, calling his name.

"Corporal Ziskind?"

10

B EN HAD once written a category's worth of questions for *American Genius* about pregnancy, to which the answers were all zygotes and blastulas and fetuses with gills. The people at the studio had joked that he knew more about pregnancy than most women did. But now that Sara was pregnant, he found it almost impossible to understand. What did it mean? he wondered as he looked around at strangers on the train and then the subway. Was it a person? A thing? An idea? Part of his sister? Or something else? And, strangest of all, wasn't this how he and Sara had first met?

Twins. When they were little, he hadn't ever imagined having a life apart from Sara—or, more precisely, he had never imagined Sara having a life apart from him. Until their father died, they had done everything together. They sat next to each other in school every day, divided their homework between them, spoke Yiddish to each other when they didn't want the other kids to listen, spent their afternoons together building elaborate cities out of blocks. Ben, slightly older and slightly smarter, was always the supervisor of their games together; Sara simply listened to his orders and obeyed. Every year the school tried to separate them by putting them in different classes, and every year their parents would call the school to ensure that they wouldn't be apart. But when the tumor in their father's lung metastasized two months before fifth grade began, no one remembered to make the call. And after their father died, something stranger happened: Sara got taller while Ben got shorter; Sara's body grew loose and lithe and beautiful while Ben's fought to grow in the confines of plastic and steel. And then Sara's imagination unfurled in paint on canvas, reaching out into the world and bringing it in, while Ben's curled tighter and tighter into his coiled brain. Now they were thirty years old, and Sara was having a baby, while Ben was still waiting for a future that might never arrive.

Looking at the pregnant woman sitting across from him on the train (why, all of a sudden, did everyone seem to be pregnant?), Ben remembered something horrible. When his father died, his mother told him and his sister that their father had a new job. Instead of being an engineer like he was before, their mother said, he was now drafted into service as an engineer of souls, interceding in the next world on the twins' behalf. He would build their futures the way he used to build roads. Ben was eleven years old, and the idea enraged him so much that he went out to the backyard with one of his father's cigarette lighters and attempted to ignite an entire can of aerosol bathroom cleaner into horrifying balls of flame.

It was a test. If his father really was building his future, Ben thought, then he would like to see how his father planned to intercede once Ben decided to burn the house down. He lit the first flame gently, pushing down on the aerosol can's button and igniting a small fireball in the air, a wavy warp of flame that quickly died. The second time the fireball was bigger, and his father still failed to stop him. The third time, Ben created a long, fantastic arc of flame that flared up in terrifying splendor along the wooden back wall of the house. When the bridge of fire slid closer to the wall, Ben held back, frightened, and released the button. The flame died, and Ben breathed with relief. But then he wondered if he had held back because his father had made him, if his father had slyly engineered his soul. No, he couldn't have. Ben was sure of it. Ben had a scientific brain, and he would prove it. Soon Ben was bearing down with full force on the button, spraying a massive fountain of chemicals right onto the house's wooden wall. If his father cared so much about his future, surely he would stop Ben from torching the house. And if he didn't, well, who needed the house? Ben thought angrily. It was the only house in the neighborhood that had just one floor, and the only reason they lived there was because of his father's leg. Maybe now that his father was dead, Ben's eleven-year-old brain imagined, they could move to a better house: a vertical house with dozens of floors and hundreds of steps, with rooms high up in towers and deep down in dungeons, with steep, spiraling, never-ending staircases leading up into the sky and down into the center of the earth. "Let's see you stop me!" Ben screamed to the skies, spraying more of the bathroom cleaner into the air. "If you're really there, you'll stop me! Let's see you stop me!" He bore down hard on the button, dousing the wall of the house. The smell was intoxicating. He breathed in, feeling giddy. It was the lightest he had felt since his father died. He watched the fan of watery chemicals as it came out of the can, waiting until he couldn't wait anymore, and then stopped waiting. "You didn't stop me!" he screamed, triumphant. He was about to ignite the spray when his mother grabbed him from behind, wrestling him to the ground and forcing his father's last cigarette lighter out of his hand.

But now he thought of Sara and remembered all the biology facts he had gathered for *American Genius*, the DNA and RNA and chromosomal combinations and matching nucleotides and Punnett squares and probabilities and genetic futures. Tiny secret blueprints of their parents were floating within her, growing, invisible and silent, engineering a soul. Every pregnant woman was carrying the dead.

―――――――

BEN HAD RETURNED to his parents' house over the weekend to search for anything he could find about the painting. If he was caught, he at least wanted to have a case, something to lighten his crime. The results were not pleasant. He had barely entered his parents' old studio when he saw the murals Sara had made as a child and felt an enormous hole open up in the floor at his feet. After spending all day flipping through piles of papers—his mother's illustration contracts for future works, his own spinal X-rays, records from a military hospital about his father's amputation, incoherent stories in Sara's grade-school handwriting, deeds to his parents' burial plots—all he had found about the painting was a one-page letter from an art dealership. The letter was so disturbing that he called Sara immediately, but when he tried to describe it on the phone, he choked. *Just come by tonight and I'll show you*, he had told her, and hung up before she could respond.

Afraid to look at it again, he had folded the letter over and over until it became a little arc of hard paper like a block of pulp (pieces of paper, Ben knew, can never be folded in half more than seven times; facts can only be reduced so much), and then stuffed it into his pocket, twiddling it with his fingers again and again on the train and the subway and then as he walked along his darkened street and at last stepped down from the sidewalk into the little sunken entryway to his building. How would he tell Sara? Just thinking about it made him sweat, though the summer night was cool. As he stepped down toward his building, he removed his glasses and wiped his eyes. Without his glasses, the world looked to Ben like an abstract painting, all vague shapes and blotches of color. He sometimes wondered which was real—the world with his glasses, or the one without them. Lately he had stopped believing in what he saw. In the days before she left him, he had too often looked at Nina with his glasses off, imagining that she was smiling.

Now, in the blur before his eyes, he could just make out the shape of a person—a woman, when he squinted—in a dark red skirt (or pants? no, a skirt) and a shirt that left her arms bare, standing between the garbage cans and the door, waiting for someone. The blur of her was lovely in the evening shadows, and for a moment he wished she were waiting for him. Better to ignore her, though. He hated acknowledging the presence of strangers. He put his glasses back on and was reaching for his key, admiring her out of the corner of his eye, when he suddenly recognized her. It was Erica Frank.

"Hello, Mr. Ziskind," she said. She smiled and stepped back from the door. She was facing him now, along the wall beside the garbage cans. "It's me, Erica, from the museum." As though he wouldn't know who she was. But was she there for him, or was it a coincidence? "Sorry to bother you," she added. For him.

Haven't you bothered me enough? Ben demanded in his brain. But her smile was so disarming, so surprisingly real, that he couldn't find the words. "Hi," he stuttered, as if she were just a friend bumping into him in the street. He planted his feet on the ground, staking out turf. To his surprise, he enjoyed hearing her voice.

"I called you earlier, but you were out. I knew I'd be in—in the neighborhood this evening, and—well, I brought this," she said.

Absurd, he thought. What did she mean? He watched as she reached into her bag. The turn of her shoulder made her hair fall away from her neck, revealing a collarbone so delicate that it made Ben think of Sara as a child, poised in front of the murals she had painted on the studio walls. Erica struggled with the zipper on her bag. He wished he could help her open it—to make her leave faster, he told himself. But then she pulled out a book and held it in front of him. It was a children's book with a snowy landscape on the cover. A woman hovered in the air above a pair of snow-covered tombstones, floating high in a watercolor sky. It was his mother's last picture book, a ghost story. The title was *The World to Come*.

"I'm a big fan of your mother's work," Erica said. "I was hoping she would be able to sign one of her books for me." She smiled.

Ben took the book in his hands, astonished. Erica watched him, and in her smile he saw something so honest that he failed to speak. Her eyebrows were raised above her pale green eyes, and as her fingers fidgeted with the strap of her bag, he saw her smooth teeth resting on her perfect lip. He couldn't remember the last time a woman had looked at him that way, besides Sara. Maybe Nina, right after they were married. But after two months Nina's smile had reversed into a sneer. He looked at Erica's smile and felt a lightness in his body, as if a stone had fallen from his heart. He had forgotten that his mother was dead.

He glanced down at the book, noticing how similar the cover was to the Chagall painting. He let his eyes follow the lines of the woman's body, the elongated curve of her hip and arm as she floated through the sky, released from the ground. As he opened the book, Erica took a step toward him. He drew in his breath, wondering what to expect.

"I know you did it, Mr. Ziskind."

He slammed the book shut. He stepped backward, edging away from her until his back was pressed against the building's stone wall. Erica moved in closer. "I saw your mother's name in the file," she said. "I know it was hers."

Ben moved his lips, but no words came out. He stared at the book and remembered how it had felt to be under the studio lights on the *Beat the Wizkind* set, sweating beneath his brace as his heart thumped inside its iron cage and his hands twitched above the buzzer, his brain fighting hard for the right answer. Suddenly he felt something unimaginably soft, cool and gentle, on the back of his hand. Thin fingers rested on his. "I understand if your mother wants it back," Erica said.

He gulped, then swatted her hand away as if it were a fly. "I don't know what you're talking about," he spat.

"I can help you, Ben. There are things you could do that would make this whole problem just go away. If you want, I can show you how to return the painting without anyone knowing it was you."

His first name sounded natural in her mouth, as if she had called him that for years. It scared him. He tried to move, but he was backed into a wall. Her breath smelled sweet and pink on his face. He hadn't been so close to a woman since his wife had told him she was leaving and, after hours of shock and pleading, he had leaned in to kiss her goodbye. She had shoved him away then, disgusted. His back felt cold against the dark gray wall. "I don't know what you're talking about," he made himself say. "If you're accusing me of something, then why don't you just call the pol—"

She tilted her head back, then grinned. "If you didn't do it, then call the police yourself!" she retorted. "Call them tonight and tell them I'm harassing you. Conspiracy to theft. If you really are innocent, nothing should stop you from turning me in." She smiled at him again, her knuckles turning white around the strap of her bag. "But if you're not, then think about it. I have my own reasons for asking you to do this. Trust me, it will be a lot easier for everyone if you just return it."

Ben noticed that her shoulders were shaking, and her nervousness comforted him. He was suddenly acutely aware of the smell of the trash in the can beside her, a thin, sweet odor of rotting fruit. Her red skirt fluttered in the evening breeze, and he caught a brief glimpse of a long, pale leg. Trust her? She smiled again, and he wondered if she could help it, if she smiled intentionally, or by mistake. She ran a hand through her hair, waiting for him to speak. He was silent. Only a moment later did he realize that his mouth was hanging open.

"I'll give you a day to think about it," she said. "Meet me tomorrow night at nine, outside the museum. If I don't see you there, I'm going to track down your mother. I'm not afraid to have them search her house."

Search the house! He felt himself starting to panic, and bit his lip. The air around her became blurry, as though he still had his glasses off. Suddenly a figure appeared behind her, a bright green flash in the orange night.

"Sara!" he called.

Erica turned around. Sara stood just behind her, one step up on the sidewalk from the sunken entrance to the building. Sara must have been teaching that day, Ben thought; she looked more presentable than usual. Her curly hair was half tied behind her head, and she was wearing a bright green blouse and dark pants that weren't jeans. There was only a single streak of blue paint on her left arm. She glanced at Erica, then stepped down beside the garbage cans, standing before them. Erica smiled, but Sara merely stared.

"Hi, I'm Erica," Erica said, sticking out a trembling hand.

Sara nodded, but didn't offer a hand in return. Erica slowly lowered her hand to her side. Ben watched as the two women looked each other over: a split second, almost invisible inspection of faces, breasts, hips, hair.

"This is my sister Sara," Ben said. He saw Erica visibly relax, her fluttering hand finding rest on the edge of her bag. "Sara, this is Erica. She, uh—we met at the museum last week."

He emphasized the word "museum," and waited to see if Sara would understand. But Sara was preoccupied, examining Erica as if Erica were one of her paintings, wondering where to add more color.

"I'm a big fan of your mother's work," Erica said to Sara, and gestured toward Ben's hands. Ben looked down, surprised to see that in his left hand he was still clutching the edge of *The World to Come*. "I just came by here tonight with a book for her to sign," Erica finished.

"To *sign*?" Sara asked. Ben saw the horror in her eyes and suddenly remembered what he had forgotten. It was like waking from a sweet dream, a brief joy forever lost. "But she—"

Ben pinched his sister's wrist with his right hand and held up the book with his left. "Don't worry, I'll give this back to you soon," he said to Erica, his voice self-consciously loud.

"Why don't you return it to me tomorrow night?" Erica intoned. Ben saw the tiny blond hairs on her forearms rise, her skin tightening in the cool night air. "Nine o'clock. I'm sure we'll be in touch," she said. She took Ben's hand.

They were in touch as he shook her hand, her soft skin warm in his palm. And then they were out of touch as Erica walked away, with Ben left holding her book and breathing her air.

11

"SHE'S BEAUTIFUL, BEN."

Ben had made Sara hurry inside and up to his apartment, but now they lounged on the couch (the couch he had just bought, a cheap used one, to replace the one Nina had commandeered) as Sara's fingers wandered over the cover of Erica's copy of *The World to Come*. Ben peered at his twin sister's stomach, trying to imagine the invisible idea within her. What did it mean? But then she propped the book up on her lap. "Who is she?" Sara asked.

Ben stiffened. Strange, he thought, how he still sometimes sat with his back rigid, his skin prickling between his shoulder blades as though he were trapped forever in his childhood cage. Especially when talking to Sara about women. Ben had first met his former wife in Sara's apartment, at a party whose main purpose had been to set him up with another artist she knew, a designer who worked in TV. The woman Sara had selected for him was pretty, but aloof. She left the party early, claiming a headache; her friend Nina stayed on, laughed at Ben's jokes, and married him. Sara had known from the beginning that the marriage was doomed. She had refused to listen to anything Ben said about his wife at the time, changing the subject whenever her name came up, and because she hadn't listened, Ben had known, too. The two twins formed a magic ring of unsaid words and thoughts, a charged circle that had stretched to include Leonid, but only barely. A fourth person might not fit. And another fourth, Ben remembered, was already on the way.

"She's the one from the museum," Ben answered. He pretended disinterest. "She works for them. She says she knows I have the painting, and she wants me to meet her outside the museum tomorrow night to give it back. She claims she won't tell anyone if I show up when she wants me to."

His twin sister listened, then tilted her head down, gazing at the cover of the book. Her hair curled in dark ropes on her neck. "She's beautiful," Sara said again.

"So that means I should believe her?"

Sara didn't answer. Ben tried to stop thinking of Erica. He kicked at a pile of recently submitted encyclopedia articles he had left on the floor the previous night, after falling asleep while reading them on the couch. As a child he had been fascinated by encyclopedias. After his father died, when he was old enough to think about it, he had reviewed the various ridiculous stories he had heard about how his father lost his leg (ranging, over the years, from a tiger to an earthquake to a barbaric family feud) and had begun looking things up, learning about the habits of various animals, the terrain of various countries, the histories of various wars—secretly imagining that he was preparing himself, readying himself to survive some even more horrible future. But now the entire idea of an encyclopedia struck him as absurd.

Sara opened the book that Erica had brought, and Ben slid down the length of the couch until he could see the pictures over his sister's shoulder. Her hands paused on a picture of a man driving a car, his lips tight as his dark inked knuckles gripped the steering wheel. Behind him, a woman with a thin smile sat in the back of the car, transparent against the seat in watercolor paint. "You didn't tell her about Mom," Sara said.

"I know," Ben answered, after a moment. "When she gave me the book, I—I don't know why I didn't." But he did know why: to maintain the illusion, to pretend that his mother existed outside of the paper pages. As long as Erica didn't know, he could believe what she believed.

"I loved the colors," Sara murmured. She ran a finger across the edge of the page. Ben looked again at the watercolor woman sitting in the back of the car, unnoticed. "The angles, with that red skirt," Sara said, thinking aloud. "And the light."

Sara always talked about everything as if it were something she had painted. If it weren't for her, Ben wondered if he would be able to see. He pictured Erica standing by the door and smiled. Would he actually go to see her tomorrow night? Suddenly he wanted to. But then he remembered why Sara had come, and yanked the book from her hands.

"This is what I needed to show you," he said, and reached into his pocket, pulling out the folded page and peeling it open. "I found this in the house." He placed the letter on top of the book and held it across the letterhead at the top, a bright red frame with the words KOMORNIK ART EXCHANGE emblazoned inside it. Sara looked down and then leaned forward, gripping the page and reading faster until Ben started reading over her shoulder, his eyes racing through the words he had already tried to forget.

December 18, 1986
Dear Mrs. Ziskind,

I'm very sorry about the tone of our telephone conversation yesterday. However, I write this note to reiterate my comments in writing. My decision concerning *Study for "Over Vitebsk"* remains final.

Your allegations about Sergei Popov's character notwithstanding (and I must admit that I find it difficult to discern their relevance, not to mention their accuracy, if you were in fact five years old when you and he last met), Mr. Popov is a major client with whom I've had numerous dealings since the beginning of *glasnost*. There has never been a problem with any other sale to him, and our relationship is one of mutual trust. The accusations he made in the telefax I read to you are not to be taken lightly. You have essentially been charged with a felony.

In no way did I intend to dishonor your father's memory. But when it comes to a sale of this magnitude, I am afraid that dead parents as evidence are simply not acceptable. I was willing to take both your word and (more significantly) that of the expert you retained through me, but I no longer intend to engage that expert's services after this incident.

Unfortunately there are large numbers of fake Chagalls on the market. Since the artist's death last year, his works are exceedingly difficult to authenticate. Every counterfeit that is sold erodes the value of the originals. Needless to say, they erode my own business as well. As for your request that the painting be returned to you, the bottom line is that even if Mr. Popov were to go to the expense of shipping the piece back to me—which he has no intention of doing, and I believe wisely so—my professional choice would be to destroy it rather than to allow the possibility of it re-entering the market. I have no reason to believe that you would not attempt to sell it elsewhere.

Having met you, Mrs. Ziskind, I understand that you've been through a lot, and I know how hard it has been on you and your children. But even if I were to take you at your word, you have placed me in an impossible situation. Mr. Popov feels that yours was a deliberate deception, and while he cannot prosecute you himself from the USSR without severe diplomatic difficulties, he has encouraged me to do so. You should understand that it is purely out of sympathy for your children that I have decided not to press charges. I hope you will be satisfied with this and will bury the matter here.

Sincerely,
Lawrence Komornik

"It's not true," Sara whispered.

Ben took the letter back into his own lap. He took off his glasses, rubbing the lenses against his shirt, and then allowed himself to say what he had been denying all the way back from the house. "Yes, it is, Sara."

Sara was silent, but Ben began to argue as if she had denied it. "I didn't believe it, either, at first. I remember how upset she was when she tried to sell it," he said, trying to sound more patient than he was. "But you know she could easily have forged that painting. And it wouldn't be the only time she did something like that." He picked up the book from Sara's lap and slammed it down on the couch. "You know she didn't write these stories herself."

It was something they never talked about, yet both of them knew. Sara blinked, and Ben could see that she was going to ignore it. "It can't be a fake," she said. "It was in a Russian museum."

"All that means is that the guy who took it wasn't a chump," Ben insisted. "He probably never told anyone in Russia that he'd been fooled, sent it straight to the museum, and kept whatever money they were giving him for the sale."

Sara shook her head. "That's not how it was. I met him."

Ben sat up, leaned forward. "You did? I mean, who? How?"

"When she was trying to sell it. I went with her to the art dealership. The man who bought it was evil."

Ben stared at her, struggling with something that fell just short of a thought. "What do you mean, 'evil'?" he finally asked. The word made him think of being a little boy, of his odd shame the first time he saw his father's fake leg—of feeling ashamed to have two legs, ashamed even to be alive. He listened, anxious.

"I mean that Mom fainted right in front of him."

Ben sat back, his surprise dissolving into disappointment. It was hard to imagine their mother passing out. "That doesn't explain anything," he said, assuming the rational voice he knew she hated. "There are a million reasons why someone would faint. And besides, this was when we were how old, eleven? You probably just misunderstood what was happening."

Sara stared at him. "You don't believe in evil," she said slowly. "For you everything is just a misunderstanding."

Ben was silent, unsure of how to put her down. At last he groaned. "People aren't inherently evil, Sara," he said. He was acutely aware of the condescension in his voice. "You can't just say that about someone you met for ten minutes almost twenty years ago."

"You're right. They aren't born evil. But they choose to be. And they are."

The line of pale blue paint on Sara's forearm quivered. For a moment Ben imagined it was a vein, and thought again of his father's veinless leg. There was no point in talking to Sara rationally, he knew. His eye fell on their mother's book between them, and the full weight of his predicament struck him in the chest.

"So what am I supposed to do?" he asked. "It doesn't change any-thing if the painting I stole is a fake to begin with. I'm as good as caught already. That woman said she would have them search Mom's house if I don't show up at the museum tomorrow night. I got the feeling that she's important over at the museum. They're going to listen to her." He gritted his teeth. "She knows I have it. And she knows where I live. She can find Mom's house in about a million ways, even just by checking where she lives in the 'about the author' section and then looking her up. She even knows where you live, from when the police talked to you. I could put it in a storage locker, but it's only a matter of time until they track it down. It's over, Sara."

Sara watched the air in front of her, then suddenly smiled. Her eyes glowed as she looked up at him. "So go meet her," she said.

Ben dug his fingernails into his palms. "But I can't. First of all, I'm not going to return the painting. It's ours, no matter who made it, and we're keeping it. And second, even if I went, I don't believe her that she wouldn't turn me in. Every time I believe someone, I get screwed. Every time *anyone* in our family believes someone, we get screwed."

"You're not going to get screwed. We're going to forge the painting ourselves."

Ben was struck dumb. He opened his mouth, and nothing came out but cold breath. At last he found his voice. "But how—how—"

Sara grabbed his hand. "Go meet her tomorrow night, and get her to show you more details about the painting. Play tough with her. Tell her you won't return it unless she shows you some evidence that proves she's for real, something that would compromise her if she tried to turn you in."

Ben was stunned. It was a side of Sara he rarely saw—a practical bent that she rarely showed him, though it was clearly visible that day when she had tagged along to Leonid's apartment. And he had seen it in some of her paintings, in shadowed landscapes with an unexpected, brilliant hidden light. "Evidence? Like what?" he asked.

"Anything about the original condition of the painting. Even though we have the original, museums still have records of things we would miss if we tried to copy it ourselves, details we wouldn't notice. We need to make sure we know everything, so it can be perfect. Then I'm going to make the copy, and you're going to bring it back."

He felt Sara's fingers on the back of his hand, the second time that evening that a woman had touched him. He shuddered. "But Sara, it's—I thought you—"

Sara grinned. "Mom did it, so why shouldn't we?"

At first Ben thought she had changed her mind, that she now believed what the letter claimed about their mother forging the painting. Then he realized what his sister really meant: their mother's books.

"Sara, you don't have to do this for me. This is my problem, not yours."

"There's no such thing as a problem that's yours and not mine."

For a moment they sat together in silence. Then Sara lifted Ben's wrist off the couch, turning it to see his watch. He wasn't wearing one. She stood up.

"I have to go home. Leonid is waiting for me," Sara said.

Ben heard Leonid's name and jolted, realizing something. *She's beautiful*, he heard Sara repeat in his head. And he wondered—after Sara's marriage to Leonid, after Ben's divorce, after the new idea growing within her—what his twin sister thought she owed him. But as he stood and moved across the room to see her out, she was already at the door.

"See you soon," she called.

The door closed before he could thank her.

————————

When a person dies, he doesn't go from one room to another, Ben's mother had once told him. *He goes to the opposite side of the same room.* Ben stood by the door and looked at the far side of the room, where his mother's book was seated on the couch like a person, propped up against the back cushions. He crossed the room carefully, afraid to disturb the air, then sat down on the couch beside it. He opened the book and began to read Erica Frank's copy of *The World to Come*.

————————————————

Let me tell you a story of how I once took on a burden that almost ruined my life, because when you're young, you do all kinds of stupid things.

One winter night, when I was still a very young man and newly married, I had to travel all alone from Metropolis, the town where I lived, to Megalopolis, the big city. It was snowing hard on the

night when I planned to go, and if I were smart I would have stayed
home. But I had just bought a brand-new car, a big one with giant
tires, and I knew I could make it. So I set out in the snow, on the
long and lonely road to Megalopolis.

I soon found out that even with a new car it's very hard to travel
all alone in the snow, and slow going, too. It wasn't long before I
became so lonely and tired and hungry that I decided to stop at
the first place I could. But the road between Metropolis and
Megalopolis is a long country road where almost no one lives.
After hours in the blizzard, I saw a tiny inn—a lonely place, like
an abandoned gravestone, but with a dim light glowing in its windows. I stopped, and though I will regret it for the rest of my life,
I went inside.

I opened the door and saw a scene I hope I'll never see again.
In a small room, a dead person was lying in the middle of the
floor, covered by a thick black cloth and with two lit candles resting above its head. A man stood at the head of the body, and many
little children surrounded it, weeping and screaming. I wanted to
close the door, get back in the car, and keep driving to
Megalopolis, but then the man saw me, and then it was too late.

"Help us! Help us! My God, my God, my God, what will we
do?!" the man cried. "My poor wife! She needs to be buried! It's
not respectful to keep her like this! She must be buried right
away! But the cemetery is all the way in Necropolis! We can't go
anywhere in this weather! My God, what will we do?!"

With that, the man broke into a strange sobbing, sobs without
tears—a weird and horrible sound from his throat, almost like
laughter. And then I forgot all about myself. What did it matter
that I was cold, and tired, and hungry, and miles away from where
I needed to be that night?

"I could give you a ride there," I said. And I told him about my
new car. "I'm on my way from Metropolis to Megalopolis. It
would be easy for me to stop in Necropolis on the way."

"But I can't leave the children alone!" the man cried.

Suddenly I felt heroic, as if I could do anything. "Don't worry,"
I said. "I can take her there myself."

"Thank you! Thank you!" the man wept. "There is no good

deed equal to burying the dead, because it is the only thing a person can do without ever expecting to be repaid in this world. For this good deed, young man, you have earned a place in the World to Come! The World to Come!"

He helped me put the body in the back of the car, and I listened carefully to all of his directions. Everyone knew him in Necropolis, he told me. All I had to do was say his name, and everything would be taken care of. Nothing to worry about. And for all that, I had earned myself a place in the World to Come!

As I drove to Necropolis, the snow came down even harder, and I could barely keep the car moving. I repeated his directions in my head, over and over again. But the entire time, all of my thoughts kept returning to one thing: I was sitting in the car with a dead body. It seemed to me that I could see the woman's half-closed eyes looking at me, as if her locked dead lips might suddenly speak. On that snowy road I thought I might die from fright alone. Soon my wonderful car got caught in a drift. It was very late, and I tried to sleep in my car, but I was afraid that if I fell asleep, I might join my passenger and never wake up. As I drifted in and out of snow and sleep, I imagined that the woman shuddered out from under her shroud to watch me. I heard the wind whistle with her voice, and I began to wonder which one of us was dead.

It didn't end well, of course. When the man arrived in Necropolis, he realized he had forgotten the name of the deceased, and when he tried to have her buried, he was accused of murdering her until, in a panic, he started claiming that the corpse was his mother-in-law's, which worked just fine until his real mother-in-law showed up and demanded to know why he was burying her alive, and then . . .

Ben read the book over and over again on the edge of that night, as if reading could somehow stave off bad dreams. When he finally fell asleep, his dreams contained no stories at all, but only the hard stones of thoughts: the unimaginably unlikely coincidence of being alive at the same time as the love of your life, the frequency with which a person was expected to bear the body and the burden of someone else, the idiocy of thinking that kindness can protect the person who is kind, and worst of all, the bottomless pit of a truth that he had suddenly, sickeningly seen: that the world to come that his parents had always talked about was not an afterlife at all, but simply this world, to come—the future world, your own future, that you were creating for yourself with every choice you made in it.

He woke up the next morning and knew he would go back to the museum.

12

A S A CHILD, Der Nister had once heard a story that the head of the rabbinic academy in Volozhin used to tell his students. One night when he was still a young man, the headmaster dreamed that he had died, and had arrived in the next world. When it was the headmaster's turn to appear before the divine throne, the Holy One took him by the hand and brought him to a small door. The door opened, and the headmaster found himself in a luminous room filled with books: shelves and tables loaded with books, manuscripts in high stacks all over the floor. The headmaster looked around the secret library and smiled. He was sure this room was the place that had been reserved for him in paradise. But as he reached to take a volume off the shelf, the divine hand suddenly grabbed his shoulder and held him back. "These are all the books you were supposed to have written," the Holy One said. "Why didn't you write them?"

In 1942, Der Nister began to live in such a room.

The wife he no longer loved had long since left him, and had taken their little boy with her. His beloved Hodele had moved to Leningrad, where there was rumored to be work in factories for young women like her. And Der Nister himself had hidden in place after place, fleeing city after city, until he finally arrived in Taskhent, Uzbekistan—where, in a tiny room in a concrete hovel outside of the clanging gongs of the bazaar, he had assembled all of the paper bridges of the book he still needed to finish while he was hiding from death.

Paper bridges stretched across the floors and walls and shelves of his room. In a town where so few people could read that no one had even bothered to erect street signs, Der Nister's room was a secret library paradise. Words hung in the air: in sheets, in scraps, in strands, black ink on white pages like the veils of blunt beads that hung in the doorways and markets in Tashkent's streets. The first volume of his novel, *The Family Crisis*, had been published in 1939, to considerable acclaim. It had been called a Yiddish masterpiece. He had cleverly positioned little pieties in the text—damning asides about how the bourgeois family in the novel was doomed, of course, because of their backward religious beliefs, their juvenile refusal to believe in progress, their exploitation of the masses—inserting them every forty pages or so to placate the censors. But in Tashkent, amid the orange smells of horses and the thick clouds of brilliant yellow dust that blew in through his broken windows and painted his eyebrows and mustache, Der Nister forgot about the censors and wrote. He was acutely aware that he was losing his mind, slowly releasing his mind from his head and emptying its contents onto scraps of paper with which he plastered the walls. He had almost completed Volume Two.

He had heard rumors of Chagall's success in America. The artist had had huge museum shows, had received commissions to decorate public halls and opera houses around the world, had stayed with his family in hotels and resort towns where other Jews couldn't even rent a room. He was hailed in papers throughout the Western world for his vast, joyous canvases filled with nothing but color and light. But the artist's wife (the woman painted in blue), Der Nister heard two years ago, had died suddenly of pneumonia on a country vacation in the mountains. Chagall had taken her to the nearest hospital, but it was a Christian hospital, and—depending on which rumor you believed— she had either been refused treatment or had seen the registration form asking for her religion and had refused to be admitted. That's what it's like in America, Der Nister's more loyal comrades claimed. They had persuaded him to join the Jewish Anti-Fascist Committee, to raise support from Jews overseas to help the Soviets defeat the Nazis. So far it hadn't helped, as far as Der Nister could tell. Later, he heard exuber-

ant reports that Chagall's old friends—Shloyme Mikhoels, the head
of the Jewish theater whose murals Chagall had painted, and Itsik
Fefer, the hack poet whose books Chagall had illustrated—had been
sent by the government on a tour of New York, Boston, Philadelphia,
Detroit, Chicago, San Francisco, and Los Angeles (with Soviet secret
police escorts, of course) to raise money and support from the American Jews. Chagall, Der Nister read in a Party newspaper, had even met
with them in New York. The tyrannical Americans had so completely
misunderstood the mission that they had sent the FBI to interrogate
Chagall immediately after the visit, but still—Der Nister read—there
was hope for a united front for triumph against the Fascist beast. Der
Nister doubted it. If it were true, he wouldn't be hiding in Tashkent.

His unfinished book had become his obsession. He rarely left his
room, which he insulated with sheaves of paper scribbled with beginnings and endings, nailing ideas to the walls and stretching long strips
of sentences from the window to the door. Tall stacks of scenes and
chapters sprouted from the floor, as if the papers had reincarnated
themselves back into trees. The paper forest around him glimmered in
the sun from the windows, weaving rays of light in yellow and purple
and blue. Hunger squeezed his throat, but he turned his ravenousness
toward writing. He almost never slept. During the shortages, he wrote
between the columns of old newspapers, or on pieces of cardboard, or
on bark pulled from trees. He traded potatoes for ink.

In the depths of the paper forest in Der Nister's room lay a shining
imaginary kingdom—the nineteenth-century town of Berdichev,
where Der Nister had lived as a child. It was a boomtown in the woods,
full of merchants and workers and students and nobles, and even more
full of the courts of the "righteous ones," the dynasties of religious lead-
ers who ruled their followers' spirits. On every piece of paper were the
members of the family in crisis: Moyshe, the scrupulous businessman
who always planned for everything and supported everyone, and had
even done the service to his children of buying his own cemetery plot
in the very first chapter of the book before his fortunes began to fade;
Luzi, the follower of the dead mystic storyteller Nachman of Bratslav,
who irritated his brother Moyshe with his religious fervor but never
failed to act as Moyshe's conscience; and Alter, the idiot savant, who
could see time and who sensed changes in his brothers Moyshe and

Luzi as he sensed changes in the seasons, and who in his rare lucid moments wrote letters to biblical figures, to the angels, and to God. In his mind, for years, Der Nister lived in nineteenth-century Berdichev. It was a place to hide.

But one day in the dust-laden summer of 1942, Der Nister received a letter, and the paper bridge tore. He sank to the floor of his room, and stopped writing.

For a week he sat in silence in the paper forest, with his shoes removed and his shirt torn, and with bright yellow dust from the windowsill rubbed on his forehead. At the end of the week he still did not write. Instead he left his room and wandered into the dust-billowed streets of Tashkent, through the bazaar with its horses and fabrics and grilled meat smells and teenage girls. He walked and walked, circling the city with his feet, afraid to ask anyone how to get where he needed to go. At last, as the sun sank in the heated yellow sky, he found what he was looking for.

He entered the synagogue—the old one, not the new one populated by his fellow refugees—where the Jews didn't even speak Yiddish, but instead spoke another Jewish language of their own. He could only communicate with them in Hebrew, and he had to listen hard to their Hebrew full of gutturals that he could barely understand. But he stayed for their prayers because he had to, and muttered words he wished he could believe. He returned every day for the rest of the year.

After thirty days of daily prayers that he wished he could believe, he began to write again. But he did not write his book. Instead, he remembered the letters his character Alter had written, and decided to write letters himself. He consulted letter-writing manuals that he had stored in the piles of papers, old pamphlets that instructed people on proper forms of address. He wrote the letters, as Alter did, in archaic formal Hebrew, and addressed his letters to those who would never write back.

To the Angel of Dreams
(may your light shine for all eternity):

Forgive me for disturbing your difficult and essential work. I am aware that you have been very busy lately, because many around the world complain of nightmares. But I hope you will indulge me with a few waking moments of your time to consider my predicament. My concern is that I have stopped dreaming.

As a child, as I am sure you recall, I dreamed all the time—long dreams, beautiful dreams. In my dreams I was always flying on air over the town. I would lie down to sleep and receive your nightly deliveries of stories like letters slipped into the mail-slots between my eyelids, and I would open each landscape as if unfolding a piece of paper before my eyes. The world unfurled at my feet, and I would rise up above it, floating above the cities between the clouds. I would wake up with a crash, as though I had fallen to the earth. Later, you began bringing me your messages while I was still awake. I don't know if you did this in error, or if you were trying to frighten me with the horrible nightmares you gave me while I failed to sleep. Yet even the most terrifying landscapes you brought me were still gifts of ferocious colors.

But now, I no longer dream at all. When I close my eyes at night, I see nothing but darkness, the same darkness that wraps me in thick blankets of shadow during the day. There are no stories and no colors, just heavy gray and black. I lie in bed trembling like a child, afraid of the closed curtain that awaits me when I sleep.

Where have you hidden my dreams?

Respectfully submitted,
The Hidden One

To Nebuchadnezzar, King of Babylonia
(may your name be erased):

I write to you on the occasion of the ninth day of the month of Av, to congratulate you in the next world—where surely you are celebrating today, the 2,528th anniversary of your destruction of the Temple in Jerusalem, where my ancestors once served as priests before God.

I send my tidings to you from the ends of the earth, from a city and country high in mountains that even your once-great empire never reached, to inform you that I am here, on the last ridge of the far end of nowhere, because of you. For it was your choice to set the House in flames that inspired all the others who followed. You were merely the first.

On this day, those with more faith than me sit on the bare ground, remove their shoes, tear their clothes, fast and weep. Even here, on the last ridge of the far end of nowhere, they mourn, pouring ashes on their heads, calling to the heavens: "Because of our sins, God cast us out from our land," just as they have done for the past 2,528 years.

I understand why. It is much easier to say that it was God—to believe that no mere human could be capable of such pointless savagery, that there must have been a reason for it, that it must have been deserved, that it must have had some kind of meaning.

But I know that it didn't. And that it wasn't God, but you.

> Respectfully submitted,
> The Hidden One

To the Eternal (may the name of your honored majesty be blessed forever and ever):

Forgive me for interrupting your divine and important work. I hope you will grant me the gift of your mercy and be particularly forgiving of my interrupting you at this juncture in the history of our world. It is my humble assumption that you are presently involved in extremely essential, unfathomably life-sanctifying creative endeavors that we shall all (may it be your will) be privileged to witness in the near future, speedily and in our time—for I cannot otherwise explain your current absence from the face of the earth.

I write regarding the letter that recently reached me (after a journey of many months) from your earthly city of Leningrad, which has been besieged and laid waste and where thousands have already starved to death, and where children and adults have begun to eat filth from the gutters and to kill insects and each other for food. The letter regretted to inform me that my daughter, my one-and-only, the one I love, my Hodele—much like all evidence of your divine presence—has died and vanished from the earth.

I am quite confident, dear God Full of Wombs, that the millions of others whose cries reach your throne—those of them who still dare to believe you will hear them, that is—demand to know why. Why, of all the millions of children in the world, did you insist on killing mine? Is there something more you wanted of me, of her, of us? Had she earned your wrath with her twenty-nine-year-old soul? Or did you want her as much as I did, and then steal her from me like a man steals another man's wife? Were you in desperate need of her particular radiance to complete the work which I am sure is engaging you at this very moment? Why—I know these other parents ask—why my child?

But I am not asking you why. Instead, I hope you will take a moment from your busy eternity to answer a different question, the only one I will ever ask of you:

What did she mean?

Respectfully submitted,
The Hidden One

There was nothing to eat in Uzbekistan, but that did not matter, because Der Nister was no longer hungry. Instead he sat in his room among the untouched stacks of paper from his book yet to be written. And he tied himself up in long ropes of memory, caged himself in with iron bars of memory, drew the curtains and hid himself in a dark tomb which he filled with an entire world of memory—until all that was missing was color and light.

1 3

I T WAS DEFINITELY him. Erica knew that now. By noon of the day after she had confronted him on the sidewalk, she knew he hadn't called the police to turn her in, which meant he was afraid. But that wasn't all. That morning she had gone through the file for the missing painting again, and had discovered two documents in plastic folders, both labeled *Found lodged in canvas frame*. The Russian gallery had probably never even exhibited the painting, she realized, since her museum was the first to find the papers in the picture's backing; if the Russian museum had bothered to display it, they would have discovered these things themselves, just as she and the others at her museum had discovered them when they began preparing for the exhibition. In the Chagall murals (big paintings, really, canvases stretched on wooden struts) from the Moscow State Jewish Theater, one of Erica's colleagues had discovered dozens of manuscript pages behind the pictures, stuffed into the edges of the canvases' wooden supports like so much insulation. The more she read through the files, the more she realized that everything about the stolen painting's condition—from the scraps of paper in the backing to the mildewed right edge where it had been left resting on a storage-room floor—suggested that it probably hadn't been displayed in fifteen years. The same was probably true of many of the works in the show. Paintings that no one looked at, left to rot in private vaults or in thieves' closets, might as well have been destroyed or never created at all. The waste infuriated her. But the papers that had been found in the frame outraged her even more.

One of the documents was a series of printed pages that looked like a chapter or story torn from a book; the other was handwritten, scribbled in ancient brown ink. She couldn't read either of them. Both were in Yiddish. The characters were the same as Hebrew, which she knew, yet she still couldn't understand a word. But Sam, one of the older curators (who had once lived on the same street as her father, and whose grandson had gone to camp with her), could. When he translated the title of the story on the printed pages and named the author, she was so bewildered that she spent her lunch break at the public library, paging through a thick anthology of translated stories and discovering one astonishing thing after another until her stomach swayed. She returned to work livid. All the anger that she hadn't let herself feel with Saul slowly gathered and rose in her throat, aimed at Benjamin Ziskind. But when the old curator saw her, he laughed.

"You've got to stop thinking about this theft, Erica," Sam said. "I know Max gave you a hard time about it, but he's over that now, trust me. He just wanted to scare you a little, whip you into shape. He's the type that flames and then fizzles. And anyway it really doesn't matter. The painting is insured. It's not a major work, relatively speaking. Everything else in this show is worth millions more. And besides, it's not your job, no matter what Max tried to tell you. The police are taking care of it."

"They're not. And I know this guy has it. I'm sure of it," she told him.

He had heard it from her before. "So tell the police," Sam said. He grinned, and in his grin she could see that he thought of her as a child, like his grandson.

"I told the police. They're doing nothing. They're convinced it's an inside job," Erica said. She decided not to mention that she had pestered them so much that they were now investigating her.

"The police already questioned him," Sam told her. His patient tone teetered on the edge of condescension. "Isn't that enough? I heard them talking to you. They said he clearly didn't fit the type, everything he told them checked out, and going after him was a waste of time. Do yourself a favor and worry about something else." He smirked.

Erica clenched her fists behind her back. Only two people had the right to talk to her like a child: her mother and her father. And her mother was dead, and her father was going insane. "You want me to worry about something else," she said, her voice rising. "All right, how about this? I'm worried that despite the absurd ease of this theft, no one at yesterday's meeting seemed to think it necessary to invest in an alarm system for the future."

Sam grimaced. "You know what the budget is like."

"But we're considering paying for bomb-sniffing dogs."

"That's important," Sam insisted. "The latest fax from the FBI said that Jewish institutions need to—"

"*Bomb-sniffing dogs,*" Erica repeated. "Is this an art museum or a fortress?"

"I don't have to tell you about the reality we're dealing with here, Erica."

"The reality we're dealing with here is that people are walking out of this building with million-dollar works of art and nobody cares, so long as the place doesn't blow up."

Sam sighed and turned back to his desk. "You should read that story that was in the painting file," he called as she left the room. "You can find it in translation. You'd like it."

But Erica had already found it, and now she was furious—not just at the thief, but at the museum, too. She almost wondered whether it was worth trying to get the painting back at all. It would serve them right, she thought, if it was never returned. But it was the principle of the thing, she felt. What made her angry was art that no one looked at, things that were hidden that needed to be seen. As the hours dragged by, her anger swelled in her gut until she couldn't wait to meet the thief that evening, to confront him about his mother's books and to catch him with the painting on the museum's new security camera— which, of course, only pointed at the street, designed not to record works of art coming out, but to record people going in.

AT NINE O'CLOCK that evening, it was strangely quiet. Outside the museum's front door, Erica waited on one of the few stretches of New York City street that could give one the illusion of being in another city, somewhere more civilized and beautiful. Twin rows of thick trees formed an arcade along the avenue to her right, their leaves rustling softly over the stone-bricked sidewalk. A block away, a woman stood waiting for a bus; over the low wall, deep in the darkness of the park, a man was singing in a drunken stupor; past the park, in her brother's apartment, her brother and sister-in-law were already kissing on the couch while her little nieces trembled through their six-year-old nightmares; in a house eighteen miles to the west, her father was swallowing his nightly pills, pacing the rooms, afraid to go to sleep alone; in the next world, her mother was watching her, worried. But on this warm late summer evening, traffic was slight. Even the doormen of the gilded apartment buildings down the street had vanished, idling indoors.

She had expected a long wait, or a never-ending one. She had even promised herself that she would wait until a quarter to ten, but no later. But she had barely positioned herself to the side of the camera when she saw a man appear across the street. Even before she could see his face, she saw the hesitation in his step, the rigid back and the stiff neck of the silhouette, and recognized him instantly. Benjamin Ziskind. He stood still, uncertain, waiting for the light to change even though the street was empty. He was holding something small and flat under one arm, a pale rectangle glowing orange under the streetlights. And then he began to cross the street.

The painting! Erica's heart danced. It was astounding, how easy this had become. As he reached her side of the street, she could make out the darkness of the landscape on the painting's lower half below his wrist, and then the shadow of the floating figure above it. But he must have removed the frame; it was smaller than she remembered. As he came closer, she saw that it was too thin, too. And then, as he stepped up onto the sidewalk where she stood, she saw the words printed across the figure in the picture. Now he was standing in front of the security camera, right where she had led him. He looked at the camera, then looked at her. In his hands he was holding her copy of *The World to Come*.

"You didn't bring the painting," she said.

"That's right, I didn't bring it," he answered. His voice was lighter than she had expected; less angry, more assured. "I'm not hiding anything. I'll even prove it." He bent down to place the book on the side-

walk at her feet, raised his arms as if he were at gunpoint, and then lowered his hands to his hips and turned the pockets of his pants inside
out. They were empty except for a few folded dollars, three keys on a
ring, and a subway pass, which he waved in front of her. It was a joke,
but he kept it up too long, pulling up his shirt out of his pants and spinning in a circle to let her admire his bare waist. Erica took advantage
of the joke to scan his body, checking for—a knife? a gun? The man
had stolen a million-dollar painting, after all. But there was nothing.
He couldn't even be hiding a weapon in his socks; his toes poked out
of ratty sandals. And there he was, spinning in front of the security
camera. She wished, for a moment, that the camera had a micro-
phone, but she knew it didn't. Meanwhile, she was surprised to find
herself enjoying the show. There was something disarming about seeing him with his shirt pulled up, the dark hair on his pale stomach bristling around his navel and above the band of his boxer shorts—and
something even more disarming about his face, the soft boyishness of
his features hardened slightly along the edges. He reminded her of her
high school boyfriend, the only boyfriend her mother had ever liked.
Her first kiss.

"That's right, I didn't bring it," he said again, picking the book up off
the ground and holding it in front of her. "I'm returning your book
instead."

What was this, she wondered, some kind of game? He was smiling
at her, a nervous smile. Maybe he didn't have the painting after all.
Could she have been wrong all this time? But then she looked down
at the book, and remembered her anger from the afternoon. The painting could wait. He held the book up toward her, offering it, but she
pushed it away.

"I discovered something disturbing today," Erica said. She pursed
her lips. "I found some stories in Yiddish that had been hidden in the
painting's frame, and a curator who reads Yiddish took a look at them
for me. Do you know what one of them was called?" She paused. He
watched her, but he didn't take the bait. " 'The Dead Town,' " she
finished.

"Your favorite," Ben said.

Erica was startled, then remembered that she had mentioned it to
him before, when she had interviewed him in her office. Why had he

remembered? She bit her lip, hiding her surprise. "But the story wasn't by Rosalie Ziskind," she said. "It was by a famous Yiddish author named I. L. Peretz."

She watched to see if he would care. He did. He winced, a subtle contraction of eyebrows and shoulders that he tried to hide by idly scratching at his stomach with his free hand underneath his shirt. But it was as if he were tugging at his own umbilical cord, trying to loosen the knot.

"So I went to the library at lunch to read the translation, to see if the title was just a coincidence," she continued. "But it wasn't. The story was almost exactly the same. And then, in the anthology with the translation, I found other stories that were familiar." She took a breath. "Like 'The Man Who Slept Through the End of the World,' which was by someone named Moyshe Nadir. And 'My Last Day in Paradise,' which was by someone named Itsik Manger. And—and this one," she said, pointing to the book in his hands, "which was by Sholem Aleichem. Even I've heard of Sholem Aleichem. I mean, his version had a wagon or something instead of a car, but otherwise it was the same. There were others, too."

She watched as Ben brushed his free hand against his forehead. His attempt at pretending disinterest was feeble; she could see that he was wiping away sweat. She heard him force a snort. "What's your point?" he asked.

"The point is that your mother, whose work I had very much admired, is a plagiarist and a fraud."

He looked down at the book, and in the streetlight she saw his knuckles whitening as he gripped the book's spine. "That's not what I thought the point was," he said.

"Why, what did you think the point was?" she snapped.

But Ben was avoiding her eyes. He held the book with both hands now, and rubbed a finger across the hair of the flying woman. "I thought the point was that my mother rescued all these stories that were buried in library vaults and that no one would ever read again."

This surprised her. "That's a very generous way of putting it," she said. She meant it to be pointed, vicious. But she thought of how the painting had been buried in the vault in the Russian museum, and her voice fell flat.

Ben wasn't finished. "And when she tried to publish them with the dead authors' names, nobody wanted them," he continued, "and when she decided to publish them under her own name, her greatest dream was that someone would notice that they weren't hers, because that would have meant that someone finally cared." He paused, breathed in the dark. "Congratulations. You are the first person in fifteen years to care."

Erica stared at the book's cover, at the dead woman hovering over the town, and thought not of Ben's mother, but of her own.

One of the pale hands holding the book moved. She looked up and saw Ben glancing over his shoulder, stepping to the side. She followed him like a shadow until they had moved a few yards away from the museum's door—and away, she realized when she began thinking again, from the security camera.

"You shouldn't even bother looking for that painting," he said under his breath. "It's a waste of your time."

The time had come. Erica was nervous, but she forced a laugh. "Why?" she asked. "Because I'll never find the thief?"

"Because the painting isn't real."

Erica jolted. Her back was against the museum's wall now, and he was leaning toward her, inches from her face. His glasses gleamed in the orange light. "What do you mean?" she asked.

"I mean it's a forgery. My mother tried to sell it, but the buyer never paid her for it. Because it's not a real Chagall."

She stared at him. "You're lying," she murmured.

"No, I'm not," he said. "Look."

Ben flipped through the book until it fell open to the page with the cover image, the floating woman in the sky. The right side of the two-page spread was covered with a wrinkled piece of paper, folded in half. He opened it, slowly, and passed it into her hands.

It was an old letter from an art dealership, one that she knew had shut down years ago. At first she skimmed it, and didn't understand. Then she read it again, and was astounded. It all made sense now. His mother was an art forger, plain and simple, a plagiarist in every medium. Erica glanced at the address at the top of the page and tried to commit it to memory, wondering if Mrs. Rosalie Ziskind still lived in the same house. If so, mother and son would both pay. In fact, the mother was more dangerous—more experienced, more talented, and at large.

But when Erica read the letter a third time, the words wavered before her eyes. Something didn't click. She looked up at Benjamin Ziskind and suddenly shook her head.

"It's impossible," she said. "It can't have been forged. That painting passed the Chagall test. We wouldn't have displayed it otherwise."

Ben's eyes bulged behind his glasses. "What Chagall test?" he asked.

She bit her lip, wondering how little she could reveal. "Chagall had a system for marking and identifying all of his paintings," she said, choosing her words. "A few years after he died, his estate started telling curators and specialists about it, to help identify counterfeits. This letter is dated only a year after he died, and probably nobody had heard about it by then. But that painting had it."

Ben opened his mouth to speak, but nothing came out. She wished she could take his hand. "That painting is real," she said, passing the letter back to him. "If your mother was never paid for it, then it was stolen from her." She was thinking aloud. "If I were her, I would—" But then she swallowed her words, realizing what she might have done.

Ben nodded, once, a subtle movement that he tried to hide by looking down at the letter again, but Erica saw it. When he knew that she had seen it, he nodded at her again, his soft lower lip glowing in the streetlight as he looked her in the eye. He folded the letter back into the book, and spoke under his breath.

"I know where the painting is now," he said. "I'm willing to find a way to bring it back."

It wasn't a confession, not quite. But for her it was enough. For an instant she looked at his dark eyes behind his glasses and felt something close to pity. Shouldn't she just let him go? But paintings didn't belong in closets, no matter whose, and here he was, willing to let it be seen again. The stone wall of the museum was cold against her back as she gulped and listened.

"If I do, though, I need to know that I'm going to be safe," he added.

She heard a tremor in his voice, and was sure it was honesty. She couldn't believe her luck. "You'll be fine. You—I—I promise," she told him, stumbling on the words. She was surprised by how hard it was to lie to him, or to tell him what she at least hoped was a lie. He was leaning so close to her now that she thought again of the boy from high school, of the touch of pure trust.

But then he straightened in front of her. "You need to prove that to me," he said. "You need to show me that if I get in trouble, you will, too. You're going down with me."

This wasn't what she had expected. He was a small man, with thin arms and shoulders narrower than hers; otherwise she might have been afraid. Saul had been too strong. "What do you mean?" she whispered.

"If you want your painting back, then you need to go into that museum right now and show me proof that it passed that test. And then you need to give me those stories."

Stories? "You mean—from the back of the painting?" she stammered.

"Yes."

"Why?"

"Because then if you try to turn me in, I can show them those papers and prove you were part of it. Accessory to theft."

Now she was frightened. She leaned against the wall of the museum, trying to steady her legs. "That wouldn't prove anything," she muttered. But her voice shook.

"Yes, it would. You just told me that you showed them to another curator. Other people at the museum know those stories were in your files. If you say anything about me to anyone, I'll just tell them I was working with you."

She held her breath. Could he be serious?

"But if you don't, I'll find a way to bring the painting back, and I'll give the stories back, too."

He was serious. But how could she do it? "No," Erica said.

"Then no painting," he snapped. "You won't find it on your own, either. And whatever you want to tell the police about me, I'll tell them about you. They'll believe me. They already did."

"No, I can't," Erica said. There had to be another way, she thought. But she already knew the police would never believe her, that no one in the museum would ever believe her, either, that everyone thought she was crazy, and that perhaps she was—that in the over fifteen years since the file claimed that Rosalie Ziskind had sold the painting to the

Russian museum, she might be the only person who had cared. But Benjamin Ziskind was already sliding the letter out of the book and folding it into his pocket. He pressed the book into her hands.

"I'm glad you liked the book," he said. Then he turned around and began to walk away.

Erica watched his rigid back as he stood just past the curb and waited for the light to change, even though no one was on the street. She wondered if he was waiting for her to change her mind. She looked down at the book, and then opened it. Inside, she leafed through the first few pages, scanning the pictures in the dim light. But what she was looking for wasn't there. Again she had been tricked.

"You didn't have your mother sign it for me," she called to Ben's silhouette.

The light had changed, but Ben stood still on the asphalt. She watched as he slowly turned around. When he looked at her, she saw the face of a different man. "I'm sorry, she couldn't," he said. "She died six months ago."

Erica looked at the woman floating on the cover of the book, then looked back at Benjamin Ziskind. And her anger disappeared. "I'll do it," she said.

———

"WE CAN'T GO in that door. The camera," she told him. She had wanted to catch him on camera with the painting, but now she had changed her mind. Was she making a mistake? As Ben stepped back onto the sidewalk and toward the museum door, she had realized what she needed to do. He had his hands in his pockets now, and she reminded herself that she had seen what was inside them and wasn't afraid. "The staff entrance has a camera, too. We have to go another way. Come."

She began walking down the street, crossing against the light and heading along the park, away from the museum. She glanced behind her and saw Ben's anxious expression as he hurried to catch up with her. She almost offered him her hand.

"Where are we going?" he asked. It was a nervousness she recognized from when he was sitting in her office. Other people's nervousness made her feel more secure. She was in control.

"In," she said.

They stopped walking about two blocks away from the museum, along the wall that held in the park. Erica stood in shadow near the wall and saw Ben illuminated in the streetlight, glowing orange and strange, like a painted figure in one of his mother's books. She peered at the street around her, and waited for a bus to pass. Then, with quick movements, she bent down until she was squatting next to a small metal grate in the ground, one of the ignored basement doors and subway vents that line the sidewalks of New York. But there were no buildings on this side of the street, and no subway line, either. She felt Ben watching her as she took a key chain out of her purse, fumbled through it in the dark, and began jiggling a key in the tiny keyhole. With his eyes on her back, she twisted the key until she heard a clank, and then reached down and pulled open the doors in the ground.

She looked up, wondering what he thought. But when she saw him, she almost laughed. His mouth hung open and his eyes bulged, as though he were absolutely certain that he was about to be killed. The maw of the sidewalk opened up like his own grave. Inside there was a narrow wooden ladder hanging from the edge of the grate, leading down to somewhere invisible to his eyes, and then nothing.

She grinned at him, sliding the book into her bag. He watched in horror, shaking his head. His fear emboldened her. She slipped her legs into the opening and then climbed down quickly, lowering herself along the ladder until she had almost disappeared into the abyss.

"Come on," she said, motioning with her hand as she stood one step short of darkness, the top of her head level with the street. "I thought you were going down with me," she joked.

"No!" he whispered.

His fear made him more handsome, she thought. She didn't need him to follow her; in fact, she had been frightened that he might. But now she saw him from the ground up, and was surprised to find that she wanted more than anything for him to follow her.

"Fine, stay there," she said, and clanged the grate shut behind her.

He wasn't coming, she saw. She would have to go herself, and hope he would still be waiting for her when she returned. And it was too late now to give him another chance. She sank down the ladder rung by rung, moving deeper and deeper into the darkness. One step more and her glimpse of him would disappear, the last glowing light of his figure in the shadows rising above the line of her vision through the iron bars. Suddenly she remembered arriving at her parents' house one night almost a year ago—rushing to make the train, pacing the train's aisles as it raced out of the city, running from the little local station past houses and trees, resting for a split second, gasping for breath, running again until she reached the house, dashing up the driveway, and then seeing her brother appearing slowly, far too slowly, in the doorway— how she had known in that instant that she had come too late, that she had missed the entire world by a hair.

But then she heard the thief's voice. "Wait for me," he called, and pulled open the door, climbing down after her.

THE LADDER WAS broken off at the bottom. It vanished about two rungs before Ben seemed to have expected, and he hung suspended in air. She watched as he stepped down, one foot groping wildly in the void until the other foot slipped, leaving him dangling in the darkness between heaven and earth.

"Just let go," she said behind him. "You're closer than you think."

He seemed afraid to believe her, but his grip was slipping and his sweat decided for him. He fell from the ladder and landed with a splash, his feet slamming and then sinking into a thick, heavy layer of slime.

The faint sounds of the street had vanished, replaced with the primeval sound of water droplets falling into quiet puddles on the ground, like the plucking of tiny strings. The air was cool and thick and furry with odors, damp cement and the faint smell of rot. His eyes hadn't adjusted yet, Erica could tell. Between the squares of light from the opening, she saw him squinting at the space in front of him. He groped in the dark, near where she stood in the shadows, afraid to step forward. A hand touched her breast, and she trembled as the hand jolted off into the air, as if jumping from an electric shock. She stood still, and her skin mourned. The hand had been perfect.

"It's only muddy by the ladder, because of the rain a few days ago," she said, trying to dispel the touch. She was surprised that her voice was shaking. "If you move away from it, there's no more mud." She stretched a hand into the light, beckoning him toward her. He stepped away from the ladder, slowly, and into the shadows. "I'm sorry about the ladder," she said in the dark, pleased that she had steadied her voice. "It was like that when I found it. The bottom rungs must have broken off at some point, or rotted away."

Now they were both standing in total darkness, and in the black ink air she felt a hand brush against her arm. An old fear rose in her throat. She fumbled in the dark for the zipper of her bag and then desperately began to rummage through it, fingertips searching for hard metal. The jangling metal rang like a tiny bell as she pulled her key chain out into the dark. Her fingers jittered, and suddenly the space beneath the street lit up, illuminated by the tiny flashlight attached to her key chain. Her hands gleamed in the dark for the briefest of instants. Then she turned the beam toward him, blinding him, disorienting him. She refused to be the one who was afraid.

"Where are we?" he asked. The lenses of his glasses gleamed.

Her light moved, slightly, shaking in her hand and falling to his chest. "Have you ever been to the Touro Synagogue?" she asked.

"The what?"

She remembered his business card for *American Genius* and was surprised he hadn't heard of it. For an instant she came close to making a joke about the show, but she refrained. "It's in Rhode Island. It's the oldest standing synagogue in the United States, from the 1700s. The people who built that synagogue were so convinced that they were going to be persecuted in America that they dug a secret passageway from the sanctuary leading underground and out of the building, so that if they were ever trapped there, they'd have a way to escape." She shifted the light, raising it to his face again. She didn't want him looking at her eyes. "The building where the museum is now used to be the home of a Sephardic family in the nineteenth century. I guess they probably felt the same way. This is an underground passageway leading out from the museum building and into the park."

Ben's eyes squinted behind his shining glasses, blinded in the bright point of Erica's flashlight. She moved the beam down quickly, crossing his chest and his hands until it shone against a wall, then glided to the floor, and down the floor over thirty feet where the beam faded, and then off the ceiling. They were standing in a tunnel, its floor covered with smooth cobwebbed stones and its walls and ceiling long and empty. The flashlight beam failed to reach the end. She heard Ben breathing in the dark: short, nervous breaths.

"I was in the storage room at the museum about a month ago, and I was moving some things around when I found a key on the floor," Erica said. Her voice seemed to warm the cold air, making it familiar. "It was underneath a loose tile. I had to move the tile when a piece of cloth we had for an exhibit got caught underneath it. The tile came out, and underneath it I found this key."

She swiveled away from the corridor as she jangled the key chain, twisting the rings so that the light flashed against the small metal key. One of her fingertips glowed red as the light pressed against it. In the glow of her finger she could see Ben watching her, his eyes soft behind his glasses in the dark. "Come," she said. When she turned around and stepped forward, she felt him moving behind her and wondered what he was thinking.

The air was thick and cold, becoming colder as they moved deeper into the abyss. He had caught up with her now, and walked beside her. For a moment, she imagined that this was normal, that they were out for a stroll, a visit to a museum. "This is like a catacomb," she heard him say.

"A what?" she asked.

"A family crypt."

She winced for a moment, feeling the embarrassment she had often felt in the past year whenever someone too casually mentioned death, as if it were a joke. But then she remembered the book in her bag, and all the other books that his mother had rescued from the library burial vaults, and smiled an invisible smile. "Wait until you see," she said.

They walked slowly, side by side. In the afterglow of the flashlight beam she could see Ben's silhouette moving, black on grayish black in the dim outline of the cave. He walked haltingly, stumbling on loose stones in the invisible floor, but Erica walked with sure, dignified steps, moving underground like a queen. Soon she could see the end of the tunnel in front of them, a flat circle of light where the flashlight beam landed against a wall some twenty feet ahead. As they moved closer, the lines on the wall emerged in the light and it became clear that it wasn't a wall, but a door—a large metal door that she was now pro-

ceeding to open with her single key. The door clanged, then rattled as
the latch unlocked. She struggled to open the door, but it was stuck.
She leaned back and pulled, the flashlight beam dangling down
toward her feet. But the door did not move. She pulled harder, puffing
in the dark, staring at her illuminated feet. But then she saw sandal-
strapped toes on either side of her feet, and felt arms enveloping her,
reaching around her until two gentle hands rested on hers. She closed
her eyes and leaned back in the dark into his chest, shocked at how
thrilled she was, how completely unafraid, leaning into him until the
door came open. Then they separated, each silent, as if they had never
touched.

Behind the door was what looked like another wall. But Erica knew
it was a giant canvas, stretched on a frame that completely covered the
door. Ben stood holding the metal door open as Erica lifted the canvas
from its sides, slightly, shifted it over, slightly, until there was an opening in the wall. And she slipped out of the tunnel and into the space
through the slot in the wall, with Ben close behind her.

"Now, this," she said, "is the family crypt."

THEY WERE STANDING in a vast room, filled with yards and yards of
metallic shelves and glass cases that stretched out in front of them like
a vault, or a library, reaching as far as Erica's flashlight beam could see.
On the shelves were endless rows of objects that glinted in the tiny
light. The first things that emerged in the light were the paintings:
rows and rows of paintings of all sizes and styles, filed vertically on
giant rolling racks one after another so that only the ones on top were
visible, gaping eyes and mouths and shapes and letters and patches of
color staring at them under the thin beam of yellow light. Past that, on
the shelves, a few sculptures revealed themselves in the shadows,
abstractions mostly, dull, stolid cubes and twists of angry rusted metal.
But most of the shelves nearest to where they were standing were filled
with silver pieces—candlesticks, wine goblets, tiny filigreed boxes for
spices, larger house-shaped boxes for collecting coins for the poor,
crowns and breastplates and miniature hands made for dressing and
reading Torah scrolls. Beneath those were endless rows of scrolls of
every kind, single and double spirals of parchment unwinding in

sequence at the level of their waists, words undulating inside them to the interrupted songs of the silent room. And beneath those were shelves filled with piles of papers—heavy, dark papers that glinted in the brief and dancing light, the occasional gold-leafed Hebrew word leaping to life from the shadows. She heard Ben holding his breath.

"We're doing an exhibit next month on illuminated manuscripts," Erica said, her voice lower than before. She turned the flashlight back toward his chest, and suddenly remembered why they had come. "Let me show you the files."

They had passed the largest shelves and had pushed open a door, arriving in a room that in the bare glow of the fading flashlight was a dim shadow of her office, with a lifeless computer sitting impotent on a desk and towering filing cabinets lining the walls. This was the part that she had been afraid of, the horrifying part of what she had agreed to do—illegal, immoral, insane. But as she entered the dark room, afraid to turn on the lights, she was surprised to find herself feeling oddly at ease. Her office seemed to glow blue in the dark. For a moment she wondered if by night the offices were occupied by curator ghosts, cataloguing works of art that the waking world had forgotten.

"I remember this room," Ben said behind her.

She turned her flashlight on him, grinning as she remembered, too. "My office," she said. "I'm buried down here Sunday through Thursday, every week. At least I have Fridays off." Suddenly she felt as though she were with a friend. But when she raised the light to his face, she saw that he wasn't smiling. Instead, his eyes blinked at her, nervous.

Erica stepped to the table on the side of the tiny office, next to her desk. The flashlight beam had begun to fade. In the dull light, she shuffled through a folder until she found the photograph she was looking for, and passed it into Ben's hands. "Chagall numbered all his paintings on the underside of the canvas, on the part where it's attached to the wooden support frame," she said. "Every real Chagall painting has those numbers."

The photograph was of the back of the painting, with the lower right corner of the canvas carefully detached from the wooden frame. Along the interior edge of the canvas, on the part that had been nailed facedown to the wood, there was a series of painted numbers connected with dashes. The numbers were painted in a curly flourish:

200-400-60-50

"He only started marking the paintings after he had his first show in Berlin," she said as Ben scrutinized the picture. "Then he backdated the ones he made earlier, in lots. All the ones in this lot have the same numbers."

She watched his eyes squinting as he stared at the picture. "What do the numbers mean?" Ben asked.

She shrugged, ashamed not to have a good answer. "It's like a bar code. It doesn't mean anything," she answered, and moved the light away. He handed the photograph back to her, and his fingers brushed against hers. She shivered, then tried to hide it. "If you want something that means something, then take these," she said.

The two paper stories from the painting were sitting right where she had left them, side by side on top of the piles of paper next to her chair. She lifted them gently with one hand, stacking them and examining them again with her flashlight. But she couldn't read a word of them.

"You can read these, right?" she asked softly. "I remember you mentioned that you know Yiddish." The flashlight beam shone through the thin paper onto the floor as she passed them into his hands. "The curator who saw these knew what the printed one was, but he didn't know who the author was for the handwritten one. He said it was something about a bridge. Do you have any idea who wrote it?"

Ben squinted in the dark, leaning toward Erica's light and holding the handwritten story up to his glasses. He shuffled the pages. "No," he murmured. "It doesn't say. But it looks old."

There was a note of fascination in his voice that surprised her. "The painting dates to 1914, and he labeled it sometime in the 1920s," she said, and then was embarrassed to hear her docent's voice.

"I—I guess so," he stuttered. He was staring at the pages now, his hands shaking slightly under the flashlight beam, as if he hadn't believed it until now.

"There were other paintings that had papers in them, too," she said, suddenly excited to be telling him. "Like those giant murals from the

Moscow State Jewish Theater. There were hundreds of pages stuffed into the backs of those, under the wooden struts the same way, in the same handwriting as this story. It's like someone tried to jam a whole novel under there. We have them down here in the files somewhere. No one's had a chance to translate them yet."

She turned the light away from the pages, toward his face. He looked up, startled, then rested the stories on her desk. "So there they are," she said. "They're real. And they're yours until you give the painting back. I'm giving you three days." She twirled the flashlight around in her palm. "Before then, I won't say anything. You can take my word on that."

She was closer to him now, standing between him and the desk without knowing how she had gotten there. In the office of the ghosts, in the fluttering beam of the flashlight, Ben's face was soft and sad and full of longing—as if happiness itself were a distant memory, something long forbidden to him.

"Why are you doing this for me?" he asked.

There were many things she might have said, and many more things that might have once been true. But in the dark vault of forgotten art, she sensed their mothers watching her. "I trust you," she said.

The trembling hand that had been twirling the flashlight lost its grip. The key chain fell from her palm to the floor, and the light blinked out. Before she could laugh or bend to pick it up, she felt hands landing softly on her shoulders, curling gently around the back of her neck, fingers branching into her hair.

The room filled with black ink, deep and wondrous pools of dark liquid beauty that seeped into the spaces between her fingers and arms and lips. And the darkness between her tongue and the roof of her mouth was flooded with color and light.

14

H AIR IN darkness doesn't feel the way it does in light. In light, you
can touch a person's hair and not feel it at all—you might think
you are feeling it, but really you are seeing its color, seeing its shape,
seeing the light and the shadows intertwined between the hair and
your own hands. But in darkness, her hair poured across his palms like
molten music between his fingers. Skin in darkness is different, too. In
light, you don't notice skin, distracted as you are by eyes watching you,
eyes you are afraid to trust, eyes that could be waiting for your shame.
But in pure darkness, her skin was warm and trembling and alive—
secret whorled passageways of ears, soft fingertips tracing circles on his
neck, the living heartbeat-shudders of falling-closed eyelids, cheeks
erupting into lips and giving way to his tongue. And in light you don't
think of how warm a person is, of how a person can enfold you, enclose
you amid arms and clothes and ribs in pure primeval underground
darkness, the heat between you glowing like an ember that you are
afraid to put out. In the dark he felt her withdraw, her hands guarded
above his clothes—not from fear, he sensed, but from hope. He held
himself back. Together they felt for the wall and sank down along it
until they were seated on the floor in the cave of the underground
room, her head on his shoulder as he breathed in her hair, inhaling
the deep delicious scent of waiting to kiss her again.

"It's strange, isn't it? Being blind?"

He was glad she spoke first; he had been too afraid of saying something wrong. But what she said was exactly right. He raised his hand in the blind air, and his fingertips stumbled on hers. He shuddered with joy.

"I can't see at all without my glasses," he heard himself say. "Or just barely. Only light and colors."

His voice rippled the shadows. He was astonished to hear how bright he sounded, syllables like sparks. Her fingers played along his skin as if pressing piano keys, slow arpeggios that traveled up his arm and across his shoulder to his neck and along the edge of his ear, closing in on a chord around the arm of his glasses. Her palm caressed his stubbled cheek.

"When I waited for you outside your place a few days ago, I noticed that you didn't recognize me," she said. Her voice floated along his ear, warm breath on his earlobe. "Even though you were looking right at me. I thought you just didn't remember who I was, but I remember now that you had just taken your glasses off."

He laughed. "See? I didn't make it up."

"You have beautiful eyes, though. You shouldn't hide them."

If she were Nina, he would have launched into his usual complaint—his legal blindness, his fear of contact lenses, his inexplicable disgust at touching his own eyes. But now, here, he stared at the darkness and reveled in her words. He turned toward her and felt along her arm, his hands brushing along her skin and sleeve until he reached her chin and at last her lips, the delicious crescent of her lips. He rested a finger in the soft dent below her nose, until she kissed his fingers and took his hand in hers. The silence shivered between them, alive. He wished he could think of something to say; he was still afraid that at any moment she might get up, turn on the lights, cast him out, disappear.

"I'm glad I met your sister," she said a moment later, breaking the silence. He breathed with relief. "Is she older or younger than you? I tried to guess, but I couldn't."

The room around him was invisible, but suddenly he felt as if his sister could be sitting right in front of him, or his parents, too, that he was only the smallest part of a whole that was much larger, much deeper. "Neither, really," he answered. "We're twins."

He heard her shift in place, the soft swish of her hair. "I never knew an adult who was a twin before," she said softly. Her voice hovered over the deep darkness. "I mean, I remember twins in my class at school when I was little. I was always jealous of them."

He would have shrugged, but her head rested on his arm, and he couldn't bear for her to move. "It's less fun when you're an adult," he said.

Her hair brushed against the inside of his elbow, strumming his skin. "I always wanted that, though," her lips murmured along his shoulder. "Most people in your life only know you as a child, or only know you as an adult. I always thought it would be wonderful to have someone who knew me all the way through, who could be with me through all of it, from the day I was born." It was strange, he thought, this intimacy—how much easier it was to speak and to listen in the absence of sight, just sound and touch. "I have a brother, but he's seven years older than me," she added. "It's like having an extra father, almost."

He thought of asking about her parents, but he decided not to. He felt the presence of his own parents in the underground room and held her more tightly, possessing her weight in his arms. He struggled to find his voice.

"Does your brother have children?" he asked. His words were more timid than he had hoped. And now he remembered that she had mentioned nieces, that she had read his mother's books to her nieces; did he sound stupid?

But she did not notice, or did not mind. "Yes," she said. He could hear her smile in her voice as her palm came to rest on his knee. "Two little girls."

He swallowed, nervous, still too afraid to trust her. But the darkness made him brave. "My sister is pregnant," he said softly. "I'm worried that I hate her for it. A few months ago I got divorced."

Why had he said it? He was sure she would curl away from him now, recoiling as if from a trap.

But she didn't. Instead she kissed him again, her soft mouth sinking into his startled lips. Before he had tasted his fill, she moved away, then returned suddenly, elsewhere, tracing his ear with her lips as his own mouth fumbled for hers in his blindness, gulping at the warm air.

"I hated my brother, too, before my first niece was born," she said. "I felt terrible about it." He marveled in the dark. How did she know exactly what to say? Her voice hung in the air, a delicate feather he was afraid to touch. "He was always talking about the baby, the baby, the baby, and I had to pretend to be excited. He was just so smug about it, so damn proud of himself, like no one in the whole world had ever had a baby before. I could've hit him. But everything changes when the baby comes." Her voice rose, floating higher, until he felt her breath along his neck. "It doesn't matter that the baby isn't yours. It's still part of you, and it means absolutely everything to you. You would gladly die for that child. And everything else just disappears."

He listened, and his whole body felt lighter, weightless. He buried his fingers in her hair and kissed the crown of her forehead, where silk sprouted from skin. They held each other for many long moments before he was able to speak. She had grown restless; the tight warm curl of her body shifted at his side. Already she was moving away. "I need to see you again," he said.

She rocked gently away from him, her legs—ah, her legs, bare legs beneath her skirt, should he have touched them? should he have tried? but no, he had waited out of hope—bumping his own knees as her head and neck rose between his hands, parting his hands until they fell to her shoulders. She was kneeling beside him, he could feel, slowly, reluctantly rising from the ground.

"After you return the painting," she said, her voice slicing the darkness. "Either bring it back or send it back. Find a post office somewhere, make up a return address. No one will know, I promise. I'm afraid to see you again before that. But after that, yes."

The painting. He had forgotten. But he wasn't going to return it, never; didn't she understand that? He remembered now that he and his sister had made a plan, a long time ago, they had already decided, yes, his sister was going to—but—

"Promise me you'll come back and find me then," she said. Now it was she whose hands were buried in his hair, she who held his skull between her fingertips, sculpting his mind. "I don't believe people so easily anymore," her blind voice whispered. "I won't go chasing after you. I need you to promise that you'll come back and find me."

He breathed in, exulting. "I will," he said, then raised his fingers to her face. "But only if you promise not to leave just yet."

She laughed, but did not promise. Instead she pressed her mouth to his, and he breathed her in, trust pouring back into his silent ribs, into the cage that held his heart.

15

THE SAGES once taught that three things hang above a person's head every day of his life: an eye that sees, and an ear that hears, and a book in which all of the person's deeds are recorded. Chagall and Der Nister had learned this as children, forced to repeat and memorize it word by word. At the time, they had laughed. But now, as they reached middle age, only Der Nister remembered it.

The eye above Chagall saw all of the paintings that he created and displayed from 1948 onward as his fame crested toward the sky. It saw the major retrospective in New York, the one in Chicago, the one in Paris, the big exhibition of new works in Amsterdam, the bigger one in London, the first prize the artist received at the Biennale in Venice. It saw the windows he made for churches around the world, and it watched as his flying lovers soared to the top of the Paris opera house. The eye also saw Chagall fall in love with his married British housekeeper, saw the child that he had with her, saw him move with his new unofficial family to a castlelike home in France, and then saw the woman and their child abandon him. The ear listened to Chagall's hundreds of interviews with magazines and newspapers around the globe, his dozens of lectures delivered in the world's most prestigious auditoriums, his endless greetings to every Matisse and Picasso who graced his path. And then, as each of the Yiddish writers and artists he had known in Russia disappeared one by one—Shloyme Mikhoels,

Itsik Fefer, Dovid Hofshteyn, Peretz Markish, Dovid Bergelson, Leyb Kvitko, and nearly every person who had ever taught at the Jewish Boys' Colony in Malakhovka—the book recorded his silence. Only sometimes, on sleepless nights, did the artist notice.

But Der Nister was constantly aware of the eye and the ear. He couldn't help it. When he returned to Moscow from Tashkent after the war, he could feel the eye that sees, watching his every move. And as for the ear that hears, Der Nister was beginning to suspect that his apartment had been bugged.

Nearly all of the other Yiddish writers had vanished, Der Nister knew. Since 1948, the Soviet secret police had begun collecting them one by one as if trying to assemble a living encyclopedia of Yiddish literature, arranging them alphabetically in their prison cells and then lining them up by library catalogue number in front of the firing squad. Der Nister could look through his hidden shelves of recently banned books by all the writers he and Chagall had known and rattle off the dates when each one had been arrested. Anyone with the slightest talent was already in jail. Der Nister imagined Lefortovo Prison in Moscow as a kind of artists' café. After a while he felt insulted not to have been invited.

He was almost finished with Volume Three of *The Family Crisis*, and he had never been more tired. His sixtieth birthday had passed; almost everything had changed. He had married again, after the long year of mourning in Tashkent. Lina was another refugee, another bereft parent, stripped of her own daughter and standing naked before him. They lay together in Der Nister's frigid room in Moscow and embraced in the love of last resort, to keep out the cold. Afterward, Der Nister would sit up in their narrow bed in the darkness and see their dead daughters sleeping at their feet.

But even more had changed for the family in Der Nister's book. Luzi, the brother who had joined the "dead Hasidim"—the religious sect of followers of Nachman of Bratslav—had become fanatically devoted to his ideological cult as the novel progressed, more and more convinced that his way was the only way of thinking, the only way of living. The sanest brother, Moyshe, had watched his own family business and sensible world collapse along with his own health and his own life, while the fanatical ideologues who wore him into the ground escaped unscathed. As of the end of Volume Two, things looked even bleaker for Moyshe's equally sensible grandson Mayerl, who was to be the subject of the forthcoming Volume Three. At some point the censors seemed to get the hint, because the magazine that had serially published the first two volumes suddenly began to reject Der Nister's work. And so he began to hide it.

He hid pages everywhere. Unpublished chapters lined his mattress, lay hammered beneath his floorboards, crinkled underneath his rug. Lina worried for him, but she was afraid to speak too loudly about it. The ear was listening, the eye was watching, and Der Nister became fanatical about cheap forms of disguise. He inscribed his name on each page in a different cipher, some of his own devising and some borrowed from the ones he remembered ancient rabbis using in the books he had studied as a child. He shifted each of the four Hebrew letters of NiSTeR over by one, the way some Hebrew manuscripts did; when the last two new letters spelled the Hebrew word for "fire," he felt nervous, edging too close to meaning. So he used other codes. Sometimes he signed off with the word "Priest" in Russian or in Yiddish, since his real last name was Kahanovitch and his ancestors had been priests in the temple in Jerusalem. When he felt brave, he inscribed his name as "Father of Hodele, may her memory be blessed." Other times, he hid behind the numerical equivalents of the letters of his name—50 for the *nun*, 60 for the *somekh*, 400 for the *tof*, and 200 for the *reysh*—written like his name from right to left. It was nothing more than a game, and he knew it. But perhaps games weren't worthless. On occasion he remembered his old housemate Chagall's fondness for games—for plays on words, for the little tricks and puns that he would put into each of his paintings. Surely, Der Nister reasoned, the artist had done something right. After all, he had lived to middle age, he was still painting, and he wasn't in jail.

But Lina was furious about the papers. She pulled them out in sheaves from inside the tattered sofa cushions, scraped them out from between the floorboards, and scolded her new husband as if he were the daughter she had lost.

"What is the point of this?" she whispered one night as she retrieved a new handful of papers from inside her pillowcase. They had just gone to bed, and he groaned softly beside her. Lately they were both aware of the ear suspended above them, and they always whispered. Sometimes they wrote notes to each other, which Der Nister preferred. He had almost forgotten the sound of her real voice.

He didn't answer her. Instead he turned on his back, staring at the dirty arched ceiling of their tiny alcove room, where water sometimes leaked from the apartment above.

"Do you think they're children, that they're not going to find these?" Lina hissed. "Are you aware that you've gone completely mad?"

"Yes," he murmured. Their old-fashioned room, he suddenly thought, reminded him of the way he had once pictured the Cave of Machpelah from the Bible when he was a child—the very first piece of property Abraham had ever owned in the Promised Land. The tomb of the patriarchs. He drew the blanket up around his thin body and shivered.

Lina snorted, and then held the papers in front of his face as he lay on his back. He caught a glimpse of the beginning of a chapter, a sentence about his character Mayerl. He was reading down to the next sentence just as Lina threw the papers into the air. Der Nister watched as little pieces of his unpublished book fluttered up and then floated down from the dripping ceiling.

Lina brushed them off the bed, and Der Nister sat up to watch them land on the dirty floor. "If you want these to last longer than you will, stash them somewhere else," she whispered. "Sometimes I think you want to be caught."

She put out the light and rolled over in the bed, but it was too narrow for her to move far from him. He turned toward her without intending to, observing the silhouette of her back in the dark as she pretended to sleep. She was only in her forties, much younger than he, and less hardened. Sometimes as he lay in bed with her, he remembered the story from the Bible of Avishag the Shunamite, the young concubine given to King David in his old age, to warm his bones. He reached over and gathered her hair between his fingers, and her body shuddered. She turned and curled toward him, and for a brief moment he wondered whether what he felt for her was real, or whether it was just a shadow of a memory—whether the thin hair he brushed away from her forehead was really hers, or whether it became something different in his hands, someone else's. In the dark his fingertips felt her damp cheeks. "Please, find somewhere to put them, for me," she whispered. "I can't lose someone else."

She folded her arms around him, and his bare stomach pressed against her empty womb. As they drifted toward sleep, Der Nister could feel their daughters pushing them toward each other, forcing them into one another's nightmares.

———

ONE NIGHT AFTER almost everyone had disappeared, Der Nister went to a performance at the Moscow State Jewish Theater. The play was stupid, a meaningless melodrama with a tacked-on final monologue about the bright new hope of the future. But the theater itself was a room dropped from paradise. Every wall of the auditorium was covered by enormous canvas murals, painted by Marc Chagall.

Der Nister had seen the murals before, of course. Chagall's studies for them had filled the house they had shared in Malakhovka. And he had seen them before in the theater, too. There were seven of them, stretched out on canvases that hung on the bare walls and surrounded the audience: a vast landscape of dancing figures (including theater director Shloyme Mikhoels, who had just been killed in an alleged traffic accident) that covered the entire left side of the room; a smaller abstract piece on the back wall; a frieze of a wedding banquet along the top of the right wall—and then, between the right wall's windows, four tall playful portraits of each of four arts: music, dance, theater, and literature. Watching the murals was far more interesting than watching the play.

Der Nister had a seat against the auditorium's right wall, and he spent the intermission and the play's brighter scenes gazing up at the mural representing literature, the one that towered beside his head. It was of a scribe writing on a yellow scroll against a deep blue background; the scroll itself was blank, and the man in the picture was even blanker: pure white from head to foot, as if the writer were in the process of being unpainted, vanishing, turning into a ghost. In the background was a high green hill, with a little man carrying a lectern with a few Hebrew letters written on its base. Der Nister noticed with a sudden shiver that the letters spelled the beginning of his name. In the semidarkness of the theater, he reached up and touched the can-

vas of the painting, feeling the firm wooden struts beneath it. Idly fidgeting with its edge, he was surprised when he accidentally lifted it,
shifting the bottom half of the canvas just a hair's breadth away from
the wall. And he went home with an idea.

The following week, he went to the theater again, reserving himself
a seat near the literature mural for the evening's performance. But
before leaving for the theater on the night of the show, he loosened
one of the floorboards in his tiny room and uncovered a small pile of
manuscript pages. It was a draft of the first chapter of Volume Three.
He rolled the papers into the sleeve of his thin sweater, put on his coat,
and went to the theater. The play was yet another pedantic melodrama, this time with music, and he was the only person in his row of
seats. When the house lights went down, he carefully slipped his fingers underneath the literature mural's wooden frame and slid a few of
his manuscript pages up and underneath it, until they were tucked into
the frame from behind. He repeated this process page by page, subtly,
working mostly between the play's scenes, when the room was bathed
in total darkness. By intermission, he had safely hidden all of Chapter
One. No one had noticed.

He returned every week after that. He had been a friend of
Mikhoels, and the people at the box office knew him; they never made
him pay. He sat through one melodrama after another, rotating his seat
around the theater until he had deposited all the papers from his apartment into the murals on the walls. Each time a page of the manuscript
disappeared behind the canvas, he knew he would never see it again.
But in the darkened theater, he felt happy. It was like mailing a letter
to the next world. There were rumors that the theater would shut down
soon, but Der Nister knew that even if it did, the murals wouldn't vanish so easily. Thanks to his old housemate's current fame, they were
worth far too much.

———

IT WAS EARLY 1949, wintertime, and when he came home from his
last trip to the theater, Lina knew what he had done. He met her in
their bed, the only warm place in their single room. The apartment
had become bare and flat, stripped of all its hidden scraps of paper
insulation, and Der Nister wondered if the two of them hadn't become

bare and flat, too, their clothes and their flesh pared down until they had to hide under the covers like children, skinny and raw. He had earned almost nothing in the past month, and she had barely earned more; there was nothing to eat. It was too early to go to bed, but Der Nister was cold. In their hunger they clutched each other beneath their worn blanket, holding all they had left.

"Sorele had beautiful legs," Lina whispered to him in the dark. Sometimes, for no reason and for every reason, she liked to talk about her daughter. "A dancer's legs. Sometimes I wonder about the man she would have made happy."

Der Nister gulped at the cold air in the dark, tracing a finger along Lina's cracked lips. He wanted to say something about Hodele, but he was afraid of taking her name in vain. "I once met a boy my daughter's age who buried himself alive," he said.

Lina was silent, but his fingers felt her lips part, and then felt warm startled breath seeping between them. "I met him in the orphanage in Malakhovka, where I used to teach," Der Nister continued in a whisper. He felt the curl of her nostrils in his palm, breath warming his hands. "Someone had found him half buried, in an open grave. That was twenty-nine years ago," he finished. The number astonished him. Hodele would be thirty-five now, he thought, almost thirty-six—the same age he had been when he taught at Malakhovka, when they had lived above Chagall, when he had met the boy who had buried himself alive.

"Do you think he's still living?" Lina asked.

Der Nister stared at the darkness. "Do you think I'm still living?"

Lina didn't answer. They both knew, now, despite the hidden papers, how few nights he had left. He groped at her body like a blind man, his fingertips memorizing her, cataloguing each curve and wrinkle of her weary skin. Lina was tired. Her limbs drooped under his. He moved his hands across her breasts, her hair, her face, until his finger landed in the deep dent above her lips, just below her nose. The impression of an angel. She exhaled beneath his finger, the steady breath of one lost to dreams.

"Lina," he whispered. In the colorless darkness, he had remembered the question Chagall had once asked him, the one that tormented him still. "Do you think your daughter meant something?" he asked.

The question had tortured Der Nister for years. But Lina simply let out a puff of air in the dent below her nose.

"She meant everything," she said. And then she fell asleep.

———————

THEY CAME FOR Der Nister the following night.

Der Nister was surprised by how ordinary it was, how unceremoniously shabby. In his nightmares he had pictured armies of men breaking down his door in the middle of the night, waving flags and firing shots through the ceiling. But instead the door simply opened, early in the evening, without a knock, and two men in dark suits stepped into his home. One pulled out a piece of paper, looked at Der Nister, and began to read.

"Pinkhas Mendelevitch Kahanovitch," he recited. "You are under arrest for treason under Article 64-A of the Soviet Criminal Code, for your role in the Zionist conspiracy to destroy the Soviet state."

It was the usual bogus charge, the same one he had heard reported by the other vanished writers' wives. Hearing it almost bored him. Lina had promised him that she would retain her dignity, but apparently she had forgotten. She let out a wail and doubled over with her back to the wall, convulsed by sobs.

Der Nister squeezed her hand before one of the agents grabbed him by the arm, pulling him away from her. But he felt strangely calm, calmer than he had ever felt before. For the first time in years, he had nothing to hide.

"I'm happy that you've come," he said. "I had wondered what was taking you so long."

The men looked startled. They glanced at each other quickly, until one of them grunted. "We need to collect everything here, all of your documents and manuscripts," the first one said, reciting protocol. "Hand them over."

Der Nister smiled. He glanced at Lina, who had looked up from her tears. "Forgive me, gentlemen," he said. "That matter is no concern of yours. I didn't write them for you, and my manuscripts remain in a safe place."

One of the agents kicked him, and he fell to his knees. But the other stuck out a heel, catching Der Nister before his face hit the floor.

While Der Nister knelt on the floorboards, the second agent began to look around the bare room. He opened the closet and rooted through drawers, pitching the clothes onto the floor. Der Nister watched the first agent smile as Lina's bras and underpants flew across the room, but didn't allow himself to flinch. The second agent kicked at the floorboards, his feet tapping at them like a dancer's before he pried up the hollow-sounding ones, where he found nothing but dust. He looked at the bed and the battered sofa, then opened his dark briefcase and took out a foot-long metal knife, which he inserted into the mattress. Der Nister watched from where he knelt on the floor as the man dissected the mattress piece by piece, leaving it in shreds, and then did the same to the sofa. For a moment he wondered where Lina would sleep. Then he realized the answer: on the floor, as a mourner. But she would survive, he knew as he saw her streaked face for the very last time. She had done this before.

While he was still in his own home, Lina filled the space, her wails crowding the air of the room as the two men chained his arms back and forced him out the door. But now, as the door clicked closed behind him, Der Nister looked up from the floor and saw Hodele standing in the stairwell, waiting for him.

She looked older than the last time he had seen her—closer to thirty-five, and not nearly as thin. She wore a bright red dress that he had never seen before, and her black hair rippled along her ears and neck. Her face was luminous. She stood just a few steps ahead of him, so close that he could have touched her, but his arms were pinned at his back. He had dragged his legs earlier, making the agents pull him from the room, but now he stood straight, transfixed, hurrying forward to reach her. But she kept stepping backward, still smiling at him, moving down the stairs always just a few steps beyond his reach. When they arrived at the street, her red dress and her black hair flew high behind her in the cold wind. But then the men threw him into the back of a small truck, and his head slammed into the metal floor as they bolted him inside.

The darkness was total, pooling around him like thick black ink. His bruised sixty-three-year-old body sank into the shadows, knocked unconscious. In the delirium that followed as the truck lurched into motion, Der Nister watched as Hodele unbolted the door. Moonlight

poured into the darkness the way it did in his old housemate's paintings, changing the colors of his hands and face until he glowed green
and purple and blue. Hodele unfurled a long scroll covered with
words, latching one end to the truck's open door and then casting the
rest of it up into the air until it caught hold of a cloud, stretching out
before them. And then she took her father by the hand and flew with
him, crossing the paper bridge he had built from the earth to the sky.

1 6

MY LAST DAY IN PARADISE
by Rosalie Ziskind

The days I spent in paradise were the most beautiful days of my life. Even today, my heart flutters a bit and tears come to my eyes when I remember that joyful time. I often close my eyes and relive those years which will never return. In those dreaming moments I even forget how my wings were shorn off before I left that other world, and I spread out my arms and try to fly. It's only when I fall on the floor in pain that I remember that I only had wings in paradise. Why did I leave, you might ask, if I was so happy there? Well, I'll tell you one thing: it wasn't up to me.

On the day I found out that I was going to be removed from paradise, I was sitting under a paradise tree listening to the singing of the paradise canaries. If you think the singing of those canaries is like the canaries on earth, you couldn't be more wrong. I would tell you what their singing is like, but you can't describe singing like that in human language. It was twilight. My teacher, an angel with heavyset dark gray wings, had disappeared for the day, and the students had all run off. Most went to play angelic games, but I went to sit under my tree, to listen to the canaries and to chat with the paradise butterflies. If you think those butterflies are like the butterflies on earth, you're quite mistaken. The truth is, I can't even describe what colors they were, because you don't have colors like those outside of paradise.

As I lay there under the tree, I suddenly heard a familiar voice calling my name: "Sammy! Sammy!"

I looked up and saw my friend Pissant—or so he was called because he was so small, a little angel who fluttered over me with his tiny wings.

"What's going on, Pissant?" I asked.

Pissant raised his wing and spoke to me from underneath it. "Sammy, it's bad. I heard that you're going to be born."

My heart thumped in my chest. "What are you talking about, Pissant? Who told you that?"

Pissant told me that he was flying by the paradise bar when he spotted Simon, the biggest drunk of all the angels, and overheard him muttering to himself. "I saw that he was annoyed," Pissant said. "He had just gotten the message that he has to bring you down to earth. It's his job to smack you on the nose right before you're born so that you forget all this—paradise, everything you've learned here, and even me! You won't even remember your best friend Pissant!" And Pissant started to cry.

"Don't cry, Pissant," I said. "All you heard was a drunk old angel in a bar. If he tries to bring me to earth, I'll smack his nose before he smacks mine."

"You know how Simon is," Pissant cried, still sobbing. "He's a beast, a murderer!"

I knew that Pissant was right. Everyone was afraid of Simon. All of the other angels were too kind. He was the only one willing to bring us down to earth to be born, and smack us on the nose to make us forget our paradise. Every time you see a dent below someone's nose on earth, it's Simon's fault. And whenever you see someone on earth with a pug nose, you can be sure Simon smacked him even harder than most. "What can I do?" I asked.

"Nothing," Pissant sobbed. "Your fate is sealed. You'll forget everything. Just don't cry, because if you do, he'll hit you so hard you'll be born noseless." Then, suddenly, he stopped crying and had a twinkle in his eye. "Wait, Sammy, I have an idea."

"What?" I asked.

He took a piece of clay out of his pocket. "Put this on your face," he said, "on your nose and right below it. When Simon comes, he'll be so drunk that he won't notice it's not your real nose. He'll smack the clay, and then you'll be born without forgetting anything." He put the clay in my hand. "Go meet him at the bar yourself. It will be easier to trick him if he doesn't take you by surprise."

I took the clay and flew with Pissant—our last flight over paradise—until I reached his home and said goodbye. "Whatever happens, don't forget me," Pissant sobbed. "Promise me that wherever you go on earth, you'll remember that somewhere in paradise, your best friend Pissant is thinking of you." Pissant always was a crybaby. As for me, I was just lucky that the wind blew by and wiped away my tears as I flew to meet Simon.

When I arrived, Simon was sitting at the bar as usual. His face was almost as red as his beard. I stood at the door for a long time before I found the courage to go inside. "Hello, Simon!" I called, my voice shaking.

Simon saw me and tried to stand and greet me, but he had drunk so much that his wings were twisted together and he fell over. I went to him and straightened out his wings. Though he couldn't stand straight, unfortunately he could fly. And what's worse, his head was clear enough to know why I had come.

"Good, you're here. Let's go," he grumbled. And before I could say another word, he had taken me under his wing and began flying me to the border between the two worlds.

Don't think it was easy. Simon was dead drunk, and he kept losing his way. At first we flew for three hours and wound up right where we'd started. Not only that, but it was a dark night in paradise and Simon had forgotten his flashlight at the bar, so we were flying blind. In the dark we crashed into the angel of dreams, who was just beginning his nightly trip to earth, and we damaged one of his wings. That night everyone on earth slept without dreams. I thought of Pissant, safe in his bed in paradise, and wanted to cry. But I didn't, because I remembered what Pissant had told me—that Simon hated tears.

When we finally reached the border, the winds were freezing. "Ugh, what cold," Simon muttered, fluttering his wings. But he was still pretty unsteady, wobbling in the air. "All right, Sammy, it's time to throw you down below!" he growled, and put me down on the very last acre of paradise. At that moment, he became a bit giddy, and gave me a pinch on the cheek. "You're a great guy, Sammy. A great guy. Now stand on one foot and recite for me everything you've learned in paradise."

I did as I was told. When I finally finished, he took out an enormous pair of scissors, turned me around, and cut off my wings. I was far too nervous to cry.

"Okay, kid," he bellowed, "now let's see that snout of yours and get this over with quick."

But while Simon was busy cutting off my wings, I had already placed the clay nose onto my face. He was so tipsy that he didn't even notice.

"Simon, don't hit me too hard, please!" I begged. I guess he was listening, because he gave me just a little tap. I almost didn't feel it.

"Now scat!" he said.

For the last time I looked behind me, and saw all of paradise, the whole scene bathed in golden light. I looked at my wings for one last time, lying on the last acre of paradise.

"Goodbye, Simon!" I said to the angel with the twisted wings, and fell to the earth. He looked at me as I fell, shocked, but it was too late. I had remembered his name.

And to this day, I still remember everything.

It used to be Sara's favorite book, this little watercolor treasure her mother had created. When *My Last Day in Paradise* was published (long ago, when Sara was still in college, counting the days between Leonid's visits, days that might as well not have been days for all they mattered to her), Sara remembered thinking that she would someday read it to herself when she was pregnant. She even imagined reading it to her children. But now that the time had actually come—her pregnancy still invisible, barely a shadowed hint on her imperceptibly radiant cheek—she read the book and was simply horrified. She knew she was supposed to be happy, and in rare moments she was. But late at night, waiting for Leonid to finish putting in his long hours at work, and then even later, lying beside him, holding him, making love to him (for how much longer?), turning out the lights and trying to sleep beside him, she was paralyzed by fear.

Sheer terror. Sometimes she thought of the person inside her, the not-yet person, and felt herself shudder at the thought that it was a separate person, a person she didn't know and didn't trust, and therefore someone who might tear her apart, before birth or after. The person could gnaw through her body too early and die. Or the person could wait silently inside her until the appointed hour, but then be born ghastly, distorted, without hands, without eyes, without legs. Or worse, he could be born perfect, and then, through some error she would never perceive, grow up to destroy someone else's life—for there are thousands of ways to destroy someone's life, Sara knew, but to improve someone's life, there are so few, so few! Or worse, he could be a she, and suffer as she had, forced to drag the future with her in her body, to wait for the world to come. When she thought of it she shook with fear.

And for good reasons, she was beginning to think. When she saw people with babies on the streets, she never once saw any of the parents smiling. Instead they grimaced. Not just frowned, but actually grimaced, bracing their faces and their babies as they stormed into stores and back out into a day so beautiful that the sun laughed out loud at the tight lines on their faces. Even the babies themselves looked exhausted, burned out. They squinted out of their baby seats like elderly men, shriveled and bald, three months old and already bored by the world. She kept hoping that with her baby it would be different. Late at night, though, as she lay next to the immense, slumbering Leonid—a sleeping giant, a solid rock that trembled with each breath like a shifting tectonic plate, slow and inevitable and certain, as if he slept without dreams—she realized that she didn't believe it. And then she would struggle not to cry until Leonid heard her thinking and woke up.

"Are you worrying about the baby?" he asked her in the dark. He slurred his words the way he used to back in high school, his accent like a cage around his tongue. She remembered walking home with him and Ben from the high school once, not long after they had met. Ben had offered to walk Leonid home—a gesture of goodwill, helping Leonid carry his things while his arm was still in the cast—and Sara had joined them. But when they reached the deserted path behind Leonid's building, Ben had stammered that he had left a book at school, and ran back to get it. Sara and Leonid were alone. And then Leonid, previously sullen and silent, suddenly started talking to Sara in that slurred voice, nonstop, words tumbling out of his mouth in random order, without articles or conjunctions or the past tense: about Chernobyl, about his school there, about his teachers, about his friends, about the junior boxing club where he had almost won the championship, about the nuclear meltdown, about fleeing the city, about the vast industrial warehouse where they stayed for endless days with thousands of strangers, sleeping on concrete and waiting in lines for hours to use the outdoor toilets and icy showers while they waited for the poison to go away, about his aunt's illness which his mother was sure was from the poison, about the same aunt's death which his mother was sure was from the poison, about his father and mother screaming at each other in the warehouse in front of everyone—about how his father called his mother a fat cow with no imagination and his mother screamed that he was a male whore who did nothing but sleep with teenage girls and did he really honestly think she didn't know about Katya because the whole world knew about Katya and there was hardly a person in their communal apartment who hadn't heard every single groan that that little slut let out every time his "unimaginative" fat cow of a wife of eighteen years was out teaching her night class for adults and actually making something of her life, which is what people do who don't feel the need to have an "imagination," and if he was stupid enough to think that Lenya didn't know about his little slut then he might as well be a cow himself for all he knew about children, because children see everything, and maybe he could hide his little slut from all his "imaginative" friends at work but no one can hide from a child, and it had deeply offended Leonid to be considered a child, particularly since he in fact did not know about Katya at all and this was the first time he had ever heard of her, and he adored his father and quickly decided that it was a lie and that his mother was a liar and a fraud and a fat cow like his father had said, and he therefore had sat silently raging at his mother while wrapped in a dirty government-issued blanket on the cold bare concrete floor in the giant industrial warehouse in front of thousands of other meltdown refugees who had begun watching the fight like it was a boxing match, cheering for one side or another while the poison continued to quietly leach its way into their homes hundreds of miles away—and then about returning to the city, months later, about going back to all the old things like his school (which had itself moved to a warehouse on the far end of the city) and his friends and his junior boxing club and pretending that everything was the same even though everything had changed, about being afraid, about being afraid to eat anything, about losing weight because he was afraid to eat anything, about being afraid to put on his clothes or brush his teeth or even to bathe because everything might have been poisoned, about starting to think that everything really had been poisoned and not just what the government said had been poisoned, about finding his father and Katya making love in his parents' bed the night he returned from losing the championship (which his father had profusely apologized for being unable to attend) and knowing for certain that everything had been poisoned, about punching his father, about his father punching him back, twice as hard, many times, his father pinning him to the floor and pummeling him and then slapping the floor and counting like a referee while Leonid jerked in and out of consciousness, one, two, three, ten, about how he was a whole lot bigger now and if his father were here he could easily destroy him, absolutely destroy him, tear him into pieces (exactly as he was now destroying the already frayed edge of his canvas sling, the enormous fingers of his good left hand shredding tiny pieces of it over his right hand's shriveled knuckles), but he was fifteen already and life wasn't long enough, because what do you end up with when you fight someone, usually nothing, since you never know when someone who looks like a little weakling might actually be wearing a steel brace under his clothes and then all you get for it is a broken hand, so maybe it was time to stop fighting, and to stop being afraid. Sara listened and saw the giant in front of her shrinking down in her mind from a giant to a person, the way her father used to do when he would take off his prosthesis at the end of the day. "You took the words right out of my mouth," she finally said. Then Leonid smiled at her, and asked, "Can I put them back?" She wasn't sure what he meant until an instant later, when he leaned his enormous body toward her, cast and all, and slipped his tongue between her lips.

"You're worrying about the baby. I can tell," he said.

"No," Sara lied in the dark.

She felt Leonid's arm drift across her breasts. "It will be wonderful," he said. "It's different when it's your child."

That was what her mother would have said, of course: "It's different when it's your child." Yes, Sara was beginning to think. Very different. It's much worse.

But Sara was thinking of other things, too, now, as she lay in Leonid's arms. She thought of the Chagall painting Ben had brought at last to her apartment, and how he had told her in a rush of words about the woman at the museum and about the numbers underneath the canvas. Sara and Ben had delicately detached the canvas from the lower right corner of the frame until the numbers appeared, as if formed from a void. The numbers slithered through her thoughts along with the shadow of a person in her womb, blending in her mind with the cryptic columns from her medical reports: the baby's heart rate, the baby's growth rate, the codes imprinted on the baby's genes.

She turned in the bed beside the mountainous Leonid, and kept thinking. She thought of the painting she had bought at an antique shop earlier that day, identical in size and age to the Chagall, and of how she had found a book called *The Art Forger's Handbook* at a used book store, and of how she had followed the book's advice and scrubbed the surface of the other painting with steel wool and dipped it in bleach until it was burnished and blank. She thought of how afraid she had been that her apartment would be searched, or that her mother's house would be searched, and of how Leonid had given her the keys to his mother's apartment in New Jersey, since his mother had gone to Russia for the week—and then she thought of how Leonid wasn't worried at all, was never worried about anything, not even the baby, because ever since he had met her when he was fifteen years old, he had decided to stop being afraid. And she thought, too, of the papers from the inside of the painting, the ones the woman from the museum had given to Ben—the ones he had mentioned, but hadn't shown her. *Pay attention to the shape of the dents in the canvas on the original*, he had muttered, all business. *You can replicate them by stuffing some paper into the frame to make it sag when you're done. Don't forget, or they'll notice. And whatever you do, don't forget the numbers. The numbers are the most important part.* And then Sara thought of how strange Ben had seemed when he had given her the painting: how reluctant to talk, how hurried, how preoccupied, how distracted, how ashamed. Sara always knew when her twin brother was in love.

"Sara, stop thinking," Leonid said. He ran his fingers through her hair in the dark, and then wrapped his arms around her, resting his hand on her belly as he cupped the shadow of a future person in the palm of his giant hand. "Please, stop thinking and sleep."

Near dawn, she did.

————

COLOR, COLOR, BOLD, loud colors, colors that sang, colors that hummed, colors that screamed, colors that sobbed, or more often than anything else, colors that seethed, angry, bitter, unlooked at, unnoticed, darkening not from age but from loneliness, from knowing that they do not exist without someone to see them—Sara did not merely see them, but heard them, smelled them, tasted them, touched them. But when she started painting the Chagall in the newspaper-covered studio she had created in her mother-in-law's kitchen—Leonid's mother would never know, and Ben and Leonid had reasoned that hers was one address that the police would never trace—she found painting, for the first time, painful. She began with the meaningless numbers, detaching the canvas in exactly the right place and copying the shape of them exactly, down to the wisps of brushstrokes that grew from them like hairs. But she had to wait for the numbers to dry before she could reattach the canvas and continue, and the morning sickness she had staved off earlier had returned with the smell of the paint. She rushed to the bathroom and tried to vomit, but nothing came out. Instead she wandered into her mother-in-law's bedroom and lay down on the bed, trying to feel better, staring at the blank white ceiling as though it were a canvas. But she was still afraid.

Long ago, in a dream, Sara had climbed up a ladder into the night sky. It was the night of the Day of Atonement. She was twelve years old, fasting for the first time—and for the first time watching her hair turn from straight to curly, her body from straight to curved. She had worried that she would already be hungry and thirsty lying in bed that night, but she wasn't. Instead she felt as light as a leaf driven by the wind, as if the world had released her. In her dream that night she ascended the ladder, climbing higher and higher until she reached a door that stood between the stars. She knocked, but no one answered. She knocked again, and still there was no response. But the third time that she knocked, dipping her feet into the night sky, the door opened and she found herself standing in an artists' studio.

It wasn't at all like her parents' studio, with its neat piles of paper, or even like the art room at school, though in one corner there were large slabs of clay. Instead it was a vast workshop with dark wooden floors and walls, filled with all kinds of equipment—potter's wheels, anvils, kilns, looms. Sparks jumped in the air. The equipment hummed in the room's buzzing space with speed, energy, power, urgency; the shuttle of the loom shot back and forth through the shifting threads, the heavy clank of glowing iron into solid metal and the tight taps of a chisel into stone rattled the air, bubbles of glass and clay grew and contracted in the heat as molten silver dripped like hot tears. The people working there were both men and women, most of them old, though one of them, kneading a slab of clay, was a man in his forties, a short, thin man with a bald head and something disturbingly familiar about his expression. All of the artists looked familiar, actually—not in the sense that she knew any of them, but there was something more comfortable about them than typical strangers. They noticed her and smiled, nodding quickly before returning to their work.

Sara moved into the room on delicate bare feet, not wanting to disturb them but fascinated to see what they were making. With soft steps she approached the bald man, who was engrossed in the mound of clay in front of him. She edged closer until she stood beside him, her eyes following his expert fingers as they nudged the clay into a face, a narrow face with a thin nose and narrow, anxious eyes. She watched the delicate fingernails scraping eyelids into existence, and then suddenly recognized the face. It was Ben.

Now Sara looked around the room in awe. There was her mother: her hair, eyes, nose, and mouth were woven into a long, detailed tapestry that a weaver was just now completing along the bottom of her chin. A few feet away, Ben appeared again, this time being freed from a block of marble, his heavy brow merging with his nose as his curved spine slowly announced itself, protruding amid chipped rock and dust. Her mother's features emerged once more from molten silver, a sheet of gleaming metal pooling into soft lips and narrow cheeks. And then she saw herself, taking form in the shape of blown bubbles of sculpted glass, her smooth child's body glowing and growing into a woman's before dissolving into her own reflection on its surface.

She stepped back toward the door, afraid, suddenly, that one of the works of art might see her, fully formed. But as she edged away, she saw her father enter the workshop through another door. Like the other artists, he wore a dirty apron, but the dirt on his was colorful, splashed with bright streaks of paint. He wore the same large glasses he had worn while he was alive, but he walked with two legs. When he at last squinted to look at her, it seemed to her that he wasn't seeing her, but someone else—or, perhaps, as if he weren't seeing who she actually was, but who she could be. He opened a wooden cabinet and took out a palette and paintbrush. Before she could wonder what he was going to paint, he approached her, still looking through her, the way she would later look at her own canvases before painting them. He dipped his brush in brown paint and raised it to her head, holding her shoulder with his free hand and brushing curls into her hair, his eyes focused on his subject as she leaned against the door. Then the door opened behind her and Sara plummeted to the earth, waking an instant before reaching the ground.

The next day, late in a long morning of fasting and prayer, came the memorial service for the dead. Sara watched as all the other children in the congregation, everyone but her and Ben, filed quickly out of the room, shooed away by their parents. With no one to mourn for, the other children had no reason to stay at the service; they were granted a recess from God. Sara watched them out the window as they raced each other into the parking lot on the bright fall day, playing under the rain of shining colored leaves.

"A *shvarts yor*," her mother said under her breath, "that you should have to stand here next to me."

A *shvarts yor*, Sara thought. A *black year*. A black year? And suddenly Sara had words to understand what she had been seeing all along: time.

It was true what Ben had often said, that Sara didn't remember things. But that was because for Sara it had become impossible to "remember" things, just as it was impossible to "predict" the future— impossible because there was nothing to remember or predict, but only things to see, a vast landscape of time spread out all around her, the months and years and days assembling and crowding her vision with colors. From that moment forward, Sara did not imagine the past, present, or future, but saw them. She stood among her days, assembling them around her like her mother and brother at the dinner table, and she watched them just as cautiously. Some were pale, grayish, and dull; some shimmered green in dim light; others throbbed red or flamed orange. But the last year was black, like her mother had said, and Sara entered it now, walking slowly past scattered minutes from the past and future that fluttered down from the trees of hours—moments of different colors, different shapes, different degrees of delicacy and softness against her cheeks—and stepping into the cave of a black year.

Inside that black year, the darkness was almost total. But there were nuances, subtleties, perceptible only to the trained eye that has learned to see time for what it really is. A black year comes in many shades. In places—near the entrance, yes, but also elsewhere, unexpectedly—the cave was filled with black smoke. Sara gagged as she moved through it, and sometimes found herself crawling on the floor to breathe, swallowing black mud as she pressed her lips to the ground. In these places she glanced up and saw the air burning in the darkness, a thick smothering smoke that coated her face and filled her brain until it was impossible to imagine light. But in other places the smoke dissipated, leaving a polished hard darkness like an onyx stone, alternately smooth and jagged under her fingers. Still elsewhere, as she proceeded through the year, the black shadows softened into something like pools of ink that squished as she moved through them, with even softer dark holes where she could sit and almost feel comforted, bathed in the soft black air. At some points bits of light leaked through—not directly, but vaguely, announcing their presence through the graying of the rock, the shift from black ink to graphite pencil shades. In those places she could stand, squinting among the shadows until she felt like she could walk for miles and no black year could hold her back. She would stride with shabby confidence across the pools of shadows until, without fail, her head would slam into a gray stalactite, and she would fall back into a dark black hole. But that was hardly the worst. In the deepest part of the cave (just past this point, Sara knew, there was an opening to the light—a small one, a narrow aperture that she could barely squeeze herself through, but an opening all the same) was the wide yawning mouth of the abyss. Sara knew it was there because during that year, she had seen it—blacker than black, not a black made from a mix of colors but a black made from the pure absence of light, a throat, a void. It was featureless, textureless, and worst of all, bottomless. If one fell into it, there was no end, not even laughter. And one could get dangerously close.

Of course, beyond the cave stood an entire world of years. Indigo years, yellow years, orange years, years that blossomed like roses and years that froze like snow and years that dissolved like sand, weeks that rooted themselves and grew and rose and towered out of the earth, and months and months of hard pebble days that bit into sensitive soles and callused them for good. There were times Sara could never have dreamed of—looming pink cliffs of seasons that had to be scaled on their faces or climbed on treacherous paths, roaring iridescent cataracts of entire decades thrown over the edge, vague yellow dunes of sleeping hours, sudden eclipses of nightmares. A few weeks were hard shining apples, or thick bread. One year, her first, was pure white milk. And there were tiny instants, fractions of a second—glances, touches, kisses, sounds, words—that flooded over the time around them, raging, surging with churning currents, and washing entire years away. Yet even these, if you rode their currents, often led into caves. Sara circumnavigated her lifetime and found that it had borders—not borders she could see, but borders she could perceive as she wandered each path through the seasons and found herself at another cavern of black years. She didn't know, of course, what these moments meant or how they might come to be—she often suspected, in fact, that the timescape wasn't pre-existent, but was brought into being by her presence, that each step she took determined the next, that perhaps the route that led up the side of a cliff was her own fault, that she might have taken a different path into a different kind of time, that, frighteningly, it was all up to her—but here they were, wordless and undeniable. And no one else was there. The time was hers alone.

Once Sara discovered how to see time, she rarely closed her eyes. As she grew older, everything, not merely time, but everything, turned into color, or light and shadow. Sounds were colors, flavors were colors, even the touch of her mother and Ben and Leonid—Ben's narrow arms around her, her mother's gentle shoulder above her head, Leonid's soft lips on her skin—were colors, shimmering colors, her brother a sturdy gray-green of a growing tree, the segue between gray

and green from a fluttering leaf to a branch, her mother a deep, resonating blue, like a square of sky caught in a windowpane just after
sundown, and Leonid was the gleam of light on water, a glimmering
orange reflection of a brightening sun. More often, though, Sara saw
shadows, deep shadows that she moved through from moment to
moment, astonished each time to see how little light there was in the
world. But after exploring the black years, Sara was no longer afraid of
the dark. She remembered once contemplating her own face in the
mirror on the eighth black day of the first black year, long ago, when
the mirrors were uncovered again. She had stared at her own eyes. Her
eyes were mostly white, of course, with a dark part in the middle,
divided by a small ring of blue. It seemed to her that a person should
see out of the white part of the eye, not the dark part. But that was not
how things were. It was only through the deep hole of darkness that she
could even perceive herself in the mirror.

Sara rose from her mother-in-law's bed and returned to the painting.
Steeling her stomach against another wave of nausea, she mechanically reattached the canvas to the frame. Then she placed the grayish
canvas on the folding easel she had brought with her and pulled open
the window blind. The canvas lit up instantly, a block of solid glowing
light. Sara saw it and stood transfixed, as if she herself were the primer
on the canvas—pallid and dull until suddenly made radiant by the
light of the world, a pure brilliant rectangle of light. So much beauty
in the world, and no one sees it! She stood for a long time looking at
the blank canvas, captivated by light and beauty. Yet when she finally
allowed herself to think of what needed to be done, she had to look
away. It was as if she had just been told to execute someone, and now
the condemned man stood before her, bending his neck across her
easel and waiting for her to slash it with her brush. But then she
thought of her brother, of her mother, of her father, and forced herself
to paint.

She worked without stopping even as the day began fading, darkening the colors, adjusting the lines. She examined the original constantly, afraid to trust the eye within her mind. With a delicate hand,
she constructed the layers of buildings on the dark silent street, the
arches of the windows, the street itself, the bricks and iron rods of the
fences. She painted in the planks of the wooden fence and the tight

strokes of the two narrow tombstones before it, sliding her brush along the shiny tin roofs and steeples. With a knifeful of white, she caked snow onto the road and the shiny rooftops, going over the surface again with a wide brush to create furrows in the paint. She let the texture of the canvas peek through the mottled surface of the round brown towers in the foreground, imitating precisely the stick-man shadow on the left and the cobweblike wheel on the right. She alternated thin umbers, stained even darker and moistened with linseed to swirl the surface, with thick grays and whites on the tree whose bare branches (she suddenly noticed) were twisted into the shape of the Hebrew letter that begins one of the names of God. Every brushstroke was exact, every color perfect. Sara was shocked by how easy it was. She felt preoccupied, in the literal sense—as if someone else had previously occupied her hand, and now that former occupier had returned, painting with her until the preoccupied canvas was occupied, effortlessly, by something new. But she also sensed that this was a false feeling, a moment that seemed to be solid ground but melted into quicksand underfoot. And she was right. The feeling vanished as soon as she began to paint the central subject: the man with the pack and cane floating behind the cross of the church steeple in the sky.

The man was the hardest part of all. His proportions were surreal, the length of his body covering several buildings on the street. The lines of his silhouetted profile were drawn as if he were standing straight, his pack sagging and his coat wrinkled as if by gravity, but he was oriented nearly facedown, almost horizontal over the town. Only the angle of his cane suggested that he knew he had been released from the earth. What made him so difficult to paint was the darkness. In the original, he floated entirely in shadow, backlit by an invisible sun on a bare yellow and white winter sky, with only the dimmest suggestions of colors, of an arm, a beard, an eye. The only feature with the slightest light in it was the man's hand, a set of fingers curled in perfect order around the cane planted in the earth. Sara squinted at that hand and suddenly saw—she didn't remember or imagine, she saw—her father's fingers curled tight around the handle of his crutches, pink knuckles in perfect rows except for the straightened index finger that he was now stretching toward her, about to press it into her soft eleven-year-old palm, until he disappeared.

After that, she couldn't paint anymore. She managed to complete the man, wisping in the white strands of his barely visible beard, but her movements were automatic. She was applying paint to canvas, but she wasn't painting. When she had at last finished and stepped back, it was obvious to her that she had failed. The man was an exact replica of the one in the original painting, down to the uneven edges of his cloak and the shadows of his face. But Sara could see that her man was a dead body, propped up by a rotting wooden cane. A floating corpse.

Biting her lower lip, she tried to ignore it. She set about decorating the back of the canvas with age marks, meticulously replicating the stains on the wooden canvas frame. She consulted *The Art Forger's Handbook* again and gently drenched the left edge of the canvas in water to reflect damage from damp storage conditions. At the very end, mixing the perfect proportions of yellow ochre and burnt sienna, she forged the signature of Marc Chagall.

Yet she had failed, and she knew it. When Sara made her own paintings, she always knew when they worked, because she could look at the picture and see that something had been found. Or not "found," exactly. More like *recovered*—as if she were suddenly recognizing something she had seen a long time ago, like a dream that returns in fragments: a phrase, a room, a feeling of intense fear, a smell. But here, in this dead town shadowed by a dead man, there was nothing to recover, nothing to find. There was scarcely anything to see. As she backed away from the canvas, she noticed the two tombstones in the foreground and realized whose they were.

She staggered to the bathroom and vomited, then crouched on the bathroom floor, gasping for breath. Surrounded by blank white tiles, she struggled against the tug of the not-yet child within her, pulling her into the future.

———

BEN ARRIVED THAT evening, too anxious to wait to see it, and Leonid came with him. Sara was still sitting on the bathroom floor when they knocked at the door. When she dragged herself up to let them in, she saw her husband and her twin brother standing in the doorway, a framed confluence of loves.

"You look—colorful," Leonid said, and reached for her. As she raised her arms to hug him, she saw what she thought he meant. Her skin was streaked with paint.

But Ben was more blunt. "Sara, you look sick. What's wrong?"

"It's the baby, that's all. I'm fine," she muttered. Even now the smells in the hallway were orange and green.

Leonid bent down to kiss her, and then sniffed at the air. "The fumes are probably bad. I should have thought of the fumes."

She shrugged, feeling ill. "I paint every day, and it doesn't bother me," she said weakly.

"This is worse for some reason," Leonid answered. He turned his head, sniffed again in the apartment's narrow hallway, and then wandered off toward the window. As he occupied himself with trying to pry the window open, Ben touched her paint-stained arm, glancing up to gauge Leonid's distance from his voice.

"I don't know if I can do this, Sara," he said softly.

"Why not?"

"Because—because of Erica. The one you met, from the museum," he stammered.

Sara watched as the red color that had drained from her own skin seeped into her brother's, dyeing his neck and ears. She held back a smile.

"She's going to think it's real," he said quickly, glancing across the room. Leonid had finally managed to throw the window open. "She—she believes me. I just don't know if I can—"

"You'll do it," Sara said as Leonid returned. "It's already done."

"I need to fix that window," Leonid announced as he returned to the twins. Sara watched with quiet awe as he casually inspected the room on his way back to them, testing the air conditioner and the closet doors. He had never lived in this apartment, but he had helped his mother buy it the previous year. His enormous shoulders were built for burdens. He reached the doorway and stooped before her, executing an absurdly sweeping mock bow. "Your highness, may we have the privilege of observing the masterpiece?"

"In the kitchen," she said, then edged along with them toward the little newspaper-covered room. She glanced at the real painting, and then at the canvas she had made. When she saw the forgery, she could hear the heavy thunk of dirty colors, the rattle and thud of the dead man and his cane. It was a joke, she realized. The two weren't even close.

"I'm sorry," she said. But then she turned around to see her husband's and brother's faces frozen in shock.

Ben was the first to find his voice. "What are you talking about, Sara?" he breathed. "I don't even know which one is real."

Leonid wasn't one for guessing. He moved closer to the canvases before Ben did, shifting his towering head until he could see the glare reflected off the forgery's wet paint. "It's incredible," he murmured. He turned and embraced her, nearly crushing her in his arms. "Absolutely incredible."

But Sara was watching her brother. Ben had stepped back again from the two canvases, his eyes wide. He turned his head from one painting to the other, and Sara found herself hoping that he would notice something missing from the one she had made — not something one could see, but something one could feel. When he opened his mouth to speak, Sara's heart thumped out a prayer. But it was pointless.

"It's perfect," Ben whispered. "Thank you."

He stepped toward her, his arms open, waiting for her. Sara let him wrap his arms around her and kiss her cheeks along with Leonid, again and again. But then she wrenched herself free. She turned around without a word and hurried back to the bathroom, closing the door tight behind her.

———

ON THE TRAIN home, she sat on a three-person bench seat between her brother and her husband, with her head leaning on Leonid's shoulder and Ben's hand resting on her painted palm and the future person inside her tugging at her gut. The train moved slowly, and the three of them had fallen into silence. Sara stared at the blank brown back of the seat in front of her and tried to picture how the painting had looked in her parents' house. To her horror she saw that her memories had changed colors, that her former life with her mother and father had paled into faded browns and blues. It was as if it had never really been. Everything left that she loved in the world was contained on this train, on this single seat. Leonid stroked her hair as she watched Ben gaze out the window, his nostrils stiff and his eyebrows tight as he wrestled with something she couldn't see.

In the lull of the train's rattle along the tracks, wedged between the only loves left, Sara slipped into sleep. In her dream, she was walking through a landscape filled not with objects but with colors, pure colors—not red and green and yellow and blue, but colors she had never seen before. When Leonid woke her up, she barely remembered the dream. Later, she struggled to fall asleep again in their bed, her body encircling the future and Leonid's body encircling hers, and she tried to recall what those colors had looked like. But she found that she couldn't even describe those colors to herself, because colors like those don't exist outside of paradise.

17

I T ASTOUNDED Boris Kulbak, thirty years after he had met Chagall and Der Nister and had guessed which one would survive and which one would disappear, when he turned out to be right. The Hidden One had vanished.

As Boris grew older, leaving Malakhovka for Moscow to live his adult life, he eventually read all of Der Nister's stories—stories so weird that he always needed to read them three times before he even could follow what was going on, but which haunted him for a long time afterward. Later, after he was married—after he was married the second time, that is, since he had woken up one morning less than a year after his first wedding to discover that his first bride had disappeared—he came across a very different work by the Hidden One. It was a trilogy, two volumes thus far, called *The Family Crisis*. The second volume was dedicated to the memory of "my child, my tragically perished daughter, Hodele. Born July 1913, in Zhitomir, died spring 1942, in Leningrad. May your father's broken heart be the tombstone on your lost grave." It was a weird book, weird because it seemed so utterly normal. Unlike most of the stories the Hidden One had written, which were full of angels and demons and objects that came to life, *The Family Crisis* was completely realistic. It was as if Chagall had suddenly started painting like Vermeer. Still, he read Volume One and Volume Two, and was eager to find out what would happen in Volume

Three. But in recent years the Hidden One had become more hidden, and Volume Three never surfaced. The story remained unfinished. Now it was already 1951, and no one had heard from the Hidden One since 1949.

He wasn't the only one to vanish into the abyss. Shloyme Mikhoels, the director of the State Jewish Theater that Chagall had so lavishly decorated, had been run down and killed in a traffic accident a few years before—which wouldn't have been odd if the actor who succeeded him hadn't also vanished the following year in an unexplained arrest. The same was true of Dovid Hofshteyn and Itsik Fefer, the latter of whom had briefly taught literature at the Boys' Colony, and both of whom, Boris remembered when he began to hear the rumors, had had books of patriotic poetry illustrated by Chagall. Boris recognized their names when he heard the rumors, not only from the orphanage, but also from a strange Yiddish letter he had received eight years earlier, in 1943.

"My dear comrade," the letter had begun,

> Please excuse the impersonal nature of this letter. I obtained your address from the records of the Soviet Jewish Boys' Colony of Malakhovka, of which you are one of many proud graduates, in the hopes that your noble patriotic background might encourage you to lend your strength to a crucial aspect of the war effort. Although you have exceeded the age for service in the Red Army, I am certain that you understand the importance of contributing anything and everything you can to the defeat of the Fascist menace.
>
> As one of the many young men rescued from the civil war pogroms by the patriotic efforts of the Soviet Jewish Boys' Colony of Malakhovka, you surely appreciate the dire circumstances to which our people have been reduced in those areas now subject to Fascist domination. Though reports have been suppressed, you have doubtless heard rumors of the humiliations and torments our Jewish comrades have suffered. Those of us who have relatives in the occupied regions know that these are not rumors. In fact they are grossly understated. Entire communities have been slaughtered.
>
> It is under this dark sky that I ask you to join the efforts of the Jewish Anti-Fascist Committee, a group operating under the supervision of the

Soviet Information Bureau and dedicated to building support among Jews overseas for Soviet efforts to destroy the Fascist beast. Along with the noted Yiddish poet Itsik Fefer, I have recently completed a tour of the United States, where we were welcomed by over 50,000 people at a Jewish Anti-Fascist Committee rally in New York. Our efforts have been productive, but more must be done. The need is urgent.

As one of those children who courageously survived another assault upon our people, you know that brutality against the Jews will not stop unless we take measures to save ourselves. We are too old to fight with our hands. I implore you to join us in fighting with our hearts.

Sincerely,
Comrade Shloyme Mikhoels
Jewish Anti-Fascist Committee

A list of names followed, including those of several Yiddish writers and other public figures he had heard of. Boris had taken the letter seriously, though his talent for expressing himself had not developed much since Malakhovka. In the end he hadn't become an artist, but rather what the state had needed, an engineer. But he felt guilty for being too old to fight. Following further instructions from Mikhoels and the others, he had written several letters—mostly to Yiddish journals and newspapers in the United States, though some to politicians in Washington as well—based largely on the form letters that the committee provided. He had even organized meetings in support of the Jewish Anti-Fascist Committee within the engineers' union, and raised money in every way he could think of during lean times. He could never tell if it had done any good. But when the names on the bottom of that letter began to disappear, along with others, after the war, Boris tried not to be disturbed. They were mostly artists and politicians, after all, which was always a tricky business. He told himself that they had probably followed Chagall to France, though some small buried part of him knew better. Meanwhile, he was just an engineer and a patriot, building roads and bridges to which no one could object.

———

CHILDREN ARE OFTEN envied for their supposed imaginations, but the truth is that adults imagine things far more often than children do.

Most adults, Boris knew, wander the world deliberately blind, living only inside their heads, in their fantasies, in their memories and worries, oblivious to the present, only aware of the past or future.

Boris had been astounded to be married—the first time, that is—to find himself suddenly in a world of families, of people who actually had parents, whose parents had parents even, whose lives did not start at the age of eleven, but centuries before their own births. But that astonishment had been too shocking to be love, too shocking even to be real, and when it proved false, Tatiana, an old friend from his university days—pretty, Jewish, fresh from her own divorce—had rescued him. She was a biologist, and when she became pregnant, she refused to allow him to consider the pregnancy anything more than what it was, cells multiplying, differentiating, turning into some sort of life, yes, but not in any way that someone like Boris could readily think of as real. Everything, even her own pregnancy, was simply a process to her, a cliché. In a dark way Boris found it comforting.

The actual child, however, had proven to be quite real, and frightening. At five years old, Raisya was tiny for her age, with smooth black hair and enormous dark eyes, and she saw things that no one else could see. Sitting with her on a train or a park bench made him realize the thickness of the veil that age and willful ignorance had lowered in front of his eyes, the percentage of each moment obscured by menial memories or predictable worries, the thick scrim of pointless thoughts that hung between him and the world. To Boris, the city park was cold and gray, its grass nothing more than blocks of hardened mud and its trees bare sticks for nine months of the year. But to Raisya, the mud itself was alive, full of ants and beetles for whom she constructed roads and bridges out of twigs, making way for a blind worm searching for a path, taking off her shoes and sinking her feet into the mud. To Boris, the communal kitchen of their apartment was a hassle that added hours to his days as he and Tatiana waited their turn for the oven and stove and wondered which of their neighbors was the official informant—every apartment had one (theirs, they had decided, was Semyon, the old man with the dyed black hair), though neither Boris nor Tatiana had ever talked enough about politics to worry. But to Raisya, it was a world of intrigue, where the ten people who occupied it ran a free market of paybacks and betrayals, of unwashed plates left intentionally in the sink that Raisya never failed to see, charred food left defiantly stuck to shared pots that Raisya never failed to smell, muttered curses that Raisya never failed to hear. To Boris, a train was a place to pretend to sleep, to brood, to be reminded of unpleasant train rides past and to dread the imminent future, when he would have to smile at his insane mother-in-law as she yelled obscenities at his wife. But to Raisya it was a wonderland where every stranger's beard was a new and unpredictable color, where discarded ticket stubs could be assembled into a complete map of the USSR, where words in Polish and Ukrainian and Uzbek floated through the air and landed on her lips. She was like the blood beneath his skin, flowing and raging blue and beautiful while his own bloodless skin paled and shriveled, unworthy of being in her presence. For the first time in his life, Boris had fallen in love.

Irina and Sergei Popov lived directly below the Kulbaks, and Raisya noticed their chubby, red-haired, five-year-old son Tolya wandering the hallways and became his friend almost instantaneously. The boy's parents had asked Raisya to bring her parents with her the next time she visited, but Tatiana was so busy in her lab, regularly returning home well after midnight in recent weeks, that it was impossible for her to come along. So it was Boris who arrived at the Popovs' door with Raisya one cold spring evening.

When the door opened, he found himself welcomed by the young couple with lavish kisses and embraces, as if he were an old friend. Irina, the mother, was tiny and red-haired, with a meek grin that made Boris grateful that Tatiana couldn't come; she could have eaten this woman alive. Sergei, the father, a thick-chested man with an easy laugh, led Boris into a corner of the room almost immediately, sitting him down as Irina busied herself with the children, distributing toys.

"When we heard you lived right upstairs, we had to have you over," he told Boris, almost gushing. He was a man who seemed to speak with his chest as much as with his mouth, leaning forward with every word. "There are so few children in this building. It's wonderful that Tolya has someone to play with."

"We're delighted, too," Boris said honestly, wishing that Tatiana were with him. "When did you move here?"

"Oh, we've lived here for years," Sergei said with a deep, disarming sigh. "I've been in this place since right after the war. Nice to be first, huh?" He smiled, waving his hand.

Boris looked around. Unlike the Kulbaks, who shared their apartment with three other couples and one elderly man, the Popovs had the whole place to themselves, and the walls were covered almost completely with framed pictures and framed medals. Obviously Sergei was a man whom the government liked. Such people often made others nervous, but Boris was a patriot who prided himself on not being afraid. "It's amazing that we've never seen each other before," Boris said.

"Not so amazing," Sergei said with a grin. "It's a big building. And I'm sure you're so busy that you never notice who's coming and going." In fact, Boris was nowhere near as busy as his wife, but he liked Sergei's assumption about his productivity. There was nothing better, Boris had absorbed since his days at Malakhovka, than being perceived as useful. "What's your field?" Sergei asked.

"I'm a civil engineer," Boris said.

"Designing sewers?" Sergei said, still grinning.

Boris tried not to squirm. He had done some templates for rerouting and repair of sewer lines about five or six years ago, a redesign of an outdated system that had been damaged during the war. He had enjoyed it. He had just started seeing Tatiana then, and each morning seemed full of possibilities, and each evening he came home with a sense of happiness he had never had before, knowing that he was doing his share of washing away the filth of the past, of creating a brand-new world. "No, mostly roads and bridges for the new highway system," he said.

"The city really is changing so quickly," Sergei said. "Did you grow up here in Moscow?"

"No, outside the city—in Malakhovka."

Sergei drew his eyebrows together. "Were your parents farmworkers?"

Boris cleared his throat. He often lied about this, particularly to strangers, but seeing this man's child playing with Raisya had softened him. Raisya and Tolya were coloring with chalk on a slate easel in the corner of the room; Irina seemed to have wandered away. "I was in an orphanage there," he said, too low for the children to hear.

Sergei reached over, putting his hand down on top of Boris's. He was a somewhat ugly man, with heavy dark hair, a thick torso, and a wide mouth, and his ugliness made Boris feel confident. Sergei's palm was warm on Boris's hand. "My father died in the Polish campaign," Sergei said, looking Boris in the eye. "Just before I was born."

The two men sat for the next seven seconds in heavy silence. There was nothing to do in this life, Boris thought, except to pick up the pieces of a shattered world. Suddenly, as he stared awkwardly at Sergei's hand, he heard Raisya burst into laughter, a ridiculous cackle that never failed to make strangers smile. He looked up and saw Sergei smiling, and knew he had found a friend.

"So what do you do that you have this gorgeous art collection?" Boris asked, glancing at the pictures that crowded the walls. He had only asked to find out more about Sergei, but now that he looked more carefully, he saw that the paintings really were impressive, or at least impressive-looking. From a distance he had assumed they were prints, but now he saw that they were all real oil paintings, some of them cracked through with age.

"Oh, they're all reproductions," Sergei said with a wave of his hand. "My wife and I are administrators for the state museum."

Senior administrators, Boris thought, judging by the apartment. Near the end of the evening, Sergei offered him some vodka. He accepted, and together they toasted the Party and their children. With a few more drinks, Boris found himself talking freely—about Raisya, about Tatiana, about the new supervisor in his office. Sergei's laughter encouraged him. They traded story after story, until Sergei started spouting battle tales about the war and Boris fell silent. When Sergei asked him about where he had been during the war, he blushed, embarrassed to be too old, embarrassed about all his private failures over the last ten years, ashamed, suddenly, of his too-young daughter and his too-young wife. Afraid to say nothing, he told Sergei embellished stories about the Anti-Fascist Committee, though he neglected to mention the Jewish aspect of it. It didn't seem important.

———

"DID YOU AND Tolya have fun?" he asked Raisya later, as they climbed up the stairs on their way home. The staircase was poorly lit, with iron railings and dank gray tiles that smelled of disinfectant, a deep throaty stench that reminded Boris of the clinic at Malakhovka, of shivering and screaming as a pregnant woman who was not his mother tried to take off his clothes and shave his head. He looked down at Raisya as she skipped up the steps beside him, and felt a tremendous ache in his chest. He wished he could hold her entire body in his hands. Instead he put his hand down on his daughter's head, cupping her skull in his palm.

Raisya nodded eagerly, her head wriggling underneath his hand. Already she was trying to escape. "I told Tolya lots of stories," she said. "I made him laugh so hard he almost died."

As Raisya began babbling, Boris's mind began to wander, and he found himself thinking of Tatiana. They had been friends, years ago, but now their friendship seemed long past. Lately he had started becoming furious with Tatiana each time she came home late, which only made things worse. When Tatiana came home the previous night, it had been close to two in the morning, and he had growled at her. He would have shouted, but he was afraid to wake Raisya. Then Tatiana had cried, weeping into Boris's chest and sputtering that she missed him, that she felt like a prisoner at work, that Raisya was growing up without her. Her face crumpled, and her hot tears seemed real. But it could all be a ruse, she could have been out with a lover night after night like his first wife had been, and Boris would never know. He had held her head to his chest with his eyes on the ceiling, seeing, in his mind's eye, the starry sky beyond the room that had hovered over him during all the previous hours while he was frustrated and alone, unreachable from where he lay in the abyss. He trusted no one in this world anymore, except for Raisya.

"Tolya says he wants to meet the other kids in the building," he heard Raisya say through his own thoughts. Suddenly he was ashamed that he hadn't been paying attention, noticing, again, the thick veil of thoughts that hung before his eyes and passed for life. "Tolya says he just moved in. He hates being the new kid."

"Tolya is making things up, baby," Boris said, and stroked her hair. Sheaths of black silk grew out of his daughter's head. "Tolya's father told me they've lived here even longer than we have."

"But Tolya says he doesn't know any other kids here."

"Well, you didn't, either, until you met him."

Raisya pulled at her own hair, twisting a lock around her finger. Boris glanced at her tiny finger, wrapped in black hair, and marveled. So much beauty in the world, and no one notices it! "That's not true," Raisya pouted. "I know Basha down the hall."

"Fine, you know Basha down the hall," Boris said, fumbling for his key and imagining that Tatiana was already home, even though he knew for a fact she wasn't. Was it really her work that kept her out so late? Was it possible to ask her? Was it possible not to?

Raisya stuck out her tongue, pointing it toward Basha's apartment. "I hate Basha down the hall."

Boris turned the key in the lock. "You shouldn't hate people, Raisya," he heard himself saying. It was something Tatiana liked to say.

"Why not?" Raisya asked.

To Boris's surprise, he couldn't think of a good answer. Fortunately, Raisya soon forgot she had asked and wandered into the tiny alcove, walled off with a bookcase, that served as her room. But after she left for school the next morning, Boris took down the little painting his art teacher had once given him, removed it from its frame, checked that Der Nister's folded story was still tucked into the wooden canvas struts, and slid it behind his daughter's rows of children's books. The Popovs worked for the museum, and you couldn't be too careful about things like that.

BORIS'S WORK HAD inexplicably slowed down. He was being assigned to fewer and fewer projects; his supervisor claimed it was a slow season for everyone, but Boris heard his colleagues complaining of having too much to do. There had been a pay cut, too, which Boris assumed was universal; it would have been capitalistic to ask. He started coming home earlier, afraid of the hours spent doodling at his desk. Meanwhile, Tatiana was staying even later at her lab. So Boris and Raisya spent more of their evenings with the Popovs. It was much roomier than their shared apartment upstairs with all of its annoying neighbors, where there was no space for her to play, and Boris was grateful to have Raisya with him, at least. The children's center where she spent her afternoons reminded him a bit too much of Malakhovka.

Besides, he was beginning to like Sergei. With Tatiana gone all evening, it was rare that he had a chance to talk to another adult about anything besides work. And Raisya seemed to like it there. Tolya's supply of toys, and Tolya himself, were a source of endless fascination.

Sergei's toys fascinated Boris, too. Being a senior state museum administrator—along with having what Boris gathered to be an impressive military record, judging by all the medals displayed on the walls and shelves—was apparently a job that conferred far more privileges than being a lowly civil engineer who never once served in the Red Army, and while the rational part of Boris's brain took pride in the fact that his country rewarded anti-fascists and placed such value on art, the stark contrast between Sergei's life and his own life one flight up pained him more than he would admit. First there was the apartment itself, an unfathomably private one which consisted of three small rooms that the family had all to themselves, with a private bath and kitchen and even a separate bedroom for the child, who would grow up without hearing his parents' fights. Then there was the abundance within the home—the cabinets always stocked with the high-quality liquor that Sergei shared with Boris; the bowls always full of candies that made Raisya salivate from the moment she walked in the door; the electric refrigerator (no communal iceboxes here) that, when Boris once sneaked a look, revealed itself to be a treasure chest of foods a child could grow on: rows of milk bottles standing like soldiers, shining heaps of fruits and vegetables, meat and fish ready to be roasted in the Popovs' private oven. Boris often wished, for Raisya's sake, that they would be invited to stay for supper, but somehow they never were. And then there were the dozens of paintings, which Boris was beginning to suspect might not be copies at all.

"You have some remarkable reproductions here," he ventured one day in front of the paintings in Sergei's living room, after a few shots of vodka had loosened his tongue. He smiled, trying to sound friendly rather than suspicious. They were alone, as was becoming typical in these early evenings. Irina was out with her friends, and Tolya and Raisya had run off to Tolya's bedroom, their arms loaded with paper and tubes of paint.

Sergei laughed, an odd snort restrained by a frown. "That's because they're professional fakes," he said.

"What do you mean?" Boris asked, and suddenly in Sergei's living room he sensed the presence of the veil, the film of vague memories and worries separating him from the moment he was living through. It horrified him. He looked at Sergei and saw nothing at all. Only the paintings on the walls seemed real.

"Officially I'm an administrator at the museum, but informally I supervise appraisals," Sergei was saying. "When I was in the army I was in charge of forging documents for espionage, and I became a bit of an expert on how to make something look authentic when it isn't. So now I can spot a lot of things that most people wouldn't notice."

"It's nice that that sort of thing has civilian applications," Boris murmured, attempting to say something pleasant but not exactly complimentary. Every time Sergei mentioned the army, Boris felt himself becoming just a bit older, his hairline sneaking even farther back.

"You'd be surprised how many times the museum acquires pieces that turn out to be fakes," Sergei said. "Especially when there are so many ways to spot a bad one. Turn it upside down, for example. An upside-down fake almost always looks unnatural. The professionals know about the easy tricks like that."

"Professionals?" Boris asked.

"Most people don't know that there's such a thing as professional art forgers," Sergei said, leaning toward Boris as if sharing a secret. His breath smelled less like vodka than like milk. "The country has been flooded with art since the war, but then there are the opportunists who pollute the supply with counterfeits. You've got to sort out the real ones from the fakes. Cheap fakes are easy to catch. The ones I have here are from the real talent, the people who are actually artists in real life, and then they also have a bit of the science background to age the canvas and all that. These are trophy pieces for me. Look at this Rembrandt, for instance," he said, standing up and lifting what looked like a small antique painting off the wall. "This guy knew what he was doing. Period canvas, period frame, aged paint, and the image is pretty good. He's a real artist. But I have a feel for these things. It was my idea to strip it down in the corner under the frame until we came to the layer where the primer was anachronistic."

"Hmph," Boris said, letting out a puff of air in awe.

Sergei returned the painting to the wall. "Of course, with a child at home, I'm better off without originals anyway. With these, I wouldn't feel so bad if Tolya decided to decorate one of them with Irina's lipstick."

Boris laughed, relieved that the conversation had moved back to something he understood. "It's amazing how many things kids can destroy," he said. "My wife is always terrified that Raisya's going to stick her finger into an electrical socket."

"Yes, or tear apart your documents." Sergei grinned. "If I didn't keep mine in a safe place, Tolya would have turned them into paintings by now." He leaned in toward Boris, miming a conspiracy. "Judging by your daughter's energy, I should hope you do the same."

Boris laughed again. "Of course," he said, thrilled by the acknowledgment of his own worth. But just then Raisya and Tolya suddenly ran into the room, bounding toward their fathers' arms. At the last second, Tolya cut Raisya off and leapt up to where Boris was sitting, laughing hysterically as Raisya remained on the floor. Boris jumped as the red-haired boy landed heavily in his lap, but Raisya was laughing, too. The chubby boy had already slipped off of Boris's knees when Sergei swooped down behind Boris's featherweight daughter and swept her up into the sky above his head.

Sergei laughed along with his son, but Raisya, midair, had stopped laughing. For an instant, looking at her held aloft by Sergei, her black hair momentarily floating on air, Boris remembered a painting in his art teacher's private room, the one of the artist's wife flying like a flag on the wind. Her hair fell to her suspended shoulders, and Raisya made a face.

"Put me down," she said, her voice strangely dark.

Sergei laughed again, a forced laugh. He had heard that she meant it. Still, he waited a moment longer before lowering her to his waist. "Why don't you bring this one home?" he said quickly, passing her to Boris as Irina appeared in the doorway. Amid handshakes and kisses, Boris and an oddly sullen Raisya went back upstairs.

It was another long night that night. After Raisya went to sleep, Boris, inspired by Sergei, lifted his mattress off the bed frame and examined all that passed for his own "documents," the treasures underneath. It had been a long time since he had looked. Most of their photographs were in albums, but here were a few that he had somehow never put away: a picture of himself and Tatiana on a trip to Odessa (when had his hair begun to disappear?), one of Tatiana pregnant, frowning at the person behind the camera, a small portrait of Tatiana's mother, wearing a smile that Boris had never seen her wear in real life, several pictures of Tatiana as a girl, a group portrait of Boris with the engineering union, and finally a picture of Raisya as a baby, her mouth open and her eyes wide. The rest of the things under the mattress were papers. His and Tatiana's identity papers (Nationality: Jewish), Raisya's (the same), two sets of divorce papers, one marriage certificate, three thin scientific periodicals with articles Tatiana had written, typescripts of several studies Tatiana had done years ago, notices from various government agencies pertaining to their apartment, and finally, piles of clippings Boris had received during the war from the American newspapers that published his letters on behalf of the Anti-Fascist Committee, and responses from people who had pledged their support. They were the closest things he had to the medals on Sergei's wall.

Tatiana arrived well after midnight. They made love mechanically, the way one eats after a fast—not seeking pleasure, but merely relief. It ended quickly, and Boris drifted into sleep. Tatiana no longer even appeared in his dreams. Instead, he dreamed of walking with Raisya, running hand in hand with her, taking off with her like airplanes into the air, and then flying with her, for miles, over the town.

"I DON'T LIKE Tolya's daddy," Raisya said one evening as they sat down to another private dinner together. They had been spending evenings at the Popovs' for almost two months, and they had still never been invited to stay for supper. Privately Boris blamed Irina, who probably took Tatiana's constant absence as some sort of insult. Meanwhile, as Tatiana continued to linger in her lab, Boris had started serving Raisya meals at a little card table in their room, unwilling to share her company with the other couples who crowded the table in the communal kitchen. The long table there reminded him too much of Malakhovka, of being elbowed out of the way by the other boys. But his cooking skills came from Malakhovka, too. Most of their meals consisted of fried potatoes with onions, and sometimes red cabbage salad. That night the potatoes had come out slightly burned.

"I don't like Tolya's daddy," Raisya repeated. "He's mean."

Boris reached across the table and served her some cabbage that he knew she would not eat. "That's a terrible thing to say, Raisya. The Popovs are very nice to you."

"Tolya says his daddy once ran someone over with a truck. On purpose. For his *job*."

Boris held back a sigh. "Baby, I told you before, Tolya likes to make things up. He imagines things. Tolya's daddy doesn't even drive a truck. His parents work for the museum."

"But he told me."

"Maybe Tolya was remembering something his daddy told him about the war," Boris said. He decided to ask Sergei whether he had ever been in the tank corps. Still, it disturbed him that Raisya had to live in a world where other children didn't hesitate to lie to her, where things she was told about the workings of the world would later turn out to be grossly untrue.

Raisya ignored him and gulped down her milk—the milk, Boris now remembered, that he had diluted with water from the sink, to make it last until the next time Tatiana was paid. He was an engineer, married to a biologist, working in the most progressive country in the world, and he could barely afford to feed his five-year-old daughter. He watched the thin gray liquid sliding between her perfect lips and remembered the bottles of milk in Sergei's refrigerator, an entire army of milk. Suddenly he felt nauseated at himself, at the whole world.

"I think it's mean to run over someone with a truck," Raisya said.

"It certainly is," Boris replied absently, picking at his food. Thinking of the milk made his own hunger seem dirty and cheap. Was Tatiana really at her lab all this time, or was he absurdly naive? Boris thought for a moment of leaving the dishes in the communal kitchen for Tatiana to do when she came home, but it would be too directly hostile. He looked back up at Raisya. Her nose was narrow like Tatiana's, but her lips were soft and full. The dent below her nose was shallow, like his mother's.

"Tolya says the person his daddy ran over was trying to run over the whole country, so his daddy had to run him over first," Raisya said. Bits of potato leaked between her lips. "How could somebody run over the whole country with a truck? It would take forever."

"Reyzele," Boris said, putting down his fork. It was his Yiddish nickname for her, and he almost never used it because Tatiana hated it. But when he called her that, he felt as if they were secret lovers, speaking a language all their own. "Reyzele."

"What?" she said in Russian, irritated. She was engrossed in stabbing an uncooperative potato with a fork.

"Reyzele, Tolya likes to imagine things. He makes things up that aren't really there."

"I told Tolya that nobody should ever run over anybody with a truck," she said, missing the potato again. "No matter *what* the run-over person did."

Boris put his hands on the table. "Reyzele, I want to tell you something. I know some people think it's important to have a good imagination, but I don't want you to imagine things like Tolya does. I want you to see what's really there. It's really hard sometimes to see what's really there."

The potato finally surrendered to her fork. She looked up at him, and her eyes were so dark and penetrating that he leaned back in his seat. "I do see things," she said slowly. "I see everything."

Boris sighed, frustrated. It was the same feeling he had had a few weeks ago while trying to help her learn how to add, the bleak realization that something important was simply not getting through. "Let's clean up these dishes," he said. But when he saw her slide down from her seat, her chin level with the tabletop, he couldn't help but swoop down and lift her off the ground, flying her through the air. This time she laughed.

His usual strategy was to eat with her late before putting her straight to bed; she seemed to fall asleep more quickly that way. After he finished the dishes, he helped her into her nightgown, wedged himself onto her tiny bed, and read aloud to her from a picture book. That night the book was one Tatiana had brought home from the library. It was something about a cat who tormented the mice who lived in his house, stealing their cheese and crushing them in his paws. In the end, predictably, the mice united, rose up, and killed the cat so that they could rule the house in peace and brotherhood. When he finished reading, Raisya frowned.

"I hate that book," she said.

Boris closed the book. "I didn't really like it, either," he confessed. The illustrations had been ugly. "Do you want me to read you something else?"

"No," she said with a yawn. "I hate all books."

This surprised him. The last report from her school had claimed that she was becoming an excellent reader. "Why?"

"Because they're made up. Tell me a real story."

"What do you mean, a real story?"

"A real thing that really happened to you. When you were little." She closed her eyes, waiting.

Boris looked at her eyelashes, dark seals over her perfect face. What could he possibly tell her? He didn't know how to make things up. "When I was little," he began. He felt his stomach clench, burned potatoes and ugly memories churning his gut. At last he thought of something.

"When I was little," he began again, "I used to like to paint pictures. Once there was a famous artist who liked a picture I made, and he wanted to keep it."

Raisya's lips moved, perfect lips like dark fallen petals of a flower, her eyes still closed. "What was your picture?" she asked.

Boris paused. "A baby," he said. "It was a picture of a baby." He waited for her to ask for details, but she didn't. He continued. "This artist wanted to keep it, but I said I wouldn't give it to him unless he gave me one of his. So he gave me a picture he made of a man floating in the sky. It's the one we had hanging on the wall, but right now it's—it's put away," he finished.

"Mmm," Raisya breathed, and turned on her side. Boris put his hand on her head, stroking her hair. Suddenly she opened her eyes. "Did your parents ever tell you stories before bed?" she asked.

Boris stared at her. He had never told her about his parents, and had long dreaded the day when she might ask. Even Tatiana barely knew; he had claimed to have been too young to remember, and she had believed him. "Sometimes," he said, his voice low.

Raisya closed her eyes again. "I bet you miss them a lot," she said.

Boris didn't move. Tatiana must have told her they were dead, he thought, maybe during their last visit to Tatiana's mother. Or else she simply knew. He cleared his throat.

"I don't need to miss them anymore," Boris said softly. "I have you."

He leaned down to kiss her good night, but she had already fallen asleep.

———

IT IS DIFFICULT to sleep alone. Boris lay in bed for three hours, trying to sleep and failing, before someone finally knocked on his door.

"Tanya?" he whispered, afraid to wake Raisya. Tatiana must have forgotten her key, he thought. Or her hands were full. At least she was here.

"No, not her," a man's voice said behind the door. Boris sat up. Before he could rise from the bed, a key turned in the lock and four men came into the room: the old man Semyon from their shared apartment, two large men he had never seen before, and Sergei Popov. It took a long time for Boris to realize that he was not dreaming.

"I had wondered if you really had a wife. It seems you do," Sergei said. He took a snapshot out of his pocket, turning it quickly toward Boris. It was the picture from under his mattress, of him and Tatiana at the beach. Boris jumped out of bed in his pajamas, staring at the mattress as if it were alive.

"You are under arrest in capital violation of Article 64-A of the Soviet Criminal Code," he heard Sergei say. "The charge is treason, for your role in the Zionist conspiracy to bring down the Soviet state."

"Conspiracy?" Boris repeated. He heard Sergei's words slowly, as if listening underwater.

"Yes, for your activity on your Zionist committee, where you conspired with the Americans to destroy the USSR."

Suddenly Boris's brain began working again. The Anti-Fascist Committee?

Sergei turned to Semyon. "Do we need to look around here anymore?"

Semyon shook his head as Boris stared. "I already cleaned everything out. We turned in the evidence this morning."

"Evidence," Boris whispered. He looked again at Sergei's hand, which had rolled the picture of him and Tatiana into a small scroll.

"We don't have time to discuss this now," Sergei said quickly. "Your wife will be home soon, and I imagine you'd prefer if she didn't have to see you this way. Unless you'd like to make this harder for her, I suggest you allow these gentlemen to bring you downstairs."

The two large men approached Boris, moving slowly, as if in a dream. Like a dream, Boris tried to raise his arms quickly, but they moved only slowly, as if shackled by weights. The men with their slow movements seized his arms and twisted them, slowly, backward, shackled them, slowly, behind his back. Boris struggled, slowly, shoved one of the men with his shoulder, slowly, until the other man slowly, very slowly, punched him in the eye.

"Let's go," Sergei said, glancing at his watch. And then a still, small voice shuddered in the room.

"Daddy?"

From where Boris stood slumped against one of the men, he could just see Raisya standing next to the bookcase. She squinted in the light, her threadbare nightgown trailing on the floor. She squinted again, then opened her eyes wide, seeing Boris with his left eye swelling shut, seeing the two large men, seeing the old man Semyon from down the hall, and then, suddenly, seeing Sergei Popov.

"Daddy!"

Sergei turned to face her, and Boris watched as his little daughter backed herself against the wall. "Raisya, your father has done something very bad, so he has to go away for a while. Go back to bed and wait for your mother."

Boris tried to speak. "Raisya, I—" But the man next to him slowly raised his hand, and Boris fell silent, because even though his daughter could see everything, that was one thing he couldn't let her see.

Raisya turned to Sergei, and through his good eye Boris could see her trembling. "Are you going to run over him with a truck?"

"We're leaving. Now." Sergei opened the door of the room.

"Please don't run over him with a truck!"

Sergei turned to Semyon. "Lock it from the outside. Her mother has the key." The men began pulling Boris toward the door.

"Daddy, don't go!" Raisya screamed.

What do you say to a child you will never see again? That there really is an abyss? That it is easy to fall into it? That the only way to stay out of the filth is to learn how to fly, or to collect the broken rungs of that ladder and build them back again? That the whole world is nothing more than a very narrow bridge, and the most important thing is not to be afraid? Boris could think of nothing; his imagination failed him. He looked at Raisya and said only what he saw.

"Baby," he whispered. And walked out the door.

———

AFTER YOU WALK out that door, the veil of imagination vanishes and you become like a child. You don't think about anything, you don't remember anything, you don't predict anything, you don't imagine anything. You just see the walls, the bars, the floor, the pliers, the strap, the club, the knife, the wires, the acid bath, the electric spark, the revolving sword, and then after that you stop seeing, stop seeing, and you only feel, feel your hair, your scalp, your skull, your skin, your nails, your eyes, your groin, your legs. And when the time arrives, a year and a half later, for everything to end (because things do end, in the end), you still think of nothing—not your wife, not your daughter, not even your mother or father—except perhaps of a baby you once saw flying through the air, or of the secrets that that baby had not yet forgotten, or of a God who is not full of mercy but rather full of wombs, or of your own blood, which, when it bursts from your chest onto the front of your shirt, is no longer blue.

But what happens after doesn't matter. What matters is what happens before. Boris Kulbak's life ended when he stepped through that door, but when that door closed, with a five-year-old girl left standing behind it—standing still, eyes open, in an empty room—his daughter's life began.

18

BEN WAS racked by guilt. He had done it. Sara's forgery—dried under a heat lamp to "age" the paint, annotated with stains and a bit of clear nail polish in one corner, worn down gently with sandpaper and salt, and otherwise perfected—had been mailed back to the museum from a busy New Jersey post office with a fake return address. He knew Erica had believed it, because it was all over the newspapers a few days later: the miraculous recovery of the stolen work, the experts called in to ascertain its authenticity, the decisive announcement that it was the real thing. Sara and Leonid were thrilled, relieved. But Ben was despondent. He still felt the imprint of her lips on his neck.

For days he couldn't sleep. Late at night he lay in bed in agony, remembering that evening in the basement. What he imagined far exceeded the mere taste that had really happened, but it didn't matter. In his blind waking dreams, she pressed him against the paintings and drank him in the dark. When he opened his eyes, he remembered how he had tricked her, and the disgrace of it hung like a lead weight in his gut. His mother's books lay in a pile by his bed, and sometimes between bouts of madness he leafed through them, to distract himself. But Erica permeated every page. In the mornings he avoided looking in the mirror. At work he read through encyclopedia entries blindly, writing questions to himself on scraps of paper on his desk. He had promised her that he would find her—but what did that mean? Should he call her? Write to her? Wait for her at the museum door? But how could he do any of that, after what he and Sara had done? Shame hung before his eyes like a veil.

One day, after a week of Ben's suffering, Sara and Leonid asked him if he would like to join them to see the Chagall exhibit at the museum. To Ben's astonishment, they weren't joking. They hadn't been there yet, and Leonid was curious to see Sara's work hanging in the gallery. The suggestion sickened Ben. But Sara pressed him, persisted. "I read that the paintings are going back to Russia next week. Sunday is the last day," Sara said. Ben detected a tremor in her voice, and realized that she knew what he was feeling. She always did. "Come with us on Sunday," she pleaded.

Ben was about to say no, when he suddenly remembered something from that evening in the basement. Erica had mentioned that she worked at the museum on Sundays. Perhaps it was an open door. He had promised her—but what could he say to her when he saw her? And how could he ever say it?

Before he knew it, he had told his sister he would be there.

———

SUNDAY WAS STUNNING. Almost autumn, but still warm; a day when the tips of the leaves on the few city trees were just beginning to dip themselves into the gold light of early evenings, but before those evenings could stain them dark. At the entrance to the museum, Ben walked by the security camera quickly, but he found that the camera didn't even make him nervous anymore. He was afraid only of Erica, and he was drawn into the building by his fear. Sara and Leonid followed close behind him, as if this visit were the most normal thing in the world, smiling and laughing as they moved through the metal detectors and into the gallery.

The three of them passed most of the pictures slowly, until they came upon a picture that forced them to a halt. *The Wedding, 1918*, was a black-and-white image of a bride and groom, held together from above by a deep red angel. A tiny image of a baby lay embedded in the bride's cheek. Leonid, Sara, and Ben formed a careful semicircle around it, looking. Silence fell and deepened as each of them imagined themselves as one of the figures in the painting—the groom, the bride, the angel pushing them together, the not-yet person in the body of the bride. They looked and saw, each sunken into his own private dreams.

"I saw an exhibit like this when I was little," Leonid suddenly said.

The silence dissipated like wisps of smoke. "You were never little," Ben retorted. He smiled when Sara laughed.

"No, I'm serious," Leonid stammered. "They had a show like this once in Moscow. We were visiting from Chernobyl, and I saw the exhibit with my grandmother. I remember these," he added, jutting his giant chin at the paintings on the wall. "I was nine or ten, I think. It was a big deal. We had to wait on line for hours just to see it."

"You also had to wait on line for hours just to buy toilet paper," Sara said.

Leonid laughed, but Ben had turned back to look at the painting again, distracted. Everything was making him think of Erica, of how he had lied. He looked at the bride and groom in the picture and suddenly remembered the shame of his own divorce. There had been a humiliating divorce ceremony in a rabbi's office, where he had tried to avoid eye contact with his wife for forty-five minutes while the two of them and three rabbis watched a scribe write out the bill of divorce with a quill pen. The ink took a long time to dry, giving Ben ample time to imagine his wife naked in her lover's bed. Then Ben had to roll up the bill of divorce and throw it into his wife's hands, and once she had caught it, he had to watch her walk across the room with it before he could leave. As he saw her walk away from him, he told himself that he wouldn't ever make the same mistakes again. With each step she took, he had silently repeated his new vow for the future: don't assume, don't believe, don't trust. But now he thought of Erica—and of his astonishment when he realized that she wasn't going to turn him in— and wondered if he had been wrong: if, just maybe, the entire world wasn't bent on betrayal, if, just possibly, every person he had ever met wasn't actually out to destroy him. If nothing ever became of him and Erica, he suddenly knew, then at least she had made him see his own mistake. He wanted to thank her.

But how would he find her? He had hoped that he would see her in the gallery, that coincidence would be on his side, but so far there was no trace of her. She must be in the basement. But to go there he would need to make up a reason, or ask for her by name, and he was hesitant. Maybe he could wait outside afterward, stop her before she left. But what would he tell her? He looked around the gallery and saw a painting he remembered from the night of the theft, a small square canvas with a man and a woman against a deep blue background, their faces blending into the luminous colors of the sky. Beauty was the property of the loved.

"Ben, are you done looking here? We want to go upstairs," he heard Leonid say through his thoughts.

"Sure," he muttered. Maybe Erica was in the upstairs gallery, where he had first met her, but he doubted it. Suddenly he remembered the first thing she had ever said to him, on the night of the theft: *And what about you, Benjamin Ziskind?* When he thought of it now, it sounded like a challenge, a harder question than any question he had ever written. He followed his sister and brother-in-law up to the second floor of the exhibit like a sleepwalker, obsessed with something no one but he could see.

Upstairs, they wandered into a large room where all of the paintings—the text on the wall explained—had once hung as murals in the Moscow State Jewish Theater, enormous canvases painted with figures representing theater, music, dance, and literature. The man in the literature mural was writing on a long blank scroll.

"Look at this." Sara pointed at the lower edge of mural, near the man's foot. "Sag marks."

Ben and Leonid bent down to look, and saw that she was right. The canvas bulged just slightly a few inches from the bottom edge, the way their own painting had. Something had been stuffed into the frame.

"Erica told me about this," Ben said, suddenly excited. "She said they found hundreds of manuscript pages stuffed behind it." He had mailed the stories from his mother's painting back to Erica, too, with another fake return address, after making copies for himself. When he read the handwritten one, he still couldn't figure out what it was or where it had come from. It maddened him to know that the secret had died with his mother. He looked again at the mural. "I should ask her if anyone translated them yet," he added, then felt himself blush. Sara smiled. Suddenly he was very aware of the floor beneath his feet, of the gallery below him, and of the basement below that. He could feel her presence in the building. She was under this roof, he thought—under this roof! His father had gone halfway around the world for his mother, into the pits of hell, but Ben couldn't walk down the steps to the basement. He was too afraid.

Most of the other visitors were chained to their audio guides, looking only at what their little headsets told them was worth seeing. But in the back of the museum, in a small room usually reserved for the final text of the exhibit and a few leftover works, Sara's painting hung centered on the wall, alone. A few laminated sheets of paper describing the theft and recovery were tacked to the wall beside it, next to a bright red exit sign above a stairwell door.

The three of them stood in a ring around it, afraid to dip their toes into the holy of holies. The painting looked almost exactly as it had on their living room wall, Ben thought. But only almost. A shudder ran through his stomach as he realized that he liked Sara's painting better than the original. In Sara's version, the lines were more supple, the motion more alive.

"Sara, it's beautiful," Leonid said.

The three of them were alone in the room, and Ben watched as Leonid reached for Sara's shoulders, folding her into his arms. Leonid almost never held her like this in front of him, Ben realized. Since Ben's divorce, Sara always shrugged her husband away in front of Ben, embarrassed for her brother. But now Ben watched Leonid's enormous arms embrace his sister and didn't feel jealousy, but wonder and awe. Here was the hand that had once punched him in the chest, and now it was caressing his sister's shoulders, wiping his sister's tears, holding his parents' future grandchild as it clasped her around her waist. It was possible, probable even, that the world could be rebuilt.

"I'm going to go downstairs," Ben said.

Sara and Leonid released each other, and Ben saw the outline of the floating man between them. "What?" Sara asked.

"I want to tell Erica," Ben stammered, and pointed carefully at the painting. He glanced over his shoulder, but no one was there. He lowered his voice. "I want to bring the real one back."

Leonid's jaw drooped. "Why?"

Sara stared at him. "Ben, are you crazy?" she whispered. "She'll turn you in."

"No, she won't," he said. "I trust her."

Leonid and Sara looked at each other, then at him. They opened their mouths to stop him, but Ben didn't hear it. The air around him seemed to be rising, quivering with a sudden freedom. Ben's body loosened and lightened the way it had years ago, when he removed his brace for the very last time. He was floating on air. He stepped toward the exit, and reached out to push open the stairwell door. And then all three of them were thrown to the floor by the force of the bomb.

IT DETONATED AT the museum's main entrance, one story down on the other side of the building: a truck packed with explosives that drove straight through the museum's front doors and then blasted through walls, floors, ceilings, paintings, sculptures, scrolls, books, records, and the eyes, brains, limbs, and bones of thirty-six people who were admiring the Chagall exhibit on the ground floor of the Museum of Hebraic Art.

There was silence for a moment, a hard, leaden silence, before people started screaming. After that it was hard to tell apart the human screams from the alarms. When Ben raised his face from where he had been thrown to the floor, the lights in the windowless gallery blinked out and the room went dark. The air stood still. Ben struggled to breathe. In the blind blackness an acrid smell seeped into the dead air around him—a chemical smell, tar and ash like thin threads pulled through his nostrils. The room was growing hot.

"What was—what was—what was—what was—" someone began stammering in the dark, burbling between the moans from downstairs. A few seconds passed before Ben recognized that it was his own voice, distorted—the high boy's voice that had once cried when his mother and sister locked him into his brace.

"What happened?"

"What happened?"

"What happened?"

At the far end of the gallery, a loud crack resonated above the screaming voices, then a deep rumble as part of the floor caved in, opening through to the gallery below. Thick black smoke began to billow up in clouds through the hole in the floor, as though a volcano had erupted. The glow from the fires downstairs cast a thin orange light in the upstairs galleries, illuminated the squares of glass on the paintings into panels of sick light, like the eyes of a nocturnal animal. The cloud thickened above the strange fire, a pillar of smoke.

Someone took Ben's hand. He groped with his other hand for a wall or a bit of floor where he could push himself to his feet. Instead his fingers found shaking shoulders, and a chin coated with drool. Someone grabbed his other hand and pulled him up. Standing, he now smelled something thicker, ash and dust. The room seemed to move. The screams coming through the floor grew louder, anguished moans of men and piercing shrieks that sounded like children. The air had become furry in the dark. Suddenly he heard a man's voice wail beside him, a sound he had never heard before. It was Leonid. "Sara, the baby—"

"The baby's fine," he heard Sara's voice crack near his knees. "Get us out."

A thin line of light emerged in the glowing darkness, and Ben saw Leonid throwing himself against the exit door, heaving it open. In the newfound light from the staircase, Ben found Sara crouched on the floor in front of him, and hauled her to her feet. When Leonid grabbed her other hand, Ben stumbled, and then looked behind him. There were more people in the room with them now, a confused crowd moving toward the stairwell door. A thick film of smoke billowed out of a vent near the ceiling, not far above Sara's painting. Instantly everyone crushed toward the exit. As he piled with the others at the door, Ben heard a hissing noise behind him and looked back one last time. The sprinklers on the ceiling had turned on, drenching the room and the painting in a thick jungle mist. The painting's glass cover clouded over with mist, then with smoke, as the museum burst into tears. The floating man vanished. Ben stood paralyzed at the sight, until Sara yanked him down the stairs.

Leonid led them as they pushed their way down the concrete stairwell with dozens of other people, pulled through the pinkish glow of the emergency lights. They reached the ground floor quickly, with people pushing them from behind. The doors on the bottom were open, revealing a short foyer and then another door leading to the alleyway outside. The crowds in the stairwell coming through from the ground floor were burned and bleeding. A woman pushed by with deep gashes on her bare arms and a thin wedge of glass embedded in her cheek. One man was running, bleeding from the head, carrying a little boy without legs. As the doors flipped open, Ben looked into the first-floor gallery. By the blackened walls he saw someone seated calmly in a wheelchair, facing a charred painting. The chair stood perfectly still. Nearby an arm rested on the floor.

The chain of Leonid, Sara, and Ben pushed its way through the doors until Leonid burst through into daylight. But as Ben saw the outdoor alleyway looming before him, he suddenly dropped Sara's hand.

"I'm going down to get Erica," he said.

"What?" Sara turned around in the doorway, and was quickly shoved to the side by other people coming down the stairs.

"Erica's office is in the basement. She's there now. I'm going to go get her."

Sara stared. "How do you know she's there?"

He coughed, feeling dizzy. He gripped the railing on the wall. "She is."

Sara's eyes widened. "Ben, that's insane. She—she'll be fine. They'll have rescue people there."

"No, they won't. It'll be the last place they look."

The stairwell was growing hot. More people started pushing through, this time people covered with ash and cement dust as well as blood. As the door to the first floor opened again behind another knot of people, thin wisps of smoke crept out with them. Ben looked up as a screaming little girl, her braids burned into gray sticks and her jeans coated with ashes, tried to turn around and run back into the gallery. Someone caught her and shoved her out the door.

"There's smoke here," Sara said quickly. Her lips were shaking. "You won't be able to get out this way again."

"There's another way out from the basement. A tunnel to the park."

"What?"

"Two blocks down, through the grate in the sidewalk. Meet me there."

She squinted, gagged. "Ben—"

"Sara, you're pregnant and you're breathing smoke. Get out."

"Ben, no! You—"

But he had already pushed her out the door, and soon another avalanche of people splattered with blood had made their way through the first-floor doors and shoved her outside with them, where Leonid's red hair towered in the blue sky. As his sister's face disappeared into the crowd, Ben squeezed back around the panicked people in the stairwell toward a door marked "Staff Only." He pulled it open and raced down the emergency-lit steps, as the stairwell by the door filled up with smoke behind him.

THE BASEMENT WAS a dark cave of burning ash. The bomb had blown a crater in the main floor clear through to the basement, and in the dim light from the hole to the smoldering lobby, Ben could see large boulders of ceiling that had crushed the plastic swivel chairs and half the desks to the floor. Soot filled his nostrils as a broken sprinkler pipe dribbled water from what remained of the ceiling. He began picking his way around the broken desks, trying hard to remember where her office had been. But with half the walls blown through, it was impossible. A cell phone started to ring nearby, but no one answered it. The phone chirped in the dark and fell silent.

He was suddenly frightened to call her name, terrified of waiting for an answer. Even if Erica was somewhere else, he thought frantically, shouldn't there be other people here, other curators, other staff? But no, he was sure she was here. The cave of the basement seemed deserted, reeking with the dizzying smell of smoke. He knelt on the floor, trying to see beneath the smashed tables and chairs. Next to his knee, he saw a man's leg, detached from its body.

Ben rose to his feet, backing away in slow steps. Then he whirled around, tripped, and began rushing through the ruined basement. He pushed through blown-out walls, moving toward what he thought might be the entrance to the tunnel.

The smashed desks and computers had given way to the storage room, a long chasm of twisted metal shelves that Ben could just barely see in the dim light shining through the broken ceiling. Curled, burnt pages of Hebrew manuscripts were blown against the walls, charred and smoldering; piles of charred paper lay in heaps. Singed handwritten sheets drifted in the dark, and suddenly Ben thought of the papers from the paintings, the entire novel rescued from the murals' frames. Lost. A pipe had burst, and the floor was covered with a thick clumpy liquid exuding a heavy odor of human waste. Ben sucked in his breath. The sewage on the floor pooled in swirls of black ink, and his shoes sank into the slime. In his confused mind, he thought of the little boy in his mother's book as he squinted at the floor, looking for a magic ring that he could use to bring the snow and wash it away. Instead all he saw were the glinting rings of silver wine goblets, and partly submerged candlesticks, and the wooden handles of scrolls sunken in the waste. The entrance to the tunnel, Ben saw, was blocked by a large contorted piece of metal that might at one point have been a sculpture or a shelf. So she hadn't left that way, he thought. Where was she?

Now he remembered where her office was—through the rows of sludge-covered manuscripts and blasted scrolls, to the right, where her flashlight that evening had led them to a dark paradise. Was she still there? She hadn't left up the stairs; he would have seen her, or at least heard her moving in the dark. The basement was strangely quiet. In the dim light that glowed through the broken ceiling as he made his way toward the row of offices past the storage room, he could see that this part of the basement was less damaged than where he had first come in. Most of the walls and doors were intact, though the floor was still flooded with slime. Might she have stayed in her office, unable to escape, the door blocked from behind? Might she be trapped there, underground, her voice muffled by debris? It was possible. Many more things were possible than he had ever previously imagined.

He slipped on the waste-flooded floor, regained his balance, and then saw the first door on the right—the same door he had entered that day when she interrogated him, and again when she kissed him. The door was charred near the cracked ceiling, but it was all in one piece. He pressed a hand to the metal surface: it was cool. As he glanced around the door's edges, he thought of the encyclopedia entry on Schrödinger's cat, the strange imaginary impossible world where each potential outcome, both life and death, was actually taking place simultaneously, until the moment one opened the door. But how was it possible to be both dead and alive? It was. *No one in our town has ever really died*, he remembered, *because no one in our town has ever really lived!* He slipped in the mud again, pawed at the walls, pulled himself up to stand, and reached for the doorknob.

Later, in the time she had created for him, the laws of gravity would be repealed and Ben would hover over the city, looking down and seeing every possibility, all at once: the buildings crooked and straight, the trees stunted and flourishing, the streets cast in shadows and sunlight, the invisible tombstones pushing through the sidewalks beneath leaves and a cloud. And then he would soar through the blue and black and orange sky, and he would know what she meant, even if it was only what she meant to him. But right now, he stood at the door that was not yet open.

"Erica?" he called, and listened for her answer. And then he opened the door and entered the world to come.

1 9

I T IS a great injustice that those who die are often people we know, while those who are born are people we don't know at all. We name children after the dead in the dim hope that they will resemble them, pretending to blunt the loss of the person we knew while struggling to make the person we don't know into less of a stranger. It's compelling, this idea that the new person is so tightly bound to the old, but most of us are afraid to believe it. But what if we are right? Not that the new person is the reincarnation of the old, but rather, more subtly, that they know each other, that the already-weres and the not-yets of our world, the mortals and the natals, are bound together somewhere just past where we can see, in a knot of eternal life?

In our world, we are free to wonder about this for a lifetime. But the world to come is a busy place, and the not-yets in it have only nine months to wonder. All of them have been sentenced to birth. And Daniel—his parents don't yet know that he is Daniel; in fact, no one anywhere on earth knows yet that he is Daniel—is afraid of being born.

———

AT THE HOUR when the future Daniel Ziskind Shcharansky was conceived, he hurried, with all of the other not-yets conceived in the same hour, to his first day of school. He and the others had hardly taken their celestial seats when the teacher—an ancient already-was who had lived centuries ago, though Daniel, knowing nothing, didn't recognize his name—entered the room, carrying an enormous book.

"Welcome to the world to come," the teacher announced. He opened the book in front of the students, and its enormous pages fluttered above them. Each page had a single name written at the top, and nothing else. The teacher turned the pages and called the roll. One by one, each of the not-yets rose as their names were called. Daniel listened, not sure what he was listening for. But when the teacher called his name, he recognized it, and rose.

"Daniel, son of Leonid and Sara." It was the first time that anyone had ever spoken his name.

"Here I am," he said.

Daniel's name was the last on the list, and he trembled with the others as all of them, not yet people, but already known by name, hovered in the air. He peered around the room. Were there some who were absent, who were cutting class, who had chosen not to exist?

"All present and accounted for," the teacher muttered to himself, making a note in the book. As the not-yets settled into their seats, bewildered, their teacher held the book up in the air. "Each of your names is written in this book, and every single one of you will sign it with your deeds," he said. Then he slammed the book shut. "I suspect you've heard it's paradise here. It is. But that doesn't mean you don't have a lot to learn. So pay close attention to everything we teach you here during the next nine months. At the end, there will be a test."

A test? Daniel shuddered, horrified. He knew nothing. He didn't even know how to learn. How could he pass a test? But an instant later, the lesson had already begun.

What do they learn in the world to come? Much of the school day is devoted to studying history. But of course it isn't anything like history classes on earth. The famous figures here are unheard of there. Instead, the not-yets study the people who really did create the history of the world: mothers, teachers, brothers, sisters, fathers, aunts, uncles, friends—because, as one of Daniel's teachers was fond of saying, "Time itself is created through deeds of true kindness." Daniel found these lessons particularly difficult; he had trouble sorting out the important from the unimportant, and it was hard to tell what mattered

out of all the things the teacher brought up in class. Worried about the
test, though, he listened carefully to every word.

"Late in the spring of 1987," his teacher began one morning, writing the names and dates on the celestial blackboard before them,
"Leonid Shcharansky discovered that his father had betrayed his
mother, and he vowed that when he grew up, he would never betray
his own wife. It wasn't until the winter of 1991, however, that he finally
vowed not to betray himself."

Not to betray himself, Daniel wrote down. He underlined it twice,
suspecting that it might be on the test. After all, the name and date
were on the board. But the teacher was already moving ahead, or backward, in a pattern he couldn't quite follow. He took notes as quickly as
possible, trying his best to keep up.

"In the winter of 1986, a revolution occurred when Sara Ziskind's
mother told her that once you are alive, there are no rehearsals for life.
From that moment forward, Sara began to really see."

No rehearsals for life, Daniel noted. But why not? He raised his
hand, but the class had already moved on.

"Shortly after his mother died and his first wife left him, Benjamin
Ziskind decided that he had been cheated too many times, and that he
wouldn't believe anyone anymore. It's true that trust is dangerous.
More dangerous than anything else. But eventually someone reminded
him that trust is also the only thing that makes life worth living."

Trust—dangerous, but makes life worth living, Daniel scribbled. But
why? And if—

"During the course of his life, which lasted from 1909 to 1952, Boris
Kulbak once met a painter and a writer, and he learned about the dan-
gers of people who imagine more than they see. Imagination can be a
beautiful thing, but it's also a trap. The wisest people are those who use
their imaginations when they are children, and then learn to see the
actual as adults. Boris Kulbak did it backwards. He saw too much as a
child, then imagined too much as an adult."

Imagination: beautiful, but trap, Daniel noted. But what did it
mean? He glanced over his shoulder at the notebook of the not-yet sitting next to him, wondering if he was writing down the right things. To
his surprise, though, he saw that the not-yet next to him had taken a
completely different set of notes, with completely different names and

dates. *Enrique Calderon, 1971, accident,* she had written. Then she
had underlined: *Memory is less important than happiness.* He stared
again at his own notes, puzzled. Were they really in the same class? He
shrugged. If she wanted to fail the test, that was her problem.

"On June thirteenth, 1965, Daniel Ziskind tore up the letter his
father had sent him in Vietnam, in which his father had sworn never
to read Daniel's letters ever again. He regretted it for days afterward.
Even when he returned home crippled, he still regretted it, but he
didn't forgive his father, or do anything to try to win back his father's
love. By the time he realized that he should have tried harder, that there
was no reason to exclude his own father from his children's lives, his
father had already passed away. When something matters, don't wait."

Don't wait, Daniel scribbled. Would this be on the test?

DANIEL WAS A good student, but history was his least favorite subject.
He much preferred science classes, where the secrets of the universe
were revealed one by one. He especially liked the lab experiments. One
time they had to plant microscopic cells of betrayal in petri dishes,
inspecting their growth over the course of the class. Daniel stared at
the dish and was astonished by how quickly the cells multiplied, by
how a surface that was pristine moments before metamorphosed
within minutes into a gangrenous plate of rot. A similar experiment
was done involving a grudge, with identical results. Envy, on the other
hand, proved itself not to be contagious at all; instead, it ate its carrier
alive. Another lab result that intrigued Daniel was when the class
measured the speed of gossip as it traveled through various media,
determining how its speed was affected by whether it was transmitted
through speech, writing, broadcast, or silence. To his surprise, the
fastest means of travel was silence, which allowed the gossip to move
faster simply by refusing to stop it, facilitated through listeners who
should have created some kind of friction to slow it down but instead
failed to rise to the subject's defense. Daniel was slightly repulsed by
the lab involving the dissection of lies, a gory procedure in which he
and a partner had to slice through layers of smooth skinlike surfaces
and pin them back to reveal the innards, which mostly consisted of disgusting rotting guts of self-loathing and fear. (Some not-yets had asked

for permission to sit out the dissections, claiming that it was against their religious beliefs. Permission was never granted.)

But what Daniel loved best about school were the field trips. One night he and his fellow not-yets were flown, in a long chain riding high across the sky, up to the storehouses of snow. They arrived at the coldest corner of the night sky, a black void in the universe where nothing could even be imagined; even his fellow not-yets seemed to vanish into deep barrels of frigid darkness. But then their teacher— this time, a humble, contented already-was named Job—knocked at the edge of the universe, and a giant door creaked open. Behind it was a cavernous room, radiant with an almost blinding light that refracted through millions of icicles that hung from its ceiling and grew from its floor like the stalactites of the earth, forming bars of ice cages that held in enormous heaps of snow, marked for future winters. The silence in that room of snow, the white peace that would fall to the earth overnight in the future when people would wake up and find their world changed, lingered in Daniel's ears until the day he was born. On another trip, their teacher showed them the gates of the seas—towering portals made of thick bars of moonlight and wind, invisible to the mortal eye, perched on the seashores of the world below and swinging closed just as the tides swelled too high, declaring to the oceans, "This far, and no farther!" Daniel's class went on voyages down to the depths of the abyss, and to the highest heights of heaven, and into the recesses of the heart. Every moment delighted Daniel, thrilled him. When Daniel and his classmates had six months to go, their teacher even took them on a tour of the gardens of paradise. They ate from the tree of knowledge of good and evil—sweet fruits that made Daniel hungry, and left a sour aftertaste in his mouth. But there was one place that their teacher would only tell them about, and refused to show them.

"Until you are born, all of paradise is yours, so enjoy it," their teacher said. "The only thing in paradise forbidden to you is the tree of life."

Daniel and his classmates looked at each other in awe. "Where's that?" one of the not-yets asked.

The teacher pressed his lips together, then sighed. "On the farthest eastern side of nowhere," he said, "where no one can ever reach it. It's

guarded by angels with four faces and six wings each, and the path to the tree is blocked by the bright blade of a revolving sword."

A revolving sword?

"But everywhere else, you can go," the teacher said.

And then the teacher began showing the class all of the cures for lung cancer. Unfortunately, that was when Daniel stopped paying attention.

———

THE IDEA THAT something lay beyond the limits of his paradise bothered Daniel, haunted him. He was an obedient not-yet, though, and never dreamed of trying to go there himself. Instead he busied himself in other parts of paradise. He still went to school every day, but the secrets of the universe he learned there no longer impressed him. As Daniel's uncle Benjamin once told Daniel's father (in one of the many letters Daniel's father never read), actually school was very easy for him, and mostly he learned things outside of school. Like at the public baths.

The public baths of paradise, like those in the world below, have many chambers, some with water, some with steam, at many temperatures. But while the baths below are purportedly good for the skin, intended to rejuvenate the body, the baths above are good for the character, a soak in liquid emotions intended to age the soul. At the paradise bath that Daniel visited daily, he always headed straight for the warm pool of love, a crowded tank in which the not-yets wallowed in mobs, body to body along the benches lining its sides and splashing each other in the center. On long white nights in the world to come, Daniel would sink down on his knees in the warm waters, tipping his head back until love filled his ears and buoyed up his wings. He would close his eyes and slip down beneath the still waters, hoping that no one would notice if he remained there forever, submerged in the blind, warm depths. But the already-weres who ran the place weren't supposed to allow them to stay there long. It wasn't healthy, the signs on the walls read. Those at risk of heart disease, or those who had a family history of broken hearts, were especially warned not to linger. But most did anyway, wrenching themselves out only when they absolutely had to, shivering off to school with their wings shriveled and shrunken.

Daniel had barely just arrived one night, sinking himself into the sweet warm pool, when the bath attendant assigned to watch him, a bald, thin man named Boris, sneaked up behind him and hauled him out by his wings.

"What are you doing?" Daniel sputtered as Boris raised him into the frigid air. Daniel had only discovered the bath a few weeks before, and he was livid.

"You can't just sit in that pool all night. You need to get used to the other temperatures," the bald man told him, his voice gruff. "You don't want to be surprised after you're born. If you never feel it here, there's no way you'll survive it there."

"But what about everybody else?" Daniel protested, waving his arm at the other not-yets splashing and laughing in the water. "Nobody's making them leave!" Drops of warm water still lingered in his ears.

Boris looked around at the other bath attendants, most of whom were lounging on the sides of the pool of love, dawdling, dangling their toes in with their charges. "That's because their attendants are idiots," he whispered. "Come with me, and I'll show you how to really take a bath." Then he took Daniel under his wing and whisked him off to a deserted room on the far end of the bathhouse. Before Daniel knew what was happening, Boris had plunged him, feet first, into a tub of ice-filled hate.

Daniel screamed. Boris refused to let him out, holding his shoulders down under the ice. The pain was terrifying. Daniel screamed himself hoarse, but Boris just watched him scream, his face immobile at the edge of the bath. Slowly Daniel's limbs began to go numb, and with the numbness, his screams subsided. He could no longer move, but he could also no longer feel. He sank deeper into the ice, frozen and silent.

"That's enough," Boris said, and wrenched him out of the water. Still numb, Daniel rode on Boris's shoulders like a block of ice, more silent and cold than the storehouses of snow, until Boris opened another door, this time to a small, deep tank. He closed the door and gently lowered Daniel into a cold still pool of grief.

Daniel remained frozen, but he was no longer numb. This time he could feel the cold water seeping into his prebirth nose and ears and mouth, chilling his limbs. He tried to float, but he sank like a waterlogged book to the bottom, submerged in the cold. The ice had scalded him until he couldn't feel, but here there was no shield against the deep chill that seeped into him, tugging on his spine. He struggled in the water, but the more he moved, the more the cold soaked his bones. Boris watched him writhing beneath the surface and held his breath. At last he could no longer stand to watch, and pulled Daniel out. "A lot of people like to jump into the hot tub as soon as possible after the cold, but it's not a good idea," he advised Daniel. Daniel barely heard him. His blue face was streaked with tears. "Let's get you to one of the steam rooms instead."

Daniel wept on Boris's shoulder as Boris carried him into another room, this one thick with a gently heated mist. How wonderful it was! The steam of friendship—warm, mostly, but with a slightly cool edge—gathered on his limbs until they thawed. Slowly, movement returned, and he breathed in deeply, inhaling the refreshing moisture until his body tingled with life. He tipped his head back and felt the cozy mist tickle the insides of his ears until he started laughing. He was still laughing when Boris lifted him up again and carried him to another room, this one with a narrow pool divided in half, partitioned between desire and lust.

When he slipped into the half nearest to the door, Daniel found the water so hot that he almost climbed out, afraid of being scalded. But the more parts of his body he slipped into it, the less he wanted to leave. Bit by bit, his body took the drug and lulled itself into the burning pool. He enjoyed the tug of the heavy heat, allowing it to pull his head below the surface, allowing his eyes and mouth to ease open— and then, underwater, he screamed. Salt! He felt the salt blind him, searing his eyes and gagging his tongue. If I keep my eyes and mouth closed, it will be fine, he thought. He squinted his eyes and pursed his lips, but the damage had been done. His head burned, reeled. This time he climbed out and jumped into the next pool without Boris's help— a churning hot tub where he rinsed his eyes and mouth, swallowing the tumbling whirlpool of boiling water until his head went weak in the heat. It was only after that, when Daniel had stayed in the hot tub so long that he nearly burst his own tiny heart, that Boris took him out and brought him back to the main room, where he gently floated him on his back into the pool of love.

"Much better, isn't it?" Boris asked.

But Daniel could no longer speak. The water that had simply been warm before now overwhelmed him with ecstasy, caressing him from every side, buoying him to the surface, embracing him around the neck. When Boris lifted him out, much later, he didn't even protest. This time the warmth had entered him forever, saturating his bones and his heart.

"Now you understand why you needed that," Boris told him as he wrapped him in towels far from the water's edge. Daniel felt Boris's strong arms around his shoulders and marveled that he didn't miss the water. It was as if he were still in the pool, on dry land.

"Yes," Daniel murmured, still in a daze. He looked back at the pool and saw all of the other not-yets swimming in it, splashing in it, chasing each other in it, playing games in it. Taking it for granted.

"Because once you're born, you might feel all of those things," Boris was saying. "In any order. And you can't control it." Daniel looked up, but Boris had turned away from him, his eyes staring at the ground. He held him tighter. "Maybe it will never happen," Boris said, and blinked. "I hope it never will. But if it does, I want you to be prepared."

———

SOME OF THE not-yets love to sleep. The beds and hammocks in paradise are made out of music, chained melodies and woven symphonies and firm fanfare mattresses and ropy-netted ballads and strong percussive massages. The not-yets swing and rock to sleep to all kinds of rhythms, resonating with sounds that they will listen for again someday in the world below. But some, like Daniel, are more restless. And they are the ones who love to eat.

The museums of paradise are restaurants filled with masterworks of art, served daily à la carte to the not-yets until they have eaten and seen it all. There are many museums to choose from, and the menus are diverse, stocked with every possible medium and style, from origami to watercolors to tapestries to monuments, from the most realistic to the most abstract. The curator-waiters, know-it-all mortals that they are, encourage the not-yets to eat nutritiously. But most of the not-yets are picky eaters. It's hard for them to eat something besides the clichéd pictures, the sweet comfort food that tastes exactly the way they have learned to expect. The already-weres tell them to try some surrealism for a change, taste just a tiny piece of a distorted cartoon, just a few bites of abstract art. They try to warn the not-yets, when they see them ordering too many unoriginal landscapes and still lifes and portraits and nudes, that they are going to need to be prepared to see things differently after they're born, that there is more than one way of seeing. Without nourishing preparation, the already-weres inform them, they will be born without any taste for new experiences; their eyes will never be starved for fresh perspectives in waking life, never hungering for visions of what might be.

So the waiters and chefs fill the daily menu with farm-fresh images and aged meaty works, sweet-and-sour sculptures and subtly seasoned visions of things in the world below. Sometimes they succeed, and the braver not-yets develop a hunger for beauty. At the end of the meal, though, it remains a matter of taste. Some love the salty, salacious paintings best; others prefer the spicy portraits of the winking woman or the ethereal landscape or the man seen from behind. A rare few appreciate the bitter, ghastly images in all media, finding in them something closer to bittersweet. A few not-yets are ascetics who simply don't enjoy eating—weak anorexics of experience who refuse to taste even the sweetest of sights. The waiters are forced to serve them kindergarten drawings, stick figures and happy faces, just to keep them from starving to birth. They are born with their eyes closed, and until they die, they see less than the blind. But even though the already-weres try to promote healthy eating habits, decadent photographs are still always served for dessert. Like the realistic paintings, they are sweet. Rumor among the waiters has it that they are the more accurate depictions of what the not-yets might see after they are born, and most not-yets crave them, gorging themselves on pictures of their future parents and brothers and sisters. But some of these pictures prove hard to swallow. It is a sad not-yet who orders a sweet snapshot of some mortal parent or sibling, only to discover a bitter aftertaste lingering on his tongue. Even worse, though infinitely more common, is the not-yet who eats a picture of a future mortal lover, gobbling it greedily and licking the frame, and then finds himself suffering all night long, vomiting as he clutches his gut. Desserts are the most likely part of the meal to cause stomachaches, though most not-yets still wolf them down. They haven't yet learned how to be afraid.

For Daniel, the world to come was an endless feast. He was always hungry, and he devoured pictures of people and landscapes almost indiscriminately, ordering whatever the not-yet at the next table was having. His palate expanded to every color, and he never saw a picture he wouldn't eat. Unlike the other not-yets, who relished the desserts, Daniel delighted in every part of the meal, from nutritious oils to high-fiber wooden statues to crunchy candy comics. The curator who served his meals in his favorite museum—a grinning already-was, also named Daniel—at first took little interest in him. Most curators were too busy coaxing the dieters to eat another stick figure. But once the natal Daniel had eaten there a few times, the mortal Daniel began to linger at his table, trying to broaden his palate and cultivate his tastes.

"Two panels of water lilies," Daniel ordered one day at lunch, "and two of those woodblock prints with Mount Fuji in the distance."

"There are fifty variations on that," the already-was Daniel advised, consulting the menu of the day. He frowned, then leaned forward, rested a hand on Daniel's table, and whispered in his ear. "I'm afraid they're all a little stale," he confided. "May I recommend something fresher?"

"Like what?" Daniel asked.

"Let me show you," the curator said. He rushed back to the studio kitchen, returning with a small watercolor. It was of a woman flying horizontally in the sky, suspended over a little town. Daniel looked, and began to salivate.

"Who's the artist?" Daniel asked.

"Oh, I'm sure you've never heard of her."

But Daniel had already taken a mouthful of it, and soon he had devoured the whole thing—salty, thick, intense. He was full.

As the days passed, Daniel grew more adventurous in his eating habits. Meaty flying goats, spicy splashes of color, refreshing silkscreened mountains, well-seasoned melted clocks—there was nothing the already-was Daniel suggested that the not-yet Daniel wouldn't try. He even wolfed down funerary art. Most of the not-yets shunned the art of tombs and graves, finding the flavor too bitter and intense. But it was an acquired taste, Daniel discovered. As he nibbled on sarcophagi and tombstones and terra-cotta warriors, he found that the dry, earthy flavors hid within them a bittersweet aftertaste of eternity.

"Hm," the already-was Daniel mused during one lunch, when his unborn charge ordered a series of mortuary murals from a tomb in lower Egypt. "I guess a taste for that stuff runs in the family." But later, when the not-yet Daniel requested an entire meal of funerary sculptures from the imperial tombs in Hue, the curator closed his notepad and refused.

"Why not?" the not-yet Daniel wailed.

"It really isn't healthy to eat so much of it," the mortal Daniel insisted. "It'll give you heartburn. Let me get you something with a little more fiber." And he brought out a feast of illuminated manuscripts, salted and spiced with gold-leafed names of God.

The natal Daniel enjoyed his meals, despite the dietary restrictions imposed by the curator. But he was beginning to suspect the mortal Daniel of deliberately giving him the saltiest works of art to eat. As he ate more regularly at the mortal Daniel's table, devouring strange surreal pictures, he noticed that he was becoming increasingly thirsty. Even between meals, he felt a dryness in the back of his throat, and soon the artwork failed to satisfy him. He needed something more. When he asked at the restaurant for something to drink, the mortal Daniel only laughed.

Daniel began wandering around paradise restlessly, climbing on the stars. No form of music could rock him to sleep. He ate again from the tree of knowledge of good and evil, hoping for refreshment. But he was surprised to find that its fruit had become bland and dry. He stole a few mouthfuls of storm water from the storehouses of rain, but they left him bloated and anxious about causing droughts below. The gardens of paradise bored him. It seemed to him that there was nothing worth doing anymore, that he might as well just sit and wait for his birth. And then, three weeks before he was due to be born, he found something to satisfy his thirst.

THE DRINKING AGE in the world to come is twenty-one. Twenty-one days, that is—three weeks until one's time has come to be born. At that point, the not-yets are allowed into the famous bars of the world to come, where they must choose for themselves whether to remain sober, to let themselves get a bit tipsy, or to drink themselves to birth. But the drinks in these bars aren't like the poor, dark, dingy ones in the world below. Instead, the vast wine cellars of the world to come are filled with bottled books.

They are arranged, the wine cellars, like libraries, by vineyard, varietal, vintage—author, genre, date. The librarian-sommeliers bring up the requested bottles carefully. Some are meant to be drunk warm, heated with love; others are plunged into icy buckets of hatred or chilled slightly in anger before drinking. Most are served at room temperature, objectively tasted; while some (cheap titles, usually, avoided at least in public by the smarter not-yets) are served lust-hot. Wary drinkers usually ask to see the label before opening the bottle, inspecting the title and the author's name to make sure it matches what they ordered. (" 'Deuteronomy,' " Daniel cried once when a drowsy bartender brought out a flinty screw-capped carafe. "I asked for 'Deuteronomy,' not for 'The New Economy.' ") The true bibliophiles are also offered a drop to sample first, to swivel under their tongues, testing for basic quality. ("Tfu!" Daniel once spat. "Plagiarism!") After that, it is simply a matter of taste, and of how long one takes to get drunk.

Most of the visitors to the paradise bar drink cheap pints of newspapers and magazines, microbrewed advertising copy, and, lately, Internet screeds on tap. Some like fancy anthology cocktails, readers' digests of different works that make them seem more sophisticated than they are. Others prefer the hard stuff that needs no particular vintage, tossing back murder mystery shots and swilling down romances and thrillers that leave them plastered on the floor for days. Of course, many of the not-yets take one look into the bars of paradise, at the frightening effects of stories on the soul, and vow to stay sober until the day they are born. They hold themselves back for twenty-one days, and then they are born contented, living their entire lives on earth without ever thirsting to read. But others—the thirsty ones, the ones who aren't satisfied with the meals at the museum and long to wash them down with something bigger, bolder—are drawn to the bar, believing that behind the crowds swallowing cheap words, there might be something worthy of their not-yet lips. And those are the ones who meet the librarian-sommeliers.

It wasn't long after his twenty-first prebirthday that Daniel met Rosalie, an already-was who worked as a sommelier at his local paradise bar. Turned off by the crowd of natals at the counter—one of whom had just vomited the plot of an entire soap opera onto his celestial barstool—Daniel had wandered off into a corner, a shady nook of the kind many paradise bars make available to the most antisocial bibliophiles, though he didn't know that he was one yet. Rosalie found him there, sulking, his head in his wings.

"Would you like to see the wine list?" she asked.

"Wine list?" he repeated, confused. He was, after all, new.

"Let me show you," she said, and landed softly at his side. He watched her fluttering beside him. The presence of this mortal felt different from the other bartenders, he noticed. It reminded him of the attendant at the bathhouse: stern, stirring, somehow slightly too close. His wings tingled beside hers as she unfurled a long scroll before him.

"You're one lucky guy," she said. "We've got the best wine list this side of paradise."

Daniel looked over her shoulder, squinting to see the long list of names in the bar's low light. "Don't tell me you've never had a drink before," she scolded. Daniel shook his head shyly, but something told him that she already knew the answer. For a moment, she held his wing and looked him in the eye. "You're going to want something sophisticated, I can tell," she said. "I would recommend this one, for starters." He followed her fingertips along the scroll until she pointed at a name that he couldn't read in the dark. "Sound good to you?"

"Sure," he shrugged, feigning nonchalance. But a fire had entered him. A thirst.

"I'll bring it right up," she said, and flew away.

A few moments later—moments that felt to Daniel like eons, and perhaps they were—she returned from the cellar, landing in his nook with a bottle in one hand. "Here it is," she said, and brandished the bottle's glowing label in his face: *Genesis*.

Clueless, Daniel nodded as she poured a few drops into his glass. "You have to drink it slowly to appreciate it," she said. "A lot of people just chug it down and miss the whole point."

He raised the glass to his lips and sipped the liquid carefully, holding it under his tongue, unsure of what to expect. At first it was sickly sweet, reminding him of some of the more cloying paintings at the museum—darkness, water, light, earth, sun, moon, stars. Typical. But then it heated up, then burned with spices, then turned creamy, then grassy, then suddenly flattened into a bitter tannin. Just before he swallowed, it reared itself up into a final burst of flavor, fruit from the tree of knowledge, which fruitfully multiplied before flowing down his throat.

"This is *very good*," he muttered a moment later, and poured himself a full glass.

"This whole vintage is exceptional," Rosalie told him as he slurped it down, swallowing a vast flood of pure rainwater and the chalky remnants of a collapsing tower before bracing his stomach against the flinty tannin of a man holding a knife to his son's throat. "You'd be surprised, though. There are people who take one sip and spit the whole thing out." Daniel kept drinking, relishing the spicy hints of jealous siblings on his tongue. "Would you like to try some of the other varietals? Same vintage, different mouth-feel?"

"Mm," Daniel murmured. He had begun drinking directly from the bottle, curling up with it like the baby he was about to become, dreaming sweet drunken dreams of eleven stars and sheaves of grain bowing down before him. A hint of flint again as jealous siblings attacked on his tongue; then a soft note, later, of sour grapes.

"Great, I'll go bring up some more." Rosalie flew down to the cellar and then back up, carrying several bottles with her that she put down on the table in front of him—Exodus, Isaiah, Ezekiel. "Watch out for this one," she said, holding up a bottle of Ecclesiastes. "It's kind of a downer. But still worth a taste. Eat, drink, and be merry."

Daniel popped the cork and poured himself a glass, spilling sour vanities into his mouth, one vain sip after another until all was vanity. As his eyes grew dim, he agreed with Rosalie. A downer. What really made him dizzy, though, was the peculiarly balanced sweet-and-sour flavor, the time to be born and the time to die, the time to weep and the time to laugh, the time to mourn and the time to dance. And the residue at the bottom of the bottle was particularly hard to swallow, when he tasted the hint that of the making of many books there is no end, and that much study is wearying of the flesh. It was a little too heavy, and made him thirsty for something simpler. He reached for the bottle of Psalms.

"Want a new glass?" Rosalie asked.

"Renew it as in days of old," he said, and hiccuped.

Before he knew it, his cup had runneth over.

————

IT WASN'T LONG before Daniel became a regular at Rosalie's bar. There were some bottles he would request again and again—he was fond, for instance, of certain appellations of Talmudic vintage pertaining to life before birth (they had a comforting, familiar flavor)—but it was mostly Rosalie's tastes that guided his literary binges. She had a particular fondness for Hebrew and Yiddish vineyards, which was convenient, since few other patrons at the bar chose to sample those languages. Even the true bibliophiles usually stuck to the products of presses from the larger, more standard book-growing regions: English, Russian, French, Spanish, German, Arabic, Chinese. The Yiddish vintages in particular Daniel could count on having all to himself. It wasn't long before his reading habit became the only thing on his mind, turning into an addiction. He would sit in school waiting for the day to end, then race to the paradise bar. Rosalie was almost always waiting for him, ready with a glass of poetry on the house.

Sometimes they would get together for a few comedies, and he would become so drunk that he would stumble out the door still laughing. Other times, she would pour out tales of lost love and tragedy until he was crying into his glass. More often, sweet laughter and bitter tannins would blend in the same cup, and each alternating sip made him thirsty for more. She never provided a bottle without commentary or at least an opinion—a sommelier's note on the vintage, or a suggestion on how to enjoy it. One day she stood beside his table as he sipped a fresh, fruit-tinged poem from a bottle by Itsik Manger:

> Eve stands before the apple tree
> The sunset sky is red.
> What do you know, mother Eve,
> What do you know of death?

Adam is gone for the day
In the wild wood alone.
Adam says, "The wood is wild,
And beauty is all that's unknown."

But Eve is afraid of the wild wood.
She is drawn to the apple tree.
And when she doesn't go to it,
It comes to her in dreams.

"This is just the kind of thing that everyone gulps down wrong, if they bother tasting it at all," Rosalie told him as she sampled a sip from the copper cup around her neck. "People taste the apple flavor and think they're drinking juice. They say, 'Oh, it's about sex.' No one ever understands what happened with Adam and Eve. That story isn't about sex. It's about death. The forbidden desire isn't love or lust—you can get that stuff anytime down at the public bath, even on earth. The forbidden desire is immortality."

"Hm," Daniel murmured. Intellectual discussions, he had noticed, tended to sound more profound when he was drunk. He took another swig and finished off his glass, then poured himself a refreshing sip of Psalms. "Yet mine is the faith," he slurred, "that I shall behold the goodness of God in the land of the living." He belched, then snored.

Rosalie laughed. "Don't count on it," she said, and carried him out.

———

BECOMING A BIBLIOHOLIC changed Daniel's eating habits. Prior to that, he had loved to eat, but now he lost his appetite. Long periods passed when he wouldn't even taste a work of art. Every painting, no matter how delicately seasoned, soured in comparison to the drunken rapture of reading. Instead he would drink himself into a stupor and then wander into the bath, where he would try to loosen his hangover by throwing himself into a chilled sulfur tub of loneliness. One morning, after drinking a particularly disturbing bottle whose town full of dead people left him feeling wasted and worthless, he skulked off to the sulfur tub and soaked there for a long time, sunken and shivering. But then Boris discovered him, and slapped him across the face.

"Daniel, what are you doing? Get out of that bath," he shouted.

Daniel lolled in the cold, smelly water. The slap barely registered; he was still drunk. "Why?" he muttered.

Boris leaned over him, his wings folded at his sides. "Because if you stay in there, your skin will soak up the stench, and then when you're born, no one will want to go near you."

Daniel slouched down farther into the pool. "I don't care," he said.

Boris watched him for a moment, then snorted. "That's your problem," he snapped. "You don't care. I haven't seen such a stupid not-yet since your uncle was born. Now get out of that bath."

Daniel still didn't budge. Boris stood for a moment, sighed, and then reached down and hauled him out of the water, carrying him over his shoulder to a warm steam room. He sat Daniel down on a bench near the vent that billowed white clouds of trust, leaving a faithful film of dewdrops on Daniel's wings.

Boris sat down and leaned toward him, then pinched his own nose. "Ugh, that explains it. I can smell Lamentations on your breath." Daniel's face began turning red, though perhaps it was only from the steam. "Don't tell me Rosalie has been getting you drunk."

Daniel looked up, his surprise dulled by the roar of words between his temples. "You know Rosalie?" he asked.

Boris snorted, then evaded. "It's not healthy to drink all those books. It's like all the not-yets who sit in the warm pool and never try the other ones. You're going to be born addicted to those stories. And then you're going to go through life thirsty for things that don't exist."

Daniel inhaled the clean, pure mist and wailed. "Trust me," he sighed, "if you knew what those books were like—"

Boris sighed, a deep sigh that sucked in some of Daniel's trust, making him wonder what Boris really knew, whether he might not have had a few drinks himself, long ago, before he was born and died. "What I know is that you haven't been eating," Boris said.

Trust seeped back up into Daniel's nostrils. "There's nothing worth eating anymore," he cried. "Once you've had those books, all the landscapes and portraits and photographs in the whole world to come just seem like—nothing. Even the photographs. Even the abstract ones. Even the surreal ones. Especially the postmodern ones. Nothing *happens* in them. They're just—" Daniel began, and choked.

"But don't you see?" Boris demanded over Daniel's sobs. "That's the whole point: *you are* what's going to happen in them. After you're born, you're going to be hungry for those things, those people and places, and then you're going to look for them, and see them and find them and put yourself into them. The artwork is just the settings, or the other characters. You have to make the plot yourself."

Daniel sobbed even more. "But how can anyone make a new plot?" he sputtered. His breath reeked of Ecclesiastes. "One generation goes, another comes," he rattled. "Whatever already was, will always be, and whatever has already been done will be done again. There's—there's just nothing new under the sun."

Boris sighed. "You need to eat," he said.

Daniel groaned over the rumbling of his own stomach. "But it's all just—I don't know, vanity."

Boris put his wing around Daniel. "How about this," he suggested. "Why don't you ask your curator to bring you something to eat that will complement what you've been drinking?"

Daniel lifted his head, feeling his hangover subside. "Do you think it would help?"

Boris looked at him, his eyes gleaming under his bald forehead. He embraced Daniel around the neck until Daniel leaned toward him, closer to the steam vent. "You won't know if you don't try," he said.

Under other circumstances, Daniel might have noticed that something was up. But at that moment his nostrils were clouded with deep breaths of trust, and he could see nothing but the brightest corners of paradise.

———

THAT EVENING, DANIEL entered the museum for the first time since he had started frequenting the bar. The daily specials hanging on the gallery walls nauseated him, but he forced himself to stay. As he sat down at his usual table, the already-was Daniel arrived. The mortal curator grinned, and placed that night's menu in Daniel's not-yet hands.

Daniel flipped its pages, searching desperately for something that would whet his appetite. After many long moments of searching, he saw something that at least didn't disgust him, though he still couldn't imagine swallowing it. It was a large painting of a bride and groom, black and white except for a large red angel holding them together. A tiny figure, a not-yet figure, was embedded in the bride's cheek.

"Listen," Daniel said to the curator, his wings brushing against the menu, "I—I've been drinking—"

"I suspected as much," the curator said with a smile.

Daniel felt himself turning redder than the angel in the picture. "No, I mean, I've been drinking the Song of Songs. Do you think this would go well with it?"

The mortal Daniel squinted at the red angel in the painting, then at Daniel's reddened face. "Maybe," he conceded, "but I have some better suggestions. May I recommend a few photographs tonight?"

"Photographs!" the natal Daniel shouted, trying not to retch. He pounded a fist on the table. "I'm sick of them!"

"These are different," the curator vowed. "Chef's special. They'll pair well with the drinks."

"Fine," the not-yet Daniel growled, putting his head on the table. And the curator hurried off.

When he returned, he presented a platter of two photographs that Daniel had never seen before. The first one was of a bride and groom, though nothing like the ones in the painting. In the painting the groom was short, almost shorter than the bride, a slight man with thin, uncertain hands. But the photograph's bride was dwarfed by the groom—a giant man with enormous hands, a thick chest, and flaming red hair. The bride seemed a bit stunned by it all, her dark eyes glowing under brown curls. In the other photograph the same bride and groom appeared again, this time held together not by an angel, but by another man—a thin, pale man with dark hair and glasses. The bride and groom looked straight at him, but the man between them was watching someone else behind the cameraman, someone invisible. Daniel took a bite of the photograph and was surprised to find that it was sweet. He chewed thoughtfully for a long while, relishing the taste, feeling nourished for the first time since he turned twenty-one. But as soon as he had swallowed both of them, the old loneliness and hunger returned.

"It isn't good enough, is it?" the mortal Daniel said. His voice was heavy, almost broken.

The natal Daniel swallowed the very last morsel and sighed. "No."

The mortal Daniel frowned, but the natal Daniel noticed his eye sparkling, and listened. "Maybe what you need is some real food," he offered. "Not art. Food."

Daniel looked up, astonished. What did the man mean? "Real food like what?"

"Real food like fruit," the mortal Daniel said.

The natal Daniel snorted. He could hardly contain his disgust. "Fruit from the tree of knowledge of good and evil?" He laughed, a hard jaded laugh. "I've had that a million times."

"No, not fruit from the tree of knowledge," the mortal Daniel said. He leaned down to Daniel's ear and whispered: "Fruit from the tree of life."

The not-yet Daniel's jaw dropped. He scanned the curator's face, but couldn't detect any signs of joking. Trust from the afternoon's bath still lingered in his own nostrils. He shivered, and shielded his face with one wing. It was a long time before he could speak. "We're not supposed to go there," he breathed.

The mortal Daniel laughed. "Says who?"

Daniel looked over his shoulder. Luckily, he had come to dinner early. The gallery was mostly empty; the other not-yets were still lolling in the pool of love. "The teachers, everyone," he whispered. "We're not allowed."

"Why not?" the mortal Daniel asked, one eyebrow raised.

Daniel sputtered, wondering if his brain was permanently affected by too many books. "We're just—not," he hissed. "Besides, it's dangerous. There's a revolving sword."

The mortal Daniel laughed again. "What do you care about a stupid revolving sword?" he snorted. "You're not a mortal, you're a natal. What, are you worried that your mother will miscarry you?"

This possibility had never occurred to him. He trembled in utter horror until the mortal Daniel grinned. "Trust me," the mortal Daniel said, "it would take a lot more than that for your mother to have a miscarriage. For somebody else this might do it, but your mother is tougher than she seems."

The curator knew his mother? Daniel was intrigued, but still cautious. He racked his not-yet brain for a reason not to go. "Anyway, it's on the farthest eastern side of nowhere," he muttered, trying to sound casual. "It's impossible to get there, so what's the point of talking about it?"

But then the curator sat down at the table across from him. The two Daniels faced each other, one already-was, one not-yet. "We can get there," the already-was Daniel said under his breath, and then he leaned toward the not-yet Daniel's ear. "I built a road."

Daniel breathed in and gasped. He didn't speak.

"Come with me," the already-was Daniel whispered. Excitement coursed through his words. "You're going to be born soon, and then it will be too late. Let's go, now. Tonight."

The not-yet Daniel's head whirled. The tree of life? How could he? But how could he not? And how many days did he have left in paradise? He realized with a jolt that when he had started drinking, he had stopped counting. There were fewer than twenty-one days left, of course, but how many really? Two weeks' worth? One? Suddenly he remembered something he had learned in school, months earlier: *When it matters, don't wait.*

He nodded, and held his breath. And then the two of them rose and walked on together, walking and running and flying for three whole days and nights until they reached the farthest edge of the world to come.

"EVERYBODY AROUND HERE likes to pave their roads with good intentions," the already-was Daniel muttered, "but those roads never seemed to get me anywhere. So I built this one out of stupid mistakes instead."

They had crossed most of paradise on their journey, at least most of the paradise the not-yet Daniel had seen. They took the main roads first, moving quickly along the good intentions past all of the schools in paradise, thousands of schools, one for every hour of the year of births to come. They passed the dormitories with their musical hammocks and beds, passed the baths, passed the museum restaurants and the library bars, raced by the gardens of paradise. As they hurried past it all, the not-yet Daniel realized, with a cold chill, how little time he had left. In just days he would have to face his birth sentence, dropped to the earth. But he wouldn't be like the other mortals. The curator had saved him from

that. He was going to stay on earth forever, to matter forever to the living. Immortal. That was what everyone wanted, wasn't it? *The forbidden
desire is immortality*, he remembered Rosalie saying. Or was it innatal-
ity? Which was forbidden, and which was innate?

And now, after three days and nights, they had reached the farthest
edge of paradise. Suddenly the land had stopped, and darkness loomed
before them. At the natal Daniel's feet yawned an enormous chasm,
stretching open for miles, bottomless. All that he could see before him
were the cyclones of garbage blown up from the depths by cold circling winds, hovering spirals of feathers and tears and regrets. And
blasted bones. And stretching out from the edge of the land over the
giant expanse to some unseen place beyond, out from the ends of
Daniel's feet on the brink of the precipice, was a very narrow bridge.

"Mistakes are a very durable building material," the mortal Daniel
was saying. "Most people just throw them away as soon as possible and
never realize that you can learn from them. But if you do, they can
actually hold you up pretty well." He stretched out a foot and tapped
it on the bridge. The tap resounded through the chasm, echoing
through the universe. "See? Solid. Let's go."

The natal Daniel shook his head, and backed away from the edge.
"No," he whispered, fighting not to swallow his own words. "Can't we
just fly?"

The mortal Daniel waved a wing over the abyss. "Are you kidding?"
he laughed. "This is the universe's dumping ground for human
tragedy. You'd never be able to fly in these winds. That's the whole reason I built the bridge. Just crawl over the mistakes and you'll be fine."
The not-yet Daniel began shaking his head again, and soon the head-
shaking turned into a full-bodied trembling as he hovered on the edge.
But before he knew it, the already-was Daniel had crawled onto the
bridge over the abyss.

"Come," the curator called over his shoulder. "The most important
thing is not to be afraid."

The not-yet Daniel watched the already-was Daniel pulling himself
along, moving across the mistakes one by one like rungs on a ladder.
Then he steeled himself, lowered himself onto the bridge, and clung
tight, watching feathers and agony whirl through the cold winds
around him as he struggled to catch up.

The mortal Daniel was right, the natal Daniel discovered. The mistakes themselves were pure weakness, soft elastic errors that barely seemed to support his weight. But like all great roads and bridges, this one's strength was in its construction, in the wise placement of pressure points and angles of approach. Large wars alternated structurally with smaller disasters, with struts built out of bad investments, drug addictions, and extramarital affairs. He crawled carefully across several medieval Crusades, nearly losing his balance before he regained his footing on the edge of the Chernobyl meltdown. The bridge swayed under his weight as a stock market bubble popped beneath his feet. He cringed before moving farther, keeping the already-was Daniel in his sight as he squirmed hand over foot across the Bhopal disaster, the gift of the Sudetenland, a drunk-driving accident, several bad marriages, and the First World War. He looked up and saw the already-was Daniel straight ahead of him, wriggling across the domino theory and then deftly crossing the Rubicon. And then, at last, rising from the shadows, he saw the tree of life.

————

IT WASN'T AT all what he expected. Daniel had envisioned something fantastically bright, gleaming with radiant leaves and fragrant flowers and singing birds in a brilliant cone of sunshine. But this tree was feeble, gloomy. Its thin gray trunk rose up out of the abyss, stretching up from so far down below that Daniel couldn't even see where it was rooted to the earth. There were no flowers, no birds, no sunlight. Instead, there were just a few shy, drooping branches, hanging low like a weeping willow's. A few pale yellowed leaves flickered in the cold wind. Between them, Daniel could just make out the one remaining fruit—a lonely overripe piece, burnished in dull browns and greens like an old forgotten painting with a tiny glint of polish in the corner, swinging sadly in the cold winds of the driven detritus of the universe.

"I see we're in an autumn of belief in eternal life," the already-was Daniel muttered. "Look at this. The four-faced guards aren't even here. Whenever you think you have adequate security, that's exactly when—"

Suddenly a brilliant flash of light sliced into their vision. Daniel clung to the end of the bridge as the light blinded him, searing his face. When the light shifted, he looked up and saw it: the bright blade of the revolving sword, sliding fast beside his neck. He ducked. It passed.

"I hate that thing," the mortal Daniel said, trying to laugh, as it swung back. But the natal Daniel looked up and saw the mortal Daniel shaking, covering himself with his wings before he straightened his back. "But you, of course, should have no problem at all," he added quickly, his voice stiff. "Just take the fruit."

"What?" the not-yet Daniel gasped. Just take it? He looked again at the fruit, then stared at the revolving sword. "But how can I take it?" he stuttered.

"Just take it."

The not-yet Daniel watched the revolving sword as it arced again and swooped over his head (blinding flash of light), then out toward him (he ducked again), then back above the tree. As he held his breath with the sword's movement, though, he suddenly realized it was moving in a rhythm. There was a pattern to its murderous swivel, a pace, like the churning jets of water in the pool of lust. He just had to feel its rhythms, and move against them, keeping track of them, counting in his head.

He waited one more cycle, ducking on cue as the sword moved in its rhythm like a heartbeat. Or like a breath. Breathe in, thought Daniel with his not-yet breath. He sucked in the cold hard air and closed his eyes against the blinding light. Then, after ducking below the blade, he leaned over so far that he nearly fell into the abyss, reached for the fruit, and wrenched it off the tree. Eternity rolled heavily in his hand as he fell backward onto the bridge in a blinding flash of light. He opened his eyes to see the fruit resting in his palm, foaming juice along a thin line in its sweet skin—sliced ever so slightly by the revolving sword. He closed his eyes again, breathed out, and raised the fruit to his lips.

"DANIEL!"

Both Daniels turned. A few steps behind them, a female figure floated in the darkness, standing, balanced, on the narrow bridge.

"Rosalie!" the mortal Daniel called, and smiled. The natal Daniel looked at her, puzzled, the uneaten fruit dripping juices in his hand. How did they know each other?

"Daniel!" she said again. But which one did she mean? She stepped toward the natal Daniel, leaning over him as he lay at the edge of the bridge, and stared at him, glowing with rage. "Don't you remember? You're supposed to be born tonight!"

Tonight?

His mind raced, glancing back at the revolving sword, and then at the fruit in his hand. But he wasn't ready!

Tonight?

"I'm so sorry, Rosie," the mortal Daniel murmured. "I forgot."

Rosalie snorted. "You didn't forget. You brought him here on purpose."

The mortal Daniel grinned. "Maybe."

Rosalie grimaced, then shouted at him. "What was the point of this? Are you just teasing him? So he'll spend his whole life wanting something he can't have?"

"What if I am? It's not any different from what you're doing to him in the bar," the mortal Daniel shot back.

But the words were feeble, and even the not-yet Daniel could hear that the curator didn't mean them. Rosalie listened, and then looked at the curator in genuine surprise, a sudden shock illuminating her face. "Or do you really expect him to eat it, and live forever?" she whispered.

The mortal Daniel didn't answer. He looked down at the natal Daniel, and the natal Daniel saw the flutter of the mortal Daniel's wings.

Rosalie watched, then spoke quietly, her firm voice confining a roar. "You really expect him to eat it," she said. "You actually, genuinely want him to be born and never die."

For a moment the mortal Daniel stood still. There was no sound on the edge of the abyss but the howling of winds.

Then, in a flash of the revolving sword, the mortal Daniel flew into a fury. "WHY NOT?" he shouted over the cyclone. "Why not, Rosalie? Why can't he have what we didn't have? Why should his children have to watch him die? Why should—"

"Because that's what makes it matter," Rosalie breathed.

The already-was Daniel looked down into the abyss, humbled and ashamed. She took him in her arms. The not-yet Daniel watched as they kept each other warm, and he shivered in the cold wind.

"We don't have time to go back," Rosalie said suddenly, glancing up at the sky. Daniel followed her eyes and discovered that in the thick darkness, he could just make out the stars. She bent down and pulled him to his feet by his wings, as he clutched the fruit in his hand. "We'll just have to send you down here. Now." She looked again at the already-was Daniel, who winked at her, then back at the not-yet Daniel, who was struggling to keep his balance on the edge of the narrow bridge. Something strange ran its hands over his back, a sudden chill. He looked over his shoulder and saw his wings detached from his body, blasted into bones and feathers swiveling in the cyclones of cold wind. He screamed.

"Listen to me, Daniel," Rosalie said, and grabbed the hand that held the fruit. She waved an arm behind her, at the paradise beyond the bridge. "This whole world to come is just an imitation of the real one."

"A forgery, if you will," the curator said, winking at Rosalie.

What? Daniel stared at them, bewildered. A forgery? He thought of all the things he had spit out in the past nine months—the copied paintings, the doctored photographs, the sour plagiarized wine. But surely this was the real—

"We've tried to approximate here what you might expect later. But that's all it is," the mortal Daniel told him. "A copy."

"The real world to come is down below—the world, in the future, as you create it," Rosalie said. "The world, to come."

The natal Daniel felt sickened, drunk. He reeled, and then lost his footing. He almost fell off the bridge before Rosalie grabbed him and pulled him back up. Teetering on the edge, he stared at them both, the man who had nourished him, the woman who had enriched him, and then glanced again at the tree of life, which stood motionless in the wind. Was this it? The end of paradise? Was there really no paradise at all? But surely there was something more! Suddenly he remembered something from the night he was conceived.

"What about the test?" he asked. "In school they said there would be a test."

The two mortals looked at each other for a long moment. Then both of them laughed.

"The test comes later," Rosalie said.

Later? Daniel wondered.

"Later," the mortal Daniel repeated. "During every moment of every day of your life."

Rosalie reached under her wing and brought out a large book—not a bottle this time, but a real book, a thick one with many pages. Daniel looked at it and recognized it: it was the roll call book from his first day of school. She flipped through it until she arrived at a certain page, then turned it around to face him. A long blank space stretched below his name. "Now either eat that fruit," she said, "or go down and fill this page with your deeds."

Daniel looked at the book, at the wide blank page stretching before him, and then down at the fruit. Its bruised skin was glowing now, pulsing blue beneath the surface. He dropped it into the void.

"Thank you," Rosalie whispered.

And then his grandfather Daniel pressed a finger to his lips.

As he fell off the bridge, he looked back and saw two strangers watching him fall, a man and a woman, their faces contorted with tears. But he heard laughter in the cold wind, laughter painted into the dark sky between the tears and blasted bones, laughter so loud that he started laughing himself. He turned in midair to face the earth, still laughing, and tumbled down to the land of the living.

Everyone was waiting for him.

AUTHOR'S NOTE

IN JUNE 2001, a small painting by Marc Chagall entitled *Study for "Over Vitebsk"* (1914), on loan from the State Tretyakov Gallery in Moscow, went missing from a temporary exhibition of Chagall's Russian works at the Jewish Museum in New York, after a singles' cocktail hour. In a bizarre sequence of events that would never be convincing in fiction, the painting was recovered months later in a mail room in Topeka, Kansas. This book is a work of fiction. While inspired by the story of this unusual theft, it in no way reflects the actual history or provenance of this painting; nor does it reflect any factual information or actual persons connected to any galleries or museums in Russia or the United States.

Marc Chagall did spend a period in the early 1920s living at the Jewish Boys' Colony at Malakhovka, a home for Jewish children orphaned by the massive pogroms that swept the Soviet Union during the Russian Civil War in 1919. In his early memoir, *My Life*, he described his experiences teaching art there:

> These colonies are composed of some fifty orphans each, under the supervision of intelligent teachers who dreamed of applying the most advanced pedagogic methods. These children had been the most unhappy of orphans. All of them had been thrown out on the street, beaten by thugs, terrified by the flash of the dagger that cut their parents' throats. Deafened by the whistling of bullets and the crash of broken

windowpanes, they still heard, ringing in their ears, the dying prayers of
their fathers and mothers. They had seen their fathers' beards savagely
torn out, their sisters raped, disemboweled . . . And here they are before
me . . . I taught those unfortunate little ones art. Barefoot, lightly clad,
each one shouted louder than the other: "Comrade Chagall! Comrade
Chagall!" . . . The clamor came from every side. Only their eyes would
not, or could not, smile. I loved them. They drew pictures. They flung
themselves at colors like wild beasts at meat. One of the boys seemed to
be in a perpetual frenzy of creation. He painted, composed music and
wrote verses. Another boy constructed his art calmly, like an engineer.

The colony served as a meeting point for many Yiddish writers, including Der Nister (the "Hidden One," pen name of Pinkhas Kahanovitch), who lived there with Chagall and who later perished in a Soviet
prison camp, and poets such as Dovid Hofshteyn and Itsik Fefer, who
were among those executed in 1952 for their activity in the Jewish
Anti-Fascist Committee. Chagall illustrated Yiddish poetry books and
children's books for all of these Yiddish writers. While living in
Malakhovka, he also commuted to Moscow in order to design stage
sets for the Moscow State Jewish Theater, which was under the direction of the Yiddish actor Shloyme (Solomon) Mikhoels. Mikhoels later
became the leader of the Jewish Anti-Fascist Committee; his murder
by Soviet agents in 1948 was staged to look like a traffic accident.
Chagall left the Soviet Union in 1922 and was ultimately one of the
very few Jewish artists in his circle to die a natural death. For information about the circle of Yiddish writers and artists connected with
Chagall, see Benjamin Harshav, *Marc Chagall and His Times: A
Documentary Narrative* (Stanford, California: Stanford University
Press, 2004), as well as the many biographies of the artist. For a record
of the Jewish Anti-Fascist Committee trial as well as an informative
introduction on the history of the ill-fated committee and its members,
see Joshua Rubenstein and Vladimir P. Naumov, *Stalin's Secret
Pogrom: The Postwar Inquisition of the Jewish Anti-Fascist Committee*
(New Haven: Yale University Press, 2001). For this novel, I also drew
upon Yiddish and occasionally Hebrew essays and memoirs of Der
Nister's life and art, which provide details about various incidents in
his life, such as his meeting with Peretz and how he responded to his

own arrest. Very little is available on Der Nister in English, and his few translated stories are scattered among various anthologies. However, his masterpiece, the unfinished novel *The Family Crisis*, is available in English as *The Family Mashber* (Mashber, the family's name, is the Hebrew word for "crisis"), translated by Leonard Wolf (New York: Summit Books, 1987), and includes a thorough translator's introduction addressing the author's life and work.

Yiddish is a thousand-year-old language (not a dialect) which is written in Hebrew characters. In this book I have used the standard YIVO (Yiddish Scholarly Institute) transliteration system to represent it phonetically in the Latin alphabet. Vowels are pronounced as follows: *a* as in "father," *e* as in "red," *i* as in "machine," *o* as in "home" (or somewhat closer to *aw* as in "raw"), *u* as in "blue," *ey* as in "they," and counterintuitively, *ay* as in the *i* sound in "high." The consonant pair *kh* is pronounced like the *ch* in "Bach." There are no silent letters in this transliteration system, so a name like "Reyzele" is three syllables long.

The following is a list of Yiddish sources for the Rosalie Ziskind books and other literary fragments that appear in the novel. All translations and adaptations are my own.

Chapter 2: Adapted from "Gekept" ("Beheaded") by Der Nister; available in English translation in *No Star Too Beautiful*, ed. Joachim Neugroschel (New York: W. W. Norton, 2002).

Chapter 3: Adapted from "Farshlofn a veltuntergang" ("To Sleep Through a World's Collapse") by Moyshe Nadir; available in English translation as "The Man Who Slept Through the End of the World" in *A Treasury of Yiddish Stories*, ed. Irving Howe and Eliezer Greenberg (New York: Penguin, 1953, 1990).

Chapter 4: Excerpted from "Yingl tsingl khvat" ("Young Tongue Scamp") by Mani Leyb; available in English translation in *Little Stories for Little Children*, ed. Miriam Margolin, trans. Jeffrey Shandler (Mt. Kisco, New York: Moyer Bell Ltd., 1986).

Chapter 7: Adapted from "Di toyte shtot" ("The Dead Town") by I. L. Peretz; available in English translation in *The I. L. Peretz Reader*, ed. Ruth Wisse (New York: Schocken, 1990). Song excerpted from "Reyzele," a "folk song" by Mordechai Gebirtig. Translation and music available in *Mordechai Gebirtig: His Poetic and Musical Legacy*, ed. Getrude Schneider (Westport, CT: Praeger, 2000).

Chapter 8: Der Nister's waking dreams are derived from several of his symbolist stories, including "In vayn-keler" ("In the Wine Cellar"), "Fun Mayne Giter" ("From My Estates"), and "Hinter a Ployt" ("Behind a Fence"). These can be found in English translation, respectively, in *Great Tales of Jewish Fantasy and the Occult*, ed. and trans. Joachim Neugroschel (1976; New York: Overlook, 1987), *An Anthology of Modern Yiddish Literature*, ed. Joseph Leftwich (The Hague: Mouton, 1974), and *A Treasury of Yiddish Stories*, ed. Irving Howe and Eliezer Greenberg (New York: Penguin, 1953, 1990).

Chapter 9: Adapted from "Mayse mit di zibn betlers" ("Tale of the Seven Beggars"), an unfinished tale by Nachman of Bratslav; available in English translation in *Nahman of Bratslav: The Tales*, ed. Arnold Band (New York: Paulist Press, 1978).

Chapter 11: Adapted from "Oylem habo" ("The World to Come") by Sholem Aleichem; available in English translation as "Eternal Life" in *The Best of Sholom Aleichem*, ed. Irving Howe and Ruth Wisse (Washington: New Republic Books, 1979).

Chapter 16: Adapted from Chapter 1 of *Dos bukh fun gan-eydn* ("The Book of Paradise") by Itsik Manger; available in English translation as *The Book of Paradise: The Wonderful Adventures of Shmuel-Aba Abervo*, trans. Leonard Wolf (New York: Hill and Wang, 1965, 1986).

Chapter 19: Excerpted from "Khave un der epelboym" ("Eve and the Apple Tree") by Itsik Manger; available in English translation in *The World According to Itzik*, ed. Leonard Wolf (New Haven: Yale University Press, 2002).

ACKNOWLEDGMENTS

I WOULD LIKE to thank those who first taught me Yiddish—David Braun, who taught me the language, and especially Ruth Wisse, who gave me the gift of this literature—for unwittingly inspiring this novel. (All errors in grammar and translation are entirely mine.) In the early stages of this novel, I often turned to my family's teacher of generations, Dr. Nathan Winter, whose devotion to Torah, service, and good deeds have surely earned him his place in the world to come, even as the legacy of his work remains in the land of the living. May his memory be a blessing.

I thank Gary Morris and Alane Salierno Mason—an agent and an editor, respectively, of the kind most writers only dream of. Both made time for this book during the exciting expansion of their own families, and I am very grateful.

I am, as always, indebted to my parents, Susan and Matthew Horn, who never cease to alert me to the wonders of the world, and especially to my mother as a diligent reader—and to my husband Brendan Schulman, whose patience, honesty, and optimism included a constant belief in this book in every possible version, even though I didn't give the book the title he suggested: *Unmitigated Chagall*.

This book is dedicated to my extraordinary siblings: Jordana (a wonderful writer and the first parent among us), Zachary (a professional animator who has even animated a Yiddish folk tale), and Ariel (run, do not walk, back to the bookstore and buy her first novel, *Help Wanted, Desperately*). They are my fellow artists, my partners in crime, and my lifelong friends—in prior worlds, in this world, and in every world to come.